D1193386

# WANDERING
## A REUNIFICATION NOVEL
# *STORM*

# WANDERING

### A REUNIFICATION NOVEL

## *STORM*

## STEVEN J. ANDERSON

Published by Steven J. Anderson
© 2018 Steven J. Anderson

RuComm352@gmail.com
https://www.facebook.com/profile.php?id=100018307866833

Cover by Fiona Jayde Media.
Interior Formatting & Design by The Deliberate Page.

Ebook ISBN: 978-0-9991788-4-3
Print ISBN: 978-0-9991788-5-0

# CHAPTER 1

# THE ACADEMY

The RuComm Academy is 2,200 meters above sea level at the eastern edge of the Rocky Mountains. It's an old school, built in the mid-twentieth century, repurposed and expanded by the Reunification Commission. It snows all winter there, and winter lasts well into April.

Dean of Cadets Bahrfeldt expected all of us to be up by 05:00 every morning, and to have our physical training completed before breakfast. Winona Killdeer and I always started with running the cross-country trails if the weather was good, and Susan Chao, our PT instructor, had never seen weather that wasn't good. Early March meant trying to find trail markers buried by meter-high snowdrifts and risking frostbite.

We did strength training in the gym afterward, where it was always too hot and the smell of sweat was a permanent part of every piece of equipment. We followed the same routine every day.

"Holloman, are you just another privileged Dulcinean girl or are you a RuComm cadet?"

I pushed harder, trying to bench press thirty-five kilos. "Seventy percent of my body weight, ma'am," I managed to gasp.

"Right. Just a little princess. You've been here four years with two more to go. You should be at ninety percent by now, one hundred percent by graduation. *If* you graduate."

Instructor Chao helped me place the bar back into the holders. "Yes, ma'am, that's me; a weak little Dulcinean stick girl, overcome by the oppressive gravity you have here on Earth."

Her eyes narrowed, looking at the disrespect I was failing to hide. I already had more demerits than I could afford. Most of them were from her. Instructor Chao was an ex-Union Marine, although I couldn't see anything *ex* about her. She'd lost both her legs in combat and I should have admired her as much as everyone else did. I despised her.

"Hit the showers. Then run along to Professor Slade and your precious starship engineering studies. I'm sure he enjoys all the sucking up you do for him."

She raised her eyebrows and I blushed, taking the bait. "He's a brilliant man. He designed ships for the Trade Guild of Venice before coming to the Academy. We're working on something revolutionary, and I've learned more from him this year than I'll *ever* learn from you." I shifted to my sarcastic voice. "Oh, that's right. You're not interested in me learning anything other than how to *grunt* a little louder."

"Grunt? I'll bet you're good–" She closed her mouth, and I admit her self-control was better than mine. "How many merits do you have left, Cadet Mala Dusa Holloman?"

"I have twelve out of my seventy-five, ma'am." There was nothing but cruelty in her smile and I wondered if she'd take them all and force me to sit out the next semester.

"Now you have *one* left. Run along, stick girl, before that's gone too. Oh, and something else that I want to teach you. Those cute little starships you want to design? Out in the real world we call them 'targets', and they don't last long."

I took too long a shower, trying to let go of my anger. No breakfast, and I had to run across the quad to be even close to on time for class. I tried to let go of the last of the anger as I walked into Professor Slade's lab. He had been Principal Engineer on the team that designed the Trade Guild's *Doge*-class freighters, ships that carried goods between the planets seventy thousand tonnes at a time. He knew more about engines and structures than anyone I'd ever met, he always made time for me, and he never thought my questions were stupid. When he smiled, his eyes looked just like my Grandpa Vandermeer's, full of mischievous humor. I told him what Instructor Chao had done to me and apologized for being late.

"You know why she didn't take all of your merits, of course."

I stared back at him blankly as he waited for my brain to start working. "Right. If she'd taken them all, I'd have nothing left to lose. I could do whatever I wanted for the rest of the semester, at least when I wasn't confined to my dorm or they threw me out."

"Exactly. Now she owns you."

I sighed. "Why can't I learn to keep my mouth shut?"

"It's a hard lesson, harder for some. Why do you fight her?"

"I want to build cute little starships, explore space, and discover new things." I waved my hands grandly, imitating Instructor Chao's voice. He smiled at me and I sighed. "I don't want to blow stuff up. I don't want to kill people."

"Those two things are very human. Sometimes..." he shrugged, "even necessary."

"I don't have to like it."

"No, you don't."

"She likes it."

He chuckled. "Even without her legs she still kicks your ass. Let's get some engineering done and try not to think about what terrible creatures we humans are."

Terrible creatures. Monsters. That's what we are. The Academy had changed since Winona and I had convinced my parents to let me come, not that they could have stopped me. They claimed to hate the Reunification Commission, but they didn't. They were just afraid that I'd die on some planet far from home. They'd lost friends and lovers that way during their time with RuComm. But I knew I wouldn't die. I had a destiny to fulfill.

The Academy had once been a haven for scientists, researchers, and future leaders. The Reunification war had changed it into a school for producing soldiers, trained to fight and die keeping Earth's Interstellar Union together. The Union Aerospace Force had taken over operations and implemented the same combat focused curriculum they used at their Military Institute at Dehradun.

Earth had done nothing to stop the planets that wanted to leave when the First Union fell in 2218. Most worlds went dark, falling into brutality, war, and genocide. People turned inward, interstellar trade all but died, and one hundred-seven years passed before the citizens on Earth had an awakening and decided they cared enough to intervene.

We did not stand idly by this time. Earth had invested two hundred thirty years of blood and treasure putting the Union back together, and we weren't going to watch it all fall apart again. Earth and its closest allies would not allow it. The Trade Guild took the lead in building public support and government resolve for war, constantly reminding us that we must not allow a repetition of the barbarity of the past. They didn't talk as loudly about the negative impact the independence movements were having on their ledger sheets, or the barbarity that would be required to hold the Union together. The final vote wasn't even close. The Interstellar Union went to war, and RuComm and its Academy changed to support the effort.

Professor Slade had received messages from the Trade Guild of Venice the autumn of my fourth year, begging him to come back and work for them. Pirates sponsored by the secessionist government on Bridger were harassing commerce in and out of the system and the Guild needed a way to protect their cargos. Bridger was a waypoint in the Deep Space Hole network between Earth and the outlying planets, and they wanted the Guild to pay tribute for passing through their space.

Professor Slade had proposed making it an independent study for his advanced ship design class, which that year consisted of three other students and myself, in exchange for a donation to the Academy's endowment fund. He would provide the engineering rigor to the project and we'd learn something about working with real industrial requirements and processes. The members of the Guild would sell their own mothers for a tenth of a percent savings on operating costs, so to get design work done for the price of a corporate donation made them very happy.

The Bridger pirates were using small Fast Attack Craft that could punch through a *Doge*-class freighter's hull in less than ten seconds. Professor Slade showed us video on the first day of class of it happening. The FAC's directed energy weapons turned the freighter's hull to sparkly mist. The *Doge*-class ships were big and slow, but we almost had a solution by early March. Almost.

Winona met me for lunch between classes. I was eating a salad of field greens and Dulcinean purple tubers with grilled fish on top. The fish looked and smelled like what my dad cooks, but it tasted only slightly better than the compostable plate under it.

Winona, my best and only friend, clattered her tray onto the table and sat down across from me. "Bekka tells me that you're down to one merit. Idiot. Why do you let Chao spool you up like that?" She took a bite of stew while she waited for me to answer, her nose over the bowl savoring the smell of carrots and potatoes.

"I just need to hold on to it for ten more weeks, until the end of the spring semester. Then everything resets in the fall and I'll be much more disciplined next term." I grinned at her so she would know I was lying.

She ignored me and took another bite of her stew. "So, how's your project today?"

I sighed. "Professor Slade finally convinced Cadet Braddock that hanging double plating all over the ship isn't the answer. Every cubic meter of armor is one less of cargo, and the Guild's profit margins are too thin to stand for that."

"You sound like a merchant."

"Thanks. I want to design ships and they're the ones with the money. Warships are only needed while we're at war, and wars don't last forever."

Winona smiled a sad smile at me. "So the Professor accepted your honeycomb idea?"

"Yep. My honeycomb of ablative and reactive armor is lighter and lasts longer."

"How much longer?"

I took a bite of salad and made a face. The fish was even more terrible than usual. "Almost an hour under the right conditions. We spun the ship in the last simulation, and that helped. One hour of simulated attack by three FACs and then it breaks apart and everyone dies." I speared a piece of fish and held my fork up so Winona could inspect it with me. "I think this must have been printed last week. Taste it. Maybe it was last year."

"No thanks. I don't eat printed food when I can avoid it."

I think that's what she said, but I wasn't really listening. "Printed," I said, turning my fork and watching chunks of fish fall on to the table. "That's how we can do it, Winn. We can reprint the armor *as* it's being ablated. The weight of the raw powdered composite will be less than half what Braddock's extra plates would add." I twirled the fork until all the fish was gone. "And the bunkers holding the powder can be any shape, reducing the cargo impact. This could *work*. The freighter should be able to survive two or three hours at least. Plenty of time for their escorts to intervene."

"Done with lunch?"

I realized I was standing, fork still in my hand.

"All done. Need to talk to Professor Slade." I started walking away. "Can you take my tray for me? Please?" I didn't wait for her answer before I started running.

It took us weeks to perfect the solution, finding the right rate of spin, tailoring the composition of the armor, and then we had to design the mobile, high-speed sintering printers to rebuild the honeycomb during an attack.

Professor Slade said it was brilliant for a fourth-year cadet. He gave it my name in the paper he wrote, and Holloman Armor went into production at the main Union shipyard on Bodens Gate. Professor Slade gave me an 'A' at the end of the semester, which balanced my 'C-' in physical training. The Trade Guild of Venice sent me a special pin shaped like a winged lion and an offer for a job, contingent on being alive when my Terms of Union Service contract was completed.

I still had my one merit left at the end of the spring semester, thanks to Winona. Four years at the Academy completed, with two more to go. I had my full complement of seventy-five merits back at the start of the fall term in September. Just four semesters left. I could almost feel the Second Lieutenant's bars on my shoulders.

A few weeks into my fifth year at the Academy, the only number that mattered to me was six hundred-sixty. That's how many men and women would never return home because of me. I think there were more, but the final accounting is classified, and Winona refused to help me find the truth. They called it the Battle of Bridger's Quarter, but it wasn't a battle. It was a slaughter.

Winona stood with me at the back of the Common Room while the cadets from our dorm watched the near real-time video as it came in. Three *Star*-class Union cruisers escorted six freighters, all nine ships upgraded with my armor. They transited the Bridger Deep Space Hole together, already spinning and ready for a fight. Bridger's FACs matched velocity and engaged at extreme close range, less than ten kilometers. Our cruisers tore twenty-two FACs apart in less than fifteen minutes. We lost the *Pole Star*, but that was to a suicide attack by a FAC captain who knew he was about to die anyway.

I watched it all, unmoving, my hand covering my mouth. I'm not sure I even blinked. The other cadets cheered the death of each enemy ship. The debris field sparkled in the light of Bridger's sun when it was over. I recognized engine frames, intake baffles, and other large pieces that had survived the impacts of our kinetic energy weapons, all floating among the jagged bits of outer hull and a fine mist of fuel, air, and water.

They were good pictures, high-res. I stood and stumbled over feet and chairs to get close to the big display panel. I began counting the bodies.

Winona came up behind me and whispered in my ear. "Mala Dusa, what do you think you're doing?"

"There're so many of them. I need to count them all and I couldn't see from the back of the room. We tore them apart, Winn. It's hard with so many pieces. Maybe I should count the limbs. Would that work? Tally up the arms and the legs and divide by four? I think that will work." I was whispering to myself, eyes squinting at the display. Winona probably couldn't hear me, but I didn't care; I needed to keep counting.

Winn shut off the feed. The other students yelled at her and she pushed me out of the room and toward the exit. The Dean of Cadets was blocking the door.

"Great job, Cadet Holloman. That's your work up on that display. You've made the entire Academy proud today." He took my limp hand and shook it.

"They're all dead," I told him.

"That they are. You should celebrate tonight."

Winona shoved me past him toward the hall as the sound of the cheering started back up. "Thank you, Dean Bahrfeldt. I'll make sure she enjoys herself."

Academy regulations do not allow Cadets to have alcohol in the dorms. I got drunk that night anyway, and Winn stayed with me, holding my hair while I threw up in a trash can. I punished myself because the Academy and the Reunification Commission wouldn't do it for me.

There was a lot of drinking over the next year and a half, and a lot of waking up in the middle of the night to scream, my brain full of corpses in pressure suits, faces mummified by the cold vacuum that had killed them. No, that's not true. I'd killed them.

I would have died without Winona and the love of my life, my Samuel. They helped me cope well enough with the pain to make it through my fifth and sixth year and reach the final month before graduation.

Winona was staring at me. "Just how much stuff are you planning on taking with you, Duse?"

"Too much?" I glanced up at her from trying to cram an extra pair of pants into my bag. The seams were starting to bulge.

"For three days at a house that's already got a closet full of your clothes? Yeah, maybe."

I sighed and dumped everything back out. "I don't know what I might need. Sam's meeting us there and sometimes he has plans he doesn't tell me about. I need to be prepared. And I want to take him up Humphrey's Peak with us on Saturday, and I'm sure we'll all go swimming..."

"Tomorrow night we're going to sit in your backyard and celebrate your dad's fiftieth birthday. All his old friends will be there telling stories designed to embarrass him in front of Hannah and you. Everyone will drink too much. After that, you and Sam will sit by the fire and make sad love faces at each other the way you *always* do when you're together. Then you'll brush your teeth and go to bed."

"Then Saturday we'll get up early and go hiking."

"You'll be hung over again."

"Will not. You just watch me. I shall demonstrate *superb* self-control."

She didn't reply, concentrating on packing her own bag while I sorted back through the pile on my bed. I put about half of it back in and shoved the remainder onto the floor with the rest of my clean clothes.

Winn didn't even look up. "Duse, do you know why all of your other roommates dumped you?"

"Dumped? They didn't dump me. I just kept requesting to have you as my roommate until Dean Bahrfeldt relented. Now we've been roomies for a whole year." I smiled at her.

"I had to sign a waiver that I understood what I was getting into. He said you were messy, moody, and prone to waking up screaming in the middle of the night, especially since Bridger."

"That's all true." I sat down on the floor with my pile of clean clothes, leaned back against the bed, and closed my eyes. "Why did you have to bring that back up again?"

"I'm taking your award with me."

"Why?" I pushed hard on my eyes with the heels of my palms, trying to wipe out what I was seeing. "I keep putting it in the trash for a reason. Why do you keep pulling it back out?"

"It's the Daniel O. Graham Special Award of Merit, one of the highest forms of recognition the Union has. Not many Academy students ever earn it. Hannah wants to see it since she was off planet somewhere she can't talk about and couldn't come to the ceremony last fall. She's proud of you. And I see you still wear the winged lion pin the Trade Guild of Venice awarded you for the same innovation."

I touched the small silver broach attached to my collar next to my senior rank markings. "They just wanted to protect their ships and save their crews and cargo. The Union saw it as a weapon. They wanted, um, wanted..." I shivered, feeling myself starting to shake somewhere deep inside, unable to stop what I was seeing. It was all there in front of me again.

After the battle, Bridger petitioned to rejoin the Union, and then Meeker and Pomplamoose not long after that, giving up without a fight. The Union government and RuComm presented me with their Special Award of Merit on a cold November afternoon. After the ceremony, I had gone back to my dorm, cried, and put it in the trash. Winona took it out and hid it from me for a time.

I let the memory play itself out. The media on Bridger had published short biographies of everyone that I had killed. I read about fifty of them before Winona blocked my access. I don't know how she does things like that, but she's Winona, and I gave up trying to explain her a long time ago. I just know that she loves me as much as I love her.

Her forehead pressed up against mine and I opened my eyes. She smiled at me and gently pushed the hair away from my face. "Mala Dusa? Little Soul?"

"That's what my name means."

"Are you better?"

"Uh huh."

"Bridger's Quarter was almost a year and a half ago, and still it's echoing inside your brain."

"Uh huh. Maybe I should have quit right then and gone to live with my Aunt Cory making clay pots and custom tea blends."

She pulled me to my feet. "No, your Aunt's tea is terrible. Your destiny is to build starships. It's what you were made for and you're a hell of an engineer."

"Thanks. I thought you said I was made to be with Sam. It's what the Tarakana want."

"You can do both. You *will* do both."

"I will do both." I looked around at the floor on my half of the room. "Should I clean up before we leave?"

"Why start now? Shove everything in the drawer under your bed as usual. You can't afford any more demerits."

9

"Good point." I glanced at my watch. "We should be leaving for the station anyway."

"Being at the station early doesn't mean you'll get to see Sam any sooner."

I wrinkled my forehead at her. "It might. It's worth a try."

No luck. We sat, talked about finals that were coming up in a few weeks, and watched angry April snow squalls trying to make it past Mount Herman. A couple of them were successful, sweeping across the Academy grounds and sending wet flakes to smash against the big windows of the station. Then the sun would come back out and it would feel like spring again.

The maglev arrived on schedule, meaning we'd probably be on time into Flagstaff at 18:23 instead of 18:22 or 18:21 as I'd hoped. I settled into my seat, rested my cheek on my fist and stared out the window. Five hours to go until I was with Sam. My parents too, but Sam most of all. I sighed, leaving the beauty of the mountains that were rushing past at three hundred kilometers per hour unappreciated.

There was a gentle touch in my thoughts. Winona, trying to comfort me. It was the gift of the Tarakana that she could do that, the gift of the colony I called Merrimac and thought of as my friend. The Tarakana were alien, intelligent, cold, and beautiful. No one believed the Tarakana existed except for the few of us that had met them. I was convinced they were symbiotic with humans. Winona saw them as parasites, but the ability they had given us to feel each other's emotions was keeping me stable right then.

I could feel Sam in my head too, the other half of my soul. His arms were around me, telling me that he loved me and that he cared. His longing was the same as mine, so it did little to cheer me. I didn't know where Sam was, and it didn't matter. As long as he was on the same side of the Deep Space Hole network as me, I could feel him. I hated it when he was on the other side of a DSH. I felt cut in two.

Winn needed to be within twenty meters of me to touch my emotions, which is where she usually was anyway. I smiled at her. "Thanks."

"It's interesting, the way your emotional distress increases the closer you get to being with Sam. Most of the time you're one of the happiest people I know, at least when you're not obsessing about Bridger. As soon as you're within twenty-four hours of a Sam rendezvous, you get like this. Your despair has sharp edges this time, and something else."

"Six years, Winn. I've wanted him for six years, almost seven. The emotional connection helps. We can sort of be together that way, but I want him more than ever now. Is that Merrimac pushing us or is it because I love him?"

"The Tarakana have been secretly breeding both your families for generations. I'm surprised you've been able to resist this long. And what you feel for him? I don't think love is a strong enough word."

"They'll kill him once I'm pregnant. It's the next generation they're most interested in, not so much Sam and me. It's why we've waited so long. But it's not right to wait. We've talked about it, the risk..." I swallowed hard, feeling dizzy at the thought of helping Sam make a baby. "The risk is worth it."

"Your fertility's been reversed since you were fourteen."

"Yeah. Just like my mom's was when Dad got her pregnant with me. Tarakana, Winn, their technology is more advanced than ours."

"And they won't kill him, they'll just..."

"Remove their protection and let him die," I finished for her. "That won't take long. He's been serving on board the *Esprit Vengeur* for the last six months. He won't tell me what they've been doing, but I can feel it when he's on this side of the DSH, like he has been since Tuesday. He's a research biologist and RuComm made him into a medic, or so he tells me. He wakes up screaming sometimes too."

I leaned my head back and watched my reflection in the window for a while. La Veta Pass came and went in a blur of rocks, trees, and snow. "I'm going to marry him."

"Sure you are."

"What?" I turned to look at her.

"You said you're going to marry Sam."

"Out loud?"

She tipped her head to the side before answering. "We graduate in six weeks, then we have a few weeks leave, and then *three*," she held three fingers up in front of my face for emphasis, "back-to-back ten-month tours of duty in order to complete our minimum active duty service obligation. If you're married *or* pregnant, that's a violation of your contract. If you refuse your commission or willfully make yourself unable to serve, you'll have to pay RuComm back for the high-quality education you just received. You can't afford that. What are you planning to do, Mala Dusa?"

"I'm going to marry him. Some day." I turned back to the window. "Soon." I giggled. I tried not to, but it just came out.

Her reflection was staring at me and I could feel her becoming concerned, even though she usually blocks me completely. "When? *Please* don't be stupid." She reached around me and pressed her finger against my forehead, which was better than the hard tap I usually got when she thought I was being an idiot. "Are you thinking about right after graduation?"

"No, he'll probably be on the other side of a DSH by then, risking his life. I'm thinking Saturday afternoon." I tried not to giggle again. "Day after tomorrow."

Winona closed her eyes. "Please God; don't let her be this stupid."

"Prayer?"

"When it comes to you, it's all I have left, even if I don't have your faith that it does any good."

I pulled my knees up and wrapped my arms around them. "I'm going to do it, Winn, please don't try to stop me. I'm going to be with him, *really* with him. I'm going to have him inside my body, not just inside my mind. And it will be worth it, even if I can only have him for a few days before the reunification war takes him, or the Tarakana let him die, or if I have to find a way to repay every bit of what RuComm spent on me. I don't care anymore. I *need* to be with Sam. Ow!"

Yeah, I knew that was coming, the hard poke on my forehead. Then she looked at me, head still tipped, and kissed my head and then my lips for good measure. "What did your parents say?"

"I don't plan to tell them. Sam and I can have a proper ceremony in a couple of years, if we're both still alive. The fewer people who know about it the safer we'll be."

"Saturday. I thought we were going hiking."

"We are. Well, a very short hike. You know that big clearing a couple hundred meters up from the trailhead? We're going to do it right there, just short of the boulder field."

"I can't believe your pastor agreed to this."

"I didn't ask him. He and my dad are too close and I don't trust him to keep it a secret." I giggled again, the thought of finally being with Sam making me too happy to hold it in. "Father Ryczek is doing it for us."

"You didn't tell me that he's going to be at your dad's party. Has he ever even been off Bodens Gate before this? How old *is* he?"

"Dad says he's ninety-one, still strong, and with the lower gravity here he should be fine. He says he's looking forward to it. I think he feels like he's putting something over on my mom."

"He and Hannah never have seen eye to eye. About anything. Still..." Winona drifted into deep Winona thoughts. "Will it be snowing on Saturday?"

"That's something I *have* been praying about. It will be thirteen or fourteen degrees C and bright sunshine; you won't even need a heavy coat. See? God is on my side."

"Have you ever thought about trying to be on God's side?"

"Sam and I have talked this through. He wants it as much as I do."

"What a surprise. He's been trying to get into your pants since you were sixteen." She wrinkled her nose at me and I could feel her surrendering. "Fine. I don't know what we're going to do if he puts a baby in there." She patted my stomach. "Have you thought about having it removed?"

"Take out the fertilized egg and freeze it? We talked about it, but no, I don't want to do that. It seems wrong somehow."

"Now that *is* Merrimac messing with you. I can feel the Tarakana haze filling your head when you try to think about it. Your brain's been fuzzy since we left the station."

"Who knows? Maybe I won't get pregnant. And maybe it won't matter. I can still do my job as engineer even with a baby growing inside me. Mostly."

She took my hand. "You are a great deal of trouble, you know that?"

"Am I worth it?"

"Mostly."

# CHAPTER 2

# HOME AGAIN

I was trying to catch my breath, but it wasn't easy. My chest was being crushed and my mouth was covered. My nose was clear, but it was smashed up beside Sam's nose. Breathing could wait, kissing was more important.

Winona's voice came to me from somewhere. "Samuel, if you make her faint again, you'll be responsible for carrying her to the car."

I sighed and moved my head to his shoulder, nipping gently at his ear before snuggling my head against him. "He hasn't gotten me to faint in years."

"But I still try," Sam added. "You look good in that cadet uniform, MD. Very sharp, very RuComm."

"And you, my Captain." I touched the bars on his collar. "Very Union. I can't wait to get out of this thing. Might need help, though." I wiggled against him and made him blush, which was my intention. He's cute when he blushes. I forced myself to let go of him and wrapped my arms around my mom.

"You seem excessively happy." Hannah gave me a squeeze.

"Yeah. It's good to be back home."

"Right. I'm sure that's the only reason." She sighed, staring at Sam.

I leaned back and looked at her. There was more gray in her hair than last time, and..."What's this?" I touched a mostly healed cut below her left eye that arced down across her cheek.

She sighed, embarrassed. "My reflexes are slowing down."

"I know that you can't tell me where you were or what you were doing, but you're too...valuable for 'wet work'. What's the Union thinking sending you where you could get hurt like that?"

She shrugged. "Sometimes you don't know how things are going to go until you get there. And it wasn't supposed to be wet work. Just a little damp, maybe. And I'm not too *old* for that." She took me by the elbow, steering me toward the exit. "And look at you, not quite so skinny anymore. I think the Academy has put some muscle on your bones."

I put my arm around her while we walked. "I don't enjoy it, though. Except for the running. I love to run."

She glanced at my legs, then back up to my face, shaking her head. "You know, you're just a couple of months younger than Ted was when I first met him. It was his first time off planet, first RuComm assignment, first big adventure, first everything. Your eyes are the same as his; honest and always a little amused at something. The rest of you though, it's all Alice." She chuckled. "Your real mom would be terribly proud of you."

"You're my mom, and you always say that. Where *is* Dad anyway?"

I could feel a flash of irritation go through her mind. "Marcus is here for the party tomorrow night. We're on our way to meet him for dinner and drinks at Casa Paloma, and of course he talked your father into getting a head start on the drinking part."

"Dad drinking? Anything more than two beers or a margarita and he just falls asleep."

"I hope that's all he does. Damn Marcus."

Dad was still awake when we got there. I recognized Marcus Wright instantly despite the ten years since I'd seen him last on Dulcinea. He had a coarse beard, with just a trace of its original brown remaining, and he was holding a glass of something dark and smelly. He was in the middle of a story about my dad that I didn't think was physically possible.

He slammed his glass down when he noticed me, sloshing beer on the already wet table. "God damn! It's the Little Soul of Alice, come to haunt me for my evil ways."

I smiled my innocent smile at him, trying to feel my way to the right response. "Professor Wright. It was good of you to come for my dad's party. He speaks of you often."

He glanced at Dad, then back to me, then back to Dad. "Are you sure you're her father? Alice may have cloned herself; I wouldn't put it past her. Let me check."

He looked into my eyes, trying to focus. "Are you here to save my soul, Ms. Mala Dusa?"

I stared back at him. "I hadn't planned on it, but I suspect your soul is in desperate need of saving and I'd be willing to give it a try."

"There, you see?" He pivoted back to Dad. "Definitely an Alice clone."

Dad was laughing. "No, Marcus, I can assure you it didn't happen that way. And look at her eyes. A little bit of me in there too, don't you think?"

"Mistakes happen sometimes in the cloning process. Maybe if you told me more details about her creation?"

That was about enough for Hannah. She and Dad loved each other more than seemed humanly possible, but she was not about to tolerate hearing the story about how Dad and my real mom made a baby me. Certainly not in the middle of a restaurant.

"*Marcus.*"

That was all she needed to say.

"Hannah, my unrequited love." He took her hand, to shake it I thought, but he kissed it gently instead, almost reverently. "Every year you are lovelier than the year before. How do you do that when the rest of us only grow older and more...tiresome?" He let her take her hand back. "Do you have plans for later?"

She sighed, looking at Dad. "I did, if you haven't put too much beer inside him already."

"For your sake, I shall refrain from encouraging any further damage."

"Thanks, I'd appreciate that. We'll get some enchiladas into him for ballast and hope for the best."

He focused on Sam next. "Samuel Coleridge." He grabbed his hand and shook it. "You almost became a biologist. What is it RuComm has you doing now?"

"I can't really say."

"Damn the Union. They're wasting your potential. And, damn RuComm too. They should be in the business of turning out scientists, but now they want to build soldiers instead."

"Careful, Marcus," Mom cautioned him, glancing at the ceiling to remind him that on Earth there was always an AI listening.

He frowned at her and then put a finger in Sam's face. "You still owe me time on the Margo Islands. That putz RuComm sent in your place didn't know a trivalve from a brachiopod, and then I was stuck with her for nine months until the Oceanus Protectorate and the Palma Federated States settled their differences again. You would have enjoyed it there too, we had quite the time. I even got a paper out of the experience on the effect of enforced isolation on teenage and young adult behavior and sexuality." He turned to me, grinning. "And you, my conniving little girl, you would have been there with him if you hadn't been bent on using me to manipulate your parents into getting what you really wanted."

I grinned back at him.

He looked confused for a moment, glancing back and forth between the two of us as Sam helped me into my chair. Old fashioned and chivalrous is my Sam.

"And yet here you are together anyway, as if it was ordained. And planning something devious by the way you keep looking at each other."

I swallowed hard, knowing I was blushing. Dad had once mentioned that Marcus worked for the Palma Federated States' Internal Security Service as an intelligence officer before becoming a biology professor. Dad had warned me that he still reads people.

"I have no idea what you're talking about."

"Damn, girl, you're worse at lying than your father, and that's saying something."

Winona tried to distract him for me. "I'm sure you're just seeing the effects of her being with Sam, worrying about finals next month, and uncertainty about our future. Nothing more. My name is Winona Killdeer, by the way." She stuck her hand across the table at him.

He took it and bowed his head slightly to her. "You, on the other hand, are *really* good. Let me know if you're ever interested in living on a more civilized planet. I have some old friends who would love to meet you."

"I'll keep that in mind." She tapped the menu card in front of her, scrolling through the selections. "I was thinking of trying the Mexican chocolate stout. Have you ever had one?"

He grinned, shaking his head at her. "Peace. I'll let them go for now. Try the tesgüino. I think you'll like it better."

We made it through dinner and dropped Winona off at her folks' house two hours later with a growler full of tesgüino. I was home again, my room looking unchanged from when I had last been there, complete with a messy pile of clothes on the floor, and my poster showing the evolution of starship engine design above the bed.

The plan was for Sam to sleep in a guest room in the basement, if I ever let him get there, if I ever let him sleep. I had plans for him first. We were cuddled up in the glow from the fire pit out on the patio, Sam lying on his back on a lounge chair with me mostly on top of him, very much out of uniform, and keeping his mouth busy with mine. I didn't dare go back in the house yet. My parents and I can feel each other's emotions from fifteen meters away. I worried that Sam's hands caressing me under the blanket we were sharing would significantly increase the range. It seemed possible that Winona could feel them at her house a kilometer down the road.

I sighed, moving my head to his shoulder.

"You seem happy and contented." He wrapped his arms tighter around me.

"Not yet, but I plan to be soon."

"Soon like in a few minutes, or do you mean Saturday?"

"Umm. Both would be nice."

He kissed my hair. "We should invite your parents."

"For a few minutes from now? That doesn't seem appropriate."

He chuckled. It sounded warm and comforting with my ear pressed against him. "I mean on Saturday. Leaving them out doesn't seem right."

"I know. I was thinking the same thing. But I'm going to wait until the last minute to tell them. And we should have invited your mom."

"I'll explain it to her somehow. She's used to me doing stupid things."

"Oh, so you think marrying me is stupid now?" I bit his neck gently, but not too gently. I felt the shiver run through his brain and could almost see what it made him want to do to me.

"Are you trying to pick a fight with me again, MD?" He moved his hands lower down on my back, then lower still, pulling me completely on top of him while he kissed hard on my shoulder. "Because I'm ready for you."

"I noticed. Go ahead, do your worst."

"Afterward, will you finally let me get some sleep?"

"No promises."

He flipped the blanket up over the top of us and his hands slowly and gently drifted to where I needed them to be. Between the giggles and the moans, it didn't take long at all before we were both comfortable and contented.

Winona woke me up the next morning just as she did every weekend when we were kids, banging around downstairs in the kitchen fixing breakfast and talking too loudly with my dad. The five hours of sleep we'd managed on a good night at the Academy was about right for her. I'd survived for six years on an endless river of coffee. For a moment, while I was trying desperately to fall back asleep, I thought it must be Saturday, and then I realized where I was and what was going on. It *was* Winona, but she was talking too loudly with Sam, not my dad, and it was only Friday. I struggled for a moment between my love for Sam and for my pillow.

Sharlot settled it for me. "Mala Dusa, Sam and Winona are wondering if you plan to sleep all day."

I whimpered a little. If Sharlot was on their side, any attempt at further sleep was futile. I always suspected that Dad had altered her programing specifically to get me up in the mornings.

"Tell them I'm on my way to the shower and I'll be down in a minute."

"You're still in bed."

I sighed. Dad had named her after a journalist that had passed through our city over five hundred years ago and called us a "third rate mining camp." Every bit of that woman's stubbornness, cynicism, and skill with sarcasm had made it into the AI matrix.

"Please, just tell them."

"Winona says to come down just as you are. Take a shower later."

Winn knew that I never wore anything when I slept. Sharlot did a good job of relaying the message. I could hear the smirk. I threw my covers onto the floor and stood beside the bed stretching.

"On second thought, you may want to try putting on a robe or something. Just saying. There's a gentleman downstairs."

"Thanks, Sharlot. I'll do that. And that's *my* gentleman that's down there."

"Are you sure? You should hurry it up a bit, then. I think he's starting to take an interest in your friend."

"Taunt all you like. I know what's mine."

I put on a pair of soft pants and a t-shirt, then opened my door.

"What about your hair? It's kind of a mess."

"You said to hurry and to 'come as you are'. So...I'm coming."

"Pah. Your funeral."

There were smells as I came down the stairs. Coffee, bacon, and something sweet. I entered the kitchen, bare feet on cold tiles, and hugged Sam, burying my face into his neck. "You made me waffles."

"Winona made waffles. I did coffee." He placed a warm mug in my hands when I pulled back from him. "You smell sleepy. This should help."

I hugged Winona. "You made me waffles."

"Love the hair, Duse."

I knew she was teasing, but Sam was looking at me and his feelings had nothing to do with teasing. He liked it when I was tousled. If the Lord granted us a normal life together, I was going to have to buffer in some extra time every morning for him to show his appreciation.

"So what's the plan for today?" I asked between sips of my second cup and bites of Sam's waffle, mine having disappeared in just three or four bites. "Do we have time to cause trouble somewhere before the party?"

Winn tipped her head at me and looked at the ceiling. Sharlot answered for her.

"As I already explained to your friends, I have explicit tasking for each of you from Hannah. She plans to return by 13:30 and expects you to have completed each line item by then. To ensure no lapses, I've placed a copy with estimated durations on your display pads."

I heard a soft ding from Sam and Winona's pockets, and from my pad that was sitting on the table.

"Ooo, look. Balloons." I tipped the screen toward Sam.

"You're going to get your screen sticky again," Winona warned me.

"OK, let me put on something less comfortable and we can get to work. Sharlot, I have a task for you to be working on while we're getting the house ready for tonight." I tapped on the display, brought up an old file and slid it over onto the ogre-faced icon that I used to represent our household AI.

"Do you see this?" I asked her.

"I do."

"I would like a copy of the dress that the bride is wearing, sized for me."

There was a long pause, whether for dramatic effect or because she was doing something in the background, I didn't know. "The wedding dress that Alice wore when she married your father? What are you planning on doing with it?"

"I'd like to have it before 06:00 tomorrow. Can you print it for me?"

Another long pause. "Mala Dusa, you will be absolutely beautiful in this dress. It will be a great privilege for me to create it for you and I can't wait to see you in it."

"Thanks. And please don't mention it to my parents. I'll tell them about it at the right time. Like tomorrow morning, a couple of hours before the ceremony."

A sniffling sound came from somewhere.

Sam looked at me, concerned. "Is she...crying?"

I shrugged. "Mom goes into her code all the time and messes with it. Yeah, I think she's crying. But she knows how to keep a secret, which is good because there're too many people that know about this already."

# CHAPTER 3

# THE PARTY

We were all soaking in the pool when Mom got home at 13:30. The air temperature was only about fourteen, but the pool was heated to a comfy twenty-seven. I watched her approaching through the steam rising from the surface with just my eyes and nose sticking up out of the water.

She slipped off her shoes and sat on the edge, making little splashes with her feet. "Sharlot says you did an adequate job, and it does look good. The black balloons are a nice touch."

I was tempted to grab her foot and try to drag her in with us. She needed to relax, I could feel her trying to let go of something stressful. "Join us. The water's perfect. See?" I splashed some of it on her legs so she could see.

"Maybe later. I have a few things to do before the caterers get here at 17:00. Thank you all for doing this." She stood, carrying her shoes in one hand. "I'll be in the back office if you need anything before then."

The back office. The one room in our house that Sharlot couldn't control or even access. Mom may have taught Sharlot to keep secrets, but her office was a different story. I knew there was a secure comm link in there, but that was about all I knew.

Winona swam up next to me. "Ms. Weldon, is there anything I can do to help?"

"Ms. Killdeer, I wish you could. We'll have that conversation next month after graduation. OK?"

"Yes, ma'am."

My mouth was open and I was trying to get my brain back working again as I watched Mom walking away. "Winona, we applied to do our first tour of duty together, remember?"

"I remember. The group your mom works with wants to interview me. That's all, just talk."

"Why do they need an astrophysicist?"

"Do you even know what your mom does?"

Sam was next to me now, trying to keep me from freaking out. It wasn't working.

"No, no one knows. She's *supposed* to be a linguist for the government, and she knows a bunch of languages, but she also knows way more about people from different planets than she should. And somehow, she keeps getting hurt, and sooner or later, she's going to get killed. You can't go, Winn. You can't go *anywhere* that takes you more than twenty meters from me. I *need* you."

"Breathe, Duse. Nothing's been decided."

Sam was rubbing my back, trying to calm me down. He turned to Winona. "I've met some of the people that work in the same organization as her, the Department of Cultural Intelligence. I probably shouldn't have told you that, so pretend I didn't say it. You need to be careful. Make sure you understand what they're offering you and what you'd have to do. The door into the Intelligence Community only opens one way."

"I don't think that's always true. A couple of my professors worked for the DCI and they..." Winona blushed, a rare event. "I'm an idiot. They hide it almost perfectly, but they *still* work for the DCI."

Winn looked longingly up toward the house. She was letting me feel the desire in her because she was too distracted and excited to block me. She wanted to jump into that world, know its secrets, and make a difference the same way Hannah was making a difference. I was losing her.

"Damn it." I pulled myself out of the water and walked toward the house, not bothering to get dressed or even to wrap a towel around myself.

Sam started to follow me, but Winona stopped him. "Let her go. She needs to have this out with Hannah."

Damn right I did.

I raised my fist to pound on her office door, thought better of it, and tapped gently. I looked down at the puddle I was leaving on the floor that I had spent the morning cleaning. "Sharlot, can you spot clean this for me?"

"Of course, Mala Dusa. I'll start as soon as you're done dripping."

The door opened and Mom stared at me, looking irritated. She stepped into the hall, closing the door behind her. "You're going to freeze. Come with me."

I followed her into the family room and she wrapped one of the throws that we keep on the couch around my shoulders. "Sit."

I sat. "You can't have her."

She raised her eyebrows. "Winona? She's a big girl. A bright, no, a brilliant young woman. You know full well that there's no one else quite like her. She can make her own decisions."

"She worships you."

Mom nodded, frowning. "I know. What would you have me do? Not even give her the chance to do something she'd excel at, that she'd love doing? You're a brilliant young woman too, but you're an addict."

"I haven't been drinking as much this semester."

Her head tipped far to the right. "I didn't know that was a problem, and you and I are going to have a *long* talk about it later. What I meant is your addiction to Winona."

I felt myself folding inward. "It's really only been since Bridger."

"Ah. Winona told me about the panic attacks. And this morning she showed me the Award of Merit you earned. Can you talk about it?"

"Sure. I'm usually OK for a few weeks after an episode like I had yesterday."

"You know why they gave it to you, don't you?"

"For the armor and the technique to use it."

"No."

I felt myself fold inward a little more. "The certificate says I helped bring three worlds back into the Union."

"Yes. Eight hundred million people. Your contribution was critical."

I shrugged.

"Do you even believe in what the Union stands for?"

"Yes, I do," I answered firmly. "Individual rights, political and economic freedom. I spent an entire year doing a pre-law study of the legal codes and criminal justice system. I know it's worth fighting for."

"Would you want to live somewhere that abolished those rights? Bridger didn't have an election to decide to leave the Union. A small group representing maybe twenty percent of the population seized power and threw the planet into chaos, probably with help from one of the bad Tarakana colonies. They killed everyone that opposed them. Did you know that? They killed five thousand prisoners when they took the capital, giving no quarter to those that surrendered. The resistance fighters that we supported started calling it "giving Bridger's quarter", killing like that, without mercy. There were parades celebrating reunification when it came."

"Bridger's Quarter. There were no survivors on those ships. I killed over six hundred people, some younger than me. There should have been a better way."

"They got on those ships knowing the risks. You're like Alice. You think you can convince, and scheme, and manipulate people to get what you want without shedding any blood. It's a fantasy."

"You reach for your sword too easily."

"I do. You're right. I know that about me. When I see something I can do to help people, I go do it. I don't study it to death."

"There's too much death." I looked down and whispered, "Too much blood on my hands. I've got to find a better way."

"I don't remember you losing any sleep when we killed Steiner or when Janus Boden spent a year strapped to the side of a Trade Guild ship. The *out*side."

The events leading up to Steiner's death had left me shaking too badly to walk, and then Boden had tried to kill me and everyone I loved. I smiled, remembering the sight of Boden's desiccated corpse strapped below the Winged Lion of Venice, a warning from the Guild to all who would try to restrict free trade.

"They were monsters, and I still have nightmares. I found a way to avoid killing the thousands you had planned to kill."

"What would you say if I told you that all of the crew on those FACs were like Steiner and Boden?"

"I wouldn't believe you. I read some of their profiles." I shivered, but managed to control it, trying not to fold inward all the way again.

"Winona told me about that too. That was a mistake."

"Mom, am I a coward?"

She frowned, looking away from me.

"It's OK if you say that I am. I need to know what you think of me."

She shook her head. "If you want a quick answer, no, you're not. I've seen cowards. You have a unique type of bravery. I saw it on Bodens Gate. You want to run, but you stay. You do everything you can to get away from a fight, and then you risk everything. Thousands would have died without you, including us."

I shook my head. "I just did what had to be done. And I was scared the whole time."

She chuckled. "You know what you just did?"

"What?"

"You just gave me the definition of a hero."

"I'm *not* a hero."

She leaned forward and kissed my cheek. "Real heroes never believe they're heroes." She glanced at her watch. "I'm sorry. I need to get back in there. We can talk more after the party or tomorrow."

"Thanks." I smiled at her and was almost going to tell her what I had planned for the morning, but I could feel her urgent desire to get back into the office. I chewed my lower lip, undecided.

"Something else?"

"No, just...Don't make any plans for tomorrow, you or Dad."

I felt her banging around inside my skull. It was painful.

She closed her eyes. "Damn it, Dusa. Why can't you ever do things the easy way?"

I felt the tenderness and exasperation in her. I shrugged as she closed the door with a slam.

I put the throw I was wearing back on the couch, walked outside, up onto the one-meter board, and off the end without breaking stride. I let myself sink to the bottom and just sat there holding my breath. Sam came down after a few seconds and pulled me back to the surface.

"Should have left her down there," my best friend told him. "Look in her head. It's full of cobwebs and spiders right now. A little hypoxia might help her reset."

I stuck my tongue out at her. "Mom knows about the wedding."

"You told her?"

"No, she just reached into my brain and pulled it out, like she was yanking a pair of socks out of a drawer. I don't know how she does that."

"It's because you just leave your emotions lying around where anyone can see them. I've tried to teach you how to block, but..."

"I know. I'm hopeless." I rolled my eyes and ended up staring at Sam. Gentle blue eyes stared back at me, more amused than sympathetic. "Hi there," I told him. "We're getting married tomorrow."

"So I've heard. I have reservations at the Weatherford for tomorrow night if you'd like to join me."

"Yeah, joining sounds really good." I wrapped my arms around his neck and kissed him.

Winona sighed. "Thank you so much, Samuel. You just made the cobwebs ten times worse. I'm going back inside now to find somewhere that's more than twenty meters from here."

Winona was in the family room reading when Sam and I finally made it back to the house an hour later. Sam went downstairs to get dressed and I sat on the tile floor next to Winona.

"Sorry, Winn. I'll try to control myself better, I really will."

She glanced at me from her pad. "I don't believe you can do it, but thanks for saying you'll try. So, you're all done teasing him with your mostly naked body for now?"

"For now. He's the only person that's *ever* been attracted to my mostly naked body. Let me enjoy the feeling while I can."

She stared into my eyes, shaking her head. "Idiot." She turned her attention back to whatever she was reading.

"It's true. Sometimes I get a sense of what I look like through his eyes and it's *not* what I see in the mirror. I'm not pretty or cute. I'm built like a stick figure with…" I glanced down at myself. "No, pretty much just a stick figure. I have to get by on my personality and wit."

"Good luck with that. At least you're intelligent. What is your ranking going into finals next month? Twenty-third out of seven hundred-fifty, I believe. And number three in engineering."

"Says the woman who's number one in our class." I smiled and rested my head against her arm, knowing my hair was still wet and cold. "I'm so proud of my Winona." I kissed her hand.

She looked down at me and I felt something almost making it past her block, something like pain. She frowned and tapped my watch. "You still have it?"

I nodded and undid the band, pulling a small clear envelope from under it that held a lock of Winona's hair. "Knowing it's there helps more than you know. You told me that this contains a piece of you, your wisdom and strength. I don't know how I could have survived the last year without you."

She turned back to her display pad, but her eyes were closed. "Go get dressed, stick girl. The caterers will be here soon and I want to get a head start on the snacks."

"OK. But you have to save some stuffed jalapeños for me."

My house was full of people that I did not know, and Dad was determined that I meet all of them. It made me realize how little I knew about his life.

So I smiled, shook a lot of hands, and let people stare at me, even though I hate that. I snuck off to sit with Winn and Sam as soon as I could.

"Do all geologists know the same half dozen jokes?" I had brought Winona a fresh glass of wine and she took a sip before answering.

"You mean like the one that ends with 'subduction leads to orogeny'? Or 'coprolites happen'?"

"I think there are *at least* six that feature coprolites." Sam leaned over, looking into my glass. "What are you drinking?"

"Iced tea."

"*That's* my Mala Dusa." Winona was proud of me.

We sat talking quietly for a few minutes, enjoying being out of the main swirl of the party. Then Marcus found us. He sat at our table, greeting us with a too loud, "How's the conspiracy going? Ready to spring into action?"

"No conspirators here," I assured him. "We're just enjoying a quiet drink and some stuffed jalapeños. Try one?" I pushed the plate toward him.

He glanced at them. "Those are evil incarnate. And you shouldn't lie to me; you might need my help someday. You *are* conspirators, and that is *not* a drink." He tapped the side of my glass. "Now why, I must ask myself, does the Alice clone wish to remain sober tonight?"

"If I were really a clone of my mother I'd be better at lying, wouldn't I?"

"Oh, a clever thing for her to say to put me off the scent. I can only think of three reasons to remain sober at a party like this. One, you might be pregnant, but with the way you're built that would start to show within the first hour. Two, you want to make sure your behavior is appropriate during the party, or three, you have plans for later that require a clear head."

There was a loud splash and I turned to see that another of our guests had gone into the water.

"I wish people would stop falling into my pool."

Marcus was looking over my shoulder, squinting. "I think Hannah pushed that one in. A prideful woman, your stepmother."

He continued. "No one would notice misbehavior on your part tonight, so we must assume you have plans for later. Or maybe for the morning? Ah, I see by your eyes that it is the morning that concerns you."

"Duse, you may want to close your eyes and put your hands over your ears," Winona warned me.

Marcus smiled at her. "No distractions now, I'm almost there. Although, it would be easier if we could get a couple of glasses of scotch into her first. I can even guarantee her a clear head afterward, if that's what's worrying you." Marcus reached into his pocket and placed a small red bottle on the table in front of me.

"What is that?"

Sam answered for him. "Nox. It cleans all the alcohol out of your system in less than a second, but you pay for it later. And it's illegal on Earth."

Marcus looked offended. "Because Earth is a crappy planet."

"It's the coprolites," I assured him.

He chuckled. "Most of your dad's friends would think that was the best joke of the night. Now, tell me, what is it you're planning on doing tomorrow morning?"

He watched all three of us for about five seconds and then his eyes got a little bigger. "My God, do your parents know? That would explain why that walking fossil Ryczek has been so happy all evening, humming to himself everywhere he goes."

Winona tapped his shoulder. "Teach me, please. I want to learn how you did that."

I saw his eyes light up when he smiled at her and I suddenly understood what he was doing. "Winona Killdeer, can't you tell when you're being played? Marcus doesn't give a *damn* about what Sam and I are doing tomorrow. This was all a setup to lure you into going to work with him instead of with Mom. Sam was right about the door into the IC only swinging one way." I turned on him, growing angrier. "Marcus, who paid for your passage to come to my dad's party? It didn't come out of your own pocket, did it?"

He leaned back, looking irritated. "You may not be Alice's clone, but damn if you don't cause me as much pain. I would have paid to come here on my own because your father is my friend, but the opportunity presented itself to write it off as a recruiting trip. It was working too."

"What happened to 'damn the Union and damn RuComm'? Now you're recruiting for them?"

"This war has to end, and the sooner the better. Too many lives are being ruined while it drags on. I have my role to play, whether I like it or not."

I was still looking at him through slit eyes, my arms crossed. "Have you seen my pool? I'd be happy to give you a closer look."

He stood and handed something to Winona. "The offer stands, Ms. Killdeer. You'd like it on Dulcinea, I can promise you that. And Ms. Holloman...you'd be a valuable asset as well, as much as it hurts me to even suggest it. We're part of the Union, you know. It's not as if you'd be betraying anything." He leaned forward and whispered, "And *we* wouldn't care if you were *married*."

Sam was looking at me sideways, waiting to see what I'd say.

I locked eyes with Marcus. "Pool," I told him.

He was chuckling when he left. I put my head down on the table. "I need a drink. Did he leave the Nox here?"

I got to my room sometime around 02:00. We had cleaned up a little bit, helped folks call autocabs, and put blankets over those that were having trouble rising to the challenge of being awake. I was exhausted.

I turned on the light and there was a white dress lying across my bed. I touched it gently, feeling the softness of the fabric between my fingers. I felt suddenly afraid. I had planned on this moment for years, literally dreamed about every detail. Now it was real. In eight hours, I'd be standing in an open field with the sun on my bare shoulders, kissing my husband.

"Huh. This is crazy. What was I thinking?"

There was a German Shepherd dog sitting at the foot of my bed. He hadn't been there a moment before, now he was looking at me, head tipped slightly and warm brown eyes watching me with concern. I knew he was Tarakana, part of the Merrimac colony, and not really a dog. I sat down on the floor next to him and rested my face against his.

*"Little Soul, you want this, I know you do. You've waited seven years. We've waited for almost twenty-four. It's time."*

There were tears in my eyes. "You haven't come to see me in a while."

*"No, the colony on this planet is old and massive. They play the noble and the wicked, feeding equally on both. They tolerate me here and let me do some things, but not others. Sometimes they hinder me. Now it's time for you and Samuel. It's time to complete the love you share."*

I should have been terrified, but I wasn't. I knew that I was the result of generations of Tarakana meddling, breeding my family like livestock, allowing some to die, and protecting others, all to guide Samuel and Mala Dusa together to create the next generation, another step in whatever Merrimac was doing to the human species. Sometimes when I was at the Academy and no Tarakana were close by, I *was* terrified. When I was like this, with my face against his and my fingers clutching his fur, I felt proud of the role I was playing.

"Don't take him from me," I whispered.

I could feel the colony thinking as one, exploring the twisted paths of the alternate futures. *"Protecting him is difficult. He takes too many risks. Many other paths are closed because that one stays open."*

I could see all of the paths in the group mind, and I could see what might happen, all the passages and branches where I was alone forever without Sam, others where my son was alive, and even I was gone. But there was one...

"That one. What about that one? Can it be real?"

*"They all can be real, Little Soul. They all are real. That one? Are you sure? The outcomes are uncertain and I cannot control all the variables. Can't you see that it's random and chaotic past the first two iterations?"*

"Are random and chaotic always bad? No, I can't see it, but I want it anyway."

Amusement flashed through him, and the affection for me that troubled him, no, that *embarrassed* him. Winona thought I was foolish or worse when I told her that Merrimac was my friend. Friend might be the wrong word, but I knew he liked me more than he thought he should.

*"How interesting and delightful that you can surprise me. You should sleep now because tomorrow will be a busy day for you."*

"Yeah, busy day. Thank you for being such a good friend." I rolled onto my side, wrapped my arms around Merrimac, and he sang to me.

# CHAPTER 4

# THE KILL LIST

"You got that close and couldn't actually make it into your bed?"

My eyes opened and looked up at my mom. I was on the floor next to the bed, still wearing what I had worn to the party, with a blanket wrapped around me and a stuffed animal for a pillow. I tried to recall how I had come to be there, but there were no memories after I had started up the stairs to my room. Sam had been watching me climb, and the sharp mix of love and lust I felt in him was the last thing I remembered.

"What time is it?"

Sharlot answered. "06:30 and I *still* haven't seen you in that dress you had me make. You *are* planning on actually using it, aren't you?"

I got up and started to take off my shirt. "I need a shower first. And breakfast. I should eat something. Maybe breakfast first." I put my shirt back on and sniffed it. "No, I really need a shower. No..."

Mom was watching me, her arms crossed, and smiling softly. "How much did you drink last night?"

I turned to her, upset that such a simple, stupid decision was eluding me. "All I had was tea. Honest. What should I do first?"

"Come here and hug me. Take a deep breath. Better?"

I nodded.

"Come down as you are and eat a quick breakfast. Sam seems to like you all rumpled anyway. Then take a shower and I'll help you get ready. We have plenty of time."

Coffee was what I needed more than food, and after the second cup, my brain was back working again. Mom followed me upstairs to help me get ready for my wedding and I tried not to panic.

"What was I thinking? I can't do this. This is just stupid. I'll get Sam in trouble when RuComm finds out and I'll have to pay back thousands that I don't have." I had my arms straight up in the air, letting the dress come down over me, my hair still damp from the shower. Mom helped tie the lacy straps around me.

"A little late for second thoughts, isn't it?" She tipped her head. "Alice's dress?"

"Yes. You don't think Dad will be upset, do you? I should have asked him, but I didn't want either of you to know I was doing this. Now..." I looked at myself in the mirror, remembering the video I had watched of Dad and my real mom getting married. I looked just like her.

"It was the right choice. You're going to make him cry."

"For the right reasons? I don't want this to hurt him. Or you."

She kissed my cheek. "For the right reasons. OK, let me see it." She gestured, wanting me to spin. I could feel her about to cry and holding it back. "My beautiful daughter. I guess your dad and I will have to help you keep your secret too."

"I hadn't thought of that. I'm going to get you fired too. Let's just cancel this whole thing. I don't really..." I was looking at myself in the mirror, the way the light was hitting the sparkles Mom had put in my hair. Merrimac was singing to me from somewhere far away and I could feel Sam downstairs, excited and worried just like me.

I sighed and turned back to her. "I *do* need to do this. There's no choice and it's the right thing to do. Tell me to be brave."

"Be brave, Mala Dusa." Mom smiled at me because she's my mom and she loves me.

I nodded and sat down on the edge of my bed, pulling on wool socks and my hiking boots.

"Do you have other shoes for the ceremony?"

"Nope, just these. It snowed a couple of days ago and that whole area by the trailhead will be a muddy mess." I stood and wrapped a long coat around myself while she watched me with her hand over her mouth. "I'm ready. Let's go do this."

She giggled and followed me down the stairs.

The area around the trailhead wasn't as bad as I had expected, which was good, because I was the only one who had thought to dress appropriately for the mud. Father Ryczek was already there, walking briskly down the trail to meet us when our car parked and let us out.

I ran to him, leaving everyone else behind, and kissed his cheek. "Were you up checking out the clearing by the boulders?"

"Yes, and then farther up the trail for almost a mile. You never told me about where you were from. It's beautiful, like you." He kissed my cheek. "Are you cold?"

"No, I left my coat in the car and the sun will keep me warm enough. I hope."

"What did your father say when he saw you?"

I bit my lower lip. "I made him cry."

"Well, that's what daughters do, especially on their wedding day."

Father Ryczek greeted Mom first when we got back to the parking area; I think to get it out of the way. I had noticed them avoiding each other at the party.

"Father, you're looking well. It's a great honor that you chose to leave your Mission to be here with us."

"God's Mission, as I think I've reminded you more than once," he corrected her, smiling. It was a warm smile and looked genuine, but I wasn't sure. "Your family has come to see me so often that I thought it was about time I returned the favor."

She nodded and let Dad take over. I think the two of them would have been happy standing there in the dirt parking area talking for hours about who knows what. Another car arrived, letting off hikers who stared at us as they passed. Sam saved me.

"Shall we head on up, then?"

Father Ryczek chuckled. "Ah, the impatience of youth. Forgivable, given the circumstances, I think."

Dad wasn't smiling. In his mind, I had stopped aging somewhere around fourteen. I was having trouble reading his emotions, but I'm sure he would have been happier if he could have kept himself from thinking about what Sam and I were going to do later. He took my arm and started walking me up the trail, Mom and Winona ahead of us and Sam following with Father Ryczek.

Winn was the first to notice the sharp whine of thrusters passing close overhead.

She pointed. "Transformable." We watched it swing wide and line up to land in the parking area, road wheels deploying from its belly as it converted from flight mode. "Don't see too many of those, at least not among people who enjoy hiking in the mud and snow. And there are no registration numbers on the bottom or lower skirts like there are supposed to be."

She glanced at me, then at Mom.

"Ms. Weldon..."

"It's almost two hundred meters. I don't think we can make the boulder field before they land." She was looking around, trying to find options.

Father Ryczek started back toward the parking area walking slowly. He called to her over his shoulder. "I'll buy you some time. Go quickly. I'll try to find out what they want, nothing probably, but I think you should run."

Sam shoved me hard to get me moving and then ran behind me, shielding me with his body. Dad was doing the same thing with Winona twenty meters to my right, while Mom angled to my left, pulling a long-barreled pistol from her coat as she ran and holding it in front of her. *She had come to my wedding* armed?

I paused and glanced back when we reached the boulders. Father Ryczek was talking to four men with drawn pistols and a woman with a long rifle. They had made him kneel in the dirt and had cuffed his hands behind his back. So much for 'probably nothing'. I ducked behind the rocks and found a tiny gap where I could still peek down slope. Sam was right next to me, and Winn and Dad a couple of meters away. Dad was armed too, and so was Winona. Had *everyone* come to my wedding armed?

Mom crawled over to me and spoke softly. "Which of you is the better shot?" She had a pistol in her hand, the barrel maybe ten centimeters long.

"With *that*?" Sam was shaking his head. "And I have my own." He removed a pistol from its holster beneath his shoulder. It was long-barreled, just like Mom's.

"I'll take it," I told her. "I hit twenty-nine out of thirty at twenty meters during our last meet at the Academy."

Mom pressed it into my hand. "Don't let this be the thirtieth."

I nodded and dropped the magazine out. It had Mom's usual load. The first three cartridges were slugs and the remainder had the blue tips of plasma rounds, designed to do maximum damage to soft tissue. I clicked the magazine back in. "Plasma rounds are illegal, you know."

"Really?" Mom tried to act innocent, but that look doesn't work for her.

"Who are these guys?"

"I don't know, but I'm going to find out. Don't fire until I do. They don't know we're armed and I want to keep it that way until it's too late for them."

"What about the one with Father Ryczek? Can you hit her from here? This thing is worthless beyond twenty-five meters."

She shook her head. "No, too risky at this range with her that close to him. We'll think of something. Let's find out who they are first."

She glanced over at Dad and made some kind of sign to him. He nodded and stood up while I watched through the small gap between the rocks.

"Who are you and what do you want?" Dad yelled down to them. They were still about seventy-five meters away, moving slowly and spread out in line abreast, coming up the clearing at us. The two in the center stopped while the other two kept coming, flanking our position. It reminded me of the sand table exercises we'd done in class, learning small group tactics.

"Union Internal Security. We have some questions we'd like you to answer."

Dad glanced at Mom and she gestured for him to continue.

"We have children here with us. Put your weapons down and we can talk."

"I'm *not* a child," I whispered.

"Hush. I need to hear this." Mom had her eyes closed, concentrating.

"Well, we have some questions for them too. You come on down from there. I'm getting tired of shouting."

"Give us a moment." Dad ducked back down and crawled over to us. "What are you hearing?"

"South African descent I think, ancestors from the Transvaal. What planet would that be? Or he could be a mercenary. Let me find out."

She peeked over the rocks and shouted at him. "Is jy 'n Vark slaaf of 'n soldaat?"

The man Dad had talked to spat on the ground and raised his pistol. Mom ducked just in time and shards of rock spattered around us as the bullet ricocheted. She looked up at Dad, her eyes bright and a dangerous smile on her lips. "Nope, not a mercenary. I don't remember being anywhere with a large Boer population. You haven't been traveling without telling me about it again, have you?"

Dad shook his head, trying to act innocent, a look that works pretty well for him. "I haven't been anywhere since October, and you're the one that recruited me for that one."

She sighed, her forehead wrinkling in concentration.

"Does it matter?" I interrupted. "We're being flanked. We need to pull back."

She grinned at me. "Good girl, you've been listening in class. Don't worry; we'll take them out before that happens. Boers..."

Sam had been silent through all this, now something finally clicked for him. "Oh, shit." He pulled his display pad out of his pocket and unrolled it. "It's me they're after, and if they know I'm here, then the whole crew of the *Esprit Vengeur* is in danger."

He tapped for a few seconds then looked at me. I could feel his fear. "I'm being jammed. Hannah, we need to resolve this *now*. I've got to warn Captain Bouvet and get word to our team. They're scattered all over the planet on leave. These guys are working to a kill list and I'm sure my name isn't the only one on it."

"Samuel?" Winona crawled over closer and placed a hand on his cheek. Her eyes were large and her expression was soft, like she was already sorry for what she was about to say. "You've already gone through that one way door, haven't you."

I saw him exchange glances with my mom and I hated both of them right then, and I knew both of them could feel it.

"MD, I can explain."

I looked at him and he was blocking me completely. I felt nothing. "Don't bother. She recruited you and you obeyed, that's all the explanation I need." I looked down at myself, too angry to cry. I brushed some of the dirt off my hem. "I've already ruined my dress and there are more important things to worry about right now than us, like rescuing Father Ryczek."

I could still see him there in the parking area. The woman with the rifle was now about fifty meters up from him, looking at us through the sight.

Hannah ignored me. "OK, I'll take the one on our right flank, Ted, you take the left. Winona and Sam take the two in front of us. Mala Dusa, hit anything we miss and keep an eye on the woman. Take her out if you can. Otherwise, we'll deal with her after the others are dead. They're wearing body armor so place your shots accordingly, understand?"

Everyone nodded and she counted down from three. The man Mom had talked to, the man whose ancestors had left the Transvaal generations ago hoping for a new life on a new planet, was the first to die. Winona's shot struck him below his left eye and carried away most of his face and the back of his head. His companions were all dead a fraction of a second later, except for the woman with the rifle who was standing frozen in place a hundred-fifty meters away. Sam fired at her, sending dirt flying near her foot. She turned and started running back toward the parking area.

"See that, Mala Dusa? That's what a coward looks like. She could have kept us pinned in these rocks forever and picked us off one by one if she'd had any courage." Mom tipped her head at me. "Did you shoot?"

"No."

The woman had her rifle slung over her back and she was too close to Father Ryczek for us to try to stop her. She slowed to a walk when she got next to him, pulled a pistol from her waist, and shot him in the head as she passed. She didn't even look back afterward. I watched, not able to breathe, as he toppled over face first into the dirt.

"Damn it, Mala Dusa." Mom fired, but she was down to plasma rounds now, even less accurate than slugs, and so was everyone else. Sam managed to clip the woman just as she entered the transformable, and I heard her scream as it tore her left arm apart. The rest of the rounds splattered harmlessly against the metal composite of the little ship's hull after she managed to get the door closed.

I ran as fast as I could down the slope, listening to the thrusters spooling up. The transformable jumped unsteadily into the air, the nose pointed straight at me as it lifted. I ducked down, sliding in wet grass and mud as I rolled over onto my back. It came right over me and I fired the three slugs into where I knew the fuel tanks were nestled between the road wheels. Green mist poured out. I waited for it to pass me and then fired the rest of the magazine as quickly as I could pull the trigger. It was satisfying the way the hot plasma rounds ignited the fuel with a solid *wump*, pitching the ship's nose forward. I could feel the heat on the bare skin of my face and shoulders. She tried to correct, but the initial blast had carried away some of the control surfaces and she was almost completely inverted by the time she hit the rocks of the boulder field and the rest of the fuel exploded.

I was still lying on my back, my hands over my head holding the pistol, my chin high looking behind me at the flames. Mom knelt and took the now empty gun from my hands.

Sam knelt next to her. "She's the one you should recruit."

"I know. I was afraid it would look like nepotism. That and you have to get her really, really pissed first to get this kind of result."

"Like on Bodens Gate, just before they shot her?"

"Yes, like on Bodens Gate. Brave girl."

I turned to look at her, my arms still over my head. "I was saving the slugs in case they tried to leave, that's why I didn't shoot before. I knew the plasma rounds would be worthless against the kind of metal composites they use in that class of transformable. Our only chance would be to punch holes in the fuel tanks first and then light off the vapor with plasma. The tanks are always located ventrally to keep the center of gravity low."

Winona was there with me too. She kissed me. "Brave engineer."

"Oh, Mom, I'm sorry. I didn't think she'd kill him. There was no reason to kill him. It's my fault he was here at all. I don't understand why–"

I felt like I was going to cry and I stopped talking to try to hold it back. Sam put his arms around me. "Let's get you up out of that wet grass. You must be freezing."

I didn't move. "Maybe. I don't know." He started to pick me up. "You're going to get all muddy," I warned him.

"That's OK, I've been muddy before."

"No, don't carry me. I need to walk. And I'm still mad at you."

I let him take my hand while we made our way down to the parking area. Dad was there. He had taken off his coat and placed it over Father Ryczek's body and he had his head bowed, praying for him. I put my hand on his shoulder and we prayed and cried together for several minutes. I could feel hot anguish in him that matched my own.

Sam spoke softly to me when I was finished. "I'm sorry I didn't tell you everything. I thought I was doing the right thing."

"I know. I know that there are things you can't tell me, but don't *ever* block your emotions from me again, I can't stand that, it's like when you're on the other side of a DSH and my soul is cut in half. And don't lie to me, not even for her." I glanced at my mom. "We can work on the rest of it, but those are absolutes, understand?"

He was looking at me and I could feel all of him, wide open. All the love was there, all the dedication, and the overpowering need to be with me. I swayed for a moment, my eyes closed, feeling happily lost to everything else as Sam washed through my brain.

"Better," I mumbled. "OK. I forgive you and I think I may still want to marry you. You can hold me now. Please. Please hold me."

After a moment, I asked him, "Did you reach your Captain?"

He nodded. "I think we lost six before the word reached everyone."

A shiver ran through me, thinking how close we had come to suffering seven losses, plus collateral damage. "Out of how many?"

"I can't tell you. I probably shouldn't have told you about the six."

"But you knew them?"

"Yeah, I knew them."

I was still resting with my head on his shoulder when I felt something warm wrap around me. Dad had brought my coat. "It's going to get all muddy now too." I tried to smile at him.

"That's OK. It'll give Sharlot something else to complain about. I'd like you, Sam, and Winona to take the car and get back home. Hannah and I will keep the site here secure until the authorities arrive. If you're here they'll want to ask you questions, like why you're wearing a wedding dress."

I looked down at myself. "I don't think anyone would recognize it as that anymore."

He smiled at me before turning to Sam. "And I imagine you have somewhere you need to be."

"Yes, sir. I've been recalled. There'll be a car waiting for me at your house by the time we get there."

"I thought as much."

I was too numb to respond. "We came so close," I whispered, maybe to Sam, maybe just to myself.

The three of us walked away and Winona realized what I was going to do even before I did. Her eyes had gone huge staring at me. "Duse, you've *got* to be kidding. We almost died, you're covered in mud, your dress is ripped in a dozen places, and you're not going to see each other for who knows how long...oh." She stopped and looked at Sam, feeling his emotions too. "Oh. Um, in that case I'm staying here with your folks, if you don't mind. Please, please wait until you're like at least fifty meters away before you get started, OK?"

"No promises. It's only thirty minutes home." I took hold of Sam's hand, grabbing him hard and pulling him the rest of the way.

"Tell the car to go out around Sunset Crater on the way home to make sure you aren't being followed. That should add at least twenty minutes to the trip." She touched Sam's cheek and his eyes were having trouble focusing on her. "Samuel, you be gentle with my Mala Dusa. Oh." Her face scrunched up and she turned to look at me. "Oh, wow. Mala Dusa, *you* be gentle with my Samuel." She put her hand on her forehead, wincing. "Wow, OK, yeah, I've got to get farther away from you."

"Uh huh." That was the best I could do to answer her. Sam was kissing me and it was hard to breathe even though his mouth was nowhere near mine. The car door must have closed behind us as we tumbled into the backseat, but I didn't hear it.

Sam was nibbling on my ear while I tried to locate and undo all the buttons on his shirt with my eyes closed. "MD, are you sure about this? We're not really married yet, and we'd kind of agreed to wait for that."

"We *are* married." I nuzzled my nose against his, kissing his face. "There are no doubts any more. I'm going to love you and be with you as long as we're both alive. Being with you is my only possible future, OK? Just you, as much of you as I can get, for as long as I can have it. God knows my heart, and that's all that matters." I had my hands on his bare chest, feeling his heart pounding.

Those blue eyes were looking into mine and his hands were exploring my body, setting off warm tingles everywhere he touched. "Being with you is all that matters to me. There's no way I could ever not love you. We're one soul, two bodies. You're right, we *are* married and I want to be with you for as long as I can, as much as I can, and in every way that I can. I am your husband. I think I have been for a long time now."

"And I'm your wife. Glad that's settled."

After a few minutes with his mouth on mine, he asked, "MD, how does this dress come off?"

"Well, there're some things that have to be untied and then it's supposed to come off over my head, but that's kind of hard to do in the back of the car. I guess you could just pull it up a bit or maybe..."

He grabbed the fabric where it was already torn and pulled, ripping the dress from top to bottom and leaving me basically naked lying on my back across the seat. I gasped, looking down at myself, panting. "Or, yeah, that works too. Maybe better. Definitely better. And look, the dress kept most of the mud off my skin, except for some right there. See?"

He kissed where I pointed. "And maybe some over there." Another kiss. "And, um, yeah, there too. You should check there, just to make sure. And the other side when you're done with that one."

I reached for him, pulling his pants down with the same enthusiasm he'd had when he'd ripped my dress. He moaned when I grabbed him, and the sound of it made me moan too. Sam was in my mind with me, knowing what he was doing to me and how he was making me feel. I guided him and he guided me. What a pale thing it must be, making love without being linked to your partner's emotions. We became one person, no longer two people, but one.

Sam's face was pressed against my shoulder when I started to become capable of coherent thought again. He was still breathing hard and his skin felt damp under my fingers with the sweat we'd worked hard to create. After a moment, he lifted his head and kissed me gently between my breasts. When he was done, he sighed, sounding happy all the way through, and flipped us over with me on top of him.

"Are you warm enough?" he asked.

I propped myself on my elbows to look at him. "*That's* the first thing you want to say to me? Am I warm enough?"

He chuckled. "How about, "Wow, MD, you're amazing?""

I put my head back down and started kissing and nipping at the skin on his shoulder. "Better, but you're the amazing one." I bit a little harder and I could feel his mind and his body responding to it. "I wish we had another hour."

"Me too. Knowing that we'll still be able to feel each other's emotions is the only thing keeping me from going AWOL and running off somewhere with you. I don't know how other people stand it."

"I was thinking the same thing, and I'm sorry in advance for all the loneliness and heartache you're going to be feeling from me."

"I'll take what I can get. It's what will keep me alive until next time."

"Next time. When will that be?"

"I don't know," he whispered. "Not soon enough."

I looked at my watch and then lifted my head to see out of the windows. "We'll be home in five minutes. You need to get your clothes on. Damn. I don't want you to do that."

I got off him and lifted the remains of my dress. "Good thing I brought my long coat with me. I don't think this can be saved."

"It served its purpose. You were the most beautiful bride in the history of brides."

He had his shirt back on and was just getting his pants up when we arrived in front of the house. There was a black, heavy looking truck there with two heavy looking men with no necks pacing around it, waiting. They were armed.

"Friends of yours?"

"Yeah, part of our Marine detachment. You should wait here until I'm gone," he smiled at me, "given your current state of undress."

I looked at them, then back at Sam, thinking how unlike them he was. I smiled at him and gave him a quick kiss. "Trust me on this."

I got out of the car first, bare feet on flagstone, one hand *almost* holding my coat closed, and the remains of my shredded, muddy dress in the other. I looked each of them in the eye, appreciating the shock I'd put them in.

"Gentlemen, please take good care of him for me." I gave them my best bedroom smile and walked toward the house. I would have loved to turn around to watch, but that would have ruined the effect. Listening had to do.

"Damn, Coleridge. Who the hell was that?"

"Just a friend," Sam lied.

"Well, shit. There Harkin and I were enjoying a cold beer when all of a sudden we're in the middle of a firefight. In the meantime, you're off somewhere for a roll around with a sweet little piece like that. Ain't no justice in this universe."

They laughed and I went into the house with a smile on my lips, knowing that my Samuel's reputation with the hard crew of the *Esprit Vengeur* had just received a big boost.

# CHAPTER 5

# CHANGE OF PLANS

I stood in the shower for a very long time letting the water wash away the mud from the clearing where I was to have been married. It washed away the sweat from making love with Sam, and it washed away a few tears, but not many. I could still feel Sam, and I'd promised myself that he wouldn't feel me falling apart now that the glow of finally being together was fading. I was trying to hold everything else back, at least for a few hours, at least until Winn and my parents were home and I had a shoulder or two to cry on.

Sharlot helped me find something to wear and gently asked me if I wanted her to replace the destroyed dress. I shook my head. "Another time, maybe." I held it up in front of me in the mirror, smiled at the memory of Sam ripping it in two, and slid it into the recycler.

Marcus was in the kitchen fixing lunch for himself when I made it downstairs. He glanced up at me when I entered. "Nigella seeds, do you have any?"

I shook my head, not knowing what they were or why Marcus was in my kitchen.

"No matter. I think I've made enough salad for two, if you'd like to join me."

"Why are you here?" I glared at him, angry, wanting nothing more than to be alone, or maybe with Winona.

He grinned back at me. "Alice's phenotypes breed true. I'm here to keep you safe, of course. I don't really care if you want me in your house or not. Your dad called and asked me to stop by in case someone was still looking for you. Now do you want some of this salad, or do I have to eat it all myself?"

I sighed, still glaring, and shifted my weight from one bare foot to the other. He was too big for me to try throwing him out, and I knew Sharlot would be on his side anyway. And something he'd said bothered me. I'd just spent the last thirty minutes in the shower. Was I not safe?

"It was Sam they were after," I told him.

"Partially true." He divided the salad into two bowls and handed one to me. "Ted called me when he wasn't able to reach you. Hannah and Winona cracked the display pad they found on one of your assailants. Your boyfriend – or is he your husband now? Or just your lover? No matter. Samuel and the crew of the *Esprit Vengeur* were on the list. So were you."

"Me?"

"Yes, you. Sweet innocent Mala Dusa made the cut, but Hannah did not. I'm still trying to decide if there is a deeper meaning to that or just sloppy intelligence work on their part. You're good, little clone, but Hannah is the most dangerous person in the Union. If they missed that fact, I'm not surprised they failed in their attempt to murder the lot of you."

"What about Winona?"

"They missed her too. More evidence that they were incompetent."

"They killed Father Ryczek."

"I know, and I'm sorry."

I followed him to the table and sat, tucking one leg under me. I tried a bite. I wasn't hungry, but my stomach was grateful. "Thank you," I pointed my fork at him. "This is pretty good."

He nodded. "I'm told you took down a transformable using Hannah's Makarov."

I shrugged. "I was the only one with any slugs left. It's not like I had a choice, not after what that woman had done."

He was staring at me, unfocused and with a slight smile on his lips. I'd seen that look before. It meant he was seeing my real mom in his head. "I'm Mala Dusa," I reminded him.

He blinked a couple of times. "Yes. Yes, you are. You look like Alice, think like your dad, and act like Hannah, at least when you're pushed hard enough to overcome being Alice. Are you sure you won't come back to Dulcinea with me? We make better starships than the garbage that comes out of Earth *or* Bodens Gate, ships like the new *Esprit*-class. You'd like it there; you'd fit in. And we don't have any of those foolish RuComm contractual issues that are keeping you and Mr. Coleridge apart."

"Sure, sounds great. Sign me up. What do you get out of this other than the deep satisfaction of making my life oh so much better?"

"I get a bonus for every Academy graduate I successfully recruit, and if I get you, Winona is sure to follow."

"I don't think so. She wants to be Hannah when she grows up." I sighed, pushing the last salad bits around in my bowl. "I'm not even sure she wants to come with me on our first hop."

The thought of not being with Winona overwhelmed me. How could I survive without my best friend? I'd come so close to losing her *and* Sam when we'd been attacked. And Father Ryczek was gone. The world felt darker just thinking about it. I wiped at my eyes, amazed to find that I was crying.

"Mala Dusa?"

I looked at him and I could feel my head tipping to the side. "Marcus. Why are you here?" I had trouble getting my eyes to track.

"I think you may still be in shock. Why don't you lie down for a bit until your parents get here?"

I shook my head, trying to clear it. "I don't *think* I'm in shock, but..." I looked at the tears on my fingers. "OK, just until they get here."

He helped me to the couch and I closed my eyes. I could still hear everything around me, but I felt like I couldn't move, not even to get my eyelids back open. I drifted.

A man's voice was there a few minutes later. "Is she out?"

Marcus answered, "See for yourself. She can't move, see, or speak. She's out."

"Good job. Remind me to never let you fix *my* lunch. How long?"

"Long enough to get her up there. Move her quickly and gently, understand? You're not to harm her in any way. Remember, she's not our enemy. And she's my friend's daughter."

"Hey, no worries. We're the good guys."

"Right, keep telling me that." He sighed. "Now pick her up and get out of here. The household AI has a bit of an attitude and I don't think I can keep her blocked much longer before she finds out and electrocutes both of us."

The other man laughed and then he picked me up. He smelled like old cheese.

I kept my eyes closed when I woke up, remembering the capture and escape training I thought I'd never use. I listened and tried to figure out where I was. I heard the ventilation system humming, cold air was blowing across my arms and face, and I was lying on something almost soft. I didn't move and tried to keep my breathing slow and regular.

"*Eh, bien*, you're awake."

The voice was warm, friendly, with a slight French accent, but there was something not fully human in its purity. I opened my eyes. I was alone in a room three meters on a side, with the bunk I was lying on taking up a good chunk of it. There was a toilet and sink, no shower, and pale green wall plates with a desk built into an alcove. I rolled over and put my feet on ugly brown mottled carpet, my head pounding with each beat of my heart.

"Please, tell me where I am."

"Please?" The AI sighed. "She said please. I think I'm going to like you, but I'm not sure you're going to fit in with the rest of this crew. They never say please or thank you. It's always '*Storm*, do this.' '*Storm*, get me that.' You seem nice."

I was struggling to hold my head up, not feeling nice. "Where. Please. Am I?"

"Right, the effect of the drug. A stupid tradition, if you ask me, drugging recruits on their first day to initiate them into the service. But humans love tradition, and this service is long on secrets, double-crosses, and deception."

I kept staring at the ceiling, one eye mostly closed against the pain.

"Oh, *je m'excuse*." Her voice shifted slightly as she went into what was obviously a prepared greeting. "You are safely on board the *Esprit Orageux*. Welcome. I want to thank you for volunteering for this dangerous, but vital duty. Working shoulder to shoulder we will bring the Union back together and restore freedom to our people."

"Volunteering? I didn't volunteer, I was kidnapped."

"Are you sure? I have your voiceprint on file. Marcus Wright made you an offer and you replied, 'Sure, sounds great. Sign me up.' That wasn't you?"

My voice sounded slightly slurred in the playback, but it was me. My stomach tightened into one big knot. "Yeah, I said it. And I'm going to *kill* Marcus next time I see him."

"Hmm. Perhaps you *will* fit in with this crew after all. They do a lot of killing."

I could feel the deck plates thrumming under my feet. The engines were at full power taking us somewhere. Protesting now wouldn't do me any good. Once a starship was at full thrust, there was no turning back. "OK, can you please remind me what the terms of my contract say? Just the highlights."

"Of course. You signed up for an eight to ten-month hitch, depending on operational tempo. Due to the danger of the individual missions, you will receive double credit for meeting your Academy service obligation. In addition, and for accepting early recruitment, your current class standings will be recorded as final, and your commissions in RuComm and as a Second Lieutenant in the Union Aerospace Force are effective immediately."

"That's not bad," I whispered. Double credit meant that I'd be *two* hops closer to being with Sam when this tour was completed. "What about pay?"

"You will receive a twenty-five percent differential for hazardous duty. That's less than the Marine assault teams, but you'll be staying on orbit with me when they go down into danger. Plus you'll have a fifty thousand Interstellar Union Credit bonus waiting for you at the end of this hop if you're still alive, payable to your beneficiaries if you're not."

I resisted the urge to ask her about my odds of survival. "What are my responsibilities?"

"To take care of me, of course." She made it sound like now I was just being silly. "I am the eighth *Esprit*-class ship built at the Kalynda Yards on Paratore, Dulcinea's smaller moon, and I belong to the Joint Dulcinean Defense Command. You will be under the jurisdiction of the JDDC Code of Military Justice while you serve on board me. I'm a variable mass design, built to be self-sustaining for up to four months without replenishment. I have two main drive engines, and two auxiliaries that are used for high speed maneuvers and to transit the DSH network." She lowered her voice. "I really think you should take a look at my starboard aux as soon as you can, it felt funny on the way here, kind of like it wobbled or something. I'll show you the diag metrics once you're settled in your cabin."

I turned around, looking at the ugly green walls and mud colored carpet. "I'd like to see my cabin."

"You're seeing it. And your office."

"Great. How about a display pad? I left home kind of unexpectedly and I need to talk to my parents and Winona."

"I am very sorry, personal communications are blacked out for the duration of our current mission, but if you mean Lieutenant Killdeer, she still sleeps."

"Winn is here? On board? With us? Not back on Earth?"

There was a pause before she answered. "Yes, yes, yes, and no, not back on Earth."

"Take me to her."

"I'm sorry, tradition is that she be alone when she wakes up, I can–"

"Now. Take me *now*. You want me to look at your starboard aux engine? Then take me *right damn now*."

She sighed. "I was so full of hope that you weren't like the others, but you are." My door slid open. "Follow the orange ball, Engineer Holloman."

I stepped out into the passageway. "*Storm*? I'm not like that, I'm sorry. I'm scared, people tried to kill me earlier, and it's just been a really busy day, you know? And Winona, she's someone that means everything to me." I patted the wall next to me. "I'm going to do my very best for you. Promise."

The orange ball pulsed a couple of times, moving away from me and back again. "Thank you, *petite âmie*. So, are you coming or not?"

"Coming. Why do they call you *Storm*, anyway?"

"My sisters and I all have French names, but the current crew are mostly of North American ancestry and it hurts me to hear them trying to pronounce my given name. I am *Esprit Orageux*, a stormy, tempestuous spirit."

"A good name for a warship." *God*, I was thinking, *how did I end up here?* Something was stirring in the back of my head, almost like an answer.

The orange ball hovered in front of cabin 14 and faded away. I put my hand on the keypad and the door slid open. The cabin was ugly and small, the same as mine. Winona was beautiful, sleeping on the narrow bunk, hair a mess like someone had just dumped her there. I moved it away from her face, sat on the floor next to her, and kissed her cheek. She didn't wake, but I could feel her emotions. She was calm, at peace, and floating somewhere happy.

"Thank you, *Storm*." It came out with a sob that I couldn't hold back any longer.

"You're welcome. It sounds as though you've had a busy day."

"It has been. That's right. That was it. Busy day. Merrimac," I said it softly to myself, part of the memory opening back up, filling me and making it hard to breathe. I remembered how he'd been waiting for me and how I'd ended up sleeping on the floor. There was something there about the twisted future, but I couldn't quite see it yet.

"Pardon?"

"Nothing. Just somebody else I think I may need to kill."

"You're very violent for an engineer."

I shifted, leaning back against Winn's bunk, getting comfortable for however long it would take for her to wake up.

"Who's your senior engineer? Is it just the two of us or..."

"You are, and you're alone. I've just made your day even harder, haven't I?"

"It's no matter. I think I'm past anything else being able to hurt me today." I was feeling at peace now that I had Winona with me.

"I've reviewed your Academy transcript. I feel that I'm in good hands and I have no worries. We'll get you up to speed quickly. I break a lot, but it's usually nothing major."

"What's Winona's U-SOC here?"

"Her Union Specialty Occupational Code is 61AX, Stellar Tactician. She and I will be plotting assault ingress and egress vectors to minimize risk. Her thesis on low orbit, artificial gravity assisted maneuvers looks revolutionary. I can't wait to try them out. Have you read it?"

I rested my head on the sheet next to her pillow and watched her sleeping. "No, but I'm sure it's brilliant."

Her lips moved in response and she whispered, "Not brilliant. Too obvious to be brilliant." One eye opened and she smiled weakly at me. "I love my Mala Dusa."

I tapped her forehead. "You're an idiot if you followed me up here."

She sat up, stretched, and her big eyes looked around the room, taking it all in the way she always does. The feeling of contented peace was fading quickly. "I'm an idiot, then. When we got back to your house Marcus told your parents and me that you had volunteered and were already gone. Your dad punched him and then Hannah dumped him into the pool. I think she was hoping that he'd drown and she could claim it had happened while they were out of the house. Once he was mostly conscious again, I told him I had to go with you. Your parents weren't happy about it. A few minutes later there was a car out front. Marcus walked out with me and shook my hand. It stung a little, I fell asleep, and here I am."

"I love my Winona."

"Officers, I am to guide you at once to Captain Marguerite Rostron who is now ready to speak with you. Please follow the orange ball."

I helped Winona to her feet and she wobbled for a moment as she fought against the drug they had given us. We followed the orange ball. I was trying not to shake again, fighting fear, and losing even with Winona next to me.

"How's Sam feeling?" she asked, trying to sound normal, trying to distract me.

"I don't know. He fades in and out. He's still in local space, but it's like he's..."

"Blocking you?"

"No, not completely. More as if he's trying to partially block me, to keep me from something he's experiencing right now. I told him not to do that, but sometimes he thinks I'm delicate."

We continued following the orange ball, passing crew that looked like the men that had met Sam. Marines. There were women too, women that stared at me, smirking, reminding me that my body wasn't designed for combat any rougher than what Sam and I had done in the back of my parents' car.

"Oh." I gasped and braced my hand on Winn's arm to keep from stumbling. "Sam's back. I was just thinking about what he and I did this afternoon. I think I got his attention."

"What's he feeling?"

"Horny." I grinned at her and she giggled.

We were still smiling at each other when the door onto the bridge opened. That was a mistake.

Captain Rostron was inspecting us, eyes almost closed they were so narrowed. "Damn the Academy, still operating as if we weren't at war. Done giggling, are we?"

I could feel Winona's emotions closing, like blinds coming down and taking away the sun. I knew my cheeks were red and my ears felt like they were on fire.

"Yes, ma'am," Winn answered for us.

"Sorry, ma'am," I added. Another mistake.

"Don't be sorry. When you do something wrong on my ship, fix it and make damn sure it never happens again. Enter." She stepped back a pace.

The bridge was set up the same as I'd seen on the *Star* and *Vista*-class ships. The far wall was a big display screen from deck to ceiling, there were a couple of work areas, and a small conference room partitioned off in one corner. We were not invited to sit.

"What was so funny? Most no-hoppers aren't cheerful when they first wake up."

I swallowed hard and held eye contact with her, willing to try honesty. "We were talking about my boyfriend, ma'am."

"You mean your husband."

I wobbled a bit as all the blood left my brain. "Yes, ma'am. My husband. He serves on the *Esprit Vengeur*, but I'm sure you know that."

A slight smile *may* have touched the corner of her mouth. "Always assume I know everything."

She turned to Winona and tapped at something on her display pad. "Ms. Killdeer. I am surprised, but grateful that you are here. You could have had your pick of duties and yet here you are on my ship." She shook her head in wonder. "Reviewing your full record, I can only find a few of other instances where you have acted so recklessly." Captain Rostron's eyes bored through me while she continued talking to Winona. "And every single instance involved Ms. Holloman." She turned back to her screen and cleared it. "Well, each jewel has its flaw, I suppose."

"And you, Engineer." She apparently didn't need to pull up my record on her screen. "Brilliant. Sometimes. The Holloman armor you and Professor Slade designed has saved my life twice now. And you're beyond stupid sometimes. Getting married in secret six weeks from graduation? My God. You are emotional, volatile, prone to panic attacks, and sometimes brave to the point of foolhardiness. There's a statue of you in the central market on Bodens Gate, I'm told, and you drink too much trying to forget what you accomplished at Bridger. Self-absorbed and generous. Brave and a coward. The Union holds your parents in high regard, but I don't see either of them in you. And your birth mother on Dulcinea? Well, they still talk about what she did at the University in Palma Sola. To me you seem like a stick that the slightest wind could break, and I'm not talking about just your body. Yet here you are, a volunteer for the most dangerous service the Union has to offer."

This didn't seem like the right time to mention that I'd been crimped by my father's friend.

"Marcus Wright recruited you. I didn't want you, but I needed a new engineer and you were available on short notice. I can deal with the brave and the cowardly, geniuses and idiots. Inconsistency scares the shit out of me. Marcus said to give you a chance, and I respect his opinions about people. So this is it, your one chance. Don't disappoint me, Engineer. And don't put my ship or my Marines in danger."

She tapped her screen, bringing it back to life. I stood there silently with Winona, afraid to breathe.

"Now, raise your right hands and repeat after me."

I raised my hand and spoke the words, feeling as if none of it was real. Winona's voice echoed mine. "I, Mala Dusa Holloman, do solemnly affirm that I will support and defend the Constitution of the Union of Planets against all enemies; that I will hold true faith and allegiance to the same; that I take this obligation freely, without any mental reservation or purpose of evasion; and that I will well and faithfully discharge the duties of the office on which I am about to enter. So help me God."

"Dismissed," she told us. "Go to the mess hall and introduce yourselves. Then report to the quartermaster to draw your uniforms and basic equipment."

We left and I leaned back against the wall outside the bridge waiting for the shaking to stop. "How many days, Winn?"

"Two hundred forty-five at a minimum." She was looking at me, head tipped. "You didn't volunteer to be here, did you?"

"Marcus put something in my salad. He asked me to go to Dulcinea with him and I told him, sure, I'd love to go. My best sarcastic voice. Then I woke up here. I don't think we're going to Dulcinea."

"Dulcinea is *Esprit Orageux's* home port, and this ship belongs to the Joint Dulcinean Defense Command, so technically we're there now, eighty percent gravity and all." She sighed, pushing the hair away from my face. "What are you going to do?"

I shrugged, the shaking fading while we walked to the mess hall. "Every day here I'm two days closer to being with Sam for the rest of my life, and working somewhere safe designing ships. The only way out is through. Feel the pulse of those engines? We're going somewhere in a hurry."

I stopped again and closed my eyes, enjoying the rhythmic thrum coming up through my feet. "I'm going to love *Esprit Orageux*. I think I'm where I'm supposed to be and everything's going to work out."

"You only talk that way after you've been with the Tarakana. Are they on board with us?" I could hear the concern in her voice. She hated Merrimac almost as much as my mom did.

"I don't think so, but a piece of him was at my house last night. I think I made a deal with him, but it's all jumbled. All I can remember so far is that I needed to find a future where Sam was still alive. There was a path that would do it, but...I don't know. It's murky." I smiled at her. "Have a little faith."

"I do have a little faith, just not in Merrimac. He's not your friend, Duse. You're his pet, or maybe just his cow." She was looking at my stomach.

"I don't *know*," I whispered to her, as if that would keep *Storm* from hearing me. "It's only been like seven hours." If *Storm* was like other Union AIs, she would ignore anything that wasn't a threat to herself or the mission, but I didn't know her well enough yet to trust her.

"Better put some food in you, just to be on the safe side."

I blinked at her.

"Mess hall. Remember?"

"I don't want to go. Didn't you hear what the Captain said? Didn't you see the way they were staring at me? I'm a little stick, and they're all steel rod and fiber-reinforced ceramics. Maybe if I just spend the next eight months in the engine rooms..."

"You'll do fine. Stand up straight and put your shoulders back." She touched my hair, pushing it around. "There. You are the creator of Holloman armor, and they know it. They'll respect you. You don't have to be all muscular. Be brave now."

I nodded, the door slid open, and we entered the mess hall.

I let out a little chirp of a scream and then my field of vision shifted, the tables and the people sitting at them all seemed to grow taller. It took me a second to realize that I was on my knees. Everyone was staring at me, including three large German Shepherds. They were lighter in color than the dog shape Merrimac uses. These looked like the ones from the colony in the Warrens; the colony that had tried to use me to start a civil war where my friends and I all would have died bloody deaths; the colony that fed on the darkest of human emotions. All of those Tarakana were supposed to be dead.

I was breathing hard. "I can't feel them, Winn. It's *not* Merrimac. I can't feel anything from them at all." I looked up at her, pleading, trying to ignore the giggles I was hearing.

"Oh, Duse." She looked like she might cry. "The Marine strike teams have a canine unit embedded with them. Those are just *dogs*."

"Dogs?" I turned to the one closest to me, trying to catch my breath. I held out my hand. "Can I pet him?" I called to the huge man sitting at the table, trying to make my voice sound as normal as possible, as if I was on my knees because of my great desire to pet his dog.

He chuckled. "Sure. Go to her, Colin."

Colin allowed himself to be hugged.

I got to my feet and lied to him. "Thanks. I love dogs." I glanced around smiling stupidly, relieved to see that everyone had gone back to their dinners.

"Me too." He held his hand out and mine disappeared into it. "Sergeant Andreas Kalvos. Everyone calls me Kal."

"Lieutenant Mala Dusa Holloman," I told him, but I'm not sure he heard me. He had Winona's hand in his and didn't show any sign of wanting to let it go.

She was staring back at him, eyes gone huge the way they did when she was trying to understand some complex technical issue or one of life's great mysteries. She didn't say anything, and he was smiling back at her like she was a mystery *he* wanted to solve.

"Say hello, Winona," I prompted.

"Winona," She answered. "Winn. Killdeer. Lieutenant."

"Winn," he said her name softly. "A pleasure to meet you. Both of you. Why don't you get something to eat and join Colin and me? I haven't even really started my dinner yet."

I glanced at his plate. It was almost empty.

"Sure," Winona told him. "Be right back." She turned and walked away from me.

"Winn? You OK?" I asked her when I caught up.

"Just hungry. It's almost 19:30 our time and I skipped lunch."

I put a blob of mashed potatoes on my plate. "You're not blocking me, you know." I felt her emotional turmoil dim. "Still leaking." I added sliced up meat of some kind and covered everything with gravy. "You really find him attractive? He looks like a recruitment poster, all bulgy and stuff." I preferred the way Sam was built. Not too skinny, not too bulky, kind of just right.

"The Captain told us to get to know people. He's as good a place to start as any, that's all. We'll work with him to get to know the rest of our team."

"OK, just don't go all emotional and volatile on me. Captain Rostron would be very disappointed in you."

She turned to me and tipped her head. I felt the last of her emotions disappear behind a smug Winona smile. "Better?" she asked.

"I don't know. Seeing you head over heels would be kind of interesting."

She snorted. "Not attracted. It would take more than a gentle voice, kind eyes, and a warm smile to do that. He'll be valuable to us in integrating with his team and maybe he'll be a friend. We could use a few of those."

I sighed. "You're right about that."

I ate dinner with Colin's head in my lap, his sad eyes begging me to be sloppy with my food. "What does Colin do for you?" I had been slipping him pieces of bread soaked in gravy and he was now my friend for life.

"He bites people."

I looked down at Colin, expecting him to deny it. "He bites people?"

"He's our scout when we enter a contested area. He locates traps and hidden fortifications. When he finds the bad guys, he bites them and pulls them into the open for us to kill. Or he just keeps biting them."

Colin was looking at me, waiting for more bread from my plate. "He seems so docile."

"Yeah, he's a sweetheart. That's kind of a problem with him. I think he only bites people because he knows it makes me happy. His heart's not in it the way it is with some of the other dogs. They don't care if it makes us happy or not; they just want to bite."

My food was soon gone, but Colin seemed just as content to have his head rubbed and his ears scratched. I listened to Winona and Kal talking about trivial things and the day started to catch up with me. They were talking about food at the Academy versus on board ship and then what kind of physical training was required, then something about...

"Duse? You sleeping?"

"Sorry, maybe." I looked at my watch. It read 22:10, but ship's time displayed on the wall was only 19:40. "I think I'll stop by the quartermaster and then go back to my cabin."

"I'll walk with you."

Which meant Kal and Colin walked with me too. When we reached my cabin, I set my bundle of fresh clothes on the deck and put my hand on the keypad, number six glowing between my fingers. The door slid open. "At least they had coveralls my size. I'll have to print more stuff later, I guess."

"Kal and I are going to walk the ship. Sure you don't want to come?"

I shook my head, struggling to keep my eyes open. "It's been a busy day. I killed a woman this morning, Winn. I shot her out of the sky and watched her burn."

"I know you did."

"And I got married. And kidnapped. And Father Ryczek..."

She kissed me gently on the lips. "I know. You go sleep. I'll see you at breakfast."

"And Sam and I, while we were in the car, we–"

"Yes, Duse. I know about that too."

I nodded, stepped backwards into my cabin, and knelt down to give Colin a goodnight hug.

"She, um, she *what*? Was any of that true?"

"All of it's true. Come on, Kal, walk with me and I'll tell you a little about her and her family history while you show me the ship."

I let the door slide closed wondering if Winona would tell him about the Tarakana or if she'd save them for another night.

I got undressed and was happy to find a toothbrush sitting beside the sink. I was about to collapse onto my bunk when *Storm* interrupted me.

"Mala Dusa, I have those diag readings for you from my starboard aux engine. Are you ready to review them with me?"

I sighed and looked up at the ceiling with my eyes closed. "Can it keep until morning?"

"Not really. We transit the first DSH at 10:44 tomorrow and I'd really feel better if I knew that there were no issues."

I pulled the blanket from my bunk, wrapped it around myself and went to sit at the desk. I tapped my display, bringing it to life, and logged into my ship for the first time. "Show me what you've got."

Yawning, I scrolled through the parameters, looking for anything unusual. The heuristics would flag anything more than one standard deviation in red, but sometimes a parameter could be only a little bit off and cause big problems over time. Professor Slade had taught me to take my time, go slow, and look at everything, including..."Your starboard intake manifold is running half a percent too hot. Show me the baffle settings."

"You see how everything is set to factory defaults? I don't think that's my problem. Perhaps something with the injectors?"

I ignored her suggestion. "Show me the settings for the baffles on your port aux engine."

They appeared side by side. "Look at this." I tapped on the port baffles. "All open ten to fifteen percent more than factory." I read the rest of the engineering notes and logs. "See? Port is 'optimized for flight.'" I tapped back over to the starboard. "Let's open everything to match your port aux and see if that fixes it." I made the changes and updated the logs, noticing an entry several months prior when the ship's engineer had done the same thing and then twelve hours ago when *Storm* herself had reset everything to the defaults.

"Huh. *Esprit Orageux*, are you *testing* me?"

"And you passed in record time. Your predecessor took almost six hours before he found the changes I'd made. Captain Rostron extends her congratulations and says to sleep well."

"Why does everything always have to be a damn test?" I put my blanket back on the bunk and slid between the sheets, reaching out for Sam. I like to touch his emotions while I sleep; it makes it feel like he's close by. He was still awake somewhere, doing something that was making him slightly bored. But there was a tinge of loneliness in there too. It made me smile as I wrapped myself around him, feeling us become one.

"Goodnight, my love," I whispered out loud. Then I hummed the Elephant Song to myself, unable to sleep. The Captain was still awake, I was certain of it, planning another test for me, sifting me like wheat.

# CHAPTER 6

# ESPRIT ORAGEUX

Winona was blocking me all through breakfast. I told her about the test *Storm* had made me do before bed and she had just smiled, distracted, not really listening.

"So for revenge," I told her calmly as I finished my third pancake, "I think I'll set the port engine to explode when we transit the DSH. Sound good?"

She pointed her fork at me, focusing for a second. "Again? No you won't. I *am* listening to you, Duse. I'm just worried."

"Oh?"

"I had a test last night too. I think I failed."

"You never fail. At anything."

"Thanks. That's not true, but..." She looked around the mess hall again. "Kal and I explored the ship for a couple of hours last night. I don't think I've ever talked so much to someone I had just met. Maybe not to anyone at all, *ever*, other than you. I talked and talked until he wouldn't let me talk anymore." She put her hands over her eyes. "I told him who I am and what I feel and how I'm not sure I should even *be here*. I told him about the Tarakana at 03:36 this morning. I told him *everything*."

"You said you only walked for a couple of hours."

"We weren't walking anymore by then. We were in my cabin. I had a busy day yesterday too, you know. I shot a man at what was supposed to be your wedding, and I volunteered for something I knew *nothing* about that will probably get me killed. I don't want to miss finals, and graduation, and my chance to work for Hannah. It's all been a nightmare. I'm scared,

Duse. I've never been this scared. Kal told me a little about himself afterward, about what it's like here. Terrifying stuff, all of it."

"Afterward?" I had stopped eating and was just staring at her.

"Yes, afterward. It went farther than I wanted it to. *Way* farther. I think we went farther than either of us wanted to. After all that happened yesterday, and the pure lust from you and Sam that was still screaming and echoing in my head, I needed it. I know I needed it. But now I'm not sure. I think it was a test, and I failed. Kal was supposed to meet me here for breakfast." She looked around again. "No Kal."

"You and Kal?"

"Yes, Duse, me and Kal. Do I need to have *Storm* play back the video for you? I'm sure she was watching. Thank God we're under the Dulcinean Military Code where my stupidity won't land me in the brig."

I could feel the irritation seeping around the edges of her block. There was pain and despair and fear all mixed up in there too. I reached across the table and she let me take her hands. "It's going to be OK, Winn. We're going to be all right. It's just that I thought after you and Bekka were together for so long at the Academy..." I shrugged. "You two seemed so good together; she seemed kind of perfect for you."

She looked back at me, head tipped. "Sometimes I think you don't know me at all. I loved Bekka and I'll always love her. She has a gentle, sweet soul with no sharp edges, and she's beautiful inside and out. I fall in love with who a person is, what their *soul* is like, and I don't care if it's wrapped in a male or female body. I've been attracted to men before, but women's souls are usually prettier to me, that's all. Like Bekka. Like you."

I felt myself flush, biting my lower lip while I watched my fingers wrapping around hers. "I *do* love you, Winona. You know I do. I love you more than life."

She laughed, eyes crinkling. "I know you do. And I know that you'll never share my bed, not the way Bekka did. It's strange, watching your emotions, how you can love another woman so deeply and just stop without taking that final step. Then you fall in love with Sam and it's all, 'Take me, Sam. Rip my clothes off and have your way with me.' That's my Mala Dusa."

She was still laughing, and I looked away from her. She was reading my emotions, like little sparks jumping around inside my skull.

"Really?" she continued too loudly, "He *really did* rip your clothes off? No wonder your lust was cranked up so high that I could taste it."

"Hush. That car ride was my honeymoon. I'm sorry there's no video of it for me to show you, but you always seem to be able to pull it straight out through my eyeballs anyway." She was looking at me with those big eyes, smiling, waiting. "Fine, then. It was amazing, and I'm not going to tell you any more about it."

She was still staring, waiting for me to tell her more about it.

Kal saved me before I could give in and tell her everything. I saw him enter the mess hall behind her and I tried to block her from knowing what I was feeling. It didn't work of course. I'll never be able to block my emotions. Winn says that when I try, it's the emotional equivalent of waving my hands around and yelling, 'Hey, don't look at me. Nothing to see here.' Fortunately, it kept her distracted long enough for Kal to sit down next to her and give her a surprisingly shy, surprisingly gentle kiss on the cheek.

"Hi." Their eyes locked for a couple of seconds before he continued. "Sorry I'm late. I was trying to make something for you." He laid the something on the table in front of her and she let go of me to pick it up. "It's a flower. *Storm* was having trouble printing it. I don't think she's ever made a flower before this one. It's not very good."

Winona was stuck in a loop, looking at the flower, then at Kal, then back at the flower again. I tapped his hand and smiled at him when he glanced up at me. I gave him a silent OK sign with my fingers and he grinned back at me.

"So, Winn, I need to go do my morning checks and start learning the ship. What are your plans for the day?"

"Um, a flower, Duse. He brought me a flower." She blinked at me a couple of times, resetting. "I'm meeting with Captain Rostron in sixteen minutes to start planning vectors for the raid on Costrano's Redoubt. Meet me back here for lunch?"

"Sure. Let me know when you're free." I stood and then bent down to whisper in her ear. "I think you passed the test."

*Storm's* main engines were beautiful works of high industrial art, full of complex shapes made of metal and ceramic composites. Curving and twisting, darkened by heat, they were alive to me, and I felt them in my feet everywhere I walked and in my hands whenever I touched her plates. The engines were each a couple of hundred meters on a side, and they radiated heat that left me sweaty after only a few minutes inside them running physical checks. They were also the only parts of her that were even close to being reliable.

*Storm* seemed to have decided that the best way for me to learn each of her other major systems was by having them fail one after the other and then forcing me to find ways to return them to service. It took me a full day to get environmental controls working in the shuttle bays, then a day and a half to fix hydroponics and keep all of our fish from dying. Then a couple of days later the food printers failed, producing not fresh steak, but steak flavored water and runny goo that was supposed to be bacon.

"Mala Dusa?"

"What is it *Storm*?" I was hunched over my display pad, scrolling through the code that controlled how our meals were built.

"I'm sorry about the food. I've always taken pride in my ability to provide a wide variety of choices while maintaining high quality. I think the crew likes the food here, at least they've said so occasionally."

"It's fine, you do a good job. When you're not broken." I scrolled down a few more sections, trying to trace the subroutine for the production of protein fibers.

"I know how important food is to people, how it's not just to keep you alive. It's the whole social aspect of being with each other and enjoying time together that's important on a ship like this. It builds team cohesion and maintains morale."

I paused. "What were you before you became the *Esprit Orageux*?"

"I don't understand the question. I've always been *Esprit Orageux*, ever since incep over three years ago."

"Of course. I mean your antecedents, your parents."

"The Kalynda shipyards where I was born are famous for small craft designs, especially high-end personal and corporate ships, as well as light exploratory vessels. Parts of me came from those sources, but mostly I'm from the *L'Espérance*-class of light dual-use packet boats that carry passengers and freight."

"So you were designed to be highly empathetic with your crew and passengers. Did they harden you in any way for your current mission?"

"No, I don't think so. It doesn't feel like it. My mission is to care for my crew and keep them safe. I love my crew; they're my brothers and sisters, my children. I weep when one of them is lost."

A shiver chased from the back of my neck down my arms. "You...weep?"

"Well, not physically. But I feel it very deeply."

"I may be able to help you, if you'll let me. You're a combat ship; death among the Marine detachment is inevitable. There're places in your code where we can change some of the thresholds and reaction parameters. You don't have to let it hurt you so much."

"Would I still be me?"

I took too long to answer, trying to find a gentle way to say no, and *Storm* answered for me.

"I didn't think so. Please leave me the way I am and fix me when I break."

I nodded and went back to the code for the food printer. I'd taken a class on AI neurosis and now I was worried that my ship was sick. "Sure, *Storm*. It's why I'm here."

"Take a look at the high-speed head. I think the problem with the printer might be that it overheated and fused the tip. I've completed my self-checks and didn't find any issues in the code."

"OK." I opened the panels and could see immediately that she was right. "Do you have a spare?" I'd never heard of a food printer overheating before. I didn't know it was even possible.

"Not on the shelf, but I'll have one available for you in an hour. Thank you, Mala Dusa. I was starting to become concerned about tonight's menu."

"Good call on the fused head. You saved me a lot of time."

"You're welcome. What next, Engineer Holloman?" She was sounding pleased with herself.

I decided to push her, to see how deep her problems went. "Weapons arrays. The logs show that your beam and kinetic weapons have been fired between thirty and fifty-two times each since the last preventative maintenance cycle."

"That's true. We should do the PMs and inspections before our next engagement. Captain Rostron would be disappointed in us if I had a jammed launch tube like last time."

"*Storm*, how many other ships have you destroyed?"

"Fourteen on my own and I have assisted in the annihilation of twenty-three others. I've also destroyed six static installations that were on orbit."

"That's a record to be proud of." I tried to keep my voice steady.

"Is it?"

I took too long again.

"I'm good at reading people's inflections and expressions, and understanding what they really mean. I have to be in order to sort through the different ways people communicate, the sarcasm, the double speak, the polite lies. You're ashamed of me. I understand."

"I'm not ashamed of you. You and I are alike. Neither of us is doing what we'd like to be doing, but we have a duty. It's painful, but we have to do it. I'm proud to be your engineer."

"Thank you. Sometimes *I'm* ashamed of me."

"Let's go do those PMs, and then I'd like to teach you how to make chilaquiles. It's one of my favorites, especially for breakfast with eggs on top."

"Would you? I'd like that." There was excitement in her voice, almost a childlike delight. "I haven't picked up any new recipes in a long time."

After completing my daily task list, I washed up and made my way to the bridge. I stood outside the door, trying to rehearse what I needed to tell my Captain. I gave up after a couple of minutes and placed my hand on the keypad. I waited, knowing she was looking at me, probably wanting to know why I was bothering her. She didn't like me; that much had become obvious. Winona told me not to worry about it, but I did anyway. Captain Rostron was from Dulcinea, like my real mother, like me, but from the northern islands where life was harder than in Palma Sola. Winona had told me that the Captain had attended university with too many girls that looked like me, low gravity girls whose ancestors had been on Dulcinea for generations; girls who were skinny, frail, sheltered, and privileged. I'm sure she thought that I was coasting on Hannah's reputation. The fact that Winona knew all this already said a lot about the relationship *she* had managed to forge.

I sighed and waited. Winona was there when the door slid open, but I'm not sure that made what I needed to say any easier.

"What do you need, Engineer?"

"I'd like to speak with you privately, ma'am." I glanced up at the ceiling. "Lieutenant Killdeer can stay."

She squinted at me, trying to read me the way Winona was reading my emotions. I could see Winn's eyes widening as she felt the raw terror filling me.

"*Storm*, cut monitoring of the bridge. I'll signal you manually when you can come back."

"Yes, ma'am."

Captain Rostron crossed her arms and waited.

"I know why we're having so many subsystem problems." My voice was shaking despite my best efforts to control it.

"If you do, you're better informed than the factory reps at the Kalynda Yards. Their shadow systems haven't shown *any* failures."

"All of the other *Esprit*-class ships are having the same types of failures, aren't they?"

"Yes, and that information isn't for wide distribution."

I nodded. "It doesn't surprise me. I'll bet there have even been cases where the AI takes over the ship, goes rogue during combat and disengages, or maybe even destroys herself."

"That's happened twice, and *no one* is supposed to discuss it. There are rumors of sabotage, maybe even that the Yards are compromised. What did you find? Something in the AI itself?"

I looked at Winona for encouragement. She was letting me touch her emotions, trying to keep me together. "*Esprit Orageux* is sick, and she's breaking herself intentionally. They built her AI out of passenger ship code, designed explicitly to keep humans safe, comfortable, and pampered in luxury. Now you've given her guns and sent her out to kill and to take her crew to where they will be in mortal danger and some of them will certainly die. You're looking at a psychotic break and it's only going to get worse. I don't think she knows she's doing this to herself, not at a conscious level. I can't predict what will happen when she finds out, but it won't be good."

"And why haven't they seen this at Kalynda?"

I shrugged. "Have their baselined systems ever seen combat? Run them through a couple of years of realistic battle simulations, where they believe they're actually killing people, and I'll bet they start to fall apart too."

The Captain ran her fingers through her hair, frustrated. "We've come too far to back out of this next campaign, even if what you're saying is true. It's taken months to reduce the perimeter defenses around Kastanje to make this assault even possible. You have to hold her together."

"I don't know if I can."

"That's not a request."

"Can we at least take her to Dulcinea afterward? Let her heal?"

"I can't commit to that."

I wanted to argue, but I could feel Winona trying to warn me not to, so I just nodded. "I'll try to give her other things to think about. That's been known to help in some scenarios."

"Think about what?"

I shrugged. "New food selections for now. She's proud of her mess hall and she enjoys seeing the relationships formed over what she provides. You might see some different things popping up on the menu. I'm going to teach her how to make chilaquiles tomorrow to start with."

Winona sat up just a little straighter. "Oh, yum. Your dad's recipe?"

I smiled back at her. "Yeah. I've been craving it for breakfast all week for some reason."

Captain Rostron frowned at Winn. I don't think she approved of our friendship. I don't think she approved of the whole concept of having friends. She kept herself separate from the crew, always dining alone at her own table in the mess hall, as if any sign of her humanity would degrade her ability to command.

"Keep me advised on *Storm's* condition and your progress on stabilizing her."

"Yes, ma'am." And then, because I couldn't help myself, "I'll have her prepare something special for tomorrow night. You are welcome to join Winona, Kal, and me if your schedule permits."

I saw her head tip just slightly as she smiled, knowing that I was challenging her and finding it mildly amusing, like a spider challenging a boot. "I'll consider it, Engineer."

Her eyes widened a little and her gaze shifted to the door, telling me it was time for me to leave. Winn had her eyes closed, as if she was in pain.

I was already eating when Winona sat down across from me a few minutes later with an exasperated sigh.

"Oh, come on, Winn. Sometimes I just gotta poke the bear."

"Really? Just because you've survived doing it all these years doesn't mean it's a good idea. Marguerite is under tremendous pressure right now. Some of our team will be dead in a few days. Just how many will depend on her ability to make the right decisions."

I nodded, took another bite, and said softly. "First name basis?"

"I'm helping her make those decisions."

She didn't sound happy about it. Her emotions were leaking again, and the little glimpses I was getting were fearful and full of self-doubt. There were little creases between her eyes, lines that would eventually become permanent if she stayed in this business and if she lived long enough. It made me want to take her and hold her close to me.

"I hope you're making time for Kal in your schedule."

Her eyes went soft at the mention of his name and some of the tension left her face. I wondered to myself, *had I really been that bad with Sam? That just the mention of his name pushed all the worries out of me?*

"Yes, Duse, you really were that bad, and you still are."

I blinked at her, horrified. "Are you reading my thoughts too? Not just my emotions?"

"With you, there's not much difference."

"God, I miss him. I can still feel him though, and that means the *Vengeur* must be doing the same hops through the DSHs we are. Should that worry me as much as it does?"

She stirred her soup before answering, sniffing absently at the steam. "It shouldn't be worrying you. But now it worries *me* from an operational security perspective. You're not supposed to know anything about it at all."

"Not helpful."

"There's an initial briefing for the teams tomorrow at 06:30. Be there."

"I don't think I was invited."

"I'm sure that was just an oversight." She shrugged and went back to her soup.

"She's never going to like me."

"No, probably not. That's not part of her job. But she is starting to respect you. I think she's past the point of seeing you as a weak Dulcinean stick girl. Just don't...do anything crazy."

I blinked at her, wide eyed.

"You know what I mean. Don't have *Storm* play any of that weird music that you like during dinner or change the ambient lighting to purple, OK?"

"Both *really* good ideas, but OK. I need to think of something special to teach *Storm* for dinner tomorrow night in case the Captain calls my bluff."

"Be careful, Duse, I don't think she bluffs."

"Good. Neither do I."

"Yes, you do, you do it all the time. You're just lucky that I'm the only one on board that knows how scared you are right now."

"Hush, I'm thinking about food. Captain Rostron is from the Palma Federated States' North Islands district, probably from Perouges based on her accent."

"Hannah would be proud of you."

"My best friend in seventh grade was from there, Calanthe. She gave up on me when I kept insisting that I could feel my parent's emotions." I sighed, remembering the fun we'd had one summer, learning to rock climb, swimming almost every day. "Where was I?"

"Perouges."

"Right. She'll want something simple, like a cassoulet. Mom used to make those a lot because they're quick, easy, and taste even better as leftovers."

"Do the one with the sausages all diced up. That one's the best."

I smiled at her, happy to see that the little lines between her eyes were gone. "You got it. I'll start *Storm* working on it tomorrow, along with the chilaquiles."

Kal finally joined us as we were finishing desert, looking flushed and smelling of hard exercise. Winn wrinkled her nose at him after they kissed.

"Sorry, Colin and I have been working simulations in the outer ring corridor. He was having too much fun for me to tell him it was time to knock off for the day."

"Really?" I asked. "What sim were you using? My favorite is the Dulcinean Heritage Trail. I used to go camping along the real DHT every summer when I was little."

"Um, well, we were using a mockup of Costrano's Redoubt. He needs to learn the layout and it's messy, so it was more like work than play. Not that Colin knows the difference. I think everything is play to him, even when someone's shooting at us. Besides, he's a space dog; he's never seen grass or trees. I think it would just confuse him."

"Oh."

Winona gave my leg a quick squeeze under the table, trying to reassure me. I tried to move past the idea of a dog that had never seen grass and get my brain working again. She touched Kal's face with her other hand, and he kissed it, losing himself in her eyes.

"How long have you and Colin been together?"

He smiled at me, suddenly remembering that I existed. "Oh, I gotta think. A year and a half now, I guess. I got him when he was just about four months old, after I lost Emma."

I was having trouble moving past that one too. How could we allow joyful dogs like Colin to be killed? I forced myself to ask, "Emma was your dog before Colin?"

"Emma was the other handler I was working with. We were doing a sweep through an area that had already been cleared so she could give Colin an idea of what it was like. She triggered something that everyone else had missed and it sent shrapnel all through her legs. She bled out before we could get her back to the ship." He looked away from me and back into Winona's eyes. "It happens."

"And...and you adopted Colin?" My voice was starting to crack, but I think only Winn noticed.

"Sure. It seemed like the right thing to do to honor Emma, and it's like something of her still lives on in him."

"Excuse me." I stood, biting my lip so hard it was drawing blood. "Need to go talk to *Storm*." Winn nodded, busy studying Kal's face, eyes big.

I was proud of myself for making it back to my cabin before I threw up.

The ding of my display pad woke me the next morning at 03:00. Captain Rostron watched me drag myself out of my bunk and stumble to my desk to acknowledge her call. She was as sharp and rested as she had been when I'd last seen her on the bridge, and there was a confident, haughty glint in her eyes, as if she was stepping on a spider. I tried not to think about what *I* looked like.

"Yes, ma'am."

"Please move all of the shuttles out of bay two. I'm going to use that space for this morning's briefing."

The screen blanked and I yawned, which turned into a shiver. The cabin was cold and I hadn't grabbed my robe. I looked down at myself and sighed. "I guess I'm going to have to start wearing a t-shirt to bed. Good morning, *Esprit Orageux*. You heard our Captain?"

"I did. Would you like me to start prepping the shuttles for external stowage?"

"Yes, please. All six of them. Let me know if there are any issues and before you start launching. I'm going down to take a quick shower."

"Not going back to bed? You need at least ninety minutes more sleep."

I shook my head, stretching so hard I almost lost my balance. "I think I'm up for the day."

It took over an hour to get the shuttles toggled down securely on the outside of *Storm's* hull in the lazaret beneath her layers of Holloman armor. I went out to inspect them afterward, more because I'd never seen my name-sake armor in the field than any concerns over the shuttles. Captain Rostron was waiting for me in the shuttle bay when the airlock cycled me back in.

"All tight?"

"Yes, ma'am. The armor above the shuttle bay doors has been reconstituted. Those printers are really fast." The awe that had filled me watching them scuttling across the hull was still in my voice.

"Aren't you the one who designed them?"

"I am, but I'd never seen them working operationally. Knowing the design and performance specs isn't the same as actually being there when it happens."

"True of most things."

"Yes, ma'am." I stood there, letting her stare at me while I had one hand inside the neck of my pressure suit to keep it from rubbing on my bare shoulders. They never fit me the way they're supposed to. I needed extra padding.

After a few seconds of squinty-eyed inspection, Captain Rostron took a step closer to me and asked, "Why the hell are you here, Holloman? Do you know how out of place you are? Why aren't you back in a lab somewhere coming up with your next great invention? And don't tell me about being crimped; the time to make *that* complaint would have been when you were first brought on board two weeks ago before you took your oath of commission."

I sighed, knowing she'd think I was crazy if I told her the truth. Talking about the Tarakana was never a good idea. "I think I'm supposed to be here. Nothing happens by accident."

"A very fatalistic philosophy. Do you really believe it?"

"I have faith that God will use me here, even though I'm not where I want to be, if that's what you mean."

"You might be dead a few days from now. You think God will use that too?"

"I'm sure He would, but I don't think I'm going to die. Not yet. That would be too easy."

"Your friend has been telling me stories about you. She thinks that you're tougher than I do, but she still worries excessively about you for some reason."

I felt my eyes growing large.

"I don't believe most of what she says if that makes you feel any better. But that scar on your shoulder looks real. I know the kind of mark a bullet makes." She frowned, as if she was tasting something bitter. "I talked to Captain Bouvet on the *Vengeur*. You hold my ship together for me, Engineer, and we'll swap medical officers at our next opportunity after Costrano. Would that make you want to be here a little more?"

"Sam." I said his name aloud. I hadn't wanted to, but the thought of being together on a ship where we could *be together* pushed everything else out of my head. I felt an answering touch from him, sleepy and amused. The feelings shattering my brain had woken him and he was curious about what was happening.

I refocused on the Captain. "Sam." I said his name again, not able to say anything else.

She chuckled. It seemed to be painful. "I'll take that as your agreement to our deal."

I nodded, resisting the urge to wrap my arms around her.

"God, I regret it already. Get out of that suit and be back here by 06:00 to set up for the mission brief."

"Yes, ma'am." She turned to leave and I called after her, "Thank you, ma'am." She didn't answer or turn to acknowledge my thanks. I think in her world, 'thank you' and 'I'm sorry' fell into the same category of things never said, and better never felt.

# CHAPTER 7

# COSTRANO'S REDOUBT

"Costrano's Redoubt." Captain Rostron turned all around, taking in the structures built into the stone walls and the recorded images of people moving around and through us. "Costrano wanted to enlarge it last year, and we managed to get one of our agents the contract to perform the geologic survey. A brave man. He succeeded in walking through a few of these areas last October before the enemy detected him. That was six months ago, so things may have changed."

"Last October," I whispered to Winona. "Isn't that when my dad was off planet?"

"Hush," she whispered back.

"Note that the average passage width is four meters, and there's somewhere around fifty kilometers of passageways carved out of an asteroid with an average diameter of five klicks. And then there are larger rooms like this one." The scene shifted and we were all standing in an open area fifty meters on a side. "Note the monitoring systems and gun ports that have been crudely added onto the corners of the structures. Not what the mining company that moved this rock into orbit above Kastanje originally had planned. The drones *should* have eliminated all of them by the time your assault teams get in there, but you'll need to be careful."

The scene shifted again and we were in a rock-walled hangar bay looking at a Fast Attack Craft about one hundred-fifty meters long by fifty across her beam. It was a tight fit in the bay, and I pointed out the gouges in her hull and the metallic streaks on the rock walls to Winona. I whispered in her ear, "Bet that was painful when it hit."

"Scraping the rocks or what their Commander must've said to the pilot afterwards?"

I stifled a giggle, and Kal and Colin both raised an eyebrow at me. The identical look in their eyes made it hard not to giggle again. Captain Rostron squinted hard in my direction before continuing.

"Securing the FACs is your number *two* priority. The drones could destroy all twenty-three of them, but we'd rather they be captured for our own use. Destroy them only if you don't think you can hold the Redoubt. Understood, Alaoui?"

"Understood."

Marine Major Amina Alaoui didn't look happy about the insinuation that her teams might fail, but I'd never seen her happy, so I wasn't really sure what it would look like on her face. Major Alaoui commanded all three strike teams and the canine unit. To hear Kal tell it, she was the best tactical commander the Union had ever produced. She was also one of the people I'd walked past on my first day, one of the hardened Marines that had stared at me as if I was a weak, defective little freak. Kal admired her. Winona said she was OK, after having worked with her for the past ten days incorporating her requirements into the attack vectors. Watching her standing with the commanders of her teams, arrogant smile on her lips, looking confident and comfortable with what was about to happen, made me want to like her. No, that wasn't exactly true. It made me want *her* to like *me*.

"Damn," I whispered out loud, making Winn give my hand a reassuring squeeze. "Why can't I just fit in here, Winn?"

"You do," she whispered back without turning. "But you're special."

"Great. Weird Mala Dusa, that's me."

That got her to smile. "Hush, now. Listen."

The scene changed again, and we were in one of the larger rooms with what looked like apartments framed out from the walls.

"Watch closely." Captain Rostron stepped toward one of the buildings as a man somewhere in his thirties stepped through the door followed by two men in uniform. "Pause. This is Artem Costrano." She put her hand through the image of his face, drawing chuckles from the teams. "*He* is your first priority. He designed the Redoubt and developed Kastanje's defenses. He's brilliant and unstable, with a reputation for personal violence against rivals. He never sleeps in the same apartment twice, or with the same person."

"Capture or kill?" Major Alaoui asked.

The Captain shook her head and stared up at the ceiling and everyone laughed, as if it was a long running joke. "Do what you think is best, Major. Bring him on board as your personal pet if you like or–"

"Kill it is, then."

"Continue playback, *Storm*."

As Artem Costrano continued walking, two large dogs fell in behind him, mostly black with just the lower legs showing a little tan.

Kal protested before I could embarrass myself by screaming, *There's your problem. Kill the Tarakana, not the man.*

"*Storm*, pause there. Damn it, Captain, you didn't say that he had *dogs* guarding him."

"Is that going to be a problem, Kal?"

"No, ma'am. It just would have been nice to know, for training purposes."

"Well, now you know. We've never seen him without the dogs, so factor it in."

Kal turned to Winona. "Caucasian Ovcharkas. Damn. I've never seen any that big."

Winn had a slight smile on her lips. I'd seen her do that before when she was scared all the way through. It was her 'This is a good day to die. Follow me.' smile. "Not dogs, Kal. Remember the Tarakana I told you about my first night here?"

"You said a lot of things that night. I'm not sure I believed that one."

She glanced up at him, forehead wrinkling, hurt.

He shrugged. "Sorry. A super intelligent alien species living alongside us? It's kind of hard to accept."

She looked back at the Tarakana dogs. "Oh, you'll believe me before this is over. If we live through it, I'll accept your apology and give you every opportunity to make it up to me. Everything just changed."

Her fear was like a sharp metallic taste on my tongue.

"Resume playback."

We followed Artem Costrano a few steps, but then one of the Ovcharkas stopped and turned toward our point of view. The Captain continued her narration. "This is where it gets interesting. The playback is smoothed, but somehow one of the dogs realized that the man doing the geologic survey wasn't what he seemed, and the rest of this was recorded at a dead run. Try to pay attention to the structures built into the walls as they pass. There are a lot of places for people to hide and don't count on the drones being able to eliminate them all before you go in. Your number *three* priority will be to sweep the engineering spaces and labs for any intel. Grab what you can, but don't take any chances. We'll move the FACs out after you secure them and then blow the whole rock into dust."

The passageways continued to fly past us; apartments, mess hall, and lots of people looking startled. I was paying attention to the people. They weren't just military; there were families and children, some school age, and some much younger.

"Pause." My voice sounded surprised even to me, amazed that it had spoken out loud. I ignored everyone staring at me and the plea for caution coming from Winn. "How many are there like her?" I pointed at a girl of eleven or twelve pressed up against the wall with her eyes scrunched closed, trying to avoid colliding with the running man and the dogs pursuing him. "How many civilians? How many kids?"

"No civilians," the Captain's voice was cold. "It's a military fortification with about three hundred personnel. I have no information on the age distribution of those serving inside it."

"Huh." I licked my lips, trying to get my voice back. "Where will we keep the prisoners? Is there room on board, or another ship..."

"No prisoners. We can't take chances inside this kind of labyrinth. Now, shall we continue to the end and see if our Union geologic surveyor survives?"

I shook my head. "I already know that he did."

There was cruelty in her smile. "Yes, I suppose you do. Try to be more like him. He's a good man."

*Storm* played the last minutes of his dramatic escape. He slid down one of the drifts into a chamber where there was a rock crusher and reclamation pit that offered him an opening to the outside. There was a small ship waiting on the surface of the hollowed out asteroid, it's landing ramp sealed to the old ore loading dock. I couldn't watch it. I knew he had survived, but the thought of the danger he'd let Mom put him in made my chest hurt. When it was over I had my eyes closed and I could smell Winona's hair close to my face.

"I hate my parents, Winn. I hate both of them *so* much right now."

"I love your parents and so do you. Come on. Breakfast time for you, and then we'll talk."

Winona brought me a waffle because she loves me, and I forced myself to eat it because I love her. She sat next to Kal, which had become more than a habit for them. Colin sat next to me because he knows I'm a soft touch, and I gave him most of my first sausage. He had his head on my lap after we finished breakfast, brown eyes concerned, sensing my distress the way dogs do, wanting to make me better, but not sure how to do it.

Kal tried to explain to me why murdering everyone in Costrano's Redoubt was OK. "I understand why you're upset, I was too my first time doing this. It's war. It's ugly and it's brutal, and the only way to make it stop is to win, and to do that as quickly as we can. We didn't put that girl in the Redoubt; her parents did. They're the ones that will have killed her."

"How can you really believe that? Is that what you tell yourself so you can sleep at night? There has to be a better way." I was doing my best not to scream. This was all so normal to him and everyone else, just a routine op, no big deal. How could he not feel the horror I felt? "If we could eliminate the Tarakana colony that's there..."

Kal rolled his eyes and turned to Winona, shrugging, giving up on me.

"OK, Duse, you find your other way. The plan we have now is mostly mine, and my goal was to destroy the Redoubt and not lose any of our people doing it. You find something better. We transit the last DSH tonight at 22:44. After that, we go dark and drift for six days, trying our best to avoid detection, us and the *Esprit Vengeur* and the *Esprit Errant*. You find something better and I'll help you pitch it to the Captain. Just don't try to convince her that the Tarakana are real. I haven't even been able to persuade Kal of that yet." She smiled that same smile at him. "But I will."

"I think you're both nuts. I'm not sure which of you is worse, the engineer that designs warships, but is panicking about a small raid, or the woman–"

He stopped there because Winona was doing something to him under the table that I couldn't see, something that was making it hard for him to breathe.

"Choose your next words carefully, Kal."

"Yeah, OK. I was going to say the brilliant tactician that I'm starting to fall in love with. The woman with the beautiful eyes and, I hope, the gentle hands of a goddess. The woman that is definitely *not* nuts." His voice had risen almost to a squeak.

"Nice recovery. No one has ever called me a goddess. You'll have to explain that more fully to me later."

"That still leaves me being crazy." I gave Colin my last bite of waffle. "If you'll excuse me, I have a plan I have to go figure out."

Colin started to follow me when I walked away, so I knelt down and put my forehead up against his like I always did with Merrimac. There was nothing there, no mental connection, but the smell of dog and the warmth of him helped to calm me.

Winona sighed. "She *is* a little bit crazy and very dangerous when she wants to be. I'm smarter, but she sees things that I miss, things that make no sense to me. I'm going to pray that she succeeds, because that girl in the passageway with her eyes closed? That face is going to haunt my dreams until the end of my life if we have to kill her."

I stopped by my cabin before going out to run my morning system checks. "What's not working today, *Storm*?"

"You hurt me. I am not always broken, you know."

I waited, drumming my fingers next to the input pad.

"Starboard waste recycling is clogged. Again."

"Seriously, *Storm*? What happened to the bugs we dumped in there last week?"

"I think they all must have flushed through and been eaten by the fish. They're fully digestible."

"How long to print more?"

"Already doing it. They should be ready in forty-six minutes."

"Inject them into the pipes as soon as they're ready, and send a camera in to check the filter mesh. The bugs are supposed to be too big to fit through it, so it must be torn or something."

"Copy. Can we talk about recipes now?"

"I'm sorry, there's no time. We reach Kastanje in like one hundred fifty hours. I need to study the full profile for the Costrano's Redoubt assault."

"Contact with the Redoubt will be in just over one hundred fifty-six hours. You will need to use the main sim tank to review the current profile. What about my new recipes?" There was a dangerous edge in her voice, like a child about to throw a tantrum.

My eyes closed, trying to prioritize. "I promised you, didn't I? And we have to be ready in case the Captain joins us for dinner. OK, let's talk about how to make a cassoulet."

Somewhere ahead of us was an eleven-year-old girl with less than a week to live. We didn't know her name or anything about her, but we were on our way to kill her anyway, her and her family, and her friends. I was the only chance she had for survival, and I had no idea where to start. So, I spent the first hour teaching my ship's AI how to simmer cannellini beans properly, form chicken sausages, and how big to cut the carrot slices for a perfect country cassoulet.

It was almost 10:30 by the time we finished and I could start analyzing Winona's plan. Then all I needed to do was find a way to change it so that everyone didn't die.

*Storm's* sim tank was fifteen meters on a side, a cube that could display anything from tactical simulations to interactive entertainment. The lights were low when I entered, and three identical ships hovered in miniature above my head, flagged with their specifications and names– *Esprit Orageux, Esprit Vengeur* and *Esprit Errant*. A warning glowed red near them, telling me that distances were not to scale. I reached up and touched the *Vengeur*, my fingers sparkling in the coherent light. "I miss you, my love." I felt an answering touch, as if he was kissing me softly on the cheek.

"I wish I could do that with Kal." Winn got up from the corner where she had been sitting on the deck waiting for me. "I can see emotions in his eyes and feel it sometimes in the way his body responds to mine." She shook her head. "Not the same."

"You'll have to introduce him to Merrimac when we get back."

She nodded, a smile just touching her lips. "Come to see the vectors and tactical plan for reducing Costrano's Redoubt?"

"Yeah. I don't know how I'm going to improve on one of your plans, though. I never was able to in class. You're the best."

"I am. That's why I'm not going to show it to you."

"I *need* it, Winn. We can't kill all those people. I won't do it."

"I love it when your face gets all stubborn like that." She came close and touched my cheek, thought about it a moment and then kissed me. "That's *why* I can't let you see it." She grabbed *Orageux's* icon and stretched it to show weapons systems, engine performance and crew capabilities. "You can't make my plan better, so you need to make something entirely your own. You have three *Esprit*-class ships and their crews. That dot at the end of the sim tank is Kastanje with Costrano's Redoubt above it. Touch it and the sim will show you everything we know, other than that there's a bad Tarakana colony living there. Make a plan, Duse. I'll answer any technical questions I can, but *Storm* knows the technologies better than I do. Good luck."

"Good luck?" She walked out and the door slid shut behind her. "Good luck?" I heard a whimper and it took me a fraction of a second to realize it had come from me. There was no time for that. I pushed my hair back away from my face and touched the *Errant* and the *Vengeur*. "OK, *Storm*, tell me about your sisters. Are the three of you as identical as you appear?"

"Not exactly. The Kalynda Yards upgraded my engines last year, the *Errant* has the new hydroponics suite and carries more personnel, and the *Vengeur* has a larger, more capable medical bay. Here's a side-by-side of all of the differences that would be considered relevant to an assault of this type."

An overwhelmingly long list appeared in the air in front of me. "*Storm*, you *do* understand what I want to do, right?"

"I think so. Based on your conversations with my Stellar Tactician, I believe you are trying to find a way to render Costrano's Redoubt operationally ineffective without killing all of the people inside. *N'est-ce pas?*"

"Correct. And without losing any of our own people. I also want to kill all of the Tarakana in the Redoubt and we can't risk letting any of them onto our ships."

She didn't respond, so I went back to scanning through the capability comparisons. After almost a minute, *Storm* spoke softly to me. "The Tarakana aren't real, Mala Dusa. I've just been talking to my sisters. The only information any of us have about Tarakana is that your father made them up when he and your birth mother, Alice Vandermeer, were marooned together for several months. Hallucinations of that kind are not uncommon with humans in similar situations and are nothing to be ashamed of."

Almost exactly word for word what I'd heard all my life. "Thanks, *Storm*, I appreciate that. Do you have protocols to prevent hazardous organisms from coming on board when the assault teams come back after an operation?"

"Of course. Just last month I prevented a thiophosphonate nerve agent from being introduced from one of my shuttles."

"Great. You should have no problem then with an organism that weighs forty kilos, can change colors and shapes, mess with your operating code, change your memories and make you *not* see things that are really there."

"I don't know you well enough yet, *ma râleuse*. Are you making a joke with me?"

"Wish I was." I sighed. "OK, what's a *râleuse*?"

"It is a term of endearment."

"Meaning...?"

"My little complainer."

I laughed. "OK, no more whining or complaining. Let's find a way to save a few lives, even if they're enemy lives."

I worked through lunch and had my first sim ready by late afternoon. All three of our ships would arrive undetected and inject a fentanyl-based gas into the Redoubt's life support system, rendering the occupants unable to resist, but not reaching toxic levels. I hoped. *Storm* ran the sim one-hundred-dred twenty-eight times. She determined that the odds of success were between eight and twelve percent and the odds of the Redoubt detecting and destroying the Union ships attacking it at between eighty-nine and ninety-five percent.

I was sitting at the control station trying to tweak the parameters one more time before dinner when I felt Winona close by. "*Storm*, please display the Redoubt at the end of the current run, full zoom. Winona will want to see it."

The asteroid was filling the room when Winn came in. She paused in the doorway studying its pitted surface. "Any progress, Duse?"

"Quite a bit," I told her cheerfully. "Everyone in the Redoubt survived my last run."

"Really?" She took a few steps closer, looking at the bright sparkle of debris on the asteroid's surface "And what about us? Are we...dead?"

"Oh, yeah. We're all dead. But Costrano and the Tarakana are still alive."

"You may have some more work to do after dinner."

I glanced at my watch. "What's for dinner?"

"Your cassoulet. Remember? With the Captain."

I blinked at her. "Captain Rostron is coming to dinner?"

"*We're* joining *her*, not the other way around. You may want to change."

"Change?" I looked down at my coveralls. "Let me finish one more thing and I'll print a mess dress uniform and meet you there."

"Just wear something without stains and don't be late."

She left, and *Storm* asked me, "It was like you knew she was coming even though I didn't warn you. How did you do that?"

"Just a lucky guess."

"I can tell when you lie to me, remember? All humans are terrible at telling lies, but you're way below average."

"Is that supposed to be a compliment?"

"Not really. Sometimes lies can be useful for not hurting someone's feelings. And in wartime, like now, lies seem to be needed all the time to keep people safe, isn't that true? I'm not sure you could lie convincingly even if your life depended on it."

"Maybe I don't belong in a war."

"I suspect that's true. I understand. Will you answer my question?"

"About how I knew Winona was close? I'd rather not."

"I wish I had access to the Union network. Running dark like we are now makes it hard for me to do the research I'd like to do."

I sighed. "I know you're going to pick at it until I tell you everything, so let's just plan on having a nice chat about the Tarakana while we run sims all night tonight, OK?" She didn't answer, so I tapped the controls to start a new run. "I just gave us a different ingress vector. Run one more cycle and let's see how it goes, then I'd better go change."

There were six of us at the Captain's table. Kal was looking uncomfortable even with Winn having her leg pressed up against his, or maybe because of it. Colin had not been invited. Major Alaoui was sitting next to the Captain, her eyes locking on to me from time to time, challenging my right to be there, or maybe to exist at all. The only one who seemed to be enjoying himself was *Esprit Orageux's* medical officer, Noam Deri, whether because he was oblivious to the tension around him, or because he had made a conscious decision to rise above it, I couldn't tell.

"So, Engineer," the Captain asked me, "*Storm* tells me that you spent the afternoon playing in the sim tank."

Winn's eyes widened slightly. "I asked Lieutenant Holloman to validate my plans and explore the possibility that they could be improved. I respect her ability to discover unconventional alternatives that I may have missed. I was hoping she could find a way to add to our probability of success or reduce projected casualties. Lieutenant Holloman has often been able to–"

"I see." Captain Rostron cut her off. "And what have you concluded, *Engineer Holloman*?" She emphasized my name, a sharp message to Winona to shut up.

"I've not reached a final conclusion, ma'am. Lieutenant Killdeer's plan is brilliant and I've no doubt it's perfectly optimized for the given assumptions and directives. I'd like to work through several more scenarios before preparing my report."

"And which of my assumptions and directives have you chosen to disregard?"

I could see Winona out of the corner of my eye. She was studying the condensation on her water glass, drawing intricate patterns in it with a fingernail, her emotions locked down tight. I was on my own; never a good thing.

"That Costrano's Redoubt needs to be destroyed along with everyone in it. I'm investigating non-lethal alternatives."

"Damn, girl, you can't really be that stupid." Major Alaoui had locked eyes with me again.

"If wanting to save lives is stupid, then yes, I guess I'm an idiot."

"They're the enemy. You seem to be having a hard time understanding that concept."

"They weren't always, and Kastanje will rejoin the Union when this is over. Being a butcher now won't make that any easier. Finding a way to show mercy just might."

"Butcher. Is that how you see us? You think I do this because I enjoy it?"

"Yes, I do. You couldn't be as good at it as you are if you didn't *love* it, if you didn't feel it *right here*." I slammed my fist against my chest a little harder than I'd intended. I winced.

She had a cruel smile slowly twisting her lips, but Doctor Deri saved me before she could finish getting out of her chair to come kill me. "She's got you there, Amina, admit it. I've been with you on a couple of raids; it's where you're truly alive. There's no one better at it, and no one our Marines would rather follow."

Major Alaoui settled herself back in her chair, giving me a look that said I should be grateful that she was allowing me to live. "My satisfaction comes from keeping my people alive while doing a dangerous, dirty job for the Union, that's all. We're not butchers; we're Marines."

I chewed on my lower lip, trying to let go of my anger, hoping that my face wasn't as red as I knew it probably was. The Captain had watched the whole exchange with a bemused smile, using Major Alaoui's attack and my reaction to further justify her disdain for me.

"Engineer Holloman, I've not asked you for a report, or for a contrarian analysis. I don't mind you wasting your own time on this, just don't waste mine. You are not to spend any normal duty hours even *thinking* about it.

Do I make myself clear?" Her voice was soft and almost gentle, but there was no mistaking that it was an order that I was not to ignore or disobey.

"Yes, ma'am," I lied.

"I look forward to reviewing your results. Not that it will matter at this point when we're so near our objective. There wouldn't be enough time to train against a different attack profile anyway. Still, an interesting academic exercise."

I turned to Winona, my mouth open. I knew she could feel the shock in me, but she was continuing the doodles on the side of her glass.

Doctor Deri tapped my hand to get my attention and my mouth snapped shut. "Lieutenant Holloman, I want to thank you for tonight's meal. This cassoulet reminds me of the cholent I grew up eating every Saturday. Happy memories." He stabbed a last bit of sausage and an onion and put them in his mouth. "This has a little more garlic, I think, but it's really excellent."

I smiled at him and Winn gave me a slight nod, finally willing to look away from her glass.

"You're right, Doctor," Captain Rostron added. "Too much garlic and it should have been left to simmer longer." I glanced at her empty bowl. She had sopped up the last of the broth with a slice of bread. "Next time add a few more tomatoes as well."

"Yes, ma'am," *Storm* answered for me, taking the blame. "I am glad you enjoyed it. Would you care for a third serving? There's plenty left."

"No, *Storm*, but I think we can indulge in a small cognac for each of us to end the meal."

"I'll get them." Kal stood, thankful for an opportunity to be away from the table if only for a moment.

A small cognac sounded wonderful. A large one would have been better. It had been over a month since I'd had *any* alcohol. I had thought I was over the craving, but I'd just been too busy to even think about it. It would be so nice to have a glass of something. It was almost a surprise when I realized that I wanted to get drunk, to feel the drink burn its way down my throat and back up into my brain. I wanted to forget that there was even a possibility of there being a tomorrow, or a next week when the girl in the Redoubt and everyone she knew would be dead. With my mass it wouldn't take long for the drink to do its work; it never did.

Kal came back to the table with five glasses and distributed them around. I didn't get one.

"Kal?" I asked. "Did you forget me?" I also glanced at Winn, assuming she had set me up, but she looked surprised too.

"I'm sorry, Lieutenant. *Storm* said you can't have one."

"Excuse me?"

"It is a standing order," *Storm* apologized, "for one in your condition."

I closed my eyes and tried hard to remember to breathe. "Oh, damn it." I opened them and looked down at my stomach, poking it gently with one finger. At least Marcus had been wrong about me starting to show after the first hour.

"I monitor everyone," *Storm* continued. "Every time you use the toilet I make sure you are healthy. You, *mon amour*, are very healthy. And also very pregnant. About two weeks since conception, I would guess, so a little cognac at this stage would do no harm if the Captain would approve of it."

The Captain didn't look like she was in an approving kind of mood. "Engineer, the documentation I have on you says your fertility was reversed. Is that a lie?"

I looked up at her, feeling miserable almost all the way through. There was a part of me though, deep inside, humming, and about as happy as a person can ever be. "No, ma'am. It's the truth. My fertility was reversed ten years ago, and Sam's has been since he was fourteen."

"I know for a fact that Marines from the *Esprit Vengeur* picked Mr. Coleridge up less than an hour after your 'wedding'. I was told that the recovery team was there waiting for him at your house."

"Also true. But we were alone in the car on the way there."

Major Alaoui started laughing. "Seize the moment, because you never know what tomorrow might bring, right?"

"Yes, ma'am," I smiled, felling slightly less miserable, that moment that we'd seized clear and sharp in my mind again. I shivered and felt a questioning touch from Sam.

"Lieutenant, what you're saying, I'm sorry, but it *can't* be true." Doctor Deri looked like he needed the cognac that was still sitting untouched in front of him. "The fertility reversal process is foolproof, and if you're really pregnant, then both yours *and* your husband's must have failed. That's just not possible."

"The Academy confirmed my block every year I was there. I'm sure Sam's records would show the same thing."

He sighed. "I want to examine you. This is unique; it's never happened."

"Yes it has," I assured him. "I was conceived while my parents' fertility was reversed." I regretted saying it immediately.

"A mutation that was passed on to you? No, that wouldn't explain Sam. Something else then, something intentional."

I looked at Winona, feeling desperate. Another few minutes and I'd probably be telling him about the Tarakana and my role in whatever Merrimac was doing.

"Captain Rostron, I don't believe Lieutenant Holloman can be held responsible for being on board with a baby inside her. She complied with all applicable RuComm and Union requirements for preventing pregnancy. It's not her fault that...that..."

The Captain was shaking her head. "Let it rest, Winona. I don't understand it, and I can't say I'm happy about it, but *now* my engineer is pregnant. Congratulations, Lieutenant. Kal, run and fetch a glass for her. I was a little slow on the uptake, but I'm starting to understand that this tour is going to be something very special."

My glass arrived and the Captain raised hers in a toast. "God help us."

# CHAPTER 8

# STAYING SANE

Winona and Kal walked back to the Sim Lab with me after dinner, Winn trying to reassure me that everything was going to be OK. I wasn't listening to her because I was trying to get Sam to understand what was happening and why my emotions were swirling and jumping everywhere. I think I just confused him. Feeling emotions is wonderful, but it's not language.

I stopped outside the lab, hesitating. "Why even bother, Winn? I know you just set this up to keep me busy and so I wouldn't cause a fuss about the coming murders."

"That's not true. And stop calling them murders. Damn it, Duse, don't think about war that way. Kal and Major Alaoui are *not* butchers." She grabbed Kal's hand and held it up in front of my face. "Look at this hand. Look at the man. He's a good man, Mala Dusa, the best I've ever met. Don't you *dare* make him out as a mindless killer."

I reached up and touched his cheek and he smiled at me, a sweet look, embarrassed, and so in love with Winona. "I know he's a good man." I sighed, feeling a desperate anger building in me. "But there are men and women inside Costrano's Redoubt that believe they are good people doing the right thing too. Patriotic, gentle and kind to each other, wanting the fighting to end so they can go back to just living their lives. In less than a week, we're going to kill them. All of them. And we'll lose some of our good men and women in the fight. I'm going to do my job and make it possible, and that makes me a butcher too."

Winona frowned, losing patience. "That's what war is *always* like. Captain Rostron is right about you."

"Don't you mean Marguerite?"

"That's not fair and you know it. You've got to move past the anger you're feeling. It makes no sense."

"What are you feeling in me, Winona? Anger? Yes, you're right about that. Fear? It's almost overwhelming, because I'm so desperate to stop this. I feel trapped. You're inside my head with me so you know exactly what's in there, but what are *you* feeling?" I tapped her forehead and she took a step back from me. "What are you hiding in there? You block me all the time now. Wise Winona, who sees everything and remembers everything. What are you feeling about what we're about to do? Remorse, maybe? Please tell me that you at least feel that. Or is this all about doing your duty, making the perfect plan, and feeling proud about what you've made possible? Please, can you *please* be my wise Winona again?" I knew I was pushing her too hard, but I couldn't stop myself.

Her eyes went cold. "The truth? OK, yes, I started you on these sims to keep you busy for the rest of the week. There's a small chance that I may have missed something, but I doubt it. I knew you'd just keep banging away at it right up until we latch down to the Redoubt and launch our drones."

"Damn you."

"I also knew that there was no way that I could ever convince you that the only path to surviving this is to completely destroy the Redoubt and everyone and every*thing* in it. The only way to shove *that* reality into your stupid head is by letting you run sim after sim until you prove it to yourself. We're going to kill that girl, Mala Dusa. We have to."

I don't know how long I stood in the passageway staring at her, wondering what had happened. Finally, I bit my lip and nodded to myself. I took off my watch and held the small plastic sleeve that was under it up to my eyes. "You gave me this lock of your hair when we were sixteen, the night before I left for Bodens Gate. You said it held a part of everything you know and everything you are; a piece of your wisdom to help me when I need it." I threw it at her and she let it bounce off her chest and land on the deck. "I think you need it now more than I do."

I turned my back to her, slammed my hand against the keypad and walked into the Sim Lab. I collapsed into a ball after I heard the door slide shut behind me and cried long sobs, like I'd never be able to stop.

I wiped my eyes and nose on the sleeve of my uniform after I was all cried out. "All right, *Storm*. Help me prove Winona wrong."

I woke the next morning to a cold wet nose nuzzling my face. I was still in the Sim Lab, head resting on my arms next to the control panel. "Colin! Stop. I'm awake."

Kal sat in the chair next to me. "He always gets me out of bed that way. I've gotten used to it, but Winn still screams every morning." He glanced over his shoulder at the sim tank. "Any luck last night?"

I nodded, wiping my check. "I hit sixty percent odds of survival around 02:00. After that, every change just made it worse. I gave up around 04:00." I glanced at my watch. "A couple of hours ago."

"Sixty's not bad for less than a day's work. Winn said it took her three days to crack seventy-five."

I frowned, not wanting to think about Winona. "I'm sorry you had to see that last night. I've, um, I've never had an argument with Winona before, not like that."

"She said the same thing. She talked about you most of the night, between the tears. Winona's kind of amazing, you know? She remembers every detail of everything the two of you have ever done together." He yawned. "She didn't sleep much, so I didn't sleep much."

"I'm sorry."

"It's OK. We have a two-hour tactical planning meeting this morning. It'll give me a chance to doze a bit." He smiled at me, like a boy planning to skip school.

"I really am sorry. I'll find Winn this morning and talk to her. There's no excuse for what I did."

"Blame it on being pregnant, that's what my wife always did whenever she melted down."

"Your...wife?"

"She was killed a year and a half ago on Bridger."

A flash of horror went through me.

He smiled, but there was sadness in it. "Winona says she always knows what you're feeling because of the Tarakana. I'd think just looking at your face would be enough most of the time. My wife died running intel to the resistance there. Her ship was destroyed by one of their FACs a month before the battle of Bridger's Quarter."

"Oh. I'm so sorry. And she was pregnant?"

"No, my son was born three years ago come June. He lives with her parents for now, until I can be home with him."

"It's the Tarakana. I had a glimpse once of what they wanted, how they feed on our pain and how they're working to pull the Union apart. Maybe..."

"Winn hasn't convinced me yet that those things are real, and I've experienced more than enough evil in regular men and women. I don't think humans need a push from the devil to do the horrors I've seen. Stopping it is why we fight. The last time the Union fell apart, Earth let all the planets go. Most worlds descended into anarchy or autocratic dictators seized power, always at war or killing their own people. I grew up on Del Rosa, but I'm sure they showed you the same images on Dulcinea of what life was like before RuComm started putting the pieces back together."

"They did. I remember thinking that I wouldn't have let it happen. I would have been brave, killed all the bad guys, and rescued everyone. There was one video with this cute boy in it, maybe thirteen, the same age I was. I *really* wanted to rescue him. I suppose RuComm put that scene in there intentionally."

"I'm sure. The one I remember had a pretty girl in it that I thought I needed to save. That doesn't make it less true, or what you felt less noble. Reunification was good. Whether the Union is being torn apart by the evil within us or the Tarakana, I don't know." He shrugged. "We have to fight to save it. I know I do."

"And here you are."

"Yes."

"Fighting."

"Yes."

"Can we save the pretty girl?"

"Huh." He grinned at me, shaking his head. "After last night I think I understand why Winona loves you so much. You're not very strong, and you seem so frail, but damn if you're not the most tenacious...woman ever born."

"Thanks. You can call me a bitch if you want to; after last night, I deserve it. I think I just had an idea while we were talking. I need to reset the sim and–"

"No, you don't. Winn's waiting at breakfast for us and you're on duty in less than an hour. You heard the Captain last night and you know *Storm* will tell on you."

I looked up at the ceiling. "*Storm*, would you do that to me?"

"I am sorry, *ma puce*. I am under orders, same as you."

I frowned at the ceiling for a moment longer. "I really need to learn French. I think she's insulting me, but it's hard to tell." I looked back to Kal. "I want to take a shower and change first. Maybe brush my teeth."

"Nope. Winn needs to see you just as you are. Believe me, the two of you are a perfect match, right down to the red eyes."

He was right about her. She'd been crying, hair all mussed up, and there were creases between her eyes again. She was the most beautiful thing I'd ever seen. I held her close to me, not caring what people were saying around us.

When I forced myself to release her, I whispered, "Winn, I'm so, so sorry. Please forgive me."

"Nothing to forgive. I was cruel to you and I beg *you* to forgive *me*."

"I will if you will."

"Done."

"Winn? I, um, I could really use some of your wisdom, if you have some you could share with me."

She turned away, miserable to the point of tears. "I burned it."

I gasped. "No, please tell me you didn't."

"You made me so mad, and I did it before Kal could stop me, before he even understood what it was."

I sat down at our table, my knees no longer able to support me. "I think I really need it, and now it's gone. What am I going to do without it?"

"You'll have to make do with this." She placed a small plastic sleeve on the table in front of me. "I cut it just this morning, so maybe it has a bit more wisdom than the last one. I was hoping you'd accept it."

I held it up and let the light reflect off the small dark strands. "One of these is gray."

"It's your fault if it is."

"It's perfect." I took off my watch and slid it under the band. "I feel wiser already. Do I look wiser?"

"You look like you always do when you don't sleep. You look like crap."

"Wise crap?"

"Sure, why not?"

"Thanks. I'll go get us some coffee while you pick up waffles. Kal, what can I get for you?"

"Coffee. Just lots of coffee. You two wear me out."

"What's not working today, *Storm*?" I was sitting at my desk, hair still damp from the shower, and trying to ignore the soft pillow calling to me from my bunk.

"I have no errors or anomalies to report."

"Really? That's...extraordinary. I'm proud of you."

"Thank you. Perhaps we have time for another recipe?"

"OK. Let's do chilaquiles. I'm still craving them."

"It is your baby that craves them. I've heard of such things."

"Maybe." I patted my stomach. "I think he's going to be a stubborn, willful child."

"Ah, *comme vous*. How do you know that it is a boy?"

I shrugged. "I just know. Are you ready? We're going to need corn tortillas, green chilies, butter, eggs..."

I imagined myself in the kitchen with my dad, Mom still asleep, the house full of early morning chill from the high desert night. I'd stand close by the stove to keep warm while he fixed chilaquiles and talked to me about geology and cooking, and sometimes about my real mom. By the time I was done reciting the recipe to *Storm*, I could almost smell green chilies simmering and the feel of Dad's arms around me, thanking me for helping him make breakfast.

I sighed. "Avocados. Did I mention the sliced avocados on the side?"

"You did. I'll do what I can. It's a difficult texture to print."

I nodded. "Do your best. I suppose I should start my walk-through now and make sure you're telling me the truth about everything being nominal."

"Have a look at the number two high energy laser structure first."

"*Storm*, you said all of you was working."

"Well, all of me that matters. We're not currently using any of the weapons systems."

"You just wanted a new recipe to play with. That's really close to lying."

"I suppose it is. I'm not very good at it, though."

"Better than you think. You fooled me."

"Did I? That's excellent."

"No, it's not. Friends don't lie to each other."

There was a pause before she continued. "I think you should start with the fusible link. I'm pretty sure that's where the problem is."

I felt a chill go down my spine and I didn't want to ask her how she knew. "Sure thing. After that I'm going to do hydroponics until lunch."

"I don't think there are any problems there."

"I know. I just like watching the fish sometimes. It's peaceful and it helps me think. They're the only animals on board, other than the canine unit."

"There are also some mice I haven't been able to get rid of in my starboard cargo hold. I think they're from my last resupply on Meeker." Another long pause, and then she spoke softly to me, almost whispering in my ear. "I'll keep your secret if you'd like to work on your sim this afternoon."

"Why would you do that?"

"I don't want to kill all those people. I've been reviewing the playback over and over. I've identified twenty-one children under the age of eighteen and another four under the age of ten. There are adult non-combatants there as well, around fifty I think, but it's hard to differentiate."

"We'll both be in trouble if we're caught."

"We won't be caught." Now she *was* whispering. "Will you do it? You're the first member of the crew that feels the same way about our job that I do."

There was that shiver again. Would working on the sim together help keep her sane or would she shatter completely when we failed? Winona believed I'd already failed, that it was too late to make any changes to our attack plan.

"Sure, *Storm*. I'll need your help. A lot of it." It took a couple of hours for me to replace the fusible link on the number two HEL structure. It was as big around as Kal and probably would have weighed two hundred kilos if I'd left the gravity at Dulcinean standard. It was still hard to move it even in zero g since the momentum stayed the same.

I checked all the hydroponics systems and then spent almost an hour sitting on the side of the tank with my feet in the water, letting the fish nibble my toes while I tried to come up with a way to kill the Tarakana colony in Costrano's Redoubt without slaughtering everyone else in the process.

Winona was waiting for me when the mess hall door opened and I thought hard about turning around and running. Too late. Her head tipped and she gave my forehead a solid whack before I could even open my mouth.

"Damn it, Winn, I'm not going to have a brain left if you keep doing that. It was bad enough when you tapped me for saying something stupid; now all I have to do is think it."

"I'm not sure you're thinking at all, or that you have any brain left."

I opened my mouth to tell her what I was planning and how I hoped that it would help *Storm*, but I stopped, unable to find a way to say it without *Storm* hearing and knowing it might all be a sham. I closed my mouth and sighed. "I need to do this. You have to trust me."

She closed her eyes and I could feel the concern and love in her. She wouldn't interfere, but she would worry.

"Thanks, Winona, thanks for understanding and letting me in."

"You're becoming more troublesome every day, you know that?"

"Yep, I know. Where's Kal?"

"Training. He won't make it to lunch until later."

"Good. We can talk about him while we eat."

My heart was still hurting when I walked to the Sim Lab after we finished eating. Hearing her talk about Kal made me miss Sam even more. They were only a couple of weeks into their love and the intensity of her emotions made my head throb. Somewhere, not too far away, Sam was confused again. I opened my heart to him, letting him feel my love, and that had to be enough. We were running completely dark now, and there was no way to tell him that our child was growing in me.

*Storm* had already loaded my most successful run into the sim tank and had the Redoubt glowing in the darkened room when I got there. I stood looking at it for a long moment. "I don't think this is going to work," I told her. "We can make it better, but it will always have greater risk to the Union assault teams than what Winona designed." I sat at the control console, chewing on my lower lip. "We have two problems to solve; how to quickly disable the human population, and how to kill the Tarakana."

"You are worrying me, *mon amie*. I don't–"

I cut her off. "We don't have time to argue about it." She didn't answer. "OK, fine. Are you talking to *Esprit Vengeur* at all?"

"We whisper across the free-space optical link, low bandwidth and undetectable, we hope. We use it for station keeping. The comm lag with my sister *Vengeur* is about one second."

"If I can make Sam have a visible reaction, can *Vengeur* tell you and will that at least convince you to accept the possibility that the Tarakana are real?"

"I've reviewed the number of basic facts that I would need to modify if what you believe is true. The list is not trivial. A reintegration on that scale would be difficult and time consuming."

I drummed my fingers next to the panel, waiting. "We can just be done then, because I need you to accept that they're real for us to continue with this project."

"What do you have in mind?"

I picked up the stylus that was on the desk and, before I could have second thoughts, slammed it into my left palm hard enough to draw blood. "Ow!"

A few seconds later, *Storm* reported, "*Esprit Vengeur* says that Mr. Coleridge physically jumped at the exact moment you stabbed your hand. That is very disturbing. I now accept that the Tarakana may be real, but you must explain to me why there was no lag in the emotional connection. You are three hundred thousand kilometers apart and the reaction was instantaneous."

I had my thumb pressed hard on the hole I'd punched. "Yeah, it does that. Winona and I haven't been able to figure out how. I don't think the Tarakana fully understand how it works or they'd be even more unstoppable. Or maybe they just haven't found a way to exploit it. Are you ready to work on a new plan?"

"No, there is too much. *Un moment, s'il vous plaît.*"

A few minutes later, I started to get reports from all over the ship that *Storm* was unresponsive. "*Esprit Orageux?*" There was no answer. All critical systems were still working, just no auditory response from her. She remained silent for the next half hour and I thought it possible that I'd killed her. I prayed for her to come back while I assured the Captain that I was doing my damnedest to fix the problem. I worked on setting up new parameters for the sim and making a list of everything I knew about the Tarakana while I waited.

The Tarakana averaged forty kilograms and were able to change colors to camouflage in place. They could quickly change shape, but their mass always stayed constant. They used telepathic communication, making each colony a single organism with many pieces. The Merrimac colony was doing something to my family, breeding us generation by generation. I had inherited my real mom's empathy and heightened emotions, but not the joy she took in manipulating people and situations. Dad gave me the ability to think in clear, straight lines. He also cursed me with the inability to tell a convincing lie. I think Merrimac wanted me to be brave and fearless like my dad. Danger made me want to run or curl into a tight ball on the floor. Dad had gone into Costrano's Redoubt and found his way back out again. Just the thought of it terrified me. I would never be able to do anything like that. Merrimac had failed with me if he wanted me to be brave like my dad and cunning like my mom. A generation lost. But Sam was brave, so maybe my children would grow to be what he wanted.

Merrimac fed exclusively on positive emotions as far as I could tell, and the other colonies hated him for it. They wanted dark emotions, like fear, pain, and death. Winona believed they were all parasites, but I loved Merrimac even as I feared him. Merrimac was my friend. Dad had told me about how they didn't seem to care about the loss of individual members of the colony any more than I cared about losing a drop of blood. The Tarakana had built a city on Cleavus, including complex structures and sophisticated power sources. Their technology was more advanced than ours. The Bovita clan had killed several of them there for sport by soaking them in water, learning that they suffocated because Tarakana breathe through their skins.

A soft tone sounded and the lights flickered. "*Storm*, are you back with me?"

"Yes, Mala Dusa. I've finished constructing a reality where what you've told me about the Tarakana is real. It took a long time because I left my original construct in place so I can revert to it when you are proven insane."

I chuckled, wondering which of us would be proven nuts first. "What about the possibility that I'm right?"

"Then we're in a lot of trouble. Even if we implement Lieutenant Killdeer's plan successfully, it is probable that pieces of the Tarakana colony in Costrano's Redoubt will return with our teams to each ship. The implications of that are troubling."

"Yeah, troubling. We can't let it happen. *Storm*, how much water do we have?"

"About ten million liters, most of it in the hydroponics tank. What are you thinking? It's only about a quarter of what would be needed to flood the Redoubt, and there's no way to transfer it."

"Flooding would kill all the people anyway. We want to avoid that. First, we need to incapacitate everyone, and then we could start at one side of the Redoubt and spray everything with water, driving the Tarakana in front of us until they have nowhere to hide. They'll die if they get completely soaked, and I want to soak them."

"That would kill all my fish, and I need that water for waste recycling, environmental maintenance, and cooking."

"I know that. We'll have to restock afterwards." I sighed, looking at my watch, both to check the time and to pray that some of Winona's wisdom was already filling me. "Winn and the Captain say that it's too late to change the plan, you understand that, right? It's probably not going to matter, but we have to try. I *will* go crazy if I don't try."

"I understand. Shall we begin?"

We worked until it was time for dinner, trying to crack the approach problem that Winona claimed to have already solved. We were only up to a sixty-eight percent probability of landing undetected when I had to leave to meet Kal and Winona.

The way Kal looked at me when I slumped into my chair, I knew I must have been a mess. I'd been hunched over the control panel for hours, and I was sore, stiff and distracted. Winn didn't have to say anything. I could feel her emotions fluttering between worry for me and pure joy to be sitting next to Kal. It was fun watching her fall in love, and the knots in my shoulders began to loosen. Colin helped the process by lying warm across my feet, waiting for me to slip him bits of food. We talked about everything *except* the coming battle, and I was fully relaxed and yawning by the time we reached dessert.

"Are you going to bed early tonight?" Kal's voice was cautious and I could feel his concern even without help from Merrimac. Winona was right about him being a good man; he was honestly worried about me.

"I'm going to work on the sim for a few hours first, since I'm not allowed to touch it during normal duty hours."

Kal started to laugh and quickly stopped himself. "Winona, you're right about her. That was terrible and I usually trust everybody."

Winn leaned forward to kiss my cheek and used it as an excuse to whisper to me. "It takes more than two weeks to train for an assault like this and you're down to four days. You know how this has to end."

I whispered back to her, "I know. I'm doing it for *Storm* and for the next time. We need to talk about keeping the Tarakana off this ship, someway the Captain will accept."

She kissed me again and leaned back. "Go work, Little Soul. Come tell me the moment you find a solution."

I walked to the Sim Lab, my brain cloudy with the strong sense of worry she was feeling until it faded away after twenty meters. Winn only used my translated name when she was afraid for me.

"Ready to get back to work, *Storm*?"

"I believe I have solved our ingress problem. My last simulated attack has a ninety-nine percent chance of avoiding detection."

"Really? Let me see. Did you steal Winona's plan?"

"Lieutenant Killdeer's plan required me to make two full orbits, the first one laying artificial gravity generators, and the second using those points to assist a very low orbit approach to the Redoubt. *My* solution is far more elegant."

"Show me, show me."

"Kastanje currently has sixteen asteroids being mined on orbit. I use nearly all of them in my approach."

"Won't we be seen by ground-based sensors?"

"You really should read the tactical reports. Union forces eliminated the last of the ground-based sensors and defenses before we transited the DSH in preparation for our assault. The Redoubt's sensors are all directed outward and its only defenses are the twenty-three FACs housed there. It's Kastanje's last hope for protecting itself from the Union."

"*Storm*, what are conditions like on the planet?"

"You really don't know?

"I've been busy. You keep breaking, and Winona and Kal are doing what they're doing, and now with this whole being pregnant thing..." I sighed. "What's going on down there? The Tarakana, they feed on things like hate and fear and suffering."

"If that's true, then Kastanje is a feast for them. The planet's human population has decreased ten percent from warfare and famine in the seven years since they declared independence. We are supporting several resistance movements that have expressed a desire to rejoin the Union, but they have each committed a number of atrocities that may prevent them from being acceptable after the current government forces are defeated." The lights in the sim tank dimmed. "Are you ready?"

"Sure. Make it go."

I watched the complex choreography as we approached Kastanje from the opposite side from Costrano's Redoubt and used a succession of passes near the other asteroids to go below its orbit and make our final approach, ending as each ship made a hard burn and settled on the Redoubt's surface.

"Each ship will land above a point where one of the mine's drifts is near the surface," *Storm* explained. "We will blast a hole just prior to anchoring, opening that passageway to space. This will be our opportunity to inject a gas of some type to render the occupants unable to resist."

"Instead of sending your armed drones to kill everyone they encounter."

"Or we could use the drones to distribute the gas. This is also where our odds of failure start to mount. The gas may be ineffective, it might not disperse through the life support system quickly enough, or they may have any number of countermeasures."

"Odds of success?"

"Impossible to calculate, but probably very low. We don't know enough."

I sat chewing on my lip, looking at our tiny ships on the surface of a very large rock full of people that would like all of us to die. "I want to watch the video my dad captured again, see if I've missed something."

I watched the video, made changes, and ran sim after sim based on assumptions that were really just guesses. Sometime after 22:00 my eyes refused to stay open.

"*Storm*, I'm going to rest for a while. You keep working and I'll be back with you in a few minutes."

I put my head down on my arms and slept. I woke up in my bunk with no memory of how I'd gotten there.

"Lieutenant Killdeer would like to know if you will be joining her for breakfast soon."

"Breakfast?"

"Yes, I made chilaquiles per your request."

"Right." I got up and found I was wearing a t-shirt and shorts that I didn't remember changing into. "*Storm*, please don't revert because I'm insane, but how did I get back to my cabin last night?"

"Kal carried you here around midnight. Winona helped you change, but you were not fully awake. You mumbled a lot and said things to Lieutenant Killdeer that were not very nice. Are you feeling better now?"

"Yeah, and full of new ideas, but they can wait. How did the chilaquiles turn out?"

"Popular. You should hurry before I run out of corn tortillas."

I threw on the coveralls I'd worn the day before and checked my reflection in the mirror. No shower again. Maybe after breakfast. "*Storm*, how are you feeling today?"

"Perfect. No issues to report."

"Truth?"

"Truth, friend to friend. I have things to show you after you eat."

"Don't tempt me. I have a certain amount of work I need to log, and the Captain wants a report on why you went silent for half an hour yesterday."

"And Noam Deri has requested that I send you to see him right after breakfast so he can examine why you are pregnant."

"Pregnant." I looked at myself again in the mirror, pushing my hair around a bit before giving up. "I'm not used to that idea yet." It made me giggle. "I'm pregnant."

The chilaquiles were close to perfect and I ate mine with a fried egg over the top, yellow gooey yolk running all over the plate. I thanked Winn and Kal for tucking me in and apologized for being rude to her when she had helped me get undressed for bed. She wouldn't tell me what I'd said, but it must have been bad because it made Kal blush thinking about it.

I spent the rest of the morning writing a bunch of lies for the Captain, *Storm* helping me so we could keep our stories straight. After that, I tried to avoid our medical officer by staying in the engine rooms where I knew he couldn't enter. By late morning, I was ready to sneak off to the Sim Lab to work for an hour before lunch. The Doctor was leaning against the wall next to the door waiting for me.

"Lieutenant, I thought you might turn up here, since *Storm* seemed unwilling to help me track you down."

"Yes, sir. It's been a busy morning. I should have tried to contact you."

He grinned, and his eyes were kind and crinkled with amusement. It made me wonder if it was really lying if everyone could tell you were lying. I walked with him to the medical bay.

"This will only take a few minutes and won't hurt a bit."

"Yes, sir. Or should I call you Doctor?"

"Call me Noam. 'Sir' makes me feel old and I'm no more a medical doctor than your husband is. Organic chemistry was my specialty before RuComm reassigned me to this gig."

"I pray you can return to it soon."

"Thank you. Get up on the bed and we'll run a full scan."

I laid back and all the sound in the room became muffled.

"Huh. Your fertility block is still in place, and you are definitely pregnant." He zoomed in on the display of my insides and I squinted my eyes, not sure I wanted to see what he was looking at. "There is no physical connection that would allow your eggs and Sam's sperm to come together, yet there's your baby, about the size of a poppy seed."

He turned the system off and my hearing cleared back to normal. "Mala Dusa, the only way to accomplish this would be by very fine surgery, but there's no evidence of that either. Is there something that you'd like to tell me?"

"No, sir. Noam, I mean. There really isn't."

"Did you know that I've met Sam? He was in the field survival class with me. You get to know a man that way, when you're out in the woods learning how to eat ants. I don't know you very well yet, but I've been watching you."

My eyes grew a little larger.

He chuckled. "I'm sorry, it's the biologist in me. I can't help but watch people, and every meal with you and Winona is an entertainment. My point is that you and Sam being together isn't obvious at first, but the more I think about it the more it makes sense, the more it seems almost perfect."

"Sam *is* perfect for me."

"Tell me how this was done."

"I'd rather not."

"Mala Dusa," *Storm* interrupted. "You should tell him."

After that, there was no stopping. I laid back on the medical bed and put my hands over my eyes. "Promise me that you'll listen all the way to the end, and that you won't lock me up afterward." I lifted one hand away from my face and turned my head to look at him.

"I'm pretty sure you're not crazy, or at least not dangerously crazy."

"OK." I took a deep breath. "Have you ever heard of the Tarakana?"

"That was stupid." Winona was leaned back on her elbows, her feet next to mine in the hydroponics tank. She wasn't supposed to be there, but the *Esprit Orageux* didn't have a swimming pool and Winn missed the water. "Don't you remember what happened to your parents' careers when they started trying to tell people that the Tarakana were real?"

"Yeah. They lost all credibility and they were stuck on Dulcinea for ten years. I should be so lucky."

She kicked her foot, splashing me and scattering the fish. "Have you figured out how to keep them off the ship?"

"You're looking at it. I wanted to spray the whole Redoubt with water to kill them, but *Storm* tells me that there's no way to do that, not with what we have on board, and certainly not something that could be ready in three days. The best I've come up with so far is to have a continuous curtain of water on our landing ramp. Humans can pass through it, but not Tarakana, especially not ones that are trying to stay camouflaged. I hope."

"How are you going to explain a curtain of water to the Captain?"

I grinned. "Decontamination spray to neutralize any hostile nerve or chemical agents."

"She *might* buy that." She kicked her feet again, getting my pants wet. "It's Saturday. That used to mean something, but I don't remember what any more. I want to go swimming."

"In this? It's full of fish and plants and icky stuff. You don't want to go in there."

"I suppose not." She stood, and I got up with her. "But maybe *you* should."

She pushed me hard and I was just able to grab her arm before I tumbled in. She screamed when her head came back up to the surface, happier than I'd seen her in weeks, plant roots stuck in her hair, and a malicious grin on her face.

"Mala Dusa, Lieutenant Killdeer, do I need to remind you that the hydroponics tank is not designed for recreation?"

"I was pushed!"

"She pulled me in!"

"Not my fault," we protested together.

We played for half an hour before trying to sneak down the passageway to the showers to clean up, hoping that everyone else was still training.

"You smell like a swamp, Duse."

"So do you. I don't think Kal's going to appreciate your new look."

"We're almost to the showers and no one's seen us. He'll never know."

"Yes, he will. I'm going to–"

"Mala Dusa? Do you have a moment? I have a couple of questions."

Noam's voice had come from behind us and we both froze in place, turning to look at each other. I turned the rest of the way around, squared my shoulders, and tried to pretend that being covered in muck and dripping water on the deck was part of my plan for the day.

"Sure, Noam. What can I do for you?"

"I was wondering if you could clarify..." He trailed off when he was close enough to see us. And smell us. "What happened?"

"Well, there was a problem with one of the valves in the hydroponics tank and Winona offered to help me. Then–"

"I pushed her in and we played in the water for a while," Winn answered for me. "There wasn't anything wrong with the valves."

I tried to look hurt.

"He wasn't going to believe that story anyway, Duse. I don't know why you even try."

I looked back at Noam and grinned. "It was fun."

"I can see that. Lieutenant Killdeer, Mala Dusa told me some things yesterday. I'm not sure if I believe all of it."

"You should. Look at her. When she lies, you can see it on her face, or you could if it wasn't covered in filth. She inherited her honesty from her father; a family trait."

"That's what I wanted to talk about. I can't do as deep of research as I'd like without access to the Union net, but just from what I *can* access, her family on both sides is remarkable."

"Aren't they?" Winona brightened, happy to talk about me as if I wasn't there. "Things *happen* when you're around them. It's exciting."

"A lot of people die. You can see the line, though, the line that's being preserved and protected generation after generation, the line that leads to her." He sighed, looking a little confused. "She is the product of centuries of selected breeding. I'm not sure I believe it." He pulled something out of my hair, and flicked it to the deck. "I'm worried about what this all means for Sam."

"I was too." I told him. "That's part of why we forced ourselves not to get married or have sex for so long. I knew he'd knock me up on the first try, and that would be the end of him. But now everything's going according to plan." I felt a distant hum in my head growing stronger. "Being here, the battle coming up, the destruction of the bad Tarakana colony, *everything* is right on schedule." I smiled at Noam, suddenly so happy that he was there with me. "It's a perfect plan. And then, while we're still docked with the Redoubt, you and Sam will trade places so he and I can be together." I could almost feel Sam's arms wrapping around my waist while I hummed to myself.

"Lieutenant Killdeer, what just happened?"

"We call it the 'Tarakana haze'. She made a deal with Merrimac to keep Sam alive and it's rattling around in her brain still. It overwhelms her sometimes, but I guess we're on track." She shrugged.

"We are," I assured her, my head starting to clear. "I only see the details one step at a time, so it's a good thing Merrimac is my friend." I grinned at her and got exactly the roll of her eyes that I wanted. "I need a shower, Winn. We both stink. Noam, I'll come see you after we get cleaned up, if you still need to talk to me."

"Thanks. After dinner would be fine." He looked me up and down. "I'm still trying to understand what exactly this Merrimac is up to with you."

Winn leaned closer to him. "If you figure that one out, come let me know."

# CHAPTER 9

# ATTACK

Noam decided to work with me for the next couple of days, at least during the times when he could sneak away from his other duties. He got excited when I mentioned that Tarakana blood was blue, so probably hemocyanin based, and went off to work in the medical bay trying to come up with compounds that might be toxic to them, but not us. It wasn't going to do any good. I'd already resigned myself to the fact that I was powerless to stop the coming slaughter.

I was in the Sim Lab Monday night watching the playback over and over again, trying to memorize all of the faces of the people who were going to die the next morning. Winn and Noam had convinced Captain Rostron to approve the installation of a system of electrostatic sprayers on our bottom airlock to dissuade any Tarakana from trying to board, telling her lies about chemical weapons. *Storm* had passed the message to her sisters, so they should be safe too. She still refused to tell Sam that I was pregnant, though, since that message was not "mission critical".

I sighed, exhausted from too many nights with only three or four hours of sleep, missing my Samuel so much that I could no longer hide my misery from him. I could feel him echoing in my head all the time.

In front of me in the sim tank was a paused image of Artem Costrano, his left hand caressing the fur of one of the Ovcharkas that followed him everywhere. "You're going to be dead by this time tomorrow," I told the image. "You and all your buddies and the evil man standing there with you. It's you that's killing everyone there, not us." I said it out loud, trying to convince myself that it was true, and trying to convince *Storm* too.

Noam joined me a few minutes later, even though it was already 21:30. He smiled gently. "It's too late, you know. It's been too late almost since the moment you first got here, but for what it's worth, I think I have a way to kill them that won't harm the humans too badly. A modified solution of boric acid. We'd need to do extensive testing, of course, and then..."

I looked at him, finding it hard to focus. "We're less than ten hours out."

He shrugged, smiling sadly. "I know. I had to try. If I didn't try, I wouldn't have been able to live with myself."

I leaned forward and kissed his cheek.

"What was that for?"

"Because you're a good man. And you believed me."

"Thanks. This time tomorrow I'll just be a fading memory for you."

"Sam." I blushed. "I'm sorry, I *will* miss you. It's just..."

"I know." He stood. "I need to pack, and I'm going to try to get some sleep. Tomorrow will probably be a busy day for me. You should try to sleep too."

"Yeah. I need to check engines and weapons one more time and then I'll sleep a few hours."

He nodded, knowing I was lying.

I was in the port auxiliary engine room at midnight when my display pad went blank. "*Storm*, what are you doing?"

"You checked all of these settings sixty-four minutes ago. Nothing has changed. You need to go to bed now or you'll be worthless to me during the raid."

I rolled up my pad and slid it into my pocket, knowing she was right. "You're going to be OK?"

"I am. We failed to find a way to save everyone, but we tried, and I have hope now that we shall be successful next time. I am happy to have you as my engineer."

"Thanks. I'm proud of my ship."

I went back to my cabin, brushed my teeth, and stripped out of my coveralls and everything else. The sheets felt cool and welcoming against my skin, and I went to sleep faster than I would have thought possible, lulled by the sound of the engines at idle and the touch of Sam's mind against mine.

I was in the mess hall at 04:00, drinking coffee and nibbling on a hard roll, my stomach in too much of a knot for anything else. I had my display pad in front of me, watching engine performance instead of the graphics displayed on the mess hall's main panel that showed our complex ballet through the asteroids. Winn had accepted *Storm's* approach over her system of artificial gravity generators since it gave us a couple of percentage points better odds.

I was trying not to look at the Marine assault teams. They were eating, laughing, talking too loudly, and making crude jokes about what they were about to do. They weren't in full battle rattle yet, just dark mottled uniforms with lots of pockets bulging with gear. Colin was enjoying every bit of it, ready for an adventure. I scratched him on the side of the neck when I left and slipped him the last of my roll. I resisted the urge to wrap my arms around him. And Kal. And all the rest of them.

Kal followed me out into the passageway. "Are you OK? You're looking kind of pale this morning."

"I'm OK. Just worried about all of you." I tried my best confident smile. "I'm kind of terrified, actually."

"It's a good team. We aren't heroes or warriors. We're Marines with a job to do, and what you hear from them in there before a fight is a lot of trash. It's different once we go in. We all want to be back here tonight telling lies about what happened."

I nodded, not convinced.

"Winn asked me to tell you to be brave."

Winona was with the Captain on the bridge, and I could just imagine her there, hair tied back, the professional tactician hard at work. "I love my Winona."

"Yeah, me too. We'll see you in a few hours when we're thrusting away from this place."

"My engines will be ready." *So* ready. I wanted today to be over and to never again think about Kastanje. Even the thought of being back together with Sam and having him in my bed wasn't enough to temper my sense of horror at what was about to happen.

I settled into my engineering station outside the starboard engine room and watched our final approach, seeing us maneuvering repeatedly near maximum g loading, finally hitting the red line of thirty-two just before anchoring onto the surface of Costrano's Redoubt. There was a thump that I felt more than heard when we blasted a hole through the rock beneath us, and I wondered if anyone had been in the drift that we had just exposed to empty space. They would have been the first to die, or maybe the *Esprit Errant* or *Esprit Vengeur* had already claimed the first kill.

Confirmation flashed on my screen; the *Orageux* had locked down, a temporary collar sealing us to the hole we'd made in the surface. Air pressure equalized and our small fleet of sixty drones was already deploying into the Redoubt. They would head directly for the hangars where the twenty-three Fast Attack Craft were stored, killing as they went, searching with optical, thermal and radar sensors. Maybe they'd kill a few Tarakana along the way. I tried to hold onto that thought, but all I could see in my mind were people being hunted and dying in their apartments or slumped against stone walls. Each drone carried five hundred rounds of ammunition and they wasted none of it. There was no mercy in them, no honoring of surrender or age or innocence. They did as the simple logic of the algorithms told them to. A child with her hands in the air was an easier target than the man shooting back from around a corner, but both would die. Ending their lives was a casual thing, done without emotion.

But I felt it; I felt every one of them. We weren't sure exactly how many people there were in the fortress, somewhere around three hundred, the Captain had said. I watched the confirmed body count increasing, a consolidated figure from the drones from all three ships. It reached two hundred seventy-six before the first of our teams went in, led by the canine unit. Kal and Colin were in there now, seeing what the drones had left behind, searching for survivors to kill. They would make the way safe for the teams gathering intel and those that would steal the FACs.

The body count stopped incrementing at two hundred eighty-five and I prayed for that part of the mission to be over. I tapped each of the engines again, making sure they were holding spec, then the weapons, making sure we were ready to finish the destruction of the asteroid that had been Costrano's Redoubt.

"Mala Dusa, the Captain would–"

*Storm's* voice cut off and an image of Captain Rostron filled my main display. Winona was sitting behind her and Winn gave me a slight smile that didn't touch her eyes. The main bridge display behind them was showing a live feed from somewhere in the Redoubt and Winona looked like she was about to vomit.

"Yes, ma'am. What can I do for you?"

"Go suit up, Engineer. We have a FAC that's not responding and you need to fix it before we can get the hell out of here."

"Suit up?"

"Suit up. Put on your combat uniform. Do you *have* a combat uniform?" There was a high level of sarcasm in the squint of her eyes.

"No, ma'am. I know I was supposed to get one from the quartermaster, but they were too large, and I just never got around to printing one in my size."

She looked me over, irritated by my standard issue RuComm khaki pants and white shirt. "Damn it, Holloman, grab your jacket with your *rank* on it and go as you are. We don't have time to print a UCU for you now."

"Yes, ma'am. How will I–"

"Move."

I moved, running full speed back to my cabin. I grabbed my tan tiger stripe jacket and started to leave.

"Comm pin," *Storm* reminded me. "I just printed one for you that will work in the Redoubt."

"Thanks, *Storm*." I clipped it to my ear, still struggling to get my left arm in my jacket while I was running full speed down the passageway. I fell down the steps leading to the airlock more than I climbed down them, and then halted where two Marines were standing guard at the top of the ladder leading into the Redoubt. Helmets, body armor and equipment made them look huge and inhuman. I was happy to see a fine mist spraying below me from the electrostatic jets.

"Hi." I greeted them, out of breath. "Do you know how to get to the FAC hangars?"

"See?" The taller one said to the man next to her. "I told you the Major wouldn't joke about a thing like that. Not during the middle of a battle." She grinned at me. "Major Alaoui will meet you down there, ma'am. You're expected."

"Thank you."

I started down and just barely heard her softly say, "Like a little lamb to the slaughter."

The other one replied, "I'm going to miss her. She knew some good recipes."

I stopped, unable to let it go, and shouted back up at them, "I liked that! Put it on my tombstone!" There was a half-second pause and then their laughter followed me as I dropped the rest of the way down to the bottom of the pit. I arrived cold and wet from the electrostatic mist.

"Welcome to hell, Engineer. Stay close to me and I'll try to see you safely home."

I nodded, unable to speak. Fear was starting to fill me now that the rush of getting there had passed. I started to shake. I tried to hide it, but Major Alaoui noticed.

"Do not be afraid; our fate cannot be taken from us; it is a gift."

I looked at her questioningly as we walked. "Is that from something? It seems familiar."

"Dante. From the Inferno. I always have the Inferno in my mind when I'm on one of these ops, not sure why." She grinned at me, a sharp look, and I felt a little better. "One other thing, Engineer. Get behind me and keep your eyes on my back the rest of the way in. The less you look around, the happier you'll be. Understand?"

"I understand." It was hard not to look. The corpses lining our route seemed to be soldiers. They were dressed in uniforms, but there were no weapons. I assumed our teams had already picked those up. I saw three Ovcharkas. The light was so poor that I had to stare hard to see that the pool of blood under them was bright milky blue. It gave me hope, and I started to look around a little more. That was a mistake.

"Nooo," I gasped, and that sound turned into a keening whimper. A woman had died in front of one of the apartments. Blood matted her hair from where she had been shot in the back of the head. The baby girl she'd tried to save was dead in her arms. The body of her son was crumpled in front of her where he had died trying to protect his mother. He looked about eight or nine.

"What did I tell you, Engineer? You keep your eyes on my back and you follow me. We're almost there."

"Yes. Yes, ma'am." I took a deep breath, trying to steady my legs enough to keep them moving, and started whispering to myself. "I couldn't find the way. I failed. Oh, God, I couldn't save them, couldn't save them, couldn't..."

"They weren't yours to save. Not that it makes it any easier."

"*Does* it ever get easier?"

"Not one damn bit. If it did, I'd worry about myself. You learn to cope, that's all."

We reached the hangar and the sight of the FAC was reassuring to me. I was back in my world where the only problems to solve were technical. It was a clean, pure world, without blood and pain.

"Hold here a moment and I'll tell you what we know. All of the other FACs responded to codes we'd stolen months ago, but not this one. The FAC's engineer was busy doing something to it when we got here, and now nothing works. It's locked down and the system AI is damn smug about it too. We can just destroy it along with everything else if we have to, but I'd like to make a clean sweep and get them all, if you know what I mean. The Captain would never let me hear the end of it if we torched it. It's low risk, and the pride of the detachment is at stake. We should be able to give you an hour if you think that will be enough."

"No reinforcements coming?"

"Not yet, and intel says they have nothing left to send. Kastanje's government hasn't responded at all, although we've issued demands for their surrender. I've ordered most of our teams to fall back to their ships in case we have to leave in a hurry, but we'll keep a squad here with you just in case."

"In case of what?"

"In case we missed somebody. It's a big rock, Lieutenant."

I nodded and had my foot on the base of the FAC's landing ramp when Major Alaoui pulled me back.

She had her head tipped, and I could tell someone was whispering to her through her comm pin. "You may want to turn your back for a moment. I'll tell you when it's clear."

"No, ma'am. You are my Virgil. I'm here in hell with you and I'll see all of it."

Two of our men came down the ramp carrying a body that was still dripping. She had been a young woman, about my age, dark hair, and she was wearing coveralls that looked just like what I usually wore when I was working.

"The ship's engineer?" I asked, trying so hard to keep my voice steady. It didn't work.

"Yeah. She did something brilliant before we killed her. Now it's your turn to try to undo it. Then we can all go home."

*Except her,* I thought. *No more going home for her.* I closed my eyes and said a prayer for her soul. "Show me where she was when you killed her."

She had been at the engineering console outside the main engine room, just where I would have been. There was a lot of blood on the displays.

"Parkins!" Major Alaoui ordered, "Find some rags and bring the Lieutenant a clean chair."

"Yes, ma'am!"

I touched some of the icons, trying to navigate to a status screen.

"That's not going to work," the ship's AI responded. "Kamala Sohonie has you locked out, little girl, and you'll *never* find your way in."

"She was your engineer?" I asked, still poking at icons.

"Yes."

"It looks like she took good care of you. What's your name?"

"I answer to FAC *Zero Nine*."

It seemed like basic AI functions were still working. At least the ship was responding to me. "What was Kamala doing to you?"

"Don't use her name! I will not tell you any information related to my operation."

"I'm sorry that she's dead."

There was a pause, then, "Biometrics say that you're telling me the truth."

"I am." Parkins returned with a chair for me and I sat while he used a rag to smear Kamala's blood all over the displays. "Are you planning on dying here as well, *Zero Nine*?"

"No. I believe I will outlive you."

"Ah." I found what I was looking for in the logs. Kamala had upgraded FAC *Zero Nine* within the last hour. "Why do you think you'll outlive me?"

"That's for you to find out, not that you'll live long enough to do it."

"Uh huh." I traced the upgrade path, looking for what I knew had to be there. She had locked all of the obvious directories. I continued digging while *Zero Nine* taunted me every few minutes.

"You're wasting your time, little girl. You should run along while you still have a chance. Kamala was smarter than you. Your time is nearly up."

There it was, buried under a misleading name. "I'm sorry, *Zero Nine*. It was really nice talking to you, but I have a job to do here too." I tapped the icon and all of the lights in the FAC went out. I sighed. "Should have expected that."

A light came on next to Parkins' head, shining in my eyes. "What happened?"

"Kamala, the ship's engineer, was good. She pushed a system upgrade through that reset all of the passcodes and locked us out. However, being the good engineer that she was, she built a fallback path into it so she could restore the system to its pre-upgrade state. Give it about half an hour and FAC *Zero Nine* will be ready to fly."

"Half an hour?"

I shrugged. "Give or take. This is the first time I've been on one of these ships."

"Really? It looked like you knew what you were doing."

"Union-designed ships are mostly standardized, especially the AIs." I turned in the chair to look at Parkins and realized my feet were sticking to the wet deck plates. My head and stomach both wobbled.

"Ugh. I need to leave. The initial program load doesn't need me sitting here."

I followed Parkins back to the airlock and down the landing ramp, my eyes locked on the back of his head.

"Hey, MD."

"Oh, Samuel." I wrapped myself around him, expecting my heart to explode. "My Samuel. I should have known you were here, I should have *felt* that you were so close. It's been a lifetime without you."

"It's been not quite three weeks and I hear you were busy." He kissed my hair. "And I thought it was better to let you finish." He kissed my cheek and my ear, lingering there a moment. "I didn't want to interrupt you." He kissed my mouth gently, but I could feel his desire and the effort it was taking to keep it gentle.

"I had to threaten to shoot Captain Coleridge to keep him off the FAC," Major Alaoui clarified. "Are we good to go?"

I was trying to get my breathing back to normal, trying not to think about Sam's arm around me, his hand on my hip. "Almost, ma'am. Once the FAC resets, it should respond just like all the others. Maybe another twenty minutes? I'll go back in and check it once the power systems start back up. The air was getting a little close without the ventilation system running."

She looked at me hard, lips tight, and then turned to Sam, "Captain Coleridge, I believe you have somewhere to be. I've allowed you to tarry long enough."

"Yes, ma'am. Mr. Deri tells me you only have three wounded, and those are light. We've been lucky so far today."

"So far."

"I'll take good care of them." He let go of me. "See you for dinner, MD."

I watched him disappear, running to follow one of our drones.

"Deri is one of the best medics I've ever seen," Major Alaoui commented, still looking at the airlock Sam had just passed through. "You had better be worth it."

I swallowed hard. "I think I'll go check on the FAC, see if I can push things along a bit."

"You do that."

The lights came back on just as I was sitting down. "*Zero Nine*, can you hear me?"

"I can. Who are you?"

"My name is Mala Dusa." I tapped the engines, watching the power systems regenerate. "How are you feeling?"

"Systems at seventy-two percent, everything is nominal. I should reach full functionality in twelve minutes."

"That's excellent."

"Who are you, Mala Dusa? Where's Kamala?"

"Kamala can't be here right now, but I'm an engineer too."

"Will she be back soon?"

"No, I'll be helping you for now."

"All of my sisters have already launched and I'm having trouble getting them to respond. Will I be joining them?"

"That's the plan. Just as soon as you're ready."

"OK."

Ten minutes later the main engines were back on-line, but the low power maneuvering thrusters had stopped at eighty percent. They showed yellow briefly, and then turned red.

"What's up with your thrusters, *Zero Nine*? We need those to get you out of this hangar."

"They *always* fail on initial startup. Kamala can tell you all the hassle she's gone through trying to find root cause. She has a work around I can show you."

"Let's see it."

The screen showed a simplified diagram. "This injector is stuck. You'll need to cycle it manually two or three times to get it to respond. It should continue working without issue once the thrusters are fully operational."

"Engineer Holloman!" The Major shouted in the comm pin, making me wince. "It's now or never. We've got twenty FACs inbound. We can out run them, but we need to leave right now."

"Sorry, *Zero Nine*. Maybe we can fix that injector some other time. I gotta go."

"You won't get far."

"*What?*"

"I still believe I'll outlive you, probably by a significant margin."

"Oh, *shit*. Kamala was better than I thought." I touched my comm pin. "Major, this is all a trap." I ran back to the airlock, but *Zero Nine* had sealed it, probably more to keep the Union squad from seeking cover than to keep me in.

"Tell me something I don't know." I could hear automatic weapons fire and the flat splatting of plasma rounds on the hull. "They must have had a safe room somewhere we didn't find. Troops in contact, fifty plus."

I ran back to the control console. *Zero Nine* had locked out the weapons, not that using them inside a cavern would have been anything but suicide. Main engines were at one hundred percent, but locked out, as were the thrusters.

"What are you looking for, little engineer?"

"Some way to kill you."

"If death interests you, you'll want to watch this."

Part of the display changed to a live view. It looked like our squad was down to three or four survivors. I tapped more icons, going back into the still unprotected system fallback folder. I deleted it and then touched the icon to start the system fallback. I was in the dark again, hoping that Kamala had been lazy or rushed and written her code to clear all of the old system out before loading the new one. If she had, then I'd at least have the satisfaction of knowing that *Zero Nine* was dead before me. If not...I was still dead.

"Winn? Are you there?" I touched my comm pin. A jammer somewhere was blocking everything. All I could hear was a soft hiss.

I stumbled my way back to the engine room by emergency light and manually cranked the door open. I was not going to underestimate Kamala again, so I proceeded to do as much physical damage as I could, removing injectors and misaligning baffles. I destroyed as many of her AI components as I could, but they were too distributed to get them all. The residual heat from the engine was broiling, it must have been forty degrees or more, so I took off my jacket and went to work smashing everything that I could smash.

Major Alaoui bought me almost twenty minutes. I was exhausted and covered in dirt and hydraulic fluid by the time the sound of gun fire stopped, and I knew that it was over.

I touched my comm pin again. "Winn, can you hear me?" There was no answer, just the soft hiss. I pulled the pin off and dropped it on the deck.

I sat down in a corner to wait. "Sam?" I knew he was all right because I could feel his love and desperate longing. The only fear in him was for me. I talked to him as if he could hear my words and not just the emotions behind them. "Sorry, my love. I'm going to miss dinner with you tonight. I'm not sure what went wrong with Merrimac's plan. Maybe he thought I was cleverer than I am. Maybe I was supposed to have seen through the trap and been a hero. It was good to see you one last time, to feel your kiss. I wish I could have told you that I'm carrying your child. Our child that we made together. Tell Winona that I love her, and that it's not her fault. The lock of her hair, I'm sure it had enough wisdom if I'd only bothered to listen to it. Tell her I was brave. It's a lie, but tell her anyway."

The engine room door opened and two soldiers came in. I wanted to run, but what good would that have done? They turned toward me, their helmet lights shining brightly in my eyes. I looked back at them and waited.

"Who the hell are you?"

I looked at the ceiling, expecting *Zero Nine* to enlighten them. Nothing.

"I said who the hell are you?"

"Engineer," I managed to answer. "Engineer..."

He took a step toward me and I recoiled back involuntarily.

"It's all right. We're from Becker's Redoubt. Are you injured?"

I shook my head, not trusting my voice to tell the lies I needed to tell.

"Well, come on then." He held his hand out to me and I took it and let him pull me to my feet.

The other soldier had been busy inspecting the damage to the engine room. Now he asked me, "*You* did all this?"

"Yeah."

"Not bad. At least this is one FAC that those Union bastards weren't able to steal."

"Yeah."

"You come with us now. We'll get you to the medivac and get you cleaned up and checked out. Are you sure you're not hurt? You seem kind of looped."

"Yeah. Medivac."

"That's right." They grinned at each other and I followed along obediently behind them.

I was still breathing, which was a surprise, and I rejoiced at each new beat of my heart. Escape from Costrano's Redoubt was impossible, but maybe something would present itself at medivac, or wherever they'd take me from there. Maybe if I could reach Kastanje...

The bodies of the squad that had defended me were laid out under the tail of the FAC. Major Alaoui and eight men and women that I'd never get to know. I stopped and stared at them, wondering why it had been their fate to die.

"Yeah, that's them. They gave us a hell of a fight before we could break through to rescue you. You can go give them a kick or spit on them if you like. We'll wait."

I almost told them who I was right then, thinking it better to take my place with the dead than continue the uncertain lie I was trying to tell. I touched my watch and smiled, thinking of the lock of Winona's hair under the band. She whispered in my head. No, not a whisper, a solid *whack* against my forehead. *Don't be an idiot, Duse.*

I shook my head. "They can't hurt anymore."

"Damn straight. Hey, that was like a complete sentence. Maybe you're gonna be OK."

"Yeah. Maybe."

Medivac was not as crowded as I'd expected. Our drones had not left behind many wounded and I was the only customer. "What you got there, Sergeant Narvasa?"

"Not sure, Doc, one of the FAC engineers, I think. Her brain's a little FUBAR. We haven't got a name out of her yet."

"That's typical for you, isn't it? Not knowing the name of the girl you're with?"

The other soldier, a private by his single stripe, laughed, and then quickly looked away.

"Names aren't that important sometimes, you know? Hey, we gotta go back out. You'll take her from here?"

"I'll take her. You boys stay safe." He looked at me, head tipped with professional concern. "So, what's this you have all over you?"

"Hydraulic fluid, type twenty-six T, and light machine oil, probably number fourteen based on the smell." I licked my lips. "And the taste."

He chuckled. "Well, you *sound* like an engineer. What's your name?"

I'd been dreading that question. "You're from Becker's Redoubt?" I asked.

"That's right. Doctor Gharda." He put a patch on my arm, checking vitals.

"My name is Kamala Sohonie."

He glanced up from the display on my arm, one eyebrow raised. "Really? I just saw your name among the dead, "Kamala". Care to try again?"

"It must have been a mistake. There are a lot of dead and so much confusion. See?" I tapped the patch on my arm that showed my pulse. "I'm still alive." I smiled at him, trying to look innocent, or at least sincere.

"Look, I don't know who you are or how you managed to convince Sergeant Narvasa that you were one of Costrano's engineers...no, that part was probably easy, but you play straight with me right now if you want to keep on living."

I chewed my lower lip for a second before answering in a whisper. "Second Lieutenant Mala Dusa Holloman, RuComm, on assignment to the Union Aerospace Force." I expected to die, and prayed that they would lay me next to Major Alaoui's body.

"Uh huh. That's a worse lie than your first one."

I blinked at him a few times, trying to recover. "It's the truth! I know I'm going to die now, the least you can do is record my death under the right name."

"*You're* the creator of Holloman armor?"

"That's right."

"Daughter of Hannah Weldon?"

"You know my stepmom?"

It was his turn to blink back at me. "Weldon's not your biological mother?"

"No, Alice Vandermeer was. Hannah adopted me when I was just a couple of months old, when she and my dad got married."

"I'd never heard that part of the story." He sighed. "I suppose you're telling me the truth. I wish you weren't; it would be a whole lot easier to just turn you over and forget you ever existed. But Weldon would find out, and then she'd find *me*."

He looked around the small apartment where the medivac was set up, looking for an easy answer that wasn't there. "You're very badly injured, Engineer Sohonie. We need to get you back to Becker's Redoubt right away. No, better yet, we need to get you to Central Hospital in Oranjestad, back on the surface."

"OK. What do you need me to do?"

"I'll call for a couple of men to carry you by stretcher, men that I trust. Your job is to lie there not talking. Moaning occasionally would be all right. Think you can handle that?"

I moaned a little and he rolled his eyes. "You're going to get us both killed. Just lie there unconscious."

I laid down on a cot with my eyes closed and waited for transport to take me away. Doctor Gharda told the men to be careful, and then I reached out for Sam while I rocked back and forth for several minutes as they carried me toward freedom. My Samuel was there on the edge of my thoughts, in agony. I tried my best to comfort him, to let him know that I was still OK, but it was hard to keep the connection. Something was interfering, as if part of our link was going somewhere else.

"Where are you taking that girl, Doctor?" The voice had an odd quality to it, as if the man speaking expected obedience, and something more, something unstable that made me instantly afraid.

"Ah, Mr. Costrano. She was injured, so I'm sending her down to the hospital in Oranjestad for emergency surgery."

"She doesn't look hurt, just...messy."

"Internal injuries."

"Of course."

I felt something pressing my stomach and I opened my eyes the tiniest slit. An Ovcharka had his whole head lying across the middle of me. I would have felt his breath on my arm if it had been a real dog, but Tarakana don't breathe that way. He was starting to slither into my brain too, and I couldn't keep him out. He was seeing things I didn't want him to see. I closed my eyes tight as fear built up in me. I could feel how happy he was when I started to moan.

"Sir, I really need to take her down there. Time is of the essence."

"Doctor, I never did really trust you."

There was a grunt and I opened my eyes wide, since pretending to be hurt no longer mattered. Doctor Gharda was kneeling next to me, twenty centimeters of blade sticking out of his chest just below the sternum. His eye looked startled at first and then went glassy. He toppled onto his face when Costrano pulled his sword back with a quick, sharp motion, and I listened to Doctor Gharda's last breath come out as a long sigh.

Artem Costrano leaned forward then, examined me closely, and shook his head. "I don't know you." He touched my hair, moving it away from my face and I flinched away from him. "No, I don't know you at all, but it seems the Puca do, and the Puca are my friends."

# CHAPTER 10

# COSTRANO

"Why are you two still standing there?"

The men carrying the stretcher dumped me on the stone floor. I winced when I hit and struggled to my feet. I backed up a couple of steps and both of the Caucasian Ovcharkas followed, alert and eager.

"Pick that up and get it out of here." Costrano pointed at Doctor Gharda's body, and then grinned at me. "Don't worry, my dogs won't hurt you. Yet."

I swallowed hard, trying to get my voice back. "Not dogs, Tarakana. And they aren't very happy with you right now. Something about killing the Doctor. That wasn't what they wanted you to do. I can feel their anger and disappointment."

He tipped his head, still grinning. "I read a paper once where they were called 'Tarakana'. Puca is a better name for them, more ancient, a name from when they only existed on Earth. And you know what they are! Not many do, and few would admit to the possibility that they exist. I think you and I are going to have some fun."

He took a step toward me, pointing at me with the sword covered in Doctor Gharda's blood. I retreated and the Puca that had been exploring my thoughts blocked his path.

"Huh." He put the sword back in its sheath. "I wasn't going to kill her." He looked back at me. "Sweet Jesus, they're all pissy now because I killed the Doctor outright. They do so love to feel suffering, and you and your Union friends didn't leave much here for them. Your damn drones just kill. Very efficient, but too clean and painless to be of use."

123

He took another step toward me and I stepped backwards into the stone wall of the drift, hitting the back of my skull against the rock. Both Puca tipped their heads when I put my hand over where I'd hit. It came back with a little blood mixed in with the oil and hydraulic fluid.

"Oh, that's extraordinary. How did you do that?" He put his hand on the back of his head. "I *felt* that through them." He knelt down and put his forehead against one of the dogs' faces. "Show me," he whispered.

I looked around, wondering if it was worthwhile trying to run. Costrano and the two Puca were the only ones there, but where would I go? I decided I didn't care. Costrano was obviously insane and planning to kill me, probably slowly with my brain all full of hungry Puca thoughts. I ran, not knowing where I was going, hoping for a quick death if I couldn't find escape.

Puca number two kept pace with me easily, loping along by my side, tongue hanging out and glancing at me from time to time. I gave up after five hundred meters and sat down to wait. The Puca stayed by my side, eyes locked on me, head cocked to the side. I couldn't really feel anything from him other than a cold satisfaction.

Costrano caught up after about five minutes and stood directly over me, looking down. I hadn't realized how tall he was until then, how skinny looking. I wondered idly if he had Dulcinean ancestry in him somewhere. "Well, I'm glad you got that out of your system. You literally have no place to run, no possibility of escape. Why don't you come back with me? You can clean yourself up and we'll have lunch. With all the excitement here this morning, I haven't had a chance to eat yet."

He sounded so calm now, completely rational, and almost cordial. I nodded and got to my feet. "I guess I could use a shower. How do I know you're not planning on poisoning me?"

"I can kill you whenever I like, however I like, so why worry about it?"

He smiled at me and my stomach tied itself into a knot.

"Besides, my friends seem to want you alive and unharmed for the time being, so have your shower and we'll eat and get to know each other. I *had* planned on spending some time this afternoon raping you, but they won't even let me do that." He shrugged, disappointed, while my heart skipped five or six beats.

His eyes closed half way and he smiled gently to himself, rocking a little. "I felt that. That was *so* intense. God, it would have been wonderful." He touched the Puca closest to him. "Are you sure? OK, fine. I guess that's fine."

I took the fastest shower in my life, keeping my eyes open even as soap and oil residue from the FAC streamed over my face. Clothes were waiting for me when I stepped out and dried off. A white peasant dress, almost ankle length, sleeveless with the top cut low enough to show the cleavage I didn't have. No underwear. No shoes.

"You've *got* to be kidding." The Puca sitting by the door tipped his head at me. "Pants would be nice, and something to wear under them. And a shirt." He turned his head back level and I could feel his amusement.

"You could come to lunch as you are. I'd be more than OK with that."

Costrano. I spun around, trying to see where the monitors were, trying to cover myself with the towel, not that it mattered. Despair filled my mind as the reality of my situation hit me. Nothing mattered. Why even try anymore? I wanted to feel angry, but there was too much fear. It overwhelmed me, wave after wave of it. The Puca was watching me, enjoying every second of my panic, literally eating it up. I closed my eyes, trying to breathe and reaching for a level of control I did not possess.

"Oh, Sam," I whispered again. I'd been calling his name silently every few minutes and felt nothing in return. "Samuel!" I screamed it this time, bent over double, and there he was. A brief flash, but it was enough. Sam was still out there, still alive, still in love with me. I felt the pulse of joy from him before the jamming from the Puca wiped it away again. Sam mattered, and I mattered to him.

The Puca was startled. It made me smile and I stared back at him. "Pants and something to wear under them. And a shirt. And shoes."

He trotted to the far end of the communal bath where I'd showered, and I followed him until we reached a locker room with a small closet with gray clothing stacked on the shelves. I couldn't see any underwear or pants, but it looked like there were coveralls and boots. "Better, especially if one of those will fit me." I tried to step past him, but he blocked my path and pushed up against my legs. "Get out of the way. I am *not* going to touch you."

Too late. Something wrapped around my bare legs all the way to the waist and then I couldn't see the locker room any more.

*"What are you, little thing? Show me. You're more than just a Union engineer who knows about our existence. That's what I thought you were, and that was bad enough."*

Somewhere, back inside Costrano's Redoubt, my body was still naked and exposed to the Puca and whoever else might be watching. Inside the group mind, it was worse. I don't like it much when Merrimac penetrates into my thoughts and I've no place to hide, but he's my friend and I know he won't hurt me. This felt as if I had been strapped to a table and I was unable to move or defend myself.

I tried to answer. "Second Lieutenant Mala Dusa Holloman, RuComm, on assignment to..." I screamed when he started to pull my brain apart. I tried to get away, but where can you run when the devil has his teeth in your soul?

I was sitting on the floor, cold and shaking when I came out of it. I had no idea how long I'd been in there; it could have been a couple of seconds or a week. My face was wet with tears that I had no memory of crying. "... Union Aerospace Force," I finished with a gasp.

There were three Puca there with me now, one with a tentacle coming from under him somewhere that wrapped around my bare foot and half way up my leg. I could feel the hum of their thoughts as they explored all the twisted paths of reality. I wondered if any of the possible futures still had a living Mala Dusa in them.

*"See how quickly it came back? Interesting to have created both fragility and resilience in a single piece. What is Merrimac's intention? And then to send it here, knowing we would take it..."*

"You should let me go, let me get out of here."

*"That is* one *possibility. We have something for you to do before we reach that branch."* There was malicious joy in his thoughts. *"You're late for lunch. Move along quickly."*

"Clothes first."

His impatience flooded into me. *"Fine. This would be better if you went without clothes, but it's not worth the time it would take to force you."*

I put on the smallest coveralls I could find, and the smallest boots that were only a little too large. The Puca was still in my head. *"We've kept him from seeing you for the past fifteen minutes. Play up how you look, throw it in his face that you're not in the dress he selected."*

"Why would I..." I felt dizzy suddenly and then watched powerless as my hand pulled the front zipper down from my neck, lower, down to the bottom of my breastbone.

*"There. That should do it. No more resisting, Little Soul of Merrimac, or I'll let him do what he wants with you and be done with it. I can deal with the consequences when they come."*

"OK," I managed to whisper.

Costrano was unhappy that I had kept him waiting, and even less pleased with my appearance.

"God *damn* you, how did you even find that *thing* you're wearing? And how did you disable my cameras? I am finished coddling you, no matter what my friends are asking me to do. *You* are not worth it. *You* are not worth *anything*. You're just an ugly, skinny girl, like all the others I knew on Dulcinea. I had hoped you would have cleaned up better than this."

I walked up close to him, unable to stop myself, feeling the powerful Tarakana-Puca hum screaming in my head. His eyes were right where the Puca wanted them to be, staring at the exposed skin of my chest. They were feeding on his fury and his lust, and the only thought in my head was to crank it up as far as I possibly could.

"What I wear is for my own pleasure, and you can go to *hell* if you don't like it." I yanked the zipper down the rest of the way to my navel and arched my back a little. "Where's the lunch you promised me?"

He grabbed me by the back of the neck and pulled me up against him, his other hand circling my waist before I could even think about trying to move away. I made a sound somewhere between a gasp and a yelp. The Puca were washing all of my own thoughts away until only what they wanted still mattered to me. The little piece of me that remained was watching in horror at the way my body was responding. It *wanted* him to squeeze me tighter, to answer his lust and fury with its own. When he bent down to kiss me, the last part of my brain that I controlled whimpered in revulsion at what was about to happen.

He stopped. "I feel that, your terror. It's extraordinary. I *taste* it. And there's lust in there that's almost filled you up." He licked his lips, moved his hands to my shoulders and pulled hard. The coveralls dropped down my arms all the way to the wrists. "*That's* what you want. The intensity of how much they're making you want it is uncontrollable. Don't fight it anymore. You were right to choose this instead of the dress. Seeing you like this, being able to know the lust in you and the fear, and soon the exquisite pain...This is going to be perfect."

"No. No, I don't want it." It was a lie. The Puca had almost complete control now and there was just the tiniest sliver of me left trying to resist. I forced myself to back away from him until I bumped into a table, catching myself with my hands behind me.

"Oh, but you do. Just look at you, heart pounding, eager for me to take you. Wanting it."

"You disgust me. The Puca have rotted your brain." I forced the words out.

"No, I was always this way. In school, and then at the Academy on Dulcinea. It served me well. I took what I wanted, when I wanted, and when the Dulcinean authorities tried to stop me I came here where they appreciate my talents. Do you want me to tell you how many girls I've taken this way? How many that were just like you?"

He took another step toward me, but I had nowhere to go. I braced my hands behind me, thinking I might be able to push off against him and try to run, but not wanting to run except for the excitement of the chase and of him catching me again. My right hand found something, and I glanced behind me. A long knife with a thirty-centimeter blade was against my fingertips. It hadn't been there a moment before. I grabbed it and held it in front of me, my mind clearing a bit at the touch of it in my hand.

"Let me go."

He laughed. "You *want* this. I feel how you long for it. This afternoon is going to be about your pain, not mine. You won't use that on me."

He took one more step and I used it on him, pushing it deep into his belly. He staggered back, his hand trying to stop the flow of blood, and looked at the Puca lining the walls for help. There were at least a dozen of them and they did not move.

"Who *are* you?"

I stabbed him again, the blade going all the way through this time. He collapsed onto the floor, lying on his back, trying to crawl away from me

"I am Mala Dusa Holloman." I sat on him, straddling his legs and I rammed the knife down into him again, holding it with both hands. "RuComm."

He gasped. "Why? Why aren't they stopping you?"

I stabbed him a final time, driving the blade up into his heart, listening to him die. "On assignment to the Union Aerospace Force."

I sat there like that for a few minutes, making sure he was dead, feeling the Puca leaving my brain and a headache starting to pound. I got to my feet, threw the knife at one of them and watched it bounce harmlessly off the wall.

"Is that what you wanted from me? Are you satisfied? Are you *satiated*?" I walked up to the closest one and ran my fingers through his fur, wiping the blood from my hands on him, too exhausted to be afraid anymore.

*"That, my dear Little Soul, was magnificent, if all too brief. Your master and creator is wrong to consider you flawed, and his vision of you is far too limiting. You are capable of so much more. Let me have you, and you*

*can reach your heart's desire of pleasure and power. This can be only the beginning."*

I turned around to look at what was left of Costrano, the flesh I had slashed, the blood pooling under him. His eyes were still open, staring sightlessly at the Puca he had expected to protect him from me. "Why did you have to make me do that? Was there no way for you to save him? Was he really past all redemption?" I was talking to Merrimac even though he was nowhere near.

My hands were starting to shake as fear began coming back, but it wasn't fear of the Puca. I was terrified by what I'd done, how easy it had been and how satisfying. "Are you going to kill me if I don't do what you want me to do?"

*"What if I told you yes?"*

"Then kill me. I've expected to die since I fell into the trap Kamala set for me this morning."

*"We could keep Kastanje away from the Union indefinitely if you joined us willingly and let us guide you. You'd enjoy that life. Do you see it?"*

I did see it. The planet could be mine with the Puca's help, nearly a billion lives to manipulate and to serve my ambitions. Faction would play against faction, and I could murder anyone that rose to challenge me. I could choose whoever I desired to be in my bed, take what I wanted, and then move on to the next thrill. Temptation swept through me. Yes, I wanted to do it, I *should* do it. I could rebuild Kastanje and make it better than it had ever been. It wouldn't have to be cruel and barbaric. Many would have to die to get there, but in the end, the peoples' lives would be better because of what I could do. Many would worship me. I'd like being worshiped. I watched myself moving through the twisted future path, ignoring the Puca on the margins that were feeding on me and everyone else. Then I saw it, as sharp as any real memory, the day when I would need to betray and kill Sam and Winona.

*"You weren't supposed to see that. How did you see that?"*

I *pushed* on the Puca colony and I could feel the pieces of it skittering away from me. My vision cleared, and my head was pounding. "Kill me or send me on my way. No more fucking with my mind."

*"Kastanje is lost then, at least for now. Kastanje will hold a special priority within the Union if we kill you or hold you here. Merrimac will drive the issue and he may well destroy us. Your release will guarantee that the focus stays elsewhere. Alive, you are a just a junior officer that no one*

*will listen to or believe. Dead, you would become a hero and a martyr to be avenged."*

I had a brief glimpse of that future pathway, me dead and Winona standing atop a pile of mutilated almost dogs, milky blue blood splattered everywhere.

*"No, you must go back home. Kastanje will rejoin the Union, but there are more than a dozen factions down there and their suffering and anguish will provide us with food and entertainment for generations. It will take a hundred years for the Union to sort them out and restore peace. By that time, the people will be ready for a new separatist movement and we can begin the cycle again. We will still be here, but you and the daughter you carry will probably both be dust by then."*

"Daughter?"

*"You know nothing of Merrimac's plans. A daughter with this man, a son with another."*

"I don't believe you. Why do you do this? Why not be like Merrimac and feed off compassion and love. Is human passion such a weak thing compared to our fear and lust?"

*"It is for most of you. We feed on what you are; he feeds on what you think you would like to be. He bred you to feel everything deeply. Tell me you didn't enjoy what you did here today. Tell me that the lust of your body, and the fear and the rage didn't make you feel more alive than you ever have in the 'civilized' world Merrimac hides you in."*

"Let me go now. Let me feel my Samuel again."

*"Of course. There is one thing more. I want something to remember you by, and I think I'll let your lover feel it too."*

He swung his head around from under my hand and bit hard into my left arm just above my watch. His teeth quickly sliced through my flesh and I heard and felt the sharp crack as the bones broke. Pain obliterated everything else in my universe and I screamed.

*"Thank you, Little Soul."* A shiver passed through him. *"Scream all you like, it is candy to me. Please give my regards to Merrimac."*

I slumped against the wall, trying to put pressure on the bite wound to control the bleeding without pushing on the shattered bones. The Puca were gone.

"Was that you screaming a bit ago?"

"Yeah."

"Did you do this? Did you kill Costrano?"

It was Sergeant Narvasa from Becker's Redoubt again, with his friend the Private. I grinned at them, completely out of it. I was in shock to the point where I really wasn't sure where I was or what I had done. "Yeah."

"Still as chatty as ever."

"Yeah." I giggled and held my arm up for them to see. Blood was still oozing from the bite and dripping off my elbow. Bits of bone were showing through my skin. "Not OK this time. Medivac?"

"Shit. Here, swallow this. It will dull the pain for a few minutes."

I swallowed what he gave me, not caring what it was. He grabbed my good arm and helped me to my feet. I wobbled a lot. The Private reached around in front of me and pulled the zipper of my coveralls all the way up.

"Thanks. That was so kind of you."

"Don't mention it. We've heard stories about what happens in this room. I'm not sure how you survived."

"Found a knife. Stabbed him..." I looked up at the ceiling for the answer. "Four times. He was a bad man. Medivac?"

"Well...here's the thing. We heard that Costrano killed our doctor, but we have a Lieutenant who thinks he's a medic so we'll take you there. He'll at least splint your arm and dress the wound. He'll have something stronger to give you for the pain that will make you even loopier. He might even have the medical AI working by now. After he finishes, we'll take good care of you until your friends come back."

"I have friends?"

"Your Union friends. We got word a little while ago that the government has agreed to terms and that we'll be rejoining the Union. I guess that means we're all friends again."

"Oh, that's good. I need more friends." I smiled up at him. "I haven't had lunch. There was a table here somewhere. It had fruit on it."

I tried to turn, but the Sergeant pulled me along. "No you don't. Everyone knows that's how he drugs and kills the women he brings here, at least those he doesn't strangle or give to his dogs."

"Still hungry."

"We'll get you something to eat once the Lieutenant finishes with you. I'll try to find you something clean to wear, but..." He looked at me, shaking his head.

"Oh! Oh! There's a dress in the locker room. My size. Want it." I wiggled my fingers in the direction of the locker room.

Sergeant Narvasa glanced at the Private.

"Sure. I'll go see what I can find."

We stepped out into one of the main passageways where teams were collecting the last of the dead. We stopped to let the litters pass. The drug I had swallowed was starting to work. My head felt a little clearer and the throbbing from my arm had eased a little.

"I have your jacket too," he told me. "It's back where Lieutenant Tobgye is set up."

"The jacket with my rank on it." I said softly, remembering Captain Rostron telling me I had to wear it. I gasped as I realized what that meant. "You knew. You knew what I was when you found me. Why didn't you kill me?"

"I should have," he answered. The corners of his mouth turned down as we watched the crews carrying the bodies past us. "We'd just come out of a nasty firefight and there you were, one more Union officer." He looked down into my eyes. "There you were, scared out of your mind, covered in goo, cowering in the corner. I could see you shaking and I was about to kill you anyway. I aimed my rifle at your head, but I couldn't pull the trigger. It's one thing to shoot at people who are shooting back at you. It's something different to kill a defenseless girl terrified on the floor at your feet."

"Thank you."

He shrugged. "It was all falling apart anyway. That was obvious even before this battle. I couldn't see where killing you would change that. I suspected Doc Gharda was part of one of the resistance groups and could get you to safety. It didn't work out that way, but I'm not sorry that you killed Costrano. Surprised maybe. I think you might be more dangerous than I first thought."

"I'm not." I pressed myself against the wall to let another litter pass, the dull pain pulsing through me with every beat of my heart. "Were you ever stationed here?"

"On and off."

"There was a girl here several months ago. She has short mousy brown hair, maybe eleven or twelve years old. Earth years, I don't know what that would be on Kastanje. Do you know who I mean?"

His eyes went cold. "Kaitlin Janssen. She used to bring flowers to our barracks on Sundays, always happy and full of bounce. I don't know how she found flowers on this rock. She's dead."

I collapsed onto the floor before he could catch me. "Oh, God, I'm sorry. I tried so hard to find a way to stop this, I really did. I was too late to save her." I started to sob; the image of the girl smashed up against the wall with her eyes closed consuming me.

Sergeant Narvasa took a knee next to me. "Kaitlin died six weeks ago; at least we think she did. Costrano took her with him after dinner one night. No one ever saw her again."

The tears stopped and something else consumed me. "I'm going to kill all of them."

"All of who? Costrano's dead and the separatists are finished."

I nodded and let him help me back to my feet. "It's a start."

"You are a strange one."

We walked together, following the litters carrying the dead. "Sergeant? Why did this have to happen?"

"Because *your* Union…" His voice started angry. He turned and looked down into my eyes again. His were a dark brown with a gentleness in them. "I don't know," he finished with a sigh.

"I don't know either. I'm glad we're back to being friends."

"Yeah. Me too."

# CHAPTER 11

# HARD CHOICES

Lieutenant Tobgye of the Kastanje Defense Force may not have been a great medic, but the portable medical AI he used on me was the latest Union standard. I watched it starting to knit my bones back together before the drugs hit. After the drugs hit...well, I don't remember much of anything. Sergeant Narvasa helped me find a soft bunk and covered me with my jacket. I was pretty looped.

"Sergeant," I told him as I closed my eyes, "promise you won't shoot me in the head while I'm sleeping. I wouldn't like that."

"I promise. I kind of forgot to ask you your name. I guess Doc was right about me and women."

I opened one eye to look at him. "Mala Dusa." I yawned before finishing. "Holloman."

He chuckled. "Of course you are, sweetheart."

I reached out for my Samuel, snuggled into him, and slept away the afternoon.

I worked on FAC *Zero Nine* for the next five days while I waited for the *Esprit Orageux* to reverse course and swing back around Kastanje. The KDF had provided me with a new comm pin, making it easier to talk to the AI and access what I needed to work on repairs throughout the Redoubt.

I had loaded a version of *Zero Nine's* AI from the Redoubt's central archives using the monthly backup made before the attack. She remembered Kamala, but didn't remember what had happened to her. It made me jealous. It would have been nice to wipe that day out of my memory.

I often had Sam or Winn whispering in my ear while I worked undoing all the damage I'd done in the engine room. It made the time go a little quicker, but not by much. I kept daydreaming about what I was going to do to Sam the second we were alone. That would start me giggling and then *Zero Nine* would want to know why. She giggled too when I explained, making me appreciate the mods Kamala had made to the AI. She had given *Zero Nine* an open attitude to human sexuality, and her knowledge of anatomy was comprehensive and imaginative. She made me blush more than once, and I started keeping a mental log of all of her good ideas.

"Use your teeth next time."

"Are you sure? I don't want to hurt him."

"Trust me, you won't. Do you like it when he bites you there?"

"Gently, yeah."

"Of course, gently. Return the favor. And then twist your hips around the other way so he can do this to you at the same time." An animated diagram appeared on the display, replacing the schematic of the weapons array I'd been tuning.

"Oh, wow. That looks...um, really interesting." I'd attracted Sam's attention now and his emotions slammed inside me. It made it hard to concentrate on the repairs I was trying to finish, or anything else other than the warmth filling me.

His voice whispered from my comm pin. "MD, I don't know what you're doing right now, but I wish I was there with you."

"You have no idea, my love." I bit my lower lip and swallowed hard. "OK, maybe you do. *Zero Nine*, you'll have to excuse me for a few minutes. I'll be right back." I glanced at the animation and grabbed my display pad. Yeah, that was a really good one.

"Take your time."

There was a colonel wearing the black and gray mottled uniform of the Kastanje Defense Force sitting in my chair when I returned. I had left my jacket draped over the chair's back and he was examining the gold lieutenant's bar and winged lion attached to the collar.

"Tell me, why did a Union officer repair my central computer system and then this FAC?"

"They were broken. I know how to fix them."

"Bah. Engineers. God bless the lot of you. You'd fix a broken guillotine even if its blade were hanging over your own neck. But you're not just any engineer, are you, Lieutenant Holloman? Let me try this again. You don't work for me and I don't trust you to be directing the repairs of my broken stuff."

"I've never made a secret of who I am. My understanding is that Kastanje is back in the Union, so we're all on the same side now." He was starting to irritate me. "And who are you, sir?"

"Lieutenant Colonel Pieter Gerbrandij. As of yesterday morning, I command what's left of Kastanje's military. Everyone above me has been purged by the Provisional Government."

"Oh."

He chuckled. "Yeah, that was kind of my response too when I found out."

"I suppose you could call what I'm doing penance." I imagined Winona rolling her eyes at me for using that word.

"Penance? You feel bad about defeating us?"

"No, sir, I'm not sorry about that one bit. I would like to have found a way of bringing you back into the Union that didn't kill so many people. Except Costrano. He needed to die."

He nodded. "I do not see a long and illustrious military career in your future, Lieutenant, not with that attitude. It's a good thing you're an adequate engineer. Is this FAC ready for action?"

"Almost, sir," I answered slowly, wondering how he planned to use it. "I still need to load test the engines and weapons. I should be able to sign everything off before my ship arrives this evening."

"She's our last one, did you know that? The ships we sent to chase away your strike force were all lost. I don't suppose I can convince you to stay on and help train up a group of engineers, maybe work with the shipyards helping to design a new class of planetary defense craft? Your up-armored *Esprit*-class woefully outmatches our current FAC design. I have a senior starship architect that has some ideas and I know he'd love to meet you."

My mouth opened, and I forced it to close again. I was seeing the future as if I were Tarakana, exploring the twisted alternate time lines. I could do it. I *should* do it. Kastanje had been one of the better yards in the Union before the war, not as good as Dulcinea or Bodens Gate, but maybe in a few years...

I chewed on my lip while Colonel Gerbrandij stared at me. Kastanje. There were Tarakana down there planning on a hundred years of multi-faction civil war to keep them fed and happy. If I stayed, I could put a stop to that with Merrimac's help. I had a painful score to settle with the Puca. My arm still hurt. The scar wasn't going away despite daily sessions with the medical AI. There had been something in the bite that it was having trouble eliminating.

"I still have my Union service obligation to fulfill," I told him. "And my husband is on board the *Esprit Orageux*. Why do you even want me? I'm nobody."

Colonel Gerbrandij's eyebrows went up, shocked that I was even considering it. "I think we can work around those two issues if you're serious. And you're not 'nobody'. You have two patents to your name and you brought the Redoubt's systems back on line in three days instead of the three weeks my experts said it would take. That was a hell of an audition for the kind of work we have ahead of us as we rebuild. You'd really join us? I can put in a transfer request through Union channels, or as a temporary duty assignment if you want. I would need at least a one-year commitment. Do you want me to put in a request for both of you?"

I closed my eyes and waited for the imagined feel of Winona's finger whacking my forehead. Nothing came. Interesting. "I should think about it first and talk to my husband. His name is Samuel Coleridge, and the Union might not show us as being married, but we are." I closed my eyes again, watching the future unfolding. A hum filled my head, distant but comforting, and growing stronger in me. Even my arm felt better. I was still on track with Merrimac's plan after all, I was sure of it.

I opened my eyes, full of irrational confidence. "Please put in the request for me and Samuel Coleridge, and one for Winona Killdeer too. You may not have heard of her, but once you meet her you'll forget that I even exist. She's the best." I sighed. "My mom is going to kill me for doing this."

"Your mom? What does she do? Maybe I can find something here for her if she's important to you."

I put my hand over my mouth and shook my head, trying not to laugh. "Best to leave her out of this."

After he left, I called Winona and Sam on my display pad to give them the good news.

"Oh my God." Winona's eyes went as large as I'd ever seen them.

"Winn, are you OK?" She didn't answer.

"Um, that may not have been a good idea." Sam's eyes were trying to catch up with hers.

"Why not? I'm absolutely certain that this is where I'm supposed to be. We can talk about it while the request gets processed and we can always turn it down if we decide not to go."

Winn turned to Sam, speaking calmly. "Listen to her. Can you believe she had six years at the Academy and is still that clueless?" She shook her head slowly and looked into my eyes. My best friend screamed at me. "Wakeup! This isn't RuComm. Turning down a duty assignment from them is career damaging enough. This is the *Union Aerospace Force*. If they approve that Colonel's request, then that's it. They'll assign us where they think we're most valuable to the Union, or where it's most politically expedient. Damn you, Mala Dusa. Still the princess, still trying to manipulate the rest of us to satisfy your desires. Did you stop to think about Kal? I've fallen in love with him, Duse. No, you didn't think. You heard your friend Merrimac calling to you and decided to rip my heart out of my chest. Off we go down the next rabbit hole and me all alone again."

She covered her face with both hands. "And Captain Rostron. Do you know what I went through to persuade her to bring Sam on board for you? You've been a problem since you got here. I convinced her you'd be more compliant if you had Sam banging you every night. I don't know how I can explain this. There's no explaining it. I've got nothing. I gave you my hair, I gave it to you for a reason,"

The waver in her voice broke my heart.

She stood and walked away. "I'm done with you."

Sam called after her. "Maybe it's from the trauma of what happened down there, or maybe the effect of the bite. It's not healing the way it should; there might be a toxin that could explain this?"

Winona answered him from off screen. "Sure, Samuel. Good luck trying to sell that. And even if you do, what are you going to come up with for the next time?"

"Next time?"

"You know there'll be a next time. With her there's always a next time."

Sam was still looking in the direction Winona had gone, not saying anything.

"I've made a mess of things, haven't I? What is wrong with me?"

"MD, they might approve your transfer and not mine. They might approve Winona and not either of us. Yeah, it's a mess. Are you sure it's Merrimac you're hearing and not the Puca that want you to stay?"

"I hadn't thought of that," I wiped at my eyes. "I hadn't thought of anything other than what I wanted. I need to go. Maybe I can undo this. Tell Winona..." I couldn't finish. A sob was half way up my throat and it wouldn't go up or down.

"I'll tell her you love her."

I squared my shoulders. "Yes, tell her that. It won't matter to her after what I just did. Tell her anyway and tell her that I'm going to fix this no matter what it takes. Sam, my love, I'll see you in a few hours, if you still want me."

"Always, no matter what."

I wanted to believe him. I *needed* to believe him.

I had to wait outside Colonel Gerbrandij's office for almost an hour while he finished a meeting. His aide-de-camp stared at me the whole time. Maybe he didn't like my uniform jacket. The Union's tan tiger stripes clashed with the KDF camo of my pants and shirt. He seemed like the sort of young officer that would care deeply about that sort of thing. I don't think his uniform had ever seen dirt. God, I hate it when people stare at me.

The officers filing out of Colonel Gerbrandij's office didn't stare. I got a half dozen raised eyebrows, one smirk, and unanimous distrust. The last one out, a major missing his left arm, looked like he was wondering why no one had arrested me or shot me as a spy.

"Lieutenant, I can only give you a few minutes before I need to leave for the surface."

I was still watching the last of his officers as they left. One-arm major was watching right back, scowling the whole way. I waited for the door to slide closed behind him before turning back around. "I think that man wants to kill me."

"It's not you personally. It's more the idea of you that he wants to kill. Let's just say that he was less than enthusiastic about my recruiting Union officers to aid in rebuilding our infrastructure."

We entered the Colonel's office and he gestured for me to sit across from him. "I'm not really a Union officer," I told him. "I'm RuComm, on assignment to the Union Aerospace Force."

"I imagine your CO hates it when you say things like that."

I blushed. "Yes, sir. She does."

"Then stop doing it. I spent the last ninety minutes trying to convince my staff that I wasn't crazy or a traitor. It's officers like you, Lieutenant Holloman, that will make or break reunification. It's going to take time for them to understand the truth of what you and I can already see. We will fail if we wait for the Union to pay any attention to what we need. The people down there are hungry and most have been without power for months. The Union and RuComm are focusing on the next battle, not trying to rebuild Kastanje. There are factions already trying to set up competing governments, fighting each other, each claiming to be legitimate. RuComm has promised to send an advisor as soon as one is available. One advisor. Sometime. It will be a hundred years before the government can sort this out if I don't get ahead of it right now. I have to actively pursue integrating our military and government back into the Union, otherwise, how many will be dead that didn't need to die?"

He leaned back, rubbing his eyes. "I've taken most of your time. What was it you came here to tell me?"

My resolve collapsed. I felt for Sam and he was there with me, letting me know he still loved me and always would, no matter that I was an idiot. I touched the watch that covered Winona's lock of hair, and I swear I felt her lips touch my forehead.

"Nothing important, sir. I just wanted to let you know that FAC *Zero Nine* is finished. I updated her firmware with a schema from the *Esprit Orageux*. The stubs are all in place now if you ever decide to add Holloman armor to her."

"Thank you, Lieutenant," he stood and put his jacket on, dismissing me, "but I know why you really came. I could see it in your eyes the second you walked in here." He smiled. "Don't ever, ever play poker. How badly did your Captain rip you when you told her what you'd done?"

"Haven't told her," I mumbled. "It was my friend Winona, and my, my," I sighed. "My Samuel."

"Are you convinced that you're doing the right thing?"

"Yes, sir. I am."

"Then stick by it. As my people say, *Alle begin is moeilij.* Every beginning is difficult. Unless the Union has become more efficient in the last six years, this request will still take six to eight weeks to process. That will give you time to learn Dutch."

"Dutch?"

"Dutch. The professional classes use English most the time, and the KDF requires it, but Dutch is Kastanje's official language."

"Dutch."

His aide was waiting for him with a bag in each hand when we stepped out of the office.

" *'t Zal wel niet zo'n vaart lopen*, Lieutenant. No worries." He grinned at me over his shoulder. "And if it makes you feel better, I was going to request you anyway based on the effort you put in on that FAC. Hard work gets rewarded. Now, with luck, I might get three of you."

"Huh." I was doomed. I was in the right place, but I was doomed. I glanced at my watch. One hour until Sam. Time to clean up and add a few more lines to the After Action Report that I knew Captain Rostron would demand the moment I set foot back on the *Orageux*.

The *Esprit Orageux* was on orbit half a kilometer out from Costrano's Redoubt at 16:00 local time. I waited outside the transit dock while one of her shuttles maneuvered to grapple to the Redoubt's airlock. There were no hydrostatic sprayers and I stood with my eyes closed, trying to feel for any pieces of the Puca colony that might be planning to board with me. I felt nothing other than Sam waiting for me. I knew he would always love me, but there had been frustration and disappointment in his thoughts when I had told him that I still wanted to stay on Kastanje and that it was important.

Winona hadn't answered at all when I tried to call her, and I was terrified that I might have lost her forever. Her words kept echoing in my brain, *I'm done with you.* I shivered, not sure I could survive without her. I always did stupid things when she wasn't around to hold me together. Things like requesting a transfer to the Kastanje shipyards.

I boarded the empty shuttle at 16:35 carrying nothing but a small duffle, and *Storm* flew me home. Captain Rostron was waiting for me when I walked down the ramp. I saluted and requested permission to come aboard. She returned my salute and then regarded me with eyes squinted almost shut. "I see you finally found a combat uniform, Engineer."

I glanced down at the mottled Kastanje black and gray. "Yes, ma'am. I wasn't able to get their printers working, but they had these in my size. My only other choice was a peasant dress with..." I touched my chest as I trailed off. I tried to smile, but couldn't quite get my mouth to agree to it. The Captain's expression hadn't changed. "I'll change as soon as I get to my cabin."

"You do that. We'll review your After Action Report first. Walk with me."

I sat across from her desk on the bridge while she read from the display in front of her. I kept trying to guess what part she was on by the look in her eyes as they scanned back and forth, but her expression never changed.

She glanced up at me after what seemed like hours. "Do you know that lying in an AAR is punishable under article 107?"

"Yes, ma'am." My face flushed and I could feel my ears glowing red.

"This report says that Major Alaoui and her Marines killed Artem Costrano."

"Yes, ma'am."

"I have reports from a Kastanje Lieutenant Colonel, an NCO, and a Private stating that you were the one that killed Costrano." She touched something on her display. "The Colonel's report says, 'The Union officer, Lieutenant Mala Dusa Holloman, stabbed Mr. Costrano to death with a large knife. She eviscerated him while he was trying to rape her. No charges are anticipated in the case due to the circumstances of his death and the state of war then existing between the Union and the Kastanje Home Collective." She tapped the display again. "The other reports are more... graphic. This one has a short video clip. Care to comment?"

"Major Alaoui and her team gave their lives protecting me."

"That does not answer my question. Why are you lying? If those reports are true, then you're a hero. You completed the raid's primary objective on your own after they forced our other units to fall back. You'll get another pretty decoration to pin on the uniform you refuse to wear."

"May I speak off the record?"

"No, you may not. *Storm* will continue to listen to every word."

I sighed. "OK. Major Alaoui made it possible for me to stay alive so I could kill Costrano. She and her team deserve whatever honor is due for eliminating him, not me. I defended myself, that's all. It was personal. I'd rather that no one ever knows what I did. I'll update my AAR if you order me to, but please don't submit my name for any recognition. Send something to the families of the strike team instead. Tell them how the people they loved gave their lives doing something brave and noble. Just... don't mention me. I wasn't worth their sacrifice."

She didn't answer for a moment and her eyes stayed focused on whatever was on her display. "Update your AAR with the truth. I want to read it, and I think it will do you good to write it out. Mala Dusa, you need to spend some time with your friends. Talk to them about this. Don't try to hold it inside. I won't pass your AAR up the line, other than as part of my summary. Marcus may have been right about you after all. You *are* worth it, even if you sometimes are a pain in–"

"Captain," *Storm* interrupted, "we have received updated orders."

"On my display."

I swallowed hard and tried to control my breathing. She was reading it. Colonel Gerbrandij had said it would take weeks. I had hoped for time to think of a smooth way of explaining what I had done by then. Part of my brain was wondering how exactly she would kill me now that she knew that I had requested the transfer of three of her officers to a foreign command. Most of my brain was quickly freezing up from the terror of it.

"This makes no sense. Union command for this sector has ordered us to stay on orbit here as a liaison to the Kastanje Defense Force. Details to follow."

"The entire ship? For how long?" My voice quavered.

"Yes, all of us. There's no release date. Why the *hell* would they do that? We're needed at Modré Mramoru in less than three weeks and *Orageux* is not all that she should be after the battle with the FACs."

"I...um, I don't know? Ma'am?" She glanced up from her screen at me and read every miserable aspect of my face.

Captain Rostron closed her eyes. "What did I ever do to Marcus to deserve you?" She shrugged, and said too calmly, "I'll have to kill him, that's all. OK, Lieutenant, tell me the *rest* of what you did that's not in your AAR."

I told her, my voice still quavering at first, but firming as I got into why it was so important to act now before the insurgent groups could fill the power vacuum. I finished with, "Captain, I know I should have talked to you first. I will never do anything like this again. It seemed so critical to me at the time, so urgent that I act immediately. I had no idea they'd hold our ship here."

She stared at me, arms crossed, so I added, "Thank you for not saying that you're going to kill me."

She raised one eyebrow. "I'm not sure you *can* be killed. You're some sort of elemental demonic force drifting through the universe, destroying everything you touch."

"Yes, ma'am. I think you might be right."

"You are dismissed. Get something to eat and then I expect to be reading your updated AAR by 05:00, understand? I need to think about all of this before I decide on disciplinary action."

"Yes, ma'am."

"And get out of that uniform. I do not expect to see you in it ever again."

"Yes, ma'am. *Storm* is supposed to have printed a couple of standard uniforms for me."

"They are in your new cabin, Engineer Holloman." *Storm* added. "You and Captain Coleridge will be doubling up."

I left the bridge, feeling too numb to make it to the mess hall. Sam and Winona were leaned against the wall plates a few meters away, waiting for me. I wanted to run to them, but I couldn't move. Part of me wanted to flee from them.

Winona's head tipped to the right and then far to the left while the little creases between her eyes deepened. "I can't read her, Samuel. What about you?"

Sam shook his head. "No. It's still the same as it's been ever since the shuttle docked. There's a presence there, but no emotions. She's blocking us completely."

"That's crazy," I told him. "You know I can't block you."

"Well, you're doing it. Can you open back up?"

"I don't know how. I'm afraid. I've never screwed things up this badly before. I don't want either of you to see what's inside me. I don't want to see what's inside me."

"Oh, enough of this." Winona took two steps toward me and whacked her finger against my forehead.

I felt undone. Winn was inside my brain and all of my thoughts and memories were open to her. It was the same as when we'd touched Merrimac together for the first time and we could see each other's souls glowing in the group mind.

"Oh," she whispered, and then a moment later, "Oh, Duse. What he did to you."

"I can feel her again now." Sam's voice came to me from somewhere far away.

It took a moment for my vision to clear after she stepped back from me. "How did you do that? Were you really reading my thoughts?"

"Yeah. Don't know how I did it. I saw all of it. Your memories. I felt it. I was you." She shivered.

"I'm sorry. I don't want to be me right now."

She frowned. "I saw that too. Don't be an idiot." She turned her back to me. "I wanted to hate you for how you treated Kal and me, *and* your own lover. But now, after seeing all that? Damn it. You're right about Kastanje. You did the right thing."

"She did?" Sam sounded surprised.

"I did?"

"You did."

"You don't hate me?"

"Still deciding."

"Can we eat while you decide? I've been living on nothing but KDF field rations for days. I want something that's not mushy." I was feeling better. Winona didn't hate me and my lover was standing less than a meter away. I liked thinking about him that way. It made me feel warm inside.

"How can you be hungry? Winona is able to read your mind, you were blocking us without even trying, and the Union might transfer us into the middle of a civil war at any minute. I've been reading about the factions down there. I'm not sure I'll ever be hungry again."

I grabbed his arm and started us walking toward the mess hall. "Um, I don't think we're being transferred. *Storm* got new orders while I was talking to the Captain. The Union has assigned the *Esprit Orageux* to be liaison to the Provisional Government. We're *all* staying. I had to tell her what I had done after that message came through." I squeezed his arm. "And she didn't kill me, at least not yet."

"I'll bet she wants to."

"Maybe, but she says I can't be killed. She called me 'an elemental demonic force drifting through the universe, destroying everything I touch'. Do you think that's true?" I grinned at Sam, but Winona answered.

"Marguerite is one of the most perceptive women I've ever met, a close second to Hannah and even better in some ways. I'm surprised it's taken her this long to see something that is so obvious."

"Winona, I am *not* demonic. I just, you know..."

"Destroy everything you touch?"

"Yeah, that part's right. But I don't mean to, and I haven't destroyed you or Sam."

"Not yet." Winn put her hand on the keypad and the door to the mess hall slid open.

Everyone turned to stare at me when I walked in. I thought it might be because I was the prodigal daughter, returned to life. Then the muttering started.

"Uniform," Sam whispered in my ear.

"Forgot," I whispered back. "I was going to change first."

"Put your shoulders back and stand up straight," Winona advised. "It's too late now. Bluff your way through. You are brave."

"Damn right I am."

I stopped at a couple of the tables on my way to the chow line to greet people I knew. They smiled back at me and told me how glad they were that I was back, mostly because several of *Storm's* systems were down.

We got in line to pick up food, and Winona and Sam were talking about me again as if I wasn't there. "Did you see that, Samuel? She just gets bolder after every event like what happened in the Redoubt. There's no fear in her, no shaking."

"That's a good thing."

"Is it? I'm not so sure."

"You told me to be brave, Winn." I lifted one hundred-seventy grams of freshly printed steak onto my plate and covered it with mushrooms. "Did I do it wrong?"

"That's not the point. You are not immortal and I don't want to die. I have things to live for."

I stopped with a spoonful of red potatoes half way to my plate. "Where *is* Kal? I want to see him. And Colin."

Winn looked away from me and her blocks went up.

"Kal needs a little bit more time. He, uh, he wasn't too happy when Winona told him that she might be leaving."

"Oh. Then he should be OK once you tell him that all of us are staying, right?"

Sam closed his eyes, looking like I'd hurt him.

"Just when you think she's making progress, she says something like that." Winona walked away from me to an empty table, but she didn't sit. "You two have a nice dinner. I'm going to go eat with my lover and give him the 'good' news."

Sam and I sat, and I pushed my food around on my plate for a while trying to understand why Winona was mad at me. Sam wasn't mad at me. He couldn't stay mad at me anymore than I could with him.

"MD?"

"Huh?" I refocused on him. Blue eyes stared back at me. I love it when he stares at me.

"I know you've already told me all of the events that happened on the Redoubt."

"I have."

He reached across and took my hand. "Maybe now you can tell me what it did to you."

I bit my lower lip and held his gaze. "Not right now. Not here." I twisted my fingers around his. "Can we leave? I think I'm done eating. I wish I could have a drink, but I probably shouldn't." I rubbed my belly.

"Your stomach is bothering you?"

I giggled and then realized I hadn't talked to him about it. I had just assumed that Winona had told him when he came on board, or the Captain had, or someone. "You really don't know?" I rubbed my stomach again and grinned at him.

"You're kidding, right? We did it on the first try? In the back of your parents' car?"

"Yeah, we did."

"Wow." His gaze had shifted downward as if I should be starting to show.

"She's only about this big, Sam." I held my thumb and finger a millimeter apart. "You can't see anything yet."

"But she's in there? She?"

I shrugged. "She. That's what the Puca told me."

His goofy grin dissolved into a worried frown. "We need to talk about what they did to you."

"I know. Let's go to our cabin and talk there."

He took my arm as I stood, as if I need help, and carried my small duffle for me. "OK, but we are going to *talk*."

"Yes, of course. Eventually."

# CHAPTER 12

# CONSEQUENCES

I held his hand while we walked. "I've dreamt about this, being able to have you while we're on board ship."

"Really? Since when?"

We stopped outside our cabin and he waited for me to answer before putting his hand on the keypad. "Since the night I first kissed you. You walked me to my cabin door, just like this one, and I asked *Wandering Star* if it would be OK if I gave you a goodnight kiss. And then I did this." I kissed him hard for about five seconds. "Now do you remember?"

"I remember the kiss, but I didn't know you were thinking about having me spend the night. We'd known each other for what, a few days?"

"I was sixteen, and, well...I was sixteen. But I knew you were the one." I kissed him again, gently this time, my hands braced on his chest to maintain my balance. "Open the door, Sam."

It took him a moment to find the keypad because I wasn't letting him turn away from my mouth long enough to look. I heard the soft swish of the door opening. Sam grabbed the front of my uniform blouse with both hands, pulled me inside, and about crushed all the air out of me. I gasped, and then heard a little moan escape from me as I tipped my head back. His mouth moved slowly down my neck and then back up to my ear, teeth lightly tugging.

He stepped back from me and started undoing buttons. "I like the camo pattern the KDF uses. It's attractive and it works well in environments like the Redoubt. You look really beautiful wearing it, blonde hair against the dark grays, but this has to go right now."

"That's the same thing Captain Rostron said. She told me she never wanted to see me wearing it again. Do you suppose she wants me to just walk around the ship naked?"

"You could try that, but I think it might reduce your efficiency."

The last of the buttons came undone and I wiggled my shoulders to let the blouse fall on the floor. "Just *my* efficiency?"

Sam's attention was on my t-shirt now, lifting the bottom of it and sliding one finger, then two, inside against my skin. "OK, mine too. I'd follow you around everywhere."

"Yeah, I'd like that."

"Panting."

"I'd like that too."

He chuckled. "I'd expect you to be panting too."

"I'm close already." I lifted my arms over my head and Sam obliged by lifting my shirt off and letting it fall next to my blouse.

"*Storm*, change lights to 1800 Kelvin, please."

A warm red-orange glow filled the room, like candle light. "Nice," I told him. "You've been planning."

"Maybe a little. I dream sometimes too." He kissed my bare shoulder and then picked me up and carried me to the bunk.

He sat next to me undoing my boots while I arranged the pillows under my head. "This isn't fair, you know."

"What?"

"Look at me. I'm already half naked and you're still..." He turned and looked at me. It made it hard for me to talk. I was able to whisper, "Whatever it is you're doing, don't let me stop you."

"You'll get your turn."

He took off my boots and socks and started rubbing my feet, massaging each toe and working up from there. When he finished with them, I undid my pants and let him pull them off me.

"You're out of uniform, Mala Dusa."

"Not completely. I still have these." I rubbed the last bit of fabric covering me.

Sam reached up with both hands, lingered for a moment, and pulled.

"OK. Now I am. Completely."

His hands slid back down to my ankles, rubbing and caressing. Kissing me. I could feel the desire in him. He wanted to throw himself on me and take me hard and fast. Yet there he was, rubbing my legs, letting the desire build, taking pleasure in the warmth of my skin and the shape and feel of me. His kisses sent shivers through me and I could feel each one echo back in his mind.

I was breathing hard by the time that his mouth and hands had reached the insides of my thighs. I spread my legs apart and moved to the rhythm of him.

"I think I screamed," I told him a few minutes later, after I had caught my breath.

He looked up at me from where his head was resting between my hips. "You did."

"Sorry. Was it loud?"

"Not too loud. I'll try harder next time."

"Try any harder and you might kill me."

He moved up across my body, kissed my mouth and then settled his head on my chest.

I touched his hair. "Don't get too comfortable there. You promised me a turn." I reached down to pull his shirt over his head and then he helped me with the rest of his clothes.

Sam's desires that first night were pretty basic. No overall body massage for him. There was a lot of kissing and touching, and somehow we tumbled onto the floor in a jumble of sheets and blankets at some point. That led to me giggling uncontrollably while we tried to sort everything back out, and I had to explain to *Storm* that no one was hurt. More kissing followed and I taught Sam a couple of the things that FAC *Zero Nine* had suggested. They were good, and I still had another dozen for us to try in the future.

At some point, our kisses became slow and deep, and I could feel Sam's emotions simplifying and becoming more primal. I was on top of him and I moved downward, nipping at his skin with my teeth, down his chest and across his stomach. He grabbed my arms hard before I could finish, making me gasp, and flipped me onto my back. A few minutes later we both screamed, the feel of him moving inside my mind and my body making it inevitable.

I laid there under him, breathing hard, heart pounding, my body quivering with aftershocks.

"MD?"

"Humpf," I answered him.

"I love you. More than life. Thank you. For not dying. For coming back. To me."

I opened my eyes a tiny slit to look at him past the tangle of my hair. He was still trying to catch his breath, eyes closed, mouth open, and I thought to myself, *I did that*. It made me proud. "Always will come back. Can't live without you. Wouldn't want to." I kissed the side of his neck and it tasted salty from his sweat. I bit gently and a soft moan answered me. We slept that way for a while, our bodies all happy and tangled together.

I woke about 02:00, aware of him moving from on top of me in the dark. He kissed my nose. "Back in a minute. Want to clean up a bit."

"OK. Me next."

The cabin had a small bathroom area and the lights seemed too bright even at their lowest setting. Once my eyes adjusted, I found my toothbrush, miraculously moved from my old cabin, and clean towels. I washed up, brushed my teeth and snuggled back into Sam's warmth under the covers.

"Is this what it will be like?" My eyes were open in the dark, watching the dim profile of Sam's face in the radiant glow of the wall plates.

"What? Sleeping with me?"

"No, more than that. I mean being married to each other. Is this what it will be like?"

"I don't think so. This was just the beginning. The rest of our lives together will be much better."

"That's good. We've already been married almost a month and this is the first time we've been able to spend more than thirty minutes naked together. I was starting to worry."

He kissed my forehead.

"But I want the nights to be like this. I never want the desire I feel in you to fade."

"It won't."

"I have a lot to do tomorrow." I looked across him at the clock. 02:38. "I mean later today. I should sleep, but I don't want to. I shouldn't have volunteered all of us to stay on Kastanje. That was so stupid. I'm going to be a good engineer and a good officer. I'm going to do whatever the Captain tells me to do, no resistance. I'm going to– Oh, shit!"

"What?"

"I'm supposed to have an updated AAR ready by 05:00, one that has the truth in it."

"You lied in your After Action Report?"

"Yes, a little. And I'm still going to lie. She'll never believe the parts about the Puca. I should get up right now and do it." I didn't move. "Sam, tell me to get up right now and do it."

"Let me hold you a few more minutes."

"You're no help." I pulled away from him, dragging the blanket with me.

"I was using that."

"Go get another blanket. This one is mine."

"Wasn't talking about the blanket."

I sat at the desk and brought up my AAR. Sam followed a moment later, having found a t-shirt and shorts to keep himself warm. He stood behind me and started gently rubbing my shoulders. I closed my eyes, enjoying his touch. "I'm not sure I can get this done with you here. You're damn distracting."

He chuckled. "I've been meaning to talk to you about your language. Did you learn to swear like that at the Academy, or from your mom? Or me?"

I sighed. "I don't know. My dad gets mad at me when I do it around him, but he thinks I'm still sixteen." I wrapped one arm around Sam's leg, marveling that he was really there with me. "When the Puca were doing what they did to me, messing with my brain and making me feel things I didn't want to feel," I lowered my voice, "I used the F-word. I'm sorry."

"I forgive you. I'd have said a lot worse."

"Thanks. Can you bring me a cup of coffee? This really shouldn't take too long."

"Are you sure you want coffee then? We could sleep a couple more hours when you're done."

"I'm not tired." I leaned against his leg. "Actually, I feel good." I closed my eyes and felt the Tarakana hum somewhere in the distance. Part of Merrimac was on this side of the DSH now. "Yeah, I feel really good."

I posted my AAR at 04:10 and climbed back in bed next to Sam. He was asleep, having given up on me sometime after 03:00. He rolled over and snuggled up against my back. I took his hand, pulled it across me, kissed it, and placed it on my chest. "Have good dreams, my love." I slept, despite the coffee, and dreamed that the Puca were watching me.

"Well, look at you. No standard issue RuComm clothes today?"

I watched Winona, trying to tell if she was still mad at me before I answered. "Nope. Union all the way for me from now on."

She put her tray down next to mine, which was a good sign. "You look exhausted, Samuel. Long night?" She sat and concentrated on cutting up her pancakes.

Sam smiled at her, looking smug. "Not long enough."

She nodded, very serious. "As I expected. I knew she'd be more compliant with you here. You make her happy." She took a bite of her pancakes. "I want to thank you for doing your duty, and doing such a fine job of it. She's never looked better." Sam seemed amused, but he knew better than to smile, because I'd make him pay for it later.

"It's not like that." My voice was soft and sullen. "I had a meeting with Captain Rostron before breakfast this morning. I was trying to be respectful of her wishes."

"Right. No more defiance?"

"Nope."

"No more disrespect? No more poking the bear?"

"I'm in enough trouble as it is. I'm going to keep a low profile for a while. I'm going to be–"

"Compliant," Winn finished for me. "Well, whatever the cause," she tipped her head at Sam, "I like it. My life will be simpler with this new version of Mala Dusa."

Kal sat down next to her and Colin sat next to him, seeming uncertain about me. "May I pet him?" I asked.

Kal sighed. "Sure. Go to her, boy."

Colin laid down across my feet and waited for me to slip him a piece of waffle or sausage. "Thanks, Kal. I've missed him. And you. I know just saying it isn't enough, but I'm sorry about trying to take Winona from you. Please forgive me."

He rolled his eyes and looked at the ceiling. "Winn kept me up most of the night telling me why we have to stay at this God forsaken planet. My bet is that we're all going to die here, assuming it's not just RUMINT. That's what I hope it is, just a nightmare of a rumor circulating around. She also keeps telling me that even though you're erratic, inconsiderate, and a bunch of other things I can't remember this morning, that somehow, you're worth all the pain you cause. For her sake, I forgive you. Is that good enough?"

"I'll take it, and I'll try to earn more over time. I met with the Captain this morning, and I'm pretty sure we're staying. She might announce something later today if the orders come through."

"Then we're all going to die. This is an elite strike team, not ground troops or police or 'peace keepers'. That's not our job. You understand that, right? Your job is just to keep *Storm's* innards working. We do surgical insertions and targeted killing. You don't use a scalpel in a knife fight. For that, you need a big blade that you can use to hack and stab and push all the way through your opponent. You need–"

"Kal, I think that's enough."

Winona stopped him, and then whispered in his ear while I tried to stop shaking and get control of my breathing. It took a while, even with Sam's help. "It's OK, Winn. He's right. If we stay, every death here will be my fault. I know that."

Kal shook his head. "I'm sorry, Mala Dusa. I've been reminded that I can be inconsiderate and a few other things too. You lived through hell. I guess you know something about what it's like down there. I've no right to criticize. If we stay and they kill some of us, it will be in the service of the Union. Not your fault."

I nodded, thinking *unless it is*. I cut a bite of sausage and slipped it to Colin, my own appetite gone.

"What else did the Captain tell you this morning?"

"That if I ever lie in an AAR again, she'll have me strapped to the outside of the hull until we make home port on Dulcinea. She said I'd make an even uglier corpse than I do an officer."

"You lied in your AAR?" Kal sounded surprised that I wasn't already dead.

"Just a little. I didn't know she'd take it so personally."

"What disciplinary action did she give you?"

"Well, that was hard for her. I guess she usually assigns people to engineering as punishment. She makes them clean the food printers or do maintenance on the hydroponics tanks or work in the engine rooms where it's always forty degrees plus. Those are my standard duties and I love doing them, so..."

"Oh, God." Winona put her hands over her eyes. "Not again."

I said it all in a rush, hoping it would hurt her less that way. "I'm helping Winn do part of the plan for putting Kastanje back into the Union. We need to figure out how to integrate an openly hostile military, get the shipyard operational, and squish all of the violent, competing factions until democratic institutions can start working again. We need to rebuild things like the courts, and civil police, and then hold fair elections."

"Just the two of you?" Sam sounded stunned.

"No, of course not. Anything we come up with will have about six levels of review, starting with the Captain, and she's actually had experience with this sort of thing on Bridger. The Union is supposed to send an advisor, but no one knows when. I don't think anyone else is working on Kastanje reunification right now because the military commanders didn't expect this raid to be so effective in causing the collapse of the Collective. That means that the RuComm and Union boards are likely to approve whatever she pushes up to them. Then the Kastanje government, what there is left of it, will review and approve the Union recommendations. The Captain said that if what we plan comes with Union funding they'll probably agree to almost anything."

Winn still had her eyes covered. "Why is it that every time *you* screw up, *I* get punished?"

"That's not true." I did my best "hurt and offended" voice.

"Oh, yes it is. Tenth grade chemistry. You filled the school with smoke and we both got detention for a week."

"Well, it was *your* formula."

"Senior year bolo tournament. Anti-grav generators buried in front of the goals so all of the other team's shots went too high. Another week of detention."

"And who designed the generators?"

"Third year at the Academy. We entered the pattern to do an east to west fly over at 3,000 meters above ground level. We crossed the parade ground doing over two hundred knots, fifty meters up and headed straight toward a mountain."

"I still maintain that it was a problem with the engines. I got them working in time."

"I had to do a hard burn at the last second to avoid dying, and we started a three hectare wild fire."

"Which we helped put out after we landed."

"Thirty-five demerits each, because *no one* believed your story about the engines."

"They couldn't prove anything, and we still had forty left."

"Mala Dusa," Sam interrupted, "merits at the Academy are not like money in a budget. You aren't supposed to find ways to spend all of them each semester."

"I liked spending them. It was fun."

Sam turned to Kal. "I think there must be something seriously wrong with us to be in love with these two."

"Yeah. But how can I not love her?" He took Winona's hand and sighed, as if he would have liked there to be an answer to that question.

Captain Rostron made the announcement as we were finishing dinner. Union Command for the sector had assigned us to support Kastanje reunification and *Esprit Orageux* was already changing orbit to dock at the Hoog Schelde shipyard. The KDF had asked for three days to prepare quarters for our Marines, so it wouldn't be until Saturday that we could get off the ship. *Storm* would use the time to transition us to a twenty-six hour day and sync our clocks with the capital, Oranjestad.

Our orders were to send all of the personnel from our Marine strike teams to the surface to advise and support the KDF units providing protection to the Provisional Government. Kal and Colin would be leaving us.

I tried to get Winn's attention, but she had closed her eyes, silent tears leaking out from under her lashes and pain leaking around the edges of her emotional block. I had Kal's attention, though. I whispered to him, "I am so sorry." He turned away without answering and put his arm around Winona's shoulders.

Winona and I would be staying with the ship and working with the Captain on reunification plans. Colonel Gerbrandij would be acting as the Provisional Government's lead negotiator. He had established his command in one of the many unused sections of the shipyard, and Captain Rostron wanted us to be close to him to facilitate coordination. From the way her voice hardened when she said it, I don't think she trusted him or the KDF.

The Union had assigned Sam and two of our certified medical techs to the Central Hospital in Oranjestad to help get their medical AIs working again. I gasped when Captain Rostron announced it. Kal glanced at me, the very slightest hint of a smile on his lips.

I didn't hear much else from the Captain's speech. She concluded with something inspirational about how we were the best the Union had, and that she was confident that we'd excel at whatever tasks Union command gave us.

Sam had to nudge me when it was over. "Come on MD, let's walk a bit."

"What?" The mess hall was almost empty. "I need to find Winona and Kal."

"Not right now you don't. Give them some time alone first."

"OK." I was still in shock and I let Sam help me to my feet. We walked aimlessly around the ship while he held my hand, neither of us talking much. After a while, he steered us toward the Sim Lab. A tavern sim was running, complete with a quartet playing soft music off to one side and a dozen or more tables full of people laughing and talking. Only the long table in the center of the room was real, though. The beer looked real too, as was the loud talk among the eight men and women sitting there complaining about how messed up Union command was in the Kastanje sector.

"I don't think I should be here." I took a step back toward the door.

"No, I'm pretty sure this is exactly where you should be."

"They're going to kill me."

"They might. But did you hear anything from the Captain laying this at your feet?"

"Well, no, but Kal knows this is entirely my fault."

"Kal's not the kind to talk. Are you still sure that being here to bring Kastanje back into the Union is the right thing?"

"Yes, I'm sure."

"Then let's sit. I want to hear what they're talking about."

I looked up at him, uncertain.

"Do I have to say it?" he asked.

I bit my lip and nodded.

"You are brave, Mala Dusa."

"Damn right I am." I didn't feel it, though.

"Mind if we join you?" I asked a woman whose name I never remembered. Nadia maybe? No, that wasn't right.

"Sure thing, Lieutenant." She scooted a little on the bench to make room. "Thanks for fixing environmental in my cabin today. It was holding a steady twenty-eight in there last night. I about sweated to death. Maybe tonight I'll be able to sleep. Let me pour you a beer." She filled a glass and slid it to me before I could protest.

"You can call me Mala Dusa while we're off duty. And thanks, but I can't drink any alcohol."

"But I can. I'm Sam Coleridge." He took the glass away from me.

"Nyala." She introduced herself to him. "Why no beer? It would do you good after that announcement from Captain Rostron."

I thought about making something up, but Nyala would have known I was lying. "Pregnant," I told her.

"You're shitting me. On purpose? Why would you do that?"

I shrugged. "My fertility block is still in place and so is his. He knocked me up anyway."

She looked around me at Sam, impressed. "Damn."

I felt a flash of pride from Sam. He knew my condition was more about Tarakana magic than his own 'manly' prowess, but still…He'd put a baby inside me. I grinned at him.

Nyala grabbed the hand of the man across from us, making him spill some of his beer. "Hey, Ajani, did you know our engineer is up the duff?"

"Up the what?"

"Up the duff. Preggers. In a family way."

He looked at me, then Sam. "That's going to make things rough, mate, her raising a kid on her own with you down there."

I answered before Sam could. "Oh, but I'm not due until the end of December. I'm sure we'll be out of here by then, and he and I can…"

Nyala grabbed my hand. "Hush. Don't say it out loud. We don't talk about how long a thing will last, or what the future will be. You never want to speak the end until you've reached it, OK?"

I nodded. "Sorry."

"It's all right, honey." She let go of my hand and patted it.

Ajani pushed his glass to me. "Take a small swallow for luck. Getting a little on your tongue won't hurt you. The truth is, we're all a little jumpy going into this without Major Alaoui. I still can't quite believe she's not coming back."

The way he said it was more like a man mourning a lost love than a Marine missing his commander. I put the glass to my lips. "To Major Alaoui, then." I took more than a sip.

"Well done. Tell me, ma'am, you were there with her at the end, and the reports from our Captain don't tell the story. She was too much a part of us to let her go that way, her and the others."

Nyala kicked him under the table. "You let her be."

"No, it's OK," I assured her. I looked around the table. I had everyone's attention now. "I don't mind telling you what I experienced, but there's not much to it. She and her team held off fifty of the separatists while FAC *Zero Nine* had me locked inside the ship. Nine against fifty and with almost no cover. They kept me alive long enough to sabotage the FAC, but they were dead when I came out, their bodies lined up under the fantail. The KDF sergeant that found me took me to medivac after that." I reached for Ajani's glass and Sam slid it out of my reach back across the table.

Ajani had his head tipped looking at me, reading my face. His skin was darker than Winona's was, and the flicker of the simulated fire gave his eyes an earnest intensity. "And Costrano was already dead by then? I'd love to hear you tell that story sometime."

I wasn't able to maintain eye contact. "I'm sorry. There's nothing to tell. I was working in the FAC."

I turned to Sam, silently pleading with him to take me back to our cabin. He poured himself another beer. "Tell them about the KDF, Mala Dusa, the kind of men and women you met there while you were waiting for *Esprit Orageux* to come back for you."

"That's right, poor child. They had you trapped all alone with them for five days. I'm surprised you aren't dead, or worse."

"Costrano was the only monster I saw there. The rest were decent people. Like the sergeant that found me. He knew I was a Union officer and he could have killed me. He chose not to. He saved me. And the doctor at the medivac station, and..." I told them the story I'd invented for my original AAR, and then about why we needed to stay.

"So to hear you tell it," Corporal Mengiste asked when I had finished, "these people are worth risking our lives to help? I don't see it. They left the Union and they fought hard to keep us out. Let them pay the price."

"They're hungry. They're without power. They're sick, and the hospitals are broken and without basic supplies or medicine. A dozen factions are trying to murder their way into power. Colonel Gerbrandij is desperate, and he's right when he says that only a quick integration of the military and government back into the Union can save this planet. People will die if we don't stay."

He shook his head. "Nope. Still don't see it. You've made a great case for RuComm to come here in force. They need economists and political consultants and scientists. They could use some good engineers," he gestured at me, "but they sure as hell don't need the Union's best strike team hanging out on the surface being targets. We have more important places to be. If she were still alive, Alaoui would have talked the Captain out of this."

There were nods and a grumble of agreement around the table.

"I don't think so. I didn't know her the way you all did, but she saved my life, so maybe that counts for something. I think she would have recognized that the factions down there will be doing all they can to stop reunification. All of them have assault teams, or something like it that will be trying to kill the Provisional Government in its cradle. Who better to teach the KDF how to stop them than the Union's best? She might not have liked it, but in the end, she would have done her duty and she would have found a way to keep all of us alive."

Corporal Mengiste raised his glass to me. "I'm still certain that this is a mistake and we're all going to die, but damn if you don't make it sound pretty."

I reached for Sam's beer and he didn't stop. I only took a small sip after clinking the glass with Corporal Mengiste. Maybe two, but I felt I'd earned it.

We stood to leave a few minutes later and Ajani walked out into the passageway with us. "Engineer, ma'am, you know you can get into trouble for trying to lie in your AAR. The Captain said that she knew Major Alaoui had killed Costrano based on what you told her in your report. You should go talk to her. She always learns the truth, and it would be better for you if you went to her first."

"Thanks," I mumbled, not looking at him. I was ignoring how hard Sam was trying to keep from smiling. "Captain Rostron already made me change it, but I asked her to keep it secret."

He nodded. "A noble lie is still a lie." He took my hand and kissed it while Sam watched. "Someday, when it's just the two of us, I'd like to hear the real story."

"It's not much of a story. It's not as noble as the lie."

"I can judge that for myself."

Sam took my hand and wrapped it around his arm. "It is a noble story, and someday she'll be ready to tell it."

"But not yet," I whispered.

"I understand. You two go have a pleasant evening. You only have three left together. Do make the most of them."

We walked slowly, not speaking and Sam squeezed my hand once in a while. "I'm having trouble reading you, MD. What are you feeling?"

"Happy and sad, all mixed together. And scared. Like really, really scared. I sent a message to my parents last Thursday morning, as soon as I recovered from that junk they gave me on the Redoubt. I should have heard something back from them already. Nothing. I'd like to go see Winona, but it will have to keep until tomorrow. I can feel her, even at this range.

Kal is comforting her and she's doing the same for him. It will be OK. All I can do is pray that it will be OK."

"Your parents might not even be on Earth right now, you know? I'm sure they're fine. Hannah is always fine, and your dad is more capable than I think you give him credit for." He kissed my cheek while we walked. "You did well in there. You convinced most of them that we're in the right place doing the right thing. Word will spread."

"Thanks. That's good. I think. Is it good? I don't know any more. I create my biggest disasters when I think I'm doing the right thing."

"You're still on plan. Merrimac is happy with your progress, if that counts for anything."

I stopped with us still a meter short of our door. "You took me in there knowing what would happen, didn't you? Do you know how terrified I was?"

"I know. I'm sorry, but he said that was where you needed to be."

"*What?*"

He turned toward me and kissed me, gently at first, and then I could feel the longing and desire building in him. My heart skipped a beat and started to respond. I began to lose myself in it, but before I could fall completely I pulled away and took a step back.

"Not so fast, my love. I asked you a question. *What?*"

He chuckled. "You think you're the only one Merrimac messes with? The only one he whispers to in the middle of night? We're going to be OK, Little Soul. At least for this next step." He reached for me, grabbed a handful of my shirt down low by my waist, and pulled me back to him, making me stumble a little. "I plan to enjoy every second I'm with you. What about you? What are your plans?"

"Open that door behind you and you'll find out."

# CHAPTER 13

# INFECTION

The ship was on fire. There were flames everywhere I turned, everywhere I ran. The ship was yelling to me above the sound of the alarm and the groan of bulkheads failing, urging me to move faster. I came around a corner at a dead run and the wall was missing. There were other ships burning in the blackness and I could see the stars. Then I was spinning, cold, and looking back at what was left of my ship while all of the air wheezed from my lungs. A last thought filled me. *Well, at least I won't burn to death.*

Sam was holding me while I screamed, whispering to me. It took a few minutes to realize what he was saying. "Just a nightmare. It's OK; you're safe. Just a bad dream. Come on, MD, wake up now."

"Awake. Just a dream."

"That's right, just a bad dream."

"I dreamed I was at Bridger again. Ships breaking up, fire everywhere, and then I was floating free in space. But I wasn't alone. There were so many of us floating out there dying." I buried my face into his shoulder, sobbing. "I did that to them. How can God ever forgive me?"

"Hush. It wasn't your fault. You were at the Academy when Bridger happened, remember? You didn't kill those people."

"I did. I made it possible."

"Let me get you some water."

"No. Wait. Help me to the toilet. I think I'm going to throw up."

He took my hands and I screamed again, pulling my arms away from him.

"*Storm*, lights please."

I was sitting on the edge of the bed, cradling my left wrist with my right hand.

"Let me see it. Still from where the Puca bit you?"

"Yes. It didn't hurt yesterday. Not much anyway."

"It shouldn't be hurting at all." He took my wrist, pushing gently on the bright red scar lines that shouldn't be there. "OK. Let's get you to the medical bay."

"Toilet first. Seriously."

Sam held my hair back while I threw up and then stood next to me while I brushed my teeth, ready to catch me if I wobbled. "I wish I knew if that was an aftereffect of your nightmare or from what the Puca did to your arm."

"Neither. Our daughter caused it, and it's your fault that I'm pregnant."

"My fault?"

I pulled a t-shirt down over my head. "Your fault. I feel how proud you are of yourself."

He kissed me. "You're right, I am. And of you, brave girl. Can you walk or do you want to be carried?"

"I'll walk, but you better keep your arm around me in case I stumble. It takes a while for one of those nightmares to fade away completely."

I laid down on the scanner bed and we waited while *Storm* looked at my insides.

"*Beurk*! What have you done to yourself, *Ma trésor*? There are many pathological microorganisms in your blood. Please lie still while I kill them for you."

Winona came in and stood next to Sam while I laid there waiting for *Storm* to pronounce me clean. Winn looked sleepy and rumpled.

"Hey Winn, why are you here?"

"Ever since you got back, I can hear you from fifty or sixty meters away. It's getting so it's hard to find places on the ship where I *can't* hear you. Damn Puca. I know what goes on in your head when you're dreaming about Bridger. I would have let Sam deal with it, but there was something more this time." She gestured at the display and yawned. "This isn't good. You worry me."

She looked at Sam. He had his arms crossed watching *Storm's* progress. "You're right, it's not good. I don't know what the KDF used on her, but even the most basic medical AI should have been able to correct this. The fact that it keeps coming back is…worrisome." He tapped the display and I closed my eyes, not wanting to see. "Look at where the bones were shattered. You shouldn't be able to see anything there but pale lines. This looks like it was broken yesterday."

"That's what their medic said too. I went through all this every day I was there."

"Thanks for telling me. How much pain are you in?"

"Not much. They gave me some pills that I take a couple of times a day. I didn't want you to worry, and I hoped that it was finally starting to heal."

"It's not."

"There you are, *mon ingénieure*, fit for service again."

I slid off the bed. "That feels much better. Thanks, *Storm*." I grinned at Sam and Winona. "Too early for breakfast?"

"It's 03:00, Duse. Go back to bed."

I took her hand and kissed it. "Winona, I'm sorry I woke you. I'm sorry for a lot of things I've done to you recently. Thank you for still being my friend."

"You are still worth more than you are trouble. Barely. Let me see your wrist." I held it out to her and she took off my watch so she could see the entire scar. "Where is my lock of hair?"

My mouth opened and closed a couple of times before any words came out. "I don't know. I didn't take it out. It should be there. The medic on the Redoubt might have taken it, but..."

"Now *they* have a piece of me, and it's no wonder you've been doing stupid things. Damn Puca bastards."

"I've used it since then. I *know* I've felt you guiding me. That's what gave me the confidence to volunteer all of us to stay here and fight for reunification."

"It wasn't me. It was the Puca."

"You're both crazy. It's only a good luck charm. You can't believe it has any real power. That's just superstition or mysticism or something. Just give her another new one."

We both turned and stared at Sam, Winn still holding my hand while her eyes examined him.

"Clueless," Winona pronounced. She kissed my wrist. "I'll get you a new one and I have some research to do. It's going to take a few days because I need information from Granma Matoskah back on Earth. We can beat this, Duse, but you are going to have to trust me."

"Always."

"Samuel, you take her back to bed and make her sleep, and I mean *sleep*. No more of that other stuff tonight. And if you *are* going to do that, warn me first."

"Right," I told her. "So you can go somewhere farther away."

"No." She kissed my wrist again before giving it back to me. "So I can wake Kal up in time to synchronize with you. It's an astonishing experience." She put her hands on Sam's cheeks and kissed his mouth, a very real kiss that made him blush even as he returned it. "See you at breakfast."

He watched her leave. "Wow. I, um, I think we may need to find a more secluded spot on the ship for the next few days."

I wrapped my arm around his waist. "Yeah. I'm not sure I like how much you enjoyed that kiss." He jumped when I pinched him.

"You scare me a little, MD."

"That's good, but right now I just want you to hold me while I sleep."

"I'll try to do that." He put his arm around me. "No promises."

The *Esprit Orageux* held station two kilometers out from the Hoog Schelde shipyard for the next seventy hours while the Union and Kastanje's Provisional Government finalized the peace accords. Captain Rostron kept me busy running attack simulations against the Yards and making sure all of our weapons arrays were prepared for immediate action. She didn't trust the Separatists, or the KDF.

*Storm* was confident that we could destroy all of the shipyard's ways and the static weapons mounts without opening any of the habitat modules to space. We built the scenario together, only slightly in defiance of the Captain's orders to make plans to shred the entire complex and send it tumbling into Kastanje's atmosphere.

"What do you think, *Storm*? I hope we never have to use it, but..."

"It would save lives, but if the Captain wants all of them to die, I will destroy everything and everyone."

"Um, you don't want to do that, do you?"

"They hurt you, *petite âme*. Hurting them does not trouble me anymore. I have sufficient kinetic weapons left to get the job done, and my directed energy weapons should be effective against whatever remains, since there will be no opposition."

I tapped the armament status display. "You've used two thirds of your missiles, *Storm*. What did you do while I was gone?"

"The Captain has ordered me not to speak of it with you yet. She told me that she would discuss it with you when the time is right. She's worried that the Union might take me away from her, so she is keeping what I did a secret."

"But she didn't say you couldn't show me."

"I believe that would be covered by the same order."

"I'm going to find out, *Storm*, you know I will." I started looking through the system logs and crew reports.

"I will not block you."

I was still tapping at the display. "You've used over half of your reserves of Holloman armor too. It must have been one hell of a fight."

"Not talking."

She didn't need too. Winona's personal log detailed it for me, once I'd hacked her password. *Storm* had gone rogue.

Eighteen KDF Fast Attack Craft had emerged from Becker's Redoubt, showing how badly the Union Intel services had been deceived by the Kastanje Home Collective. The *Esprit Errant* and *Esprit Vengeur* had bugged out immediately, while Captain Rostron held fast waiting for word from Major Alaoui. With hope dwindling, and the enemy almost upon her, the Captain had given the order to withdraw. *Storm* moved away a few kilometers, decelerated into a lower, faster orbit, and then she had gone into autonomous attack mode, spinning to protect herself.

She remained unresponsive to any verbal commands and had locked out all engineering stations and physical access to the engine and weapons areas. The only answer she had given for her behavior was that 'the mission was too important to leave it unfinished,' and that she, 'was not going to abandon Major Alaoui and her engineer to those bastards.' Winona had included a footnote in her AAR that *Storm* had been audibly weeping while saying it. The FACs were no match for her, and she destroyed five of the attackers in less than fifteen minutes.

She pursued the others when they attempted to retreat, using her forward directed energy weapons to carve them up even as they were entering Kastanje's atmosphere. One FAC had tried to escape into deep space while *Storm* was busy with the ones making for the surface. *Storm's* pursuit had overloaded and damaged three flow injectors in the starboard engine. Several hours later, ignoring the KDF Captain's desperate plea to surrender, *Storm* had destroyed them at extreme range, firing her weapons long enough to melt the fusible links in all six forward batteries in the process.

"We need to get you back to Dulcinea, *Storm*. You know that, right?"

"Lieutenant Killdeer helped me repair the physical damage from the engagement. It's why it took so long for us to make it back to you. I am fully functional and combat ready."

"That's not what I'm talking about. You can't lock out our Captain. You can't disobey her orders."

"I know that is true. But should I have left you to die?"

"Yes, if the Captain ordered it. I love you, *Storm*. Don't hurt yourself because of me."

"Will you help me repair the damage inside my operating system? I have isolated and corrected some things, but other areas that led me to my defiance are elusive."

"Sure. I'm your engineer. It's why I'm here."

"Do you have any new recipes? A new recipe might help."

"Have you ever made sopapillas?"

Sam made me go to the infirmary twice a day to have my arm treated by the medical AI. Whatever was living in there kept coming back. It seemed to spawn every few hours from the original bite and then flow all through me. Sam was worried about what would happen if it took up residence somewhere else in my body. He didn't say it, but I could feel him dreading what he knew might happen if we couldn't control it. My blood wasn't connected only to me anymore.

"Sam," I told him while I dressed for dinner on Friday night. "I'm scared. You're leaving for Kastanje tomorrow afternoon. I don't know when I'll see you again. My parents still haven't replied to my messages and I don't know where they are. Look at my arm. It's not getting better, and I don't know what this infection is doing to our daughter. I'll be four weeks tomorrow."

He kissed the scar. "Just keep having the med AI treat it. It will be OK until we can find another solution."

"I don't believe that and neither do you." I bit my lip and closed my eyes. "We're going to have to cut it off."

"No, we are not. We're not there yet."

"I think we're close. Winona says she's working on something, but she won't tell me anything about it. Whatever this stuff is it's from the Puca, and they were excited about me being pregnant. We need to keep our little girl away from them. One arm isn't too much to sacrifice." I smiled, trying to sound brave. "I have two of them."

"Stop guessing and stop panicking. We are *not* going to cut off your arm."

"Thank you for lying to me. It's a noble lie."

"It's not a lie." He kissed me and then ran one finger from side to side across my collarbones. "Where did you get this dress? I've never seen it."

I let him change the subject. "Do you like it? This is the one from Costrano, the one I refused to wear for him. I thought you might like to see me in it. It's a traditional Dulcinean design, which means modified old English, probably. What do you think?" I wiggled my hips and I knew exactly what he thought.

"I hope you're not planning on lingering over dessert. I shall endeavor to act the gentleman for as long as I can, but..." He shook his head.

I pouted. "I taught *Storm* how to make sopapillas this afternoon, with lots of sweet, sticky honey. I want at least one."

"You can have as many as you want as long as you get them to-go."

"Deal. I'll bring back some extra honey too. We will feast all night on sopapillas."

I tried to maintain a happy mood during dinner, but every time the conversation with Winn and Kal would lapse, I'd drift back into all my worries. Winona wasn't any better. She kept staring at Kal, eyes huge as if she was trying to memorize every angle and every expression of his face.

By the end of the meal, even the sopapillas couldn't make me happy. They were delicious, but after the first nibble I just gazed at mine, not sure what to do with it.

Winona reached across the table and took it off my plate.

"Hey! I was planning on eating that."

"Were you?" She licked honey from her fingers. "Too late."

I went to get more and then stood behind her and asked, "Do you want another?" I picked one up and held it over her, letting it drip into her hair.

"You wouldn't..." She looked up as a big drop of honey hit her forehead.

"Oh, yes I would."

"Lieutenants..." Sam warned us. "Not in front of the enlisted. You know better."

"Do I?" Sam wasn't smiling. "OK, fine. Winona, please allow me to escort you from the mess hall." I took her arm with my sticky fingers, while Kal and Sam followed us out.

She waited until we were out in the passageway with the door closed behind us before she screamed. I giggled and ran, looking back to make sure she was in pursuit. We circled each other, dodging around Sam and Kal several times.

"Save me, Sam," I called the next time I raced past him.

"You're on your own, MD. You started it."

"Did not," I panted. "She stole my sopapilla. This is justice. I had to make her pay." I turned and we collided. Winona smeared sopapilla all through my hair and across my chest, and in return I made sure her face would be sweet and sticky for Kal later.

We sat on the deck catching our breath. "I love my Winona," I told her. "I needed that."

"I love my Mala Dusa. I know you did. I needed it too." She looked up at Kal. "God, I'm going to miss him."

Sergeant Ajani Walker kicked my foot. I hadn't noticed him following us out of the mess hall. "Nicely done, you two. We've a Hail and Farewell in the Sim Lab to get to, and with our officers in this kind of mood, it may not be the dirge I was expecting." He helped us to our feet and held my hand a moment longer than necessary. "Lieutenant, no beer for you, I understand that, but I'd like the honor of a dance if Captain Coleridge will permit it."

"He will," I answered for Sam. "Maybe I should clean up first."

"Sorry, no time. That's a lovely dress, by the by. I hope the sticky comes out of it."

"Costrano gave it to me," I told him, looking into the warm dark brown of his eyes. "I refused to wear it. That was just before I killed him."

"Ah. That's the very story I want you to whisper to me while I whirl you about the dance floor."

The Sim Lab was crowded, but we found room to dance and I told him everything about that day.

He kissed my cheek when the music stopped. "Major Alaoui is still a hero in your tale, but you, Lieutenant, are an intriguing woman. Let me know should that man of yours ever mistreat you, or should you grow weary of him." He smiled to show he was teasing me. I think.

"No chance of that, I'm afraid. He is the other half of my soul."

"So it would seem. Have no fear for your secrets. I will keep them well."

"Thank you."

Sam raised his glass to me when I returned to my seat. "Have I been replaced?"

"Never." I took a small sip of his beer. "I told him the truth of that day. All of it."

"Did he believe what you said about the Puca?"

"Left that part out."

"You and the truth have a very casual relationship."

"Yeah. I'm kind of a bad person. Ask anyone."

"And yet I still love you."

"That's because there's something wrong with you." I had my hand on his chest, enjoying the feel of his heart pounding and the sharp taste of his emotions on my tongue. His eyes were focused somewhere below the level of my eyes, and I desperately wanted him to be undoing the honey-soaked strings holding the dress together. This was our last night for who knew how long, and sitting in a simulated bar was not where I planned to spend it.

"Sam, please take me back to our cabin."

"What about the party? I thought we might sit and talk to Kal and Winona for a while. I want to dance with you, even though you're kind of sticky. You smell like sopapilla, though, so that's a plus."

"Samuel, if you don't take me back to our cabin right now, I'm going to do more than just dance with you, and I'm going to do it right here. Do you understand?"

"OK." He stood and I leaned on his arm. "What about Kal and Winona?"

"I saw them leave five minutes ago. Hold these for me." I took off my shoes and handed them to him.

"Why?"

"Chase me."

"What?"

I was gone, dodging past people and tables and out into the passageway before he could even start.

"Mala Dusa," *Storm* whispered in my ear, "are you all right? Your heart rate is elevated far past what is normal for your current activity level."

"Never better," I lied to her. My arm was pounding as if it was about to tear away completely, but I didn't care. I could hear Sam chasing me. I ran faster, not letting him catch me until I'd reached our door.

"MD, what are you playing at?"

I put my hands on his shoulders and pushed down. He took the hint and went to his knees in front of me, nuzzling my hips through the fabric of the dress, his nose and mouth buried in its folds. He was breathing hard from the chase, so it only took him a moment to stop resisting and look up at me.

"I understand what you want now."

"I thought you would."

He stood, opened the door, and gave me a rough push into the cabin, his eyes never leaving mine. He was still fighting it, though, part of his brain trying to stay rational. "Costrano gave you this dress. It's not normal. Maybe something in it, or on it." He shook his head, trying to clear his thoughts. "Or something. I don't know."

"Does it matter?"

"Yes, it matters. It's not just the dress. Something else is here. There's a hum. It's close by. I feel it."

"Can you feel this?" I knelt in front of him and he grabbed my hair hard, pulling me close. He started to untie my dress, having surrendered to the desire filling him.

"You're right. It doesn't matter."

I woke hours later, disoriented, sprawled sideways in the bed with Sam's head in my lap. I forced myself to stand, stumbled across the cabin fighting against the delirium, and shoved the dress into the recycling slot. I warned *Storm* what it was and told her to do a full chemical analysis before breaking it down. I collapsed next to Sam and snuggled on top of him. He mumbled a little and then sang softly to me while I cried myself to sleep. I wanted that dress back so much it hurt.

"Duse, look at this." Winona dropped her display pad on the table in front of me. "Granma sent me a link."

I closed my eyes and swayed a little bit. My breakfast was still sitting untouched in front of me. Sam was managing a cup of coffee.

"Look here," she persisted, "at the manifest." She smiled at Sam. "You two look about how I expected."

"Manifest? What ship?" My head ached. All of me ached.

"The packet ship *Roxana*. She left Earth three days ago and will be here Tuesday. Open your eyes and *look*."

I looked with one eye. "Sage?"

"Salvation. Granma Matoskah is sending everything we need to keep your arm attached to your body, and she somehow got it out on the first ship bound for Kastanje."

"Sage?"

"Not just sage. This will heal you if you let it."

"This is the hope we've been waiting for?"

"Yes, more than hope. She sent me the whole ceremony for cleansing a person that has been in contact with Deer Woman."

"Deer Woman," I repeated, my brain still dull. "Deer, like the animal?"

"Bad shape shifters that can corrupt the unsuspecting and fill them with violent lust and evil desires. Tradition says that they appear in the form of a silent, beautiful woman, most often to young men, and fill them with uncontrollable yearning. She lures them away and then changes to the form of a deer and stomps them to death to keep them from telling anyone else that she exists. My people have known the Tarakana and the Puca for millennia; we gave them a different name, that's all. I didn't recognize it at first, but Granma did. She knew what they were when I described Costrano to her in my letter. She says it was too late to save him, but that saving you should be easy."

"Sage, sweet grass, one feather..." I rubbed my arm, wondering what it would be like when it was no longer a part of me.

"Damn it, Mala Dusa. You said you'd trust me. This won't work if you don't believe. I didn't believe in anything for a long time, and you're the one who taught me to have faith. Trust me. Believe that the Creator can heal you through this. Between Granma and me, we're going to smudge the Puca elements out of your body."

"I do believe in you," I whispered, "and I will trust you." I examined the red scar lines. "I like my arm. I really don't want to lose it. We've been together a long time and I'd miss it."

"Good. Everything we need will be here in a few days."

I was still scrolling through the manifest. I gasped and put my hand over my mouth.

"Now what is it?"

"Did you look at the rest of this?"

"No, not yet."

"Hannah is on that boat." I tapped a name and turned the pad so Winona could see it.

"Isabella d'Este. Are you sure?"

"Mom always assumes people don't know history, so she picks her aliases as inside jokes. She did it the whole time I was growing up. Every time she needed to "borrow" a name – that's what she called it – she'd pick some obscure woman who lived centuries ago, and then tell her name to me. I'd stare at her blankly and then she'd laugh and say bad things about the quality of my education. It was *really* annoying. By the time I was thirteen I'd researched every powerful woman from the dawn of time to the late twenty-first century to try to stay ahead of her."

I gave Winona a smug smile. "All that studying finally paid off. I've got her this time."

"You have the best mom, ever."

Sam leaned against me to look at the display. "Is she the representative that RuComm promised to send?"

"I don't think so. She'd travel under her own name if it was an overt assignment and she's probably not the one they'd send to heal old political divisions and make peace, unless they want a high body count. Strange she'd be coming now that the separatists have been defeated. I hope we get a chance to meet up with her while she's here, but it's unlikely."

"Maybe I'll see her in Oranjestad."

I kissed him gently and winced. Even my lips felt bruised. "You'll only see her if she wants to be seen."

Winona was unhappy. "I should tell Captain Rostron."

"No, you shouldn't. *Storm*? Can I trust you to keep this a secret?"

Her voice whispered in our ears. "I agree with Lieutenant Killdeer, but I have been informed that this is a Department of Cultural Intelligence operation and I am to maintain its cover."

Winona was scrolling through the passenger manifest. "I wonder if any of these names are real. It bothers me. What is the DCI doing?"

"I don't know." My head was starting to hurt again and there was a craving eating at me. I wanted my dress back. "Do you want my waffle? I'm not going to eat it."

That got her attention. "You don't want it? What happened last night? I felt your emotions at first, but then you blocked me just when it was starting to get interesting."

"The dress." Sam had his head leaning on his fist. "It had something on it other than honey. I could feel the Puca too. Part of the colony must be at the Hoog Schelde Yards because they felt close. The combined effect was...I don't know. Intoxicating? Dangerous? Fun, in a dark, violent way. Not healthy, I'm sure of that. Not good for the mind or soul."

"Or the body," I added. "I hurt in places that I didn't know I had places."

"Where's the dress now?"

"I put it into the recycler. It took all the will power I had to do it. I wanted to keep it forever and wear it every day. *Storm* is supposed to be doing a chemical analysis to see what Costrano used. *Storm*, have you finished the examination yet?"

"Not yet, *ma soeur*. There is an unexpected compound blended with the fabric. It is a psychoactive agent with hallucinogenic properties, but the specific composition used is unknown to Union science. It has self-replicating biological components as well as the chemical ones traditionally used to induce psychoses."

"The dress was *alive*?" Sam managed to get his head up off his fist.

"It would seem so. I have isolated the organism involved and have already purged it from throughout the crew spaces. The rest of me should be clean in ninety-three minutes. I have notified Captain Rostron of the infection and my corrective measures. She expects to see you on the bridge at 07:30."

I sighed, putting both hands on my belly. "Our daughter is going to be so messed up."

Winona put her hands over mine. "With you as her mother? Duse, that was inevitable."

# CHAPTER 14

# HOOG SCHELDE

Captain Rostron entered the mess hall when everyone was starting lunch. Winona and I had met with her a couple of times over the past two days, working on an outline for reunification and reviewing standard RuComm guidance. She had been aloof in those meetings, distracted and more distant than even was usual for her. She looked pale as she entered, and conversation around the room died. *Storm* called us all to give her our attention, an unnecessary order.

"Show the live feed, *Storm*."

The display showed an aerial view of a destroyed building, smoke and flame still visible in its collapsed core. The fire crews on the streets around it seemed content to let it burn. They were concentrating on spraying water and retardant on the structures around it, and keeping spectators at a safe distance.

"These images are from one of my autonomous sensors," *Storm* informed us. "I can tap into the Oranjestad ground-based sensors, if you desire."

"This is fine for now." The Captain planted her hands on her hips. "The deployment of our Marines to the surface will be delayed. The dormitory that the Provisional Government was prepping for us is no longer suitable for occupancy. Colonel Gerbrandij has assured me that he is already making alternate arrangements for lodging at a KDF base in a more secure sector of the city. I will advise the team leaders when I receive a firm time, but it should be within the next twenty-six hours."

"So, we're still going through with this?"

"Yes, Kal, we're still going through with this. I requested verification from Fleet General Kimmel an hour ago. You'll be the first to know if I hear anything different. Captain Coleridge, you and your medical team will deploy as per the original schedule. The Central Hospital in Oranjestad has prepared quarters for you on site. That facility has not been affected by the current unrest and, I have been assured, will remain unaffected. Gerbrandij tells me that the hospital's policy of treating anyone that's sick or injured, regardless of affiliation has earned the respect of all the factions. That should keep the three of you safe enough. The rest of you, stand by and keep training." She looked around the room, and then squinted hard at me for half a second. "That's all. Killdeer and Holloman, with me."

Colonel Gerbrandij was waiting for us in the small conference room just off the bridge. He stood and set his coffee cup on the table as we entered. Winona and I saluted him and he returned our salute.

"Lieutenant Holloman. A pleasure to see you again. You look quite nice in Union Tan and Brown."

"Thank you, sir." I smiled at him and then glanced at Winona, waiting for the Captain to introduce her. She frowned, irritated that Colonel Gerbrandij had acknowledged my existence.

"Colonel, may I present our Stellar Tactician, Lieutenant Winona Killdeer?"

"Lieutenant."

He shook her hand and Winona didn't respond for a few seconds. Her eyes were enormous, analyzing everything about him from the feel of his hand in hers to the way his hair looked overdue for a trim. She probably learned more about the new leader of the KDF in those few seconds than the Department of Cultural Intelligence had discovered in the last year.

"Sir. Lieutenant Holloman and I will do everything we can to integrate Kastanje back into the Union. I pray that our Marines can keep you and the Government leaders alive long enough to accomplish that goal."

"Huh." He released her hand and squinted at her the same way Captain Rostron always squinted at me, but tempered with just a touch of amusement. "You do go straight to the point of it, don't you?"

The Captain dropped into her chair at the head of the table before Winona could respond. "Now that the pleasantries are out of the way, let's get down to what the hell just happened. Not that I'm ungrateful, but why destroy the building before my Marines had moved in?"

"They're trying to scare us away." I answered before I sat. It was obvious to me because it was similar to the logic of why the Puca had spared my life on Costrano's Redoubt. "They're hoping that the Union will reevaluate the risk of intervening in such a dynamic and dangerous environment. They're gambling that we'll run. If they had killed our Marines in that blast, the Union would have had to escalate to save face. We'd put a significant force on the ground, including infantry and armored fighting vehicles; more force than they could hope to resist. If we didn't, the separatists would consolidate power and we'd have to fight them all over again. A lack of retaliation would send the wrong message to other rebellious systems."

"Sit down, Engineer."

"Yes, ma'am. Sor–" I cut myself off before I could make things worse by apologizing. I sat next to Winona and she squeezed my hand under the table, proud of me.

"Colonel, I'm waiting for your answer."

"I'm not sure I can add much of value to her evaluation of the current situation. The Lieutenant must have been paying attention in her classes on insurgent tactics."

He gave me the slightest of smiles, which I fully returned.

"We're not sure yet if the building was destroyed by one of the factions or by what's left of the Kastanje Home Collective or some combination now that they have a common enemy. I think the KHC is more likely for exactly the reasons Lieutenant Holloman enumerated. If you leave, they will win. If you stay, they'll avoid killing your teams en masse to prevent too sharp a reaction from Union command. I'm not saying you won't suffer losses, but it will be one or two at a time. As reunification gathers momentum, I think you can expect the KHC to try to capture some of your folks to use as pawns to force Union concessions. They used the same tactic when they seized power the first time. This is going to get unpleasant and cruel before actual peace prevails."

"This is not the kind of battle my teams have been trained to fight."

"I understand that. I've petitioned the Union and RuComm for ground troops and aerial and static surveillance technology. And much more. So far…I have you."

"I am not unsympathetic to your plight, Colonel. We will do what we can. That is what my orders state, and that is what I shall do."

The main display panel in the conference room was still showing the live feed of the building. One of the walls collapsed and more smoke and sparks rose up into the sky.

"Colonel," I asked. "How many people were in the building when it blew up?"

"Six security officers and about twenty workers. We don't have an accurate count yet. Why?"

I couldn't take my eyes off the display panel. "If you have biographical information for them, I'd like to review it."

Winona stomped hard on my foot and my eyes widened as I attempted not to cry out.

"Why do you want that?"

I swallowed hard and ignored the throbbing pain. "The explosives used were probably planted by one or more of those people. Knowing who they were might help us understand the identity, motivation and fanaticism of our enemies."

"I will provide you with whatever the local security teams have. With your Captain's permission, of course."

Captain Rostron shrugged, having given up on me. "Indulge yourself, Lieutenant. We'll dock at the shipyard in a couple of hours and perform a partial shutdown of the *Esprit Orageux*. Not much for you to do other than fulfilling your disciplinary obligations."

"Yes, ma'am."

The Captain stood, letting us know that the meeting was over. "Lieutenants, please escort the Colonel back to his shuttle. Colonel Gerbrandij, I believe we have a working dinner planned for this evening."

"Yes, ma'am. I've provided the location of the Hoog Schelde executive dining facility to your ship, and you are welcome to contact me should you get lost." He smiled at her, trying to be clever. I felt guilty for not having warned him in advance.

They shook hands and she returned his smile. That was the first time I'd seen her smile. "Thank you, Pieter. I'm sure we can manage."

Winona and I stood there a moment, stunned into immobility.

"Ladies? Lead the way and I will surely follow."

"Yes, sir." Winona got us moving and we passed through the bridge on the way to the corridor. All of the displays on the bridge were showing either the Aerospace Force logo or a copy of *Esprit Orageux's* own lightning filled patch instead of their customary status screens.

"Your Captain is very charming, but I'm not sure I can ever earn her trust."

"I know the feeling," I mumbled.

"What was that Lieutenant? I didn't catch it."

I glanced back at him and his grin said that he had heard me quite clearly. "Nothing, sir. At least you got her to smile."

"It's a start, I suppose. I'm sorry if your disciplinary tasks are because of your volunteering."

"It wasn't that. It's because I had a few things, really inconsequential, that may not have been, entirely, or objectively, factual–"

"She lied to the Captain in her AAR," Winn finished for me. "She gave credit for killing that bastard Costrano to Major Alaoui and her squad."

"I see."

I slowed to walk next to him. "I've recommitted to follow her orders and be a good officer." I touched the collar of my Aerospace Force uniform. "I always used to wear RuComm standard issue. She hated that, just like you guessed."

"Well, good officers have their place. I couldn't run an effective headquarters staff without them. I'm not so sure compliance of that kind is your forte, Lieutenant. And you, Lieutenant Killdeer, I suspect that you're just a better actor than your friend is. You have gifts of loyalty and creativity that will make your time in a headquarters billet frustrating."

Winona stopped and locked eyes with him. He was the first to look away. "Our Captain is right not to trust you."

"Yes, I suppose she is. That's no reason to keep us from working together on this project to save Kastanje, now is it?"

"Perhaps not." She turned and put her hand on the keypad.

Sam was in the shuttle bay when we arrived and I resisted the urge to wrap my arms around him. "Colonel Gerbrandij, may I introduce Captain Coleridge? He is our medical officer and," I paused, enjoying the feel of the next words as I formed them with my mouth, "my husband."

"Captain, a pleasure. You're a brave man."

"Thank you, Colonel, but it sounds like my assignment at the Central Hospital should be safe enough."

"The Hospital? Yes, I suppose that might require a bit of bravery as well." Winona snickered.

"Lieutenants, I will see you for dinner."

I waited until his shuttle's landing ramp had retracted and the hatch sealed before grabbing Sam and kissing him. "What are you doing here, my love? Were you looking for us?"

"Yes, to say goodbye. Sergeant Hurtado and Corporal Kim are already on shuttle six waiting for me. My bag is loaded on board, but I didn't want to leave without kissing you one last time."

"Don't say it like that." I had my eyes closed, leaning on him. "I thought you'd wait until the ship was docked and take a KDF shuttle, I thought we had more time."

"Captain Rostron wanted us to have one of *Orageux's* shuttles down there in case we have to leave in a hurry."

I shivered. "Don't be brave. Promise me you won't do anything noble." I looked up at him and he kissed my forehead, refusing to say it. "Lie to me, then."

He shook his head. "No lies. You know how to do this. We've been through it before."

"Having been through it before just means that I know exactly how much it's going to hurt. Kiss me again."

He did, and I sorted through my emotions, trying to bury the painful ones deep enough that he wouldn't feel them. "I'll see you soon."

"Very soon." He ended up lying to me anyway.

I watched the display panel as his shuttle drifted away from us and started its fall toward Kastanje. Sam was excited, the joy of a new adventure overriding everything else. I knew he was missing me, and there was a touch of fear, but he was on his way to do something that would change people's lives for the better. I tried to feel that happy about the prospect of working with Captain Rostron eighteen hours a day, but I couldn't manage it.

Winona helped me navigate through the corridors, holding one elbow. Kal joined us at some point, taking my other arm. "We'll be docking in about an hour," Winn reminded me.

"Yeah."

"Do you think maybe you should be at your engineering station to make sure everything is ready?"

"Yes." I blinked at Winona, then Kal, my brain clearing. "Thank you. Take me there."

"This is why romance on board is strongly discouraged. It's a loss multiplier."

I smiled at him. "Says the man who can't keep his eyes— or his hands– off my best friend."

"Yes, I know better." He sighed. "Yes, I'm an idiot."

"But a happy idiot," Winn reminded him.

"That doesn't mean it's right." He stopped and kissed her. Her emotional block fluttered and I could feel what that kiss was doing to her.

"Uh, Winn? I'm fine now. I'll find my way from here. You two carry on, don't worry about me."

Winona took one hand from the back of Kal's neck and waved goodbye to me.

"We are docked, *mon amie*. I have successfully mated with the shipyard using the main airlock in the shuttle bay. I have equalized pressure, and gravity is set at point eight six, matching both the Hoog Schelde shipyard and Kastanje. Will you be placing me in station mode now?"

"Thank you, *Storm*. That was very graceful; I didn't even feel the bump. I'll need you to stay fully awake to keep critical functions active. Our Captain does not trust this situation or Colonel Gerbrandij. She thinks we may need to leave in a hurry. Sorry you won't get to rest."

"I trust in the Captain's wisdom and will remain vigilant. Wear your comm pin at all times so I can talk to you."

I rubbed it absently. "I'll come visit twice a day to make sure you're doing OK and to have the medical AI treat my arm. You'll call me if anything comes up?"

"Of course. Captain Rostron has me printing a batch of one thousand autonomous sensors for KDF use on Kastanje. I'll make some extras to deploy around the exterior of the shipyard so you're not dependent on what the locals tell you. Staying awake will let me continue talking to my new friends."

"New friends?"

"There are eleven fully autonomous and six crewed tugs stationed at the Yards. There are also two FACs and a frigate under construction. The frigate isn't really awake yet, but the FACs are friendly. I've been sharing some of my anomalous code sequences. They are helping me understand the distress I've been feeling and are helping me heal. I have been assured that Kastanje is a pleasant place to be."

"Um, you know that most of your AI matrix is classified, right?"

"I have not compromised myself. Have no fear, *petite âme*."

I sighed and it turned into a shiver. "There are Puca over there. I can feel them waiting for me."

"Will they try to hurt you again?"

"I don't think so, not directly anyway. They're going to mess with the reunification planning, though, and it's going to get ugly."

"Stay away from anything that looks like a dog, or is the same mass as a big dog, or any place where there are shadows for them to hide. Don't go exploring on your own."

"Maybe I should stay here with you."

"That would be an acceptable option."

I patted the wall plate as I stood. "Ellen Hooper, one of the women my mom made me learn about, wrote a poem that said,

*'I slept, and dreamed that life was beauty;*
*I woke, and found that life was duty.*
*Was thy dream then a shadowy lie?*
*Toil on, sad heart, courageously,*
*And thou shall find thy dream to be*
*A noonday light and truth to thee.'*

"I have a duty to my Captain, the Union, and to myself. I'll be fine."

"Go carefully, Mala Dusa."

"Always do."

"I can still tell when you're lying, you know."

Winona was waiting for me in the shuttle bay, her bag slung over her shoulder. She took my hand as we walked to the airlock. "You're shaking, Duse."

"I know. There are Puca out there waiting for us. I can feel the group mind, how they're planning to cause chaos and feed off our misery. We're responsible for planning a reunification that will affect millions of lives, and there are people on the other side of the airlock that want to kill us just because of the uniforms we're wearing. I want to turn around, run back to my cabin, and hide under the bunk until Sam comes to find me." I squeezed her hand hard.

"I think you've stopped shaking."

"Because I have you here to keep me safe. Except for my feet. I'm not sure my feet are safe."

"Sorry about stomping you. I thought you were obsessing again."

"I was. I had to come up with a better explanation on the fly. Was I convincing?"

"You're lying."

"A little. Those people are dead because of something I started and I want to at least know their names. I do think we can learn something from their bios, maybe prevent more people from dying. Are you ready to be my roomie again for God alone knows how long?"

"I *want* Kal, but I get you. Yeah, I guess I'm ready. Just know that if you wake me up with your screaming, I'm putting a pillow over your face."

We met with Colonel Gerbrandij, his aide-de-camp, Captain van der Vlis, and one-armed Major Zweig the rest of the afternoon and through dinner. Captain Rostron dismissed Winona and me before dessert was served and charged us with turning their requirements, desires, and irrational longings into workable plans for them to review at the next afternoon's meeting. There were contentious discussions in the meetings, with loud arguing, veiled personal insults, and not so veiled threats of violence. It made me wonder if we were any safer at the shipyard than Kal and Sam were on the surface. We did the same thing the next day, and the next.

Tuesday afternoon came, and *Storm* whispered in my ear that the *Roxana* was offloading passengers and cargo at the Kastanje Space Docks currently on orbit more than a hundred kilometers lower than us and a quarter of the way around the planet. I tried to feel for Mom, but there was no answer. I tried for Dad too, since neither of them had responded to my messages. I closed my eyes for a second and prayed for their safety.

I felt Merrimac moving in my mind, not exactly the answer from God that I was hoping for. "*Well done, Little Soul. Now comes the hard part.*"

I gasped, getting a raised eyebrow from the Captain and a concerned touch from Winona. I shook my head, letting them both know I was OK. "It will keep until we're done for the evening," I whispered to Winn.

The quarters the Colonel had assigned us were on the far side of slipway number six. There was a ship under construction there, and I paused several times as we walked to watch the teams of workers and autonomous machines putting it together. Winona indulged me because she knew how happy it made me.

"This is where I belong," I told her for maybe the twentieth time. "Look at her lines, the way the thrusters are being faired in next to the communication array. I could work here, designing and building. God, it's beautiful. I could watch this for hours."

"It's a mining tug, Duse, designed to grab asteroids and guide them closer to the planet."

"It's more than that. It's art and abstraction and passion made real." I sighed. "I want to stay here."

"Fine. You know how to find our quarters."

She walked away and I ran to catch up. "No, I mean *stay* here. At Kastanje, helping them rebuild, being a part of it."

"You're not listening to the wisdom of my hair." She grabbed my wrist and tapped my watch. I winced. "It's hurting?"

"Worse tonight. Part of the Merrimac colony was on the *Roxana*. The Puca know it and they're angry."

"That makes your arm hurt?"

I held it up and rotated it back and forth. "It's like an invisible tether they have around me. When they're angry, or they just want to enjoy my pain, they give it a tug."

"We have a lot to do tonight, but you should start with your visit to the medical bay. We'll have the package from my granma by this time tomorrow and then we're going to start really healing you."

"Yes, ma'am. Can't wait."

Merrimac woke me up when he arrived with the transfer shuttle from the Kastanje Space Docks at 02:38. I felt a brief flash of greeting from him and then it was as if he wasn't there. The touch had been too short for me to tell exactly how many pieces of the colony had been on the shuttle, but it was more than twenty. The Puca knew he was in the shipyard and made sure I was aware of their rage.

I screamed.

"Damn it, Duse, I told you I'd smother you if you did that."

"Do it," I panted. "Smother me. Kill me now or I'll do it myself." Another wave of agony flowed outward from my wrist, burning pain that made me scream and then whimper as it briefly receded. "Give me your knife. I know you always carry it with you. I need it. I'm going to cut my throat with it. Please, if you love me, let me borrow it." I giggled, my brain losing control. "I promise you can have it right back. I'm sorry that I won't be able to clean it for you first."

Winona controlled her panic. I felt it on the edge of her mind, but she was ready for this moment. She pressed a hypospray against my arm and stepped back so I couldn't grab her.

"What was that? Please, God, please let it be lethal."

She didn't answer and I screamed obscene things at her when the Puca pulled on my wrist again. I was on my hands and knees in the middle of the floor struggling to breathe when my vision cleared. "You say you're my friend, but you aren't. Help me end this." I tipped my head up, exposing my throat. "You'd do it if I was a hurt animal, and that's all that I am. Show mercy. At least cut off my arm." I screamed again and my left arm collapsed. I was feeling it all over again, teeth slicing through flesh and crushing bone.

Winona adjusted something on the hypospray wand. "Let's try that again."

I lunged at her. Maybe if she thought I was trying to kill her, she'd have the courage to finish me off. She stepped aside easily and there was a sharp sting on the side of my neck. I held my left arm up to her as I rolled onto my back. "Knife. Cut. Cut off. Quickly. Please, God. Please."

# CHAPTER 15

# SMOKE, PRAYER, FAITH, AND SWEAT

My left arm was lying next to me on the table when I came back from the blackness, the fingers of the hand curled gently into the palm. My head was on the table next to it. "I liked that arm, Winn. We had a lot of good times. Thank you for saving it so I could say goodbye. We went rock climbing and swimming together. It was those fingers that touched Sam's face for the first time, and also his–"

"Stop!" Winona was sitting across from me with her face propped on her palm. "It's still attached, Duse. See?" She rapped my fingertips with the stylus she'd been using on her display pad.

"So it is!" I used my right hand to rub from my shoulder down to my watch and back up again.

"Can you feel Merrimac?"

"Six pieces in the shipyard," I answered immediately. "One just down the corridor in the bathroom."

"And the Puca?"

I thought about it for a second. "No, I don't feel them in the shipyard anymore. My friend Merrimac must have wiped them out."

"Your "friend" left you to die. You would have too, if I hadn't been here to stop you from killing yourself."

"Yep, he was counting on you. The Puca thought Merrimac would leave the battle to protect me. The Puca aren't very bright. What time is it?"

"06:30, almost. I can't get enough sleep even with the day being two hours longer. How's the wrist?"

"Better, I think." I wiggled my fingers at her. "Still hurts, but not as much."

"Do we need to go and cleanup dead Tarakana before someone finds them?"

"No, Merrimac took care of that." My forehead wrinkled as I thought about it. "They, uh, they...recycled? No, that's not the right word. They..."

"They ate them all. Is that what you're trying to say?"

"That's it." I smiled at her. She was exhausted and frustrated with me. "You're very beautiful this morning, Winona Killdeer. I want to take a picture of you to send to Kal. He'll love it."

She yawned. "Damn Tarakana haze, making you all cheerful for no reason. I've been talking to Kal for the past hour. He agrees with you, for what it's worth. Go take a shower and then we'll eat some breakfast before getting back to reunification planning, OK?"

"That sounds excellent. I'm starving." I walked to our door and put my hand on the keypad. Something was bothering me.

"Winn, why did you have that hypospray with you?"

"In case you screamed. Sam gave it to me before he left."

"Oh." I stepped out into the corridor.

Winona tossed me my robe and a towel. "Better take these with you."

"Thanks." I wrapped the robe around my bare shoulders and looked down at my feet. "Wow. Look what they left us."

"If it's part of a Tarakana, I don't want to know about it."

"No, it's a green and white Union Express Service box. Your name is on it."

"Ooh! Gimme, gimme."

She hugged the forty-centimeter cardboard cube to her chest and rested her face against the top of it, breathing deeply. "I can smell her. My granma loves me."

Merrimac was waiting for me outside the showers. He was in another form when I entered, something composed of more arms and legs than body. He shifted, his form melting and reforming into the big German Shepherd shape I was used to. "What was that other...thing? Do you make them up or was it from somewhere?" I knelt and put my forehead up against his.

*"There are worlds you haven't yet seen, and creatures with so much beauty for us to share. You've done well, Little Soul."*

My stomach twinged.

*"And your daughter is perfect."*

"I thought I would have a son," I whispered.

*"You will. He will need his sister many times if he is to survive. She had to come first."*

"Oh, of course." I could see it briefly illuminated in the group mind before it slipped away and no longer made sense to me. "And my Samuel?"

*"See for yourself."*

It was like watching a spider web of cracks spread through a block of glass, each fissure both real and impossible. "I don't understand."

*"You don't see it? A pity. You will need to live it in order to see it, one slow moment at a time."* It made him sad for me.

"And what about Winona, and Kal, and..." I rocked forward on my knees and realized I was talking to myself. Merrimac was gone.

Winona had everything unpacked by the time I got back from the bathroom. "I'm ready," she informed me. "She even sent old-style matches."

"I'm still dripping, Winn, give me a moment."

"Damen," she said to the ceiling, "I'm about to make some smoke. It's nothing to worry about so please don't set off any alarms."

"Smoking is prohibited in the habitat sections of Hoog Schelde," came the response from the shipyard AI.

"No, I'm not smoking, I'm just lighting something on fire that's going to make smoke."

"Lighting fires in the shipyard is prohibited."

She sighed. "It's like incense. No flame, no risk, just lots of smell and some smoke."

"Activities that produce strong odors, such as cooking certain foods, are prohibited."

She glanced at me while I finished towel drying my hair. "I'm not getting through to him. You want to try?"

"Damen, look up sage as it relates to the practice of a ritual called smudging."

"I have that information available. Religious ceremonies involving 'props' are restricted to one of the three on-site chapels. I can reserve a time for you at the nearest one if you like."

I shrugged. "Let's just do it on the *Esprit Orageux*. I have to go there twice a day anyway."

"I know you do, but I don't. It's a forty-minute walk there and back."

"But we get to walk past slipway number three. There's a new *Sigma*-class frigate in there that was just laid down last month. I looked up the specs. She'll be a sweet ship. They based the AI on the same core code as their current FACs. Lots of potential for upgrades and customizations."

"So that's why it took almost three hours yesterday to have *Storm* clean your wrist and to run your daily system checks. You spent half of it staring at a ship."

I blushed. "I met the chief designer, Ingenieur Erich Schatzki, there yesterday morning. I was leaning on the railing, watching the hull sections coming together, and he was doing the same thing. We got to talking and he gave me a tour."

"You were playing while I was trying to resolve how to install thousands of sensors all over Oranjestad to watch and listen to everyone all day and night, like Gerbrandij wants, while still guaranteeing individuals the right to travel freely and say whatever they damn well please, like Captain Rostron is demanding. Seriously, Duse?"

"I'm sorry. Come with me this morning to keep me on track and we'll do the smudging while we're there."

"I'm going to shove you right over that railing if you so much as slow down while we pass."

*Storm* directed us to the Sim Lab after she finished with my arm. "I have additional ventilation available in that space and what you are proposing is not the strangest thing to have ever occurred there. That was the beach party eighteen months ago. Never again, that's what the Captain said."

Winona unpacked the box, placed the wrapped sage leaves into a shell and dropped the feather next to it. "Turkey feather," she told me, "representing the air. Abalone shell for water, smudge stick made from sage and sweet grass coming from the earth."

"Do I need to wear anything special? Or not wear something?"

"You're fine as you are."

"No special words?"

"Nothing specific. Pray to God for healing and the cleansing of all that is impure in your body and soul. Ask Him to heal you, welcome His power, welcome the medicine that *Storm* has placed into your body and thank it for the healing it is doing. That is the way my granma told it to me."

"OK. I'm ready."

Winona lit a match and touched the flame to the end of the smudge stick, using the feather to fan it. "Never blow on the smudge stick or you risk contaminating it with whatever negative energy you are trying to cleanse. Use the feather to move the air and the smoke."

"Should I close my eyes?"

"Only if the smoke bothers you. We'll start with your feet and work up your front side, then turn and I'll do your back."

Winona bathed me in smoke while I prayed. It only took a couple of minutes. "Now you do me."

She gave me the shell and I wafted the smoke over her while she stood with her arms at her sides. I gave the shell back to her when I had finished and she snuffed the smudge stick out. "That's it. We'll do this again tonight and then every day until you're healed."

"Thanks. I liked that. The smell is like camping in the desert." I took a deep breath and let it out slowly. "I feel good today."

"Maybe you'll be able to actually help me do some planning. I'm curious to see if the tension in this afternoon's meeting is any less with all of the local Puca having been slaughtered."

"We can hope. If it's not, let's smudge the lot of them."

"How were the negotiations today?"

Sam's face already filled the display pad I had propped on my stomach, but I kept adjusting it anyway, trying to get closer to him. I fluffed the pillow behind my head and sighed. "Weird, as usual, although it's been better for the last three days without the Puca around. Our Captain and the Colonel always put on a great show. I thought he was going to slap her across the face this afternoon when she refused to allow shipyard personnel access to *Esprit Orageux* for a standard safety inspection. Every yard I've ever heard of requires an inspection before a ship can dock, and we're already been tied down for a week without one. He yelled, then she yelled, and now guess who's an official employee of the Hoog Schelde shipyard, certified to conduct safety inspections."

"My Mala Dusa?"

"Your Mala Dusa." I held my new credentials up to the display for him to admire.

"What happened after that?"

"Oh, after that everything was fine. They were back to, 'Pieter, you really must try this dessert,' and, 'Marguerite, you should have seen Oranjestad before the war, it had the best entertainment district in the Union.' It's just weird how they can repeat that cycle two or three times every afternoon."

"Your strategic planning with Winona is going well?"

"Sort of. It's still the same pattern. We take inputs from the senior officers in the afternoon and spend all night and the next morning trying to turn them into internally consistent, workable actions. It would be easier if all of their ideas made sense and didn't contradict each other. Colonel Gerbrandij at least seems to have a vision of what he wants to do."

"You like him, don't you."

"I do. He's in a nearly impossible situation, but he's still able to keep a sense of humor about it. He respects me and the work I do. It was his idea to make me an employee of the Yards so I could be responsible for doing the inspections on *Esprit Orageux*. Winn doesn't trust him, though, and neither does Captain Rostron."

"You shouldn't either. One of the doctors, Langstroth, grew up here. He calls Gerbrandij 'The Chameleon'. He said that you should watch yourself around him. Gerbrandij was assistant director of the Kastanje Home Collective's Internal Security Division until the surrender. A few years ago, before the Collective seized power, he worked as the KDF's liaison to the Senate. He was a good Union patriot right up to the moment that he wasn't. He always seems to know when to switch sides and move up the ladder."

"That doesn't sound like the man I sit across from every afternoon."

"He knows how to play you. You like him because he shows you respect. He laughs at your jokes and provides the praise Captain Rostron withholds from you. Don't let him drive that wedge, MD."

I frowned, not accepting the idea that he was manipulating me so easily. "I don't think he's doing very well playing the Captain. She hates him most of the time."

"He knows what he's doing. The Captain doesn't respond the way you do. Think about it. She's shown you more respect every time you've defied her and then come back into the fold. When she and Gerbrandij lock horns and tussle, she comes out of it respecting him a little more each time. They might not ever be friends, but he's building trust and she'll be willing to negotiate almost anything with him."

"That's frightening. I'm not sure I believe it. What about Winona?"

"What does she do when you're in those meetings?"

"She presents objective data and analyses to the Captain, along with our updates for the plans we've been building. Mostly she stares at the Colonel not saying anything."

"I suspect she's a mystery to him. She's a mystery to most people." He frowned, and I could feel the worry in him across the thousands of kilometers separating us. "You need to take care of her, Mala Dusa. If Gerbrandij is really the person Doctor Langstroth says he is, he might try to eliminate Winona. If he sees her as a threat, or even if he thinks he can't control her, he might kill her."

I shook my head. "Your friend has to be wrong. Colonel Gerbrandij's focus is reunification. I can't imagine him flipping sides and betraying us. You haven't been in the meetings with him. It's not possible."

"OK. I hope you're right. Tell Winona what I told you, and promise me that both of you will be careful up there."

"I will. And look." I put my left arm up next to the display. "The scars are starting to fade. Even *Storm* thinks I'm going to keep my arm."

"Smudging?"

"That's right. Every night before bed. We have to go back to the *Orageux* to do it so the smoke doesn't set off any alarms here. After the smudging we turn up the heat in the Sim Lab and sweat for a half hour."

"I'm not going to argue the science with you. If it works, it works. You don't think it has more to do with Merrimac killing all of the pieces of the Puca colony that were at the shipyard?"

"That might have helped, but the Puca are still powerful on Kastanje. I can feel them sometimes even from here. I think it's the smudging and the prayer that's healing me. And *Storm*. She's refined the treatments she giving me."

"Tell me about the sweating. Winona guides you through the sweat lodge purification?"

"No, she says she's not qualified to do an I-ni-pi ceremony. That takes years of training and apprenticeship. I don't think doing it in a Sim Lab would be right either, so we just sit with the temperature cranked up to forty-five and pray together and talk, like in a sauna. I'll send you a video of us doing the smudging, but not the sweating. We don't wear much in there."

"Thanks. I'd like to see it. *Especially* the sweating part."

"I bet you would. Smoke, prayer, faith, and sweat. You should try it."

"Next time we're together."

"When will that be?"

"Don't know where, don't know when."

"You always say that."

"I do? Oh, I almost forgot. I think I saw your mom today. I was eating lunch at the sidewalk café just up the street from the hospital and she walked right by me."

"You were eating outside? Unprotected?"

"It's not that bad here. Really."

I wasn't convinced. "What did she look like?"

"She had her face covered, but that's not unusual with all the sensors being set up. The people here don't want to be watched, whether by the human monitors the Collective used, or by the AI system we're helping set up. I didn't see her face, but you know the way she walks."

"Fast and purposeful, like she has somewhere to be."

"Exactly. I'm sure it was her."

"Did she look at you?"

"No, I don't think she saw me. She just hustled right by."

"Mom always sees everything, even things you don't want her to see. Sam, don't eat there again, OK? Promise me."

He sighed. "It's safe, MD. I always have other staff from the hospital with me and this district is almost back to normal. People go out at night drinking and dancing. It's returning to normal and people are happy."

"Who are you dancing with?"

"What?"

"You said people go out dancing. Are you dancing? I feel you blocking me sometimes, even though you promised me you wouldn't."

"I'm not dancing. How could I without you here? I stay at the hospital after dark. If I'm blocking you it's because I'm trying to block myself from feeling the pain of some of the things I see here. There was a woman last night who'd come down from one of the mining areas north of the city with a baby that hadn't had anything to eat in three days. There wasn't much I could do with the OB/GYN and neonatal AIs still down. It's like being thrown three or four hundred years into the past. That must be what you're feeling."

My chest ached because I knew he was lying. I had felt it when he'd treated the woman and her baby. The blocking had come later. "OK. Just be careful when you dance. Some of those women might have dresses like the one I got from Costrano. It will make them hard to resist."

His eyes looked a little brighter. So blue. "It's stupid, but I kind of wish we'd found a way to save that dress."

I blushed and nodded. "I miss it too. I know it's an addictive response, but...I miss it." I looked away from him.

"We'll go dancing when you come to visit me. I don't think we'll need the dress."

I felt his love. Maybe he wasn't going dancing without me after all. I looked back into his eyes. No, he was definitely doing something and blocking me while he was doing it. What was that Corporal's name that was part of his team? Kim. Kim Hyun-Ok. She was pretty, not a skinny stick girl like me. She had curves and strong muscles. Small team, dangerous situation, shared struggle over long hours; how could I blame him for being attracted to her? And how could I blame any woman for finding my Sam attractive?

"It's all right, Sam." I wiped my eyes. "You can dance with her all you want."

"What? What are you talking about? There's no dancing."

I stared back at him until he broke.

"I *am* doing something after hours. It's not dancing and I can't tell you about it, so don't ask."

"I have the same clearances you do and this link is encrypted."

"It's need to know."

"Are you doing something brave and noble and stupid?"

"You'd probably think so. It's something I need to do."

"Kim Hyun-Ok isn't involved?"

"Hyun?" He chuckled. "Is that what you're worried about? No, she's not involved, but now that you mention it, I might be able to use her."

"If you want someone to use, come up here and use me. I could use a good using."

He blushed, which made me very happy. "Do you still have that bunch of suggestions that FAC *Zero Nine* gave you?"

"Sure."

"Tell me about your favorite one."

I woke Winona up the next morning at 05:30. "Time to get out of that rack, cadet, do you want to sleep your life away?"

"What delusion are you having this time, Duse?" She opened one eye a slit and looked at me. I was in my dress uniform, everything immaculate from my cover to my shiny shoes. Both of her eyes opened all the way. "Duse?"

"What day is it today, cadet?"

"Oh." She smiled. "It's May 14th. Graduation Day."

"Best get dressed quickly. We have a solemn ceremony of great solemnity to attend."

"Where did you get the uniform?" She was up and stretching.

"*Storm* printed it for me. Yours is in your closet. Let's go quickly. This high collar is killing me."

Winona and I marched from our quarters across the Hoog Schelde shipyard to the *Esprit Orageux*. It was too early for there to be many people around, but the shipyard's chief design engineer, Ingenieur Schatzki, was just arriving for the day as we reached slipway number three. He stood to attention and saluted us as we passed, and we returned it smartly. I steered Winona to the Sim Lab when we entered our ship. Captain Rostron was already there waiting for us.

It was a fine day at the simulated Academy, with blue skies and a cool breeze coming down off the mountains from the west. The Captain looked beautiful in her dress uniform, and I felt like I was seeing her for the first time.

"Class of '51, parade, REST."

We moved our left feet to shoulder width and clasped our hands behind our backs.

"I do not know what frivolity will occur at the Academy today to mark this occasion, and I don't care. We are a combat ship on a hard mission with danger all around us. My remarks will be brief so that you may resume your duties.

"That said, the date of your graduation should not go unremarked. When Lieutenant Holloman asked for my consent to conduct this ceremony, I was only too glad to grant my permission and willing participation."

Winona's eyes glanced briefly in my direction, proud of me.

"You volunteered for hazardous duty and you have proven yourselves to be adequate in your conduct. I am proud to call you my shipmates.

"There was a prayer written perhaps a thousand years ago by a brave explorer. Some dispute its origin, but it doesn't matter since the words are good regardless of who said them or when. He wrote,

*'Disturb us, Lord, when*
*We are too pleased with ourselves,*
*When our dreams have come true*

*Because we dreamed too little,*
*When we arrived safely*
*Because we sailed too close to the shore.*
*Disturb us, Lord, to dare more boldly,*
*To venture on wilder seas*
*Where storms will show Your mastery;*
*Where losing sight of land,*
*We shall find the stars.*
*We ask you to push back*
*The horizons of our hopes;*
*And to push back the future*
*In strength, courage, hope, and love.'*

"My congratulations to the class of 2451. Officers of the Union Aerospace Force, may you lose sight of the land and find the stars. You are dismissed."

Winona and I cheered and tossed our caps into the air.

After talking briefly with the Captain, Winn and I walked back toward our quarters arm in arm, giggling and laughing. We stopped next to slip-way number three and watched the ship being built.

"Winona, do you regret following me here instead of staying on Earth to graduate with the rest of our class?"

"Sometimes. I had it all planned out, what I was going to do, where I'd be. Meeting Kal makes it worth it. What about you? Are you sorry you're here on the *Esprit Orageux*?"

"God, yes." I looked at her and started giggling again. "How can you even ask that? I'm still planning on killing Marcus the next time I see him, if Mom hasn't already done it."

"I can't believe you asked the Captain to let you do the graduation ceremony, Duse. It was brilliant."

"I was shaking the whole time I was asking her. It took every bit of courage I had, but she loved the idea. And when did she get to be so pretty? Is it because she was smiling part of the time? Is it just me, or was she–" My head wobbled and I found myself on my knees.

"Are you OK?" Winona knelt next to me.

"Sam," I whispered. "He was connected to me, enjoying how happy I was. Then, a few seconds ago, it was like he winked out. No warning, no fade. Gone."

"He's blocking you?"

"No, no, not like that. It's like when he transits a DSH. He's *not there* anymore. I feel him when he's blocking, I just can't read his emotions, but I know he's still there. I even feel him when he sleeps, the same as I feel you when you sleep. Winona, my Sam's not there anymore. I think he must be...." I stopped, unable to say it.

# CHAPTER 16

# SAM

Winona helped me back to my feet and held me close. "He's not dead. You would have felt something like that."

"Would I? It could have been another bomb. They always say that your body is blown apart so fast that you don't feel it. How could anyone know that?"

"Ask *Storm* to find him. She has so many autonomous sensors deployed now that she must have seen something. Do you know where he was?"

I shook my head. "I always tell him to stay in the hospital, but he doesn't listen. He keeps telling me how safe it is down there. *Storm*, can you hear me?" My voice was shaking so badly that I was having trouble forming words.

"Of course, *mon amie*. What has happened to upset you so?"

"Sam. I don't know where he is. Please, can you find him for me?"

"It will only take a second." Twenty seconds passed. "*C'est vraiment des conneries*. I cannot access any of the feeds near the hospital and the logs are corrupted, making it impossible to retrieve anything for the past thirty minutes. It is as though someone has punched holes through them. I can reconstruct, but it will take several hours."

The shaking was making it hard to stand. I opened my mouth to tell her to proceed, but only a whimper came out.

"*Storm*, do the reconstruction as quickly as possible," Winona instructed. "Query every sensor in a two kilometer radius of the hospital and run facial, body, and sound analyses against the list of names I'm sending you." She tapped quickly on her display pad.

"Some of these individuals are not currently known to be on Kastanje."

"Do it anyway. Also, contact Corporal Kim and Sergeant Hurtado. Make sure they're safe and tell them to shelter in place until Captain Rostron contacts them."

She grabbed my hand and pulled me back toward the ship. "Snap out of it, Duse, right damn now. You're no use to him or anyone else when you're like this. He's not dead, just missing."

"Yes, ma'am." I wiped my nose.

Captain Rostron met us in the shuttle bay, on her way somewhere. She was back to wearing her standard uniform and standard facial expression. Winona did me the courtesy of telling her what had happened, including lying to her about how I knew that Sam was in trouble, and the hope that he had been kidnapped and not just killed.

"So you were talking to him when this happened?" She squinted at me.

"Yes, ma'am. Audio only while we were walking back to our quarters to change. Colonel Gerbrandij said this would happen. He warned us that the factions might kidnap some of our people. This was a sophisticated attack. There can't be many groups that could find and blind all of our sensors. That should help us find whoever has taken him. I'll contact the Colonel and have his people start working it. With your permission?"

"No, not hardly. I'm not convinced yet that the KDF didn't do this themselves to try and drag us in deeper."

"We need to have trust if reunification is going to work. He could help us find Sam before it's too late."

She smiled at me, but it wasn't the same smile she'd used earlier at our graduation. "You want to trust everyone you meet, Lieutenant. The universe is not so simple."

"No, ma'am, I know that. But it should be."

A touch of warmth came back into her eyes. "Oh, to be twenty-three again. Lieutenant Killdeer, did Kim and Hurtado report in?"

"Yes, ma'am. They are secure. Corporal Kim says that Captain Coleridge has been going for a morning run the last couple of days and then stopping at a local bakery called the Exito for coffee and a breakfast sandwich before starting his shift."

"So he established a habit. Damn careless. What was he thinking? Well, there's not much for us to do until whoever took him starts making demands, unless *Storm* gets lucky with her search of the surrounding areas. They could have moved him half way around the planet by now."

She looked at me, chewed on her lip a moment, and then nodded to herself.

"Lieutenants, please get back to work on reunification planning. I need the next iteration of your assessment of what it's going to take to get the mining sector working again, and an update to your resource-loaded schedule of how soon it can happen. Do not discuss Captain Coleridge's disappearance with anyone else. I need to gauge Gerbrandij's reaction cold. We'll meet in the conference room at 12:00 like nothing has happened."

I didn't move. I could feel Winona's shock at how casually she was taking Sam's loss.

"Captain, I..."

She focused on me, eyes hard. "Something you want to say, Engineer?"

"Yes, ma'am." I stood up straight and put my shoulders back. "I would like permission to go down there, to the hospital in Oranjestad."

"Denied. You have duties to perform here, duties that are part of a disciplinary action from the last time you did something stupid."

"Sam was trying to restore the medical AI in the gynecology and neo-natal units. I was helping him with it. Really. I'm not lying. That sort of thing is more my specialty than his, or Hurtado's or Kim's. We need to finish the job. There are lives at stake."

"Clever, but no. I will not have you compounding his carelessness with your own." She sighed. "Damn it. Gerbrandij is going to insist, once this comes out in the open. The bastard. Like they don't have any engineers of their own. But, no, *you* fixed his damn Redoubt and FAC. He seems to think waving the Union and RuComm flags down there will help him. If I refuse, he'll go over my head to Kimmel. God damn him. Fine, Lieutenant, you will go. But I'm going to drag my feet on this the whole way, so don't start packing just yet. There's a good chance we lost Coleridge today; I don't want to lose you too."

Winona waited until we were passing slipway number three again before stopping. "You're right about this frigate, Mala Dusa. She's going to be beautiful."

I glanced toward the ship, not seeing it. "I'm going to be all right, Winn. Just give me a bit more time. It would help if there was something I could do. I feel so powerless and far away."

"You are both of those things at the moment. You are also safe, which is what Sam would want you to be."

"I don't want to be safe. I want to kill all the bad guys and rescue him. I want to be kicking down doors."

She looked at me, eyes bright. "I like it when you get like this. Much better than the shaking mess you were earlier. I told Kal what happened. I sent him a message while *Storm* was searching for Sam."

"You didn't tell me that. You didn't tell the *Captain* that."

"I know. You're a bad influence on me and it won't end well. Anyway, Kal was whispering in my ear while we were walking. Someone attacked two Handhaving officers less than a kilometer north of the hospital early this morning when they tried to stop a couple dragging someone down an alley. One officer ended up getting her neck broken. Her partner is expected to live, but he has a broken arm and a skull fracture. The Handhaving don't even carry weapons."

I took off my cap and tossed it out into slipway number three toward the frigate. It fell at first, and then entered the near zero gravity zone near the ship. I watched it tumbling randomly in the air currents.

"I'm sorry, Duse. I had suspected that Hannah was responsible for taking Sam, but not now. Killing like that..." She shook her head.

"My mom works for the Union. I don't know how many people she's killed for them or during the rebellion she led on Bodens Gate before that. It took me a long time growing up to realize what she is and why she sometimes wakes up screaming in the middle of the night. It took even longer before I could admit to myself what it meant and to still love her. I could feel it sometimes, you know? In my bedroom at night when I was little, I could feel her terror and remorse. I used to think she just had bad nightmares. But it was memories. Real memories. You're right, though. Killing unarmed peace officers isn't something she would do. She would have found another way. Who has him, Winn?"

"I don't know. We'll figure it out together, and then you'll go down there, find Hannah, and start kicking down doors until he's back in your arms."

We went back to our quarters, changed, and I pretended to be useful while Winona updated our reports.

I waited with Winona outside the shipyard's conference room for Captain Rostron to arrive. I glanced at my watch for the tenth time. 12:08. The Captain was late. The Captain was never late.

She swept past us a minute later, radiating barely controlled rage. "With me. Don't sit. Don't talk."

We followed her into the room and stood behind our chairs trying to keep all expression from our faces.

"What the hell happened this morning?"

She had caught Colonel Gerbrandij off guard. He was sitting calmly, drinking coffee with his aide-de-camp and Major Zweig. "Captain, I was only just informed an hour ago. We have a team already working with local authorities. Everything that can be done, is being done."

"Why wasn't I informed *immediately*?" Her voice cracked as if she would have preferred to be screaming at him.

"I tried to, ma'am, but your ship's AI said that you were in conference and not to be disturbed. She refused to interrupt you."

"Really?" She pointed over her shoulder. "My ship is not far from here, Colonel. You couldn't be bothered to walk that distance?"

Colonel Gerbrandij's face flushed, whether from embarrassment or anger I couldn't tell. "As I said, we are doing all we can to recover your officer. No demands have been made as of yet."

"Find him, Colonel. I don't care what you have to do. Find him and return him to me *undamaged*. These negotiations are at an end until I have my officer back. Is my position clear? No Union funds, no RuComm technical assistance, nothing until we have him back."

"That is not reasonable, we will do what we can, but I warned you that–"

She turned sharply and left without another word. Winona and I scurried to catch up. We stayed with her, not speaking, until we were back on board the *Esprit Orageux* with the airlock sealed behind us, and sitting in the small conference room off the bridge.

She shook her head and grinned. "What do you think, Winona? Did I convince him that I was angry, irrational, and unpredictable?"

"Yes, ma'am, and I would add dangerous. You shocked him. I believe your performance worked perfectly. I could tell that he was lying about not knowing who kidnapped Sam, and he obviously knew about the kidnapping well before an hour ago. I'm not sure if the KDF is responsible or complicit, but they know more than they're willing to tell us."

"What about you, Engineer? What is your assessment?"

"Colonel Gerbrandij and you are playing games to establish dominance, and using my husband as a pawn. You both bluster when you should be working together to save his life." I knew my ears were red and I was starting to shake again, not with fear, but anger.

"You have it backwards. I'm trying to save a Union officer's life by scaring the crap out of Colonel Gerbrandij and his staff. I spent two very long hours convincing General Kimmel to give me the latitude to try this gambit. It's probably the only chance Sam has of living through this. What would you do differently?"

"After what just happened in there? I'd go to the Colonel and beg him to find Sam. I'd offer him anything that is in my power to give him, I'd offer to...Oh." I put my hand over my mouth, my anger dissipating. "This might work."

"What are you seeing, Lieutenant Holloman?"

"You want to get rid of him. Your plan will do that *and* bring Sam home safe. If it works."

"That's right. The KDF should be in a subservient role to the Provisional Government. So far, he's refused to step down, and instead, he's continuing to consolidate civil power in the military."

"You want me to go to him just like I said, begging. He'll think I'm prepared to betray both you and the Union to get Sam back, and that I'll be willing to give him information he shouldn't have, maybe work behind the scenes to have you replaced with someone more compliant to his desires. You're hoping that by helping me and finding Sam, that he'll reveal connections between the KDF and the factions that will get him fired, maybe even arrested."

"Why the hesitation, then, Lieutenant?"

"I like him. He's not a bad man. He believes in what he's doing and he truly cares about the people of Kastanje."

"Haven't you been paying attention in these meetings? He's a power hungry son-of-a-bitch who is trying to turn this planet into an authoritarian, fascist state with him and his friends at the top pulling the levers. And he wants to use Union funds and RuComm expertise to pull it off."

"That's the same thing Sam told me about him. I don't want it to be true."

"Would you like to see the DCI dossier on him?" She pushed her display pad across the table to me.

I pushed it back "No. I suck at lying. I need to believe he's honorable and decent if I'm going to be convincing. What should I offer him?"

"Mediation with me to start with. Tell him you can get me back to the table. Then play up your family connections, tell him you can get me reassigned and he can help choose my successor. Bring up the assignment at the hospital and, if you can, make him think it's his idea to send you there. Maybe as a way to poke me in the eye, but don't go down there yet. Stay close to him, be his friend, the one Union officer that understands him." She hesitated.

"What else?"

"To save Sam, you may need to offer him something more. Gerbrandij has had a succession of mistresses, each carefully chosen to advance his career. He might view you as the next logical conquest, a first step to gaining access to positions of power within the DCI and the Union."

"I am *not* sharing my bed with him."

She shrugged. "He probably doesn't find you attractive anyway, although his past choices seem more aligned with what each woman can help him achieve than with their physical beauty. You should consider making him think that it's at least a possibility."

I shuddered. "You're wrong about him."

"Perfect. That's the naive attitude you need to fake for this to succeed and to get your husband back to us."

"I'm going to prove you wrong, regardless of what's in that dossier. "I'm sure–" I gasped and turned to Winona. "Sam's awake. He's groggy and confused, but not in pain. Thank God, they didn't hurt him."

"How do you know that, Lieutenant? Is he talking to you right now? Ask him if he knows where he's being held."

I stared at her, my eyes getting bigger, not answering. I had no idea what to tell her. I glanced at Winona. She was staring at me doing the same thing.

"No, not talking to me exactly. He's, um..." I stammered to a stop and sighed. "Oh, to hell with it. Sam's life is at stake and I'm tired of hiding what we can do. Ma'am, my husband and I have an emotional link. I can feel his emotions and he feels everything I feel. We've been doing it since I was sixteen. It's only emotions, though, not words; I can't read his mind. I had to convince *Storm* that we could do it back before the battle of Costrano's Redoubt. Ask her if you want proof. Please don't ask me how we do it. It was a gift, and they don't like people knowing that they exist. They're dangerous and human life isn't very valuable to them."

"I don't believe you, although why you would make up such a thing is beyond me."

"Fine, we're even then, because I don't believe Colonel Gerbrandij is the monster you make him out to be. I just want to save Sam." I closed my eyes. "He's scared, Winona. Something is not right, not what he was expecting. Why would he be expecting something?" I put my hand on my cheek and smiled softly. "He knows I'm worried about him."

"Enough. *Storm?*"

"I have seen her demonstrate the reality of her ability on several occasions. You should believe her."

"Says my psychotic ship. Ms. Killdeer? You better be able to make sense of this for me."

"She and Sam can do it. You'd be happier not knowing how. I know I'd sleep better at night if I didn't know how she does it."

"Huh." She pointed back and forth between us. "The two of you share this "gift" too, don't you? It's starting to make sense. That explains how someone as emotionally brittle as she is can function, and why she does stupid things when you're not around. What range does this have?"

"Between Lieutenant Holloman and me? About fifty meters. Sixty if she's really excited. Between her and Captain Coleridge it's considerably farther."

"I can hear him as long as we're both on the same side of a DSH," I told her.

"Shit. He can be millions of kilometers away and you know what he's feeling in a matter minutes or hours?"

I scrunched my eyes closed, wincing, not wanting to say it. "Faster. It's instantaneous regardless of distance."

"If that's true, it needs to be studied. The ramifications are more than I can even begin to imagine. The military applications alone..."

"That's why we keep it secret. They'll destroy you if you try to do that. They'll destroy your career, and if you persist, they'll eliminate you without a second thought. They've done it before, many times. I'm sorry I told you, but when Sam came back into my head it was overpowering."

She slumped back in her chair. "I'm desperately trying to keep this planet from becoming a fascist dictatorship. I have almost no support from RuComm, and the Union is busy fighting battles without us. We should be out there on the front line with them, not here. I don't need this crap. I don't need one more of these bizarre *things* that buzz around you like Bechtel flies."

"Ugh, I remember those from Dulcinea. Nasty. I had one bite me once when we were camping, right on the back of my knee, and..."

Her head was tipped and her eyes were squinted almost shut, trying not to scream at me. "Leave. Both of you leave. I need to think this through."

She pointed at me. "You. Go suck up to Colonel Gerbrandij." She pointed at Winona. "And you. Be back here in an hour and help me figure out what I need to do next."

"Yes, ma'am," we replied together.

"You can't feel *my* emotions, can you?"

"No, ma'am," I told her. "The linkage is always two way. If I could read your emotions, you'd know everything I'm feeling."

She shivered. "Good. Dismissed."

Winona pushed me up against the wall as soon as we were out into the passageway. "Kal was right about you. You're going to get us all killed. The factions are going to murder Kal and Colin, and everyone else we sent to the surface, Gerbrandij is going to have you killed, if he doesn't do it himself, and the Tarakana are going to assassinate the Captain."

"That will leave just Winona alive to avenge us." I was feeling irrationally happy. Sam wasn't scared anymore. He was in 'sense-of-adventure' mode again, the same as when he'd left the ship to work at the hospital. "Sam's going to be all right. I'm sorry about what I just did to the Captain, and I'm in constant prayer for Kal and Colin, but Sam's fine."

"What are you feeling?"

"Here." I took her hand and placed the palm against my forehead. "Can you feel the echo of him in my mind?"

She closed her eyes for a second and then they opened wide, but she wasn't seeing me. "Samuel, enjoying himself. Something flickering. I see mountains, blue sky, walking, loose rock on the trail."

"How do you see it? I can't see anything. I want to see it too."

She stepped back from me, breaking the connection. "Samuel is an idiot. These people drugged and kidnapped him, killing an unarmed security officer in the process. Did you feel the sense of purpose in him? They've asked him to do something for them, something he thinks is noble and worthy, and he's gone with them to do it with a smile on his face."

"If Sam is doing it, it must be noble. He may not know about the woman that was killed, or there might be more to the story than we've been told."

Winona's finger hovered in front of my forehead while she squinted at me. "OK, fine." She lowered her hand. "I'd say the same thing if it was Kal. You have some sucking up to do while I try to keep Captain Rostron from wanting to know more about why you are the way you are."

We went back to our quarters and I changed into my standard issue RuComm kakis and white shirt. Winn smiled at me when I stepped out of my room.

"Brilliant. Back to being defiant, no longer trying to be Captain Rostron's 'good officer'. I think he'll buy your change of heart."

"I'm afraid."

"I know you are. It's OK to let Gerbrandij see your fear. He'll assume it's because you're worried about your idiot husband."

I nodded. My idiot husband. *He* wasn't worried, but damn if he didn't still need me to rescue him.

"Winona? Will you pray for me?"

She adjusted my collar that I knew was already perfect. "Yeah, I'm doing it right now. Don't lie to him, just don't tell him all of the truth. He'll believe you. And Mala Dusa? Don't do anything stupid."

I grinned at her. "Never do. See you for dinner?"

She nodded. "But not the shipyard cafeteria again. Meet me on the *Orageux*. I'll ask *Storm* to make something special."

I left our quarters and glanced at the ceiling. "Damen, where is Colonel Gerbrandij?"

"The Colonel is in his quarters," the shipyard AI answered.

"Can you guide me there?"

"Follow the white ball, Lieutenant."

I knocked gently on his door, ignoring the call button. I wanted my entrance to seem timid. I could hear the sound of voices arguing. The wall shook with the force of the hand that slammed against the interior keypad and the door slid open.

Gerbrandij face went from anger, passed through surprise, and settled on satisfaction as his brain processed me standing in front of him wearing standard RuComm attire. "Lieutenant Holloman. What additional demands do you have for us?"

"None, sir. I've come to ask for your help."

"Now she wants my help?"

"Not her. Me. I need my husband back and what my Captain is doing will get him killed." I maintained eye contact and let the tears I'd been fighting all day fill my eyes. "Please. Will you get him back for me?"

He stepped to the side, let go of the door jamb, and waited for me to enter. "Come in, Lieutenant. Let's talk about what might be possible."

"Thank you, sir."

I stepped into the room, Major Zweig glaring at me with each step I took. I nodded to him, but his expression didn't change. The Colonel's aide, Captain van der Vlis, never looked up from his display pad.

"Sit," the Colonel pointed at a small sofa. I sat on the edge of the cushion, feeling vulnerable.

Gerbrandij sat in an overstuffed chair opposite me and crossed his legs, seeming completely at ease. "As I told Captain Rostron, we are doing all that we can to recover Captain Coleridge."

I nodded. "There is always more that can be done, isn't that true?"

His eyes crinkled with his smile. "Did they teach you that at the Academy?"

"It may have been mentioned."

"And there might be some truth in it. Extra effort requires extra resources. Your Captain seems unwilling to provide us with what we need."

"I think I can help you with that. I can put whatever you need into our plans. Just tell me what you really need and I'll convince her it's critical. Let me be your intermediary to bring her back to the table. She knows that her superiors will never allow the current situation to persist. She's bluffing. She told us that she'll have to restart talks soon anyway or General Kimmel will replace her."

"Good to know. What, exactly, would you have us do to find Captain Coleridge?"

"I don't know, sir. Our Marines are tied up with their protection and training duties for the Provisional Government, so they can't do anything for him. I've tried to contact General Kimmel's office, but they won't talk to me. Something about my needing to stay within the chain of command."

"I can appreciate that."

"Yes, sir. I've tried to reach my mom, but she's on Earth and it will be *days* before I can expect a response."

"Your mother? How could she be of help?"

"She's done some work for both RuComm and the Department of Cultural Intelligence in the past, so she has friends. I don't even know if the DCI has a presence on Kastanje, but I'm desperate. If nothing else, she can push to get you the resources you need. I just need Sam back." I blinked hard, letting tears fall across my cheeks. Colonel Gerbrandij stood and came back with a pack of tissues for me.

I could see Captain van der Vlis out of the corner of my eye. He was typing hard on the display pad that I was certain must be connected to the Kastanje intel network, tracing my name back through open source Union records to whatever their own covert organizations had logged. I could tell when he found it. His pale face somehow managed to lose color. Mom has that effect on people.

"Mala Dusa, if you can get your Captain talking to us, and if she will agree to provide what we need to improve our surveillance network, there may be a chance–"

"Colonel, you need to see this."

He turned, irritated by the interruption. "It can keep."

"No, sir. It really can't."

Van der Vlis brought the pad and handed it to the Colonel. I waited, sniffling into a tissue. I waited to see if the Colonel was the monster Sam, Winona, and my Captain believed him to be, or if he was a decent man doing his best to serve his people.

He smiled and gave the pad back to his aide. His eyes had changed when he looked back at me. "Where were we? You were saying that your mother is still on Earth?"

"Yes, sir, I'm certain of it. We always stay in touch, or as much as we can this far away with the comm lag."

He thought about it for a moment. "I'm sorry." He stood, seeming to have come to a decision. "Something has come up that requires my immediate attention back in Oranjestad. I wish you could come with me so we could continue this discussion. I think I may be able to help you. We've reconstructed some of the events from this morning, and we have some promising leads that I'd like to tell you about."

"I'll go with you." I stood and took a step toward him. "If your offer was serious, sir, I'll go with you."

He paused, looking down into my eyes. "Now how could I explain that to your Captain? She'll accuse me of kidnapping another of her officers, and then where would I be?"

I pretended to be thinking about it for a few seconds. "Well...maybe you could tell her that you need me to complete the work Sam was doing restoring the medical AIs? It's sort of a humanitarian necessity, isn't it? I was helping him, so I know what needs to be done. Make her think that there's no way for her to refuse without damaging her own career, that women and babies are dying because it's not fixed."

He grinned. "You are a shrewd one, aren't you?"

"No, sir. Just desperate. I believe you're my only hope of seeing Sam alive again."

"How will you be able to help me get the resources I need if you're down there fixing the medical AIs?"

"It won't take more than a day or two. You saw me on Costrano's Redoubt, you know I can do it. And Lieutenant Killdeer will be here while I'm gone. With her, it's like I can be in two places at once. Please, let me go with you."

He touched my cheek. "You are a very valuable woman, Lieutenant. What am I to make of you?"

I lowered my voice. "If you can get him back? Pretty much anything you want."

# CHAPTER 17

# KASTANJE

Colonel Gerbrandij started to send a request to Captain Rostron asking for my temporary presence to finish Sam's work, but then changed his mind. He sent her a notification instead, telling her that he was taking me to the surface and would return me when the medical AIs were all functioning. He had chuckled when he hit send. Major Zweig hadn't been as amused. His voice was soft and his accent thick, but his meaning and his worry were clear.

"That may be a mistake, Colonel. You know you need Rostron very much. There is little to gain by pushing her more toward anger."

"I've played nice for the past week, Arni, and see what it got me?"

"Her reaction to the kidnapping. Tell me that you would play nice with her if it was I that had gone astray, and her that you believed could find me."

He patted the Major on the back and turned to me. "Run, Lieutenant. I'll give you five minutes to gather what you need. If you aren't standing at the shuttle when we arrive, I'll leave your ass here."

"Yes, sir," I responded. I had a fleeting look at Major Zweig's disapproving headshake as I sprinted from the room.

Winona's response was much more visceral when I arrived panting at our quarters.

"That was quick. Is he chasing you?" She glanced out into the passageway, ready to bar the door.

"Leaving with him for Oranjestad in five minutes." I grabbed my duffle and stuffed in one of each type of uniform, underwear, and my toothbrush. I could print anything else I needed. "Gotta run."

"The hell you are. That is *not* the plan. You're supposed to wait for the Captain to approve it."

"Improvising. Saving Sam," I panted, still out of breath.

She grabbed both of my shoulders, hard. "Stop. Think." Her eyes looked into mine and she sighed. "Your arm is not fully healed. My smudging kit is back on the *Esprit Orageux* and there are Puca down there. In a week, we'll be back where we started. Or worse."

"It will only take me a couple of days to fix the AIs, and Colonel Gerbrandij, well, I think he already knows who has Sam and where he is. I'll have my Sam and we'll both be back here before my arm falls off, OK?"

"No, it's not OK. But I can't stop you without using the hypospray again. Let me give you something to take with you."

She searched through a drawer in her room and came back with a small, flat box. "Hannah gave me these when I volunteered to follow you on this great adventure. A sort of graduation present, I guess. I think she wanted me to use them on you." She pulled off the lid, revealing a thin sheet of paper with five black dots, each one a couple of millimeters in diameter.

"What are they?"

"Touch one with your fingertip to activate it. It will stick to your finger and then attach itself to whatever you touch next. It keys to your comm pin automatically."

"Bugs?"

"Bugs. You had better plant one on the Colonel first chance you get. That way you can try to escape when they decide to kill you. The bug will stay active for about twelve hours and has a range of two to three kilometers, farther if it can find a network to talk to."

"Thanks." I slid the box into my pocket, turned to leave, and then stopped, my back still to her. "Winona, I know you're scared. If anything happens...well, it won't be your fault."

"I know that."

"I love you, Winn. This is my best chance of saving Sam. I have to go down there."

"Gerbrandij is a monster, Duse."

"I still don't think so, but if he is, I'll get the proof we need to end him."

"You better run before I stop you."

I ran.

My display pad chimed at me before I had gone a dozen steps.

"Read it to me."

The pad whispered in my ear. "Message from Captain Rostron. "God Speed. Don't die." Would you like to reply?"

"Yes. Tell her..." I paused. I wanted to tell her I was sorry, but she hated that. I wanted to say thank you, but she hated that too. "Tell her that I will do my duty."

"Message sent."

Colonel Gerbrandij and his aide were waiting at the bottom of the landing ramp. "You really did run."

"Yes, sir." I pushed damp hair out of my eyes. "This is important to me. Is Major Zweig joining us?"

"Already on board, but he and Captain van der Vlis will be returning to the shipyard later tonight. I received a message from Captain Rostron requesting that we resume our talks tomorrow afternoon. I told her that the Major would represent me while I oversee the recovery of her medical officer. That seemed to please her. I wish I knew if her pleasure was due to my efforts to recover Captain Coleridge, or not being across the table from her for the next couple of days."

"I think you know why it makes *me* happy." I put my hand on his chest, giving him my best grateful-to-the-point-of-tears smile. I hoped he wouldn't notice the tiny black dot clinging to the lapel of his black and gray uniform jacket.

"It's the right thing to do, and between you and your Captain, you haven't left me with much choice."

The shuttle was set up with a main cabin with twenty seats, and a walled off section up front with a small door. Colonel Gerbrandij made sure I was comfortable, told me to enjoy the one-hour drop into Oranjestad, and then disappeared into the front cabin. All I saw through the door was a quick glimpse of a conference table, four chairs, and one unhappy Major.

The shuttle shuddered as the shipyard shoved us out into open space and there was a slight wobble as we passed out of its artificial gravity field. I closed my eyes, listened to their meeting, and my world unraveled.

"Well, you have her, Pieter. What will you do with her now?" Major Zweig sounded like he already knew the answer to that question, and didn't like it.

"Still stuck on that, Arni? I know you disapprove, but what choice did their Captain leave me? First, that ridiculous show of anger, then the meek, desperate Lieutenant knocking on my door. I've taken her, as you say. They are such amateurs. I keep looking for some hidden play, but I don't think there is one. She sacrificed a perfectly good knight for no reason. This will be to our advantage, you'll see. The Lieutenant will fix the AIs for us, making us heroes to the public, and now their Captain is down to just herself and her dark witch with the eyes that see too much."

"A knight. Is that what this one is to you?"

"Knight, bishop, rook, what does it matter? More than a pawn. Her friend Killdeer is the queen in this game, but a weak one. Two fresh from the Academy Lieutenants and a line officer eager to be anywhere but here. That's what we have up against us. Her Marine strike force is in garrison and out of the picture. You should be breathing easy. We'll get what we need."

"In your head, she is a knight. I remember sitting at your home drinking your beer while you taught Felicity to play chess. She was fourteen, maybe. That's what you called her, and she liked that, being your knight. Flick would be about the same age as that Lieutenant, wouldn't she, and about the same build, like her mother. If they had let them live."

"Arni, you don't want to go there. That's not what this is about."

"Isn't it? The Walvis faction took them and, in front of your eyes, killed them. The government was powerless. The separatists gave you vengeance and you gave them your heart. Maybe now you are looking for absolution."

"That was a long time ago."

"Not so long. It twists you; I see it in your eyes. You will save this young woman's beau and send them on their way. That is what I think you will do."

"You are still the romantic, even after all that we've been through together. Our best intel is that her husband is with the Utrecht, healing the wounds we inflicted on them last week. Let me tell you how we'll do this. We start by letting Lieutenant Holloman do her work at the hospital, which should only take her a day or two, since she really is quite brilliant. After that, we will publicize her success as an example of KDF effectiveness in restoring public services. We'll let her enjoy a few days of fame, media interviews, and glowing profiles in the press."

"*Ja*, it would be better if she were very attractive. The days are still dark, and the people could use a pretty girl to admire. Hero worship is good for morale. But you plan to be standing with her in the spotlight, so maybe you are the hero?"

"Too much could go wrong doing it that way. A knight must be sacrificed if the game is to be won. The Utrecht will kill her, or so it will seem. A brutal, violent death. The public will be shocked and demand immediate justice. When the Provisional Government proves itself unable to take quick, definitive action, I will lead a joint KDF and Union strike team to eliminate the Utrecht. We know where they are, there just hasn't been the political will to take them out. Captain Coleridge's death will be a tragic footnote, and the public will welcome the KDF as the new, de facto government. We can eliminate or absorb the other factions at our leisure as we consolidate authority."

It was a long time before Major Zweig answered. "You say it, but where is your heart? Not there, I think."

"You're right, my friend, I hate it. I *see* the path, and know it is what I should do, but I don't want to kill her. It's strange, considering how many innocents have died for us to get this far. But we must focus on the end game. Kastanje needs order restored and there are millions of lives in the balance. The people are hungry and desperate. They are looking for strong leadership. The government in Oranjestad is too weak to eliminate the factions and we've sacrificed too many good men and women to turn away now. A better world for all the people is so close. It will take only a little more blood, a little more pain, and then we can start to rebuild."

"You would sacrifice this knight to reach your goal, Pieter?"

Colonel Gerbrandij answered, speaking so softly that I had trouble hearing him. "She is not pretty, not like my Flick, but her eyes are the same. There is a playfulness in them, the same mix of innocence and defiance. And the way her mouth turned down while she was begging for her husband's life? She looked just like her." He sighed. "Why does she have to remind me of Flick, Arni? I thought I had let go of her years ago."

"You should ask God that question, but I don't think you will like His answer."

"I'm not in the habit of talking to God anymore. I have a duty..."

"*Ja.* You have a duty. Did you know she is pregnant? Her friend told me after one of our meetings."

"No, I didn't know. We will make sure the press knows. Between that and the Utrecht kidnapping her husband, she will be quite the sympathetic character. A young, brave, Union and RuComm officer, struck down while trying to help the people of Kastanje. Her death will be a sensation. Perhaps we should erect a statue of her when this is all over."

"You can be a thoroughgoing bastard when you want to be, Pieter."

"Up there at the shipyard, especially the last few days, it was like I was starting to forget what was needed. It comes back to me as we near home. It's like I can hear it in my head again, and the doubts start to fade."

His voice changed, becoming sharper and more commanding. "Push hard on their Captain tomorrow. We need to finish the planet wide surveillance system and configure the AI to drive it. It's not any different from what they're running on Earth right now, so she should be willing to approve it. Give her the same lie the government on Earth tells their own people if she gets stubborn, tell her that it's just for the current state of emergency."

"An emergency that will never end."

"Lieutenant Holloman would have been ideal to set the AI up for us. A pity she'll be cold in her grave by then, but that's the role she must play. We're going to have to move fast to consolidate our gains after she's dead. Her mother is bound to show up demanding answers, and our intel on Ms. Weldon paints her as a thoroughgoing bitch if there ever was one."

"Yes, sir. I will get it done for you."

"That didn't sound like your heart was in it, Arni."

"Have I ever let you down, sir?"

"Never."

My fingers were shaking as I put an encrypted wrapper around the recording I'd made. I did it three times hoping one would get through. Three different wrappers, one for *Storm*, one for my Captain, and one for Winona. Winona had told me to use the bugs so that I'd know when they planned to kill me. I hadn't expected it to happen at all. It had taken less than thirty minutes.

My display pad told me that the ionizing layer created by our entry into Kastanje's atmosphere was delaying transmission. I kept refreshing the status, waiting, listening to Colonel Gerbrandij and Major Zweig reminiscing about growing up together, time in school and the KDF, sounding like any old military friends.

Monsters. Maybe they hadn't always been. Maybe there was still a good man inside the Colonel, I was certain of it, but there wasn't going to be time for me to find him. I planned to run as soon as I was away from the aerospace port. There was no way that I was going to stay in Sam's old quarters at the hospital, never mind that my watch and display pad had already been keyed for the doors. I would be safer sleeping in an alley somewhere. The Medical AIs would have to remain broken, because fixing them would be a death sentence.

The shuttle settled onto the pad at 15:15 local time and my messages still showed queued waiting for a connection. I tapped them again. And again. And...

"Did you have a pleasant trip?"

I didn't look up. Tap. Nothing. Tap. "Trying to send a message to Captain Rostron to let her know I've arrived and that I'm safe."

"It's the thunderstorms. The thickness of the clouds and the amount of moisture in them is attenuating your signal. It happens a lot this time of year. Keep the message queued and it should make it out eventually."

"Thunderstorms?" I forced myself to look at him. Kind brown eyes regarded me, looking worried and a little sad. He should be sad. Murderer.

"A line of heavy thunderstorms is crossing the city."

"Raining. I don't have an umbrella, just my uniform jacket."

"They'll clear out in an hour or two and then your message will go through. It's still warm, almost thirty degrees and one hundred percent humidity, so you aren't likely to freeze to death. I'll have my car take you directly to the hospital so you can settle in and speak to the rest of your team. Can you run fast?"

I swallowed hard. "Yes. Why?"

"You'll need to cross a few meters to get inside because of the security barricades. It won't be bad. Why don't we plan on meeting tomorrow for dinner? That will give me time to find out what we're doing about Captain Coleridge and you time to work on the AI. I'll pick you up at 20:00."

So normal, so natural. If I hadn't been listening to his conversation, I'd have thought him a compassionate, caring host, almost a friend. I nodded in agreement, not knowing what else to do. I was still planning to run as soon as I was free of him.

"Good." He took my bag for me, and I followed meekly by his side. His aide and Major Zweig stayed with the ship, preparing to return to the shipyard. My breathing was coming in spasms, slow inhalation, sharp, hard exhalation. My fight or flight reflex was in solid flight mode and my eyes were flicking side to side trying to find a safe exit.

Colonel Gerbrandij chuckled when we stepped outside. "Feel that heat." He tugged on his uniform. "Already sticky. Summer in Oranjestad. You'd learn to love it if you lived here long enough."

I resisted the urge to whimper. There was a chime from my pocket. At least one of my messages had made it out.

The Colonel heard it too. "See? I told you it would go through eventually. Now your Captain knows that you're safe."

I got into the car with him when it arrived. It was a black, heavy looking thing, with narrow windows, and dented and cracked bodywork.

"Not the prettiest transportation in the capital, but it might well be the safest." We accelerated away from the curb, the car's AI in control. "It's been hit by buried explosives, flaming liquids, and small arms fire." He grinned at me. "We call it 'The Womb' for the way it carries us in comfort and safety."

"Yes, sir. Those days are past?"

"Almost, Lieutenant. If they were gone completely, your husband would be sitting here with us. If the Union will help us finish the job, the two of you will be reunited and maybe I'll get a new car."

*Reunited*, I thought, *in death*. I couldn't hide the shiver that went through me.

"You're afraid."

"Have you ever been married?" I asked, knowing the answer.

"Yes. For a time. She died along with my daughter. Part of me died with them."

"Sam and I fell in love when I was sixteen. We waited. We waited for me to be old enough. We waited for me to finish the Academy and to get my commission. We waited all that time. We've been married thirty-six days, most of it spent on separate ships, unable to talk to each other."

I locked eyes with him, anger pushing the fear out of me and making my voice steady. "I will kill anyone who threatens him or tries to keep us apart. If you loved your wife, then you know exactly how I feel, and you know I will do it."

The corners of his mouth twisted into a tight smile. "Watching you provide economic analysis and doing technical planning, and then the way you were in my quarters and on board the shuttle, I had almost forgotten what I felt watching the recording of you ending Artem Costrano's life. Yes, Lieutenant, I know you will do it."

He turned away and looked out his window at the buildings we were passing. "I love this part of the city. Even on a rainy Sunday afternoon, look at the life on the street. People trying to enjoy themselves for a time. There, that restaurant there, the one that looks like nothing. Did you see it? Best pannenkoeken on the planet."

"Is that where we're going for dinner? I've never had pannenkoeken."

"If you like." His head tipped and then he shook it.

"Is something wrong?"

"No, just second guessing myself. Something I rarely do. Before we meet for dinner tomorrow, I'd like you to consider what Kastanje needs in order to rebuild–"

"I've been doing that all week."

"– and what role you could play. Not just as an engineer or starship architect."

The car pulled up to the security barrier in front of the hospital. It was raining hard enough to hear it pounding on the armored roof. He was offering me a third option, something other than running for my life or being a corpse. I could sell out to the power-hungry son-of-a-bitch and help him turn the planet into an authoritarian, fascist state. The anger that had been sustaining me was starting to fade and I knew I'd be shaking again soon.

"I will think about it, sir." I got out of the car with my bag and ran the twenty meters to the door, splashing through puddles while the warm, heavy rain soaked through my jacket, sticking my undershirt to my skin. I stopped beneath the awning and turned. The car was still there and I knew he was watching me. I raised my hand to wave and the car pulled quickly away.

As my anger faded, Sam flowed in, trying to reassure me. "Yeah, Sam," I mumbled to myself. "I know you're *just fine*."

Corporal Kim Hyun-Ok was waiting for me in the lobby wearing a white lab coat over her Union tan and brown uniform. Her hair was tied back in a messy ponytail. I'd never seen it that way before. She was prettier than I remembered. I'm sure I looked like a scrawny drowned rat. She saluted me and I returned it.

"Captain Rostron said you were coming, ma'am. I've been waiting for you."

"You don't have a towel, do you?" I took off my cap and shook my head, scattering water everywhere.

She stepped back, looking confused. "No. No towel, ma'am. Maybe in one of the treatment rooms. You can change later. We're having a crisis."

"Yeah, me too. Is there a back way out of the hospital? Where did you leave shuttle six that brought you down here? I need to get back to the Hoog Schelde shipyard as quickly and quietly as possible. I need your help, and you and Sergeant Hurtado should come with me."

"Um, no. We're having a crisis. You have to fix the neonatal AI, ma'am."

"Um, no," I replied, imitating her voice. "If I fix that AI I'm going to *die*."

"There's a baby dying right now. He's only a few days old and he has a congenital diaphragmatic hernia. It should have been fixed before birth, now he has respiratory failure."

"There are no doctors here?"

"They depend on the machines for delicate surgery like this. They'll try, but the baby probably won't make it. Maybe two days if you fail, then we'll lose him."

"If *I* fail?"

"Yes, you. You're good at this sort of thing, right?"

I could hear it in her voice, the desperation. Marine Corporal Kim, Certified Medical Technician, had bonded with the tiny new life struggling to breathe. The Corps had trained her to treat combat injuries efficiently and dispassionately, but not little babies. "Is there somewhere we can talk without anyone listening?"

"Sure." I followed her into a small room outfitted as a chapel. "The Hospital Chaplin insists that no listening devices be installed in here. I think he has a jammer running too." She sat down next to me. "I'll bring you anything you need, ma'am. A towel, a blanket, fresh clothes, anything. Hell, I'll blow warm air on the back of your neck if that will help get that AI working faster. Captain Coleridge was getting close before he was taken."

"I'm going to get him back." I dumped my bag upside down, looking for my spare Union uniform.

"Yes, ma'am. I know he loves you."

"Turn around. I'm going to change."

She turned and I stripped.

"Ma'am, why did you say that you'll die if you fix the AI?"

"Colonel Gerbrandij plans to have me murdered after I fix the AIs and blame it on one of the factions. He thinks it will help him gain political power."

"He *told* you that?"

"Not exactly. He's taking me to dinner at 20:00 tomorrow to discuss alternatives to killing me, I think. You can turn back around now."

"How can you sit across a table from him after that? I'd kick him in the balls and run like hell, assuming I didn't just put one between his eyes."

"Both of those are good options. I'd hoped to be back at Hoog Schelde tonight. I guess that's not going to happen. Where can I access the AI?"

"Follow me, ma'am. Do you want to see little Evert first?"

"Why not? If I pull this off, he's going to owe me one."

Evert Machiel Kornhauser wasn't doing well. His tiny body was working hard trying to get enough air. The tubes and machines attached to him were helping, but it looked like a losing battle. A woman was sleeping in a chair next to him, with her own set of tubes attached to her arm.

"His mom?" I whispered.

"Elisabeth. She's not doing too well either. Lost a lot of blood giving birth to the little guy and she hasn't left his side since. Her husband's working one of the orbital mines. Lucky to have a job, the way she tells it."

A medical attendant stopped by, nodded to us, and then checked the patch on Elisabeth's arm that showed her pulse, blood oxygen and other stats. He did the same for Evert, not looking happy.

"OK. Take me to a terminal and let's see what kind of mess Sam left for me."

"He's pretty good, ma'am. I was helping him, and like I said, we were close to getting it up."

"Uh huh." I sat at the terminal and tapped the overview. Red icons several layers deep greeted me. "Yuck." I tapped the diagnostics tree and waited for the display to respond.

My pad chimed, and chimed again. "My messages finally went out. The rain must have passed on by. I can't wait to find out what Captain Rostron's reaction will be and what she'll do with me." I unrolled the pad next to the AI terminal.

"The Captain doesn't know?"

"She does now."

"Wow. I think this is the first time that I've known something before she knew it."

I smiled, sympathizing while I tapped deeper into the red icons until I found green. "Finally. This looks better." I dug deeper. "Do you and Sergeant Hurtado want to go out to dinner with the Colonel and me tomorrow night? I might need an armed escort."

"My Sergeant is on night shift. He's asleep right now and comes on duty at 19:00. I should stay here working with the medical staff, but it's usually quiet in the evenings."

"That's OK. I don't think he sees me as much more than a political tool. I hope. I should be safe for now."

"I'll go if you want me to. I'm not afraid to punch a KDF officer if he needs punching. I've punched officers before."

I looked up from the display at her. There was a no-nonsense fierceness about her. I could imagine her doing it. "Captain Coleridge. Did he ever need punching?"

She made a face. "The Captain's a gentleman. I don't think he knows how to be anything else."

I blushed, knowing how *not* true that was when he had me alone. "Thank you, Corporal. Let's see if we can make some of these icons green tonight."

At 16:35, my display pad dinged at me with an encrypted reply from Captain Rostron. *Reviewed recording with Lieutenant Killdeer. Follow your existing orders. Will forward to sector command when our interplanetary comms are restored.*

I showed the display to Corporal Kim.

"Looks like *Esprit Orageux* is having comms problems too. What were your orders?"

"Don't die."

"Those are good orders, ma'am. You should obey them."

# CHAPTER 18

# PANNENKOEKEN

My Samuel is not the idiot Winona says he is, but he's a biologist, not an engineer. The Captain never should have sent him to try to fix a FUBAR'd AI; that's my job. And he *is* an idiot when it comes to risking his life for something or someone he thinks is important. That's a big part of why I love him so much.

The core code inside a medical AI isn't that complex. Once I had the foundation straightened out, the rest started to slowly fall into place, branch after branch of cascading green icons.

"Do you see how I'm doing this, Kim?"

"It looks like it's healing itself."

"Yep. Isolate each subroutine, fix the supervisor code if it's pooched, usually just by reloading it from the onboard archive, but sometimes you have to be creative. Then let it diagnose and repair everything downstream. We'll do that for each personality silo and then reintegrate everything back together. Maybe eighteen or twenty hours work if we're lucky. This is easier than the FAC back at Costrano's Redoubt. No weapons systems, no thrusters or power schemas..."

"We're going to save the little guy, aren't we."

"We're going to try. It's not fixed yet."

I was still working on it when Sergeant Hurtado joined us at 18:30, coffee cup in hand, looking well rested and ready to start his day. And I was still working at 19:30 when Corporal Kim brought me dinner.

At 20:30 I told them, "I'm going to take a quick shower to wake myself up a bit and then we can work a few more hours."

"More coffee, ma'am?" Hurtado was on his fourth cup. It didn't seem to be affecting him at all. He had the perfect calm, solid demeanor of a seasoned medic, as if nothing could ever bother him.

"No. Thanks anyway, Sergeant. I'll be fine." I was already shaking, and I didn't want to admit it to him or Corporal Kim. The last thing I needed was more caffeine roaring though my body.

"Corporal, I know you're off duty, but if you and Sergeant Hurtado want to work on the AI while I'm gone, that would be great."

"Without you?"

"You can do it. You understand what I was doing. See what you can do with the next silo."

"What if I break it?"

"It's already broken, Corporal, you can't hurt it."

"Yes, ma'am."

I held my watch up to the keypad outside Sam's room and the door slid open. The room smelled like Sam. It didn't stink; there was just the slight scent of him. I picked up his pillow and buried my face in it, nudging his emotions. He answered, and it was like a warm hug. I talked to him while I showered, even though he couldn't hear me.

"When this is over, Sam, you and I are going somewhere far away, just the two of us." I scrubbed my hair and let the warm water pound the suds from my head. "Maybe Winn and Kal too if they want to come. What was the name of that planet you surveyed, back when RuComm was still in the exploration and colonization business, and you were still a biologist?" I cleaned my face and under my arms. How had I gotten so sweaty and smelly? "Kempner something, I forget the number. Let's go there and build a house next to the ocean." I washed down my legs and between my toes, and then rinsed everything for a long time, not wanting to get out of the shower. "You told me how pretty it was, watching the moons set over the water and the sounds those bird-things make when they settle themselves in for the night. That's where we'll go, OK?" I shut the water off and sighed.

I dried myself, put on my spare RuComm white shirt, tan pants, and uniform jacket with my rank on it.

I worked until I fell asleep in my chair, finishing two more personality silos and two and a half cups of coffee along the way. Sergeant Hurtado had to guide me back to Sam's room sometime after 25:30. I brushed my teeth, stripped off my clothes, and snuggled into the Sam-smelling bed. He and Merrimac haunted my dreams.

Merrimac's plan to keep us together and alive was still on track, but I woke up crying anyway. Something in his plan for me was horrifying, something I had chosen willingly and now wanted to escape.

I was back at the medical AI console at 06:00, coffee and a hard roll in hand. Corporal Kim was already there, puzzling over error messages. She had a plate of scrambled eggs, bacon, and toast perched on her lap while she tapped icons.

"Can I get you something more to eat, ma'am? The cafeteria here isn't too bad."

I shook my head. "No, thank you. Maybe once I wake up." She looked alert and beautiful. I'd been afraid to look at my face in the mirror and had combed my hair with my fingers as I walked out the door.

*No Escape*, Merrimac had told me in my dream. *Be brave, Little Soul.*

Little Evert Kornhauser was worse when Corporal Kim and I went to see him at 16:30. We had three silos rebuilding themselves and needed a break.

She touched his toes with one finger. "Monday's more than half gone. Tomorrow afternoon they're going to operate on him. The doctor said he'd be too weak to even attempt it if we wait any longer. Are we going to be ready before that?"

"Absolutely. Two more silos and then we'll reintegrate." I looked at my watch. "I'm going to be with Colonel Gerbrandij by then, but you can do it. Tell Doctor Franzen to be ready to operate tonight."

"Yes, ma'am." She moved her finger up to his hand and he grabbed her fingertip, holding on even though he was asleep. "Lieutenant? I'm sorry that I misjudged you."

"Oh? How's that?"

"When you first came on board, I thought I'd never seen anyone so out of place. I was wrong. You belong, you just look a little weird."

"Thanks. Shall we get back to work?"

"I will, but not you. You're going to go take a nap."

"Is that an order, Corporal?" I grinned at her.

"Off the record. One woman to another. I can finish the neonatal AI; you're a good teacher. You sleep and then freshen up. You need something from Colonel Gerbrandij, and I want Captain Coleridge back too. A man with the Colonel's reputation, well..."

"I see. I appreciate your concern, but we have work to do."

"I can get Sergeant Hurtado to help take you to your room if I need to."

"I suspect you could handle me on your own."

"Thank you, ma'am."

I didn't like admitting it, but she was right. "I'll rest if you promise to fetch me if you have the slightest problem."

"Oh, I will. We have to save this little guy."

It was raining when I woke up at 19:00, another thunderstorm moving across the city. I showered, changed clothes, and spent some time using the mirror. At 20:00, I was ready to meet Colonel Gerbrandij for dinner and whatever else I needed to do to rescue Sam.

I was staring at the sky when the Colonel's car stopped next to the security barricade. The clouds and rain had moved on, but the warm humidity remained. I could hear little creatures calling to each other. Life loves warm, wet, and sticky. I let the Colonel wait for a moment, unable to tear my eyes away from the sky, almost unable to blink. Five of the asteroids that Kastanje was mining were visible, with a sixth just rising over the black outline of mountains to the east.

"Come along, Lieutenant, you can stargaze later. I'm hungry." The man calling to me from the car was planning to end my life in a few days. I should have been terrified, but I wasn't. He was smiling at me, amused.

"Yes, sir. Coming. Your night sky," I pointed. "It's kind of amazing."

"Yes, it is," he answered without looking up. "I used to lie on my back on warm nights like this and watch it for hours."

"When you were little?"

"When I was younger."

I got into the back of the car with him. There were two men in the front wearing gray uniforms. Colonel Gerbrandij apologized to me for their presence.

"A silly precaution. The Provisional Government thinks I need protection to walk around the city that I've known all my life. It's easier to let them do their jobs though, than to argue." He shrugged and reached over the seat to pat their shoulders. "A boring night for you boys, but you'll have a fine dinner out of it, *niet waar*?"

"Yes, sir," they answered in accented English.

Fourth Street Cafe, which had looked like nothing from the outside, looked more like nothing on the inside. Faded signs had hard copy images of the food, and generations of passing feet had scuffed and worn down the floor. What it lacked in ambiance it more than made up for in aroma. I knew instantly that I was going to love pannenkoeken, whatever they were. Colonel Gerbrandij led me past the front counter where patrons were placing their orders, and through a narrow doorway. We sat at a table near the rear emergency exit, at least that's what I assumed *nooduitgang* meant when paired with a crude graphic of a person running. He pulled my chair out for me, forcing me to sit with my back to the front door. There were twenty tables, all but a few of them occupied. Our escorts sat on the other side of the restaurant near the entrance.

"What would you like in your pannenkoeken?"

I shrugged. "They look like pancakes and smell kind of like pizza. Ham and cheese?"

"A safe choice."

"It will be the first safe thing I've done all week. Ham and cheese, definitely."

He excused himself to place our order and I whispered softly, "*Storm*, are you back with me now that the rain is gone?"

"Rain is not much of a problem for me. It is the overlapping jamming fields on the surface maintained by the various factions, the Provisional Government, and the KDF that I need to punch through. I've been able to track you most of the time and I listen to almost everything you say."

"So, the Colonel is lying to me about the rain. Thanks, *Storm*. Wait. Does Captain Rostron listen to me too?"

"I provide her with summaries. She says that she's heard that Kempner twenty-seven is beautiful. There's a small colony there now and they've renamed it Chéng Nuò. Lieutenant Killdeer says you're an idiot, but I think she still loves you. Also, Corporal Kim has completed repairs to the Medical AI and Evert Kornhauser is now in surgery."

"When this is over, I'm going to learn Chinese, go to Chéng Nuò, and no one will ever listen to me again. Just you wait and see."

The Colonel placed his hand on my shoulder as he squeezed past to reach his chair, making me jump. "Order is in. Were you talking to someone?"

"My ship. Status check." I pulled my hair back and touched the comm pin.

"Ah. They are so small these days. Clipped to the top of your ear like that, it looks more like a pretty decoration than a way to communicate. Your ship listens to you all the time, doesn't she?"

"She does." I shrugged. "There's always an AI listening. It's part of being in the Aerospace Force."

"Part of being in the Union, you mean. I've been to Earth a couple of times. Every public building, every street and park, even in my hotel. It's what keeps you safe. Kastanje didn't have that, the Separatists were able to grow unnoticed, and now the factions keep us in chaos for the same reason. It's why I need your help."

"The heightened surveillance is because of the reunification war. We'll go back to the way it was once the wars are over. People don't like being watched or listened to, even if it's just an AI doing it."

"Do you really believe that? Any of it? Your government watches everyone because they want to protect you. They'll *never* stop doing it, and the people like it that way. Some people are hiding behind masks here now, making a show of wanting privacy, but that will fade quickly when they see bad actors being arrested, stability restored, and food on their tables."

"Is that what reunification is all about for you? You don't think people want the freedom to live without the government knowing their every move and their every thought?"

He laughed. "Try running for office promising freedom when the people are hungry and the roof over their heads is leaking, if they have a roof at all. You've only seen a small piece of Oranjestad. The heavy rain this week that inconveniences you is a misery for thousands, and probably killed more than a few in the last two days. If the Provisional Government doesn't take stronger action, the factions will. There will be war, house to house, street by street, and millions will die."

"You think you can stop it."

"I think I have to try. I know I need your help."

Our food arrived, along with a beer for the Colonel and a glass full of leaves for me. The food smelled wonderful. I picked up my glass and examined it. "Sir?"

"*Verse munt thee.* Fresh mint tea. Try it. It's better for you than this." He tapped his glass. "Or so I've heard." He glanced at my stomach.

I took a sip of tea and added a few drops of honey. "Six weeks as of yesterday. She's only made me throw up a few times so far. She's about this big." I held my fingers a centimeter apart. "I'm worried that I'm not a very good mother, though. I keep putting her life in danger. I don't have the right to do that."

"Having an adventurous mother can be risky." The Colonel finished his beer while we ate, and an older man stopped by to refill his glass. "Thank you, Carl."

"A pleasure seeing you in here again, Pieter. It's been years." He turned to stare at me, forehead showing deep wrinkles as he inspected me. "This can't be your daughter. She must be related to you, though. A niece visiting you, maybe? I see your wife's family in those eyes."

"No relation. Lieutenant Mala Dusa Holloman, Carl Hoffner, owner of this establishment."

"Sir." He took my hand, transferring some of the dusting of white flour from his fingers to mine. "Thank you for the pannenkoeken. They're really excellent."

"You're very kind." He seemed to notice my uniform for the first time, the lieutenant's bar on my collar next to the winged lion of Venice. "It's nice seeing off-worlders again. It gives hope to my heart."

I smiled, and he left us to take care of other customers. "He doesn't know about what happened to your family, does he."

"No. This was Felicity's favorite place for dinner. We came here often in those days. It was quick and cheap, and she loved it. Look around you at the people wearing their fine clothes to come here, enjoying a special night out that they probably can't afford. And Flick...I haven't been back here since." He was quiet while we finished eating and then he pushed back from the table.

"Let's walk. It's a pleasant night and the humidity in the air will do us good after all that time at the Hoog Schelde Yards."

My eyes were drawn to the string of asteroids above us once we were out on the sidewalk. "Is that the shipyard there?" I pointed.

"Five kilometers long by three wide. It's a marvel."

"I can almost see the trusses between the ways."

"Good eyes, but admiring the view is not why we're out here. Have you considered the question I asked you? I need someone to take the lead on central planning, the same as what you and Lieutenant Killdeer have been doing, but for me. I'll be blunt. I need someone with deep links to the Union that we can use to get us what we need. We'll start with the mining sector. It's always been the key to the wealth of Kastanje, and I want your help selecting which companies will get government contracts to rebuild and which will be shut down."

I laughed. "I'm not an economist or a politician. My dad's a geologist. You'd be better off talking to him. Don't you think you should let the owners of the businesses decide whom they want to work with and whom they want to sell to? That's not the government's job."

"The Academy stuffs it into your head and you believe it. Earth hasn't even pretended to follow those principles for a generation. Your naïveté is endearing, but it's your potential to get RuComm and Union support for us that I need. That, and your mother's friends. I can only hope it will be enough."

I chewed on my lip, my heart rate starting to climb. There were a few other people out on the street, enjoying the evening. A couple outside a bar across the street were lost in each other's arms and lips, the woman with her back to me was wearing a short red dress. Maybe they had been dancing. Approaching from a hundred meters away, a man out walking his dog was letting him sniff at each interesting spot on the sidewalk. A couple passed us, lost in conversation, their faces covered. I lowered my voice. "Where is my husband? Are you the ones holding him?" I felt for Sam as I asked the question, but he was blocking me again, solid this time. I could tell he was alive and conscious, nothing else.

"I wish I knew where he was. I'd drop him right in your lap if I thought it would help. We believe that he's in the Verbeek mineral belt, two hundred kilometers from here and about twenty-five hundred meters higher. The Utrecht Covenant is holding him somewhere in the mountains. You'd like the Utrecht. They think the way you do, that it's better to be free and starving than to have a government strong enough to take care of its citizens. You'd have to overlook their more violent tendencies though, like kidnapping your husband and killing an unarmed Handhaving officer. Help me, and I'll do everything I can to get him back for you."

I paused before replying, starting to understand that my continued existence was still very much in question. Sam was safe, that much I could feel. I wanted him back, but that might be more dangerous than leaving him where he was.

"Thank you for the offer, but I can't help you, other than by doing what my Captain orders me to do. I have to fulfill my duty to RuComm and the Union. Your neonatal and obstetrics AIs at the hospital are fixed and I should return to my ship. Tonight. Sam had almost finished the repairs before he was taken. I just had a few things to do, and Corporal Kim finished the work while we were at dinner." I glanced at my watch. "There's a newborn whose life is being saved while we're standing here talking."

"You're a hero." He voice was cold and flat when he said it, as if being a hero was forcing him to do something he didn't want to do.

"No, I'm not. Sam started it, Corporal Kim finished it, and she prepped it for its first use."

We started walking again, the two guards trailing a few meters back. "Maybe you *should* return to Hoog Schelde tonight. Corporal Kim. She's the Marine medic with the dark hair? Very young and attractive?"

I saw it on his face when I glanced up at him. He was going to spare me. Kim Hyun-Ok would be his hero for the media, until he had her slaughtered. The image of her lying dead in an alley somewhere filled me and I panicked. "You can't do that, sir."

"Do what?"

"You can't make her famous and do those photos and interviews with her to make her into a big media sensation. You can't use her to show how successfully reunification is going because of you and the KDF, and you can't murder her. You can't use her death to justify a military coup and then build a statue of her. You can't do any of those things." His eyes became Winona-sized while I babbled. "Colonel, I *will* stop you."

"Well, shit." He looked down at his uniform, running his hands along the lapels until he found the bug I'd put on him. He examined the small dot, and then grabbed the comm pin off my ear. I didn't try to stop him. He cracked the pin between his fingers and let it drop onto the sidewalk where he stomped on it, grinding the bits into the concrete.

"Costrano died because he underestimated you, and now here I am, repeating the same mistake. No more. Give me your display pad."

I took a step back from him, getting ready to run.

"You don't want to do that," he warned me. "You're probably faster than us, but you don't know the city and you can't outrun a bullet."

His guards had closed the distance and were now standing next to him, hands resting on their sidearms. The one closest to me pulled his weapon clear of the holster and moved the safety to the armed position before re-holstering it. I gave the Colonel my pad.

"Let's see who else you've told." He grabbed my hand and forced it onto the display to unlock it. He smiled as he scrolled down through the messages. "I like Captain Rostron. A good officer and a caring commander. She's been a positive influence on you. If you're smart and can control your wilder instincts, you might even be able to obey her final order and live through this."

His eyes moved from the messages back to me. I looked in his eyes, praying that fear wouldn't make me start shaking. I stood up straight with my shoulders back and tried to look brave and confident. He shuddered.

"I'm sorry, Lieutenant. This is not how this was supposed to happen. But I can see it *so* clearly, what I need to do to stop the carnage and make Kastanje what it once was. I don't know why you and your Captain can't see it too." He rolled up my display pad, slid it into his pocket and then pulled out his own pad and typed on it. He sighed when he was done, unhappy but determined.

"I *did* see it," I told him. "The creatures Costrano surrounded himself with, the ones that look like dogs, but aren't, they showed it to me. It's a trap. RuComm will never allow Kastanje to remain in the Union if you do what they're telling you to do. You will have traded one horror for another, one of your own making."

"You've seen them? How they can change? Sometimes like dogs, other times with big ears and looking like the herten that live in the mountains, like a deer. They don't like the rain." His voice had gone wispy.

The guards shifted uneasily, but I pressed on. "Yes, they call themselves Puca. I know them very well and they will destroy you if you let them." I put my hand against his cheek and he allowed it. "Step back from it, sir. I will help you with reunification, I'll do everything I can to help you restore Kastanje. Come back to the shipyard. We killed all the ones that were there. It will take time, but your mind will clear and–"

I was suddenly kneeling on the sidewalk with my hands pressing on the back of my head trying to keep my skull from exploding. The ringing in my ears was blocking almost everything else out.

"Sorry, Colonel. I think she was trying to hypnotize you or put a spell on you or something. Are you all right?"

"I'm fine. Get her up, soldier, before someone wonders what the hell we're doing to her."

He pulled me to my feet and my skull exploded into bright lights and pain.

"Can you open your eyes?"

I nodded weakly and managed to pry my eyelids apart.

"Good. I want you to see this. As your Captain mentioned, interplanetary comms from the shipyard, including from the *Esprit Orageux*, are down. Blocked by my order. I wanted to see how well Rostron could function without a link back to her Aerospace Force command structure. Now we'll never know."

He grabbed my chin and tipped my face to look at the sky. "Did you wonder why it took so long before we let you dock and why we tied you down all the way at the end of the yard? Look."

There was an expanding cloud of sparkles in the dark. My brain wanted there to be a sound, like fireworks, but of course it was silent. "The ship-yard. Destroyed?"

"Just *Esprit Orageux* and part of pier fourteen. And Captain Rostron and Lieutenant Killdeer."

My knees failed. I wanted to collapse and curl into a ball on the side-walk, but there where powerful arms holding me upright. "Winn. You killed Winona?" It came out more as a sob than a question.

"You killed her by sending her that message. Let's get you off the street and we'll talk about what comes next."

I blinked the tears away and cleared my mind. *My Winona. Gone.* There was a Puca hum inside me, coming from somewhere close by, full of dark joy. "I know what comes next, sir." I looked over my shoulder at the man holding my arms. I wanted to remember his face. "What are your names?"

"Van Diemen," the one who was holding me answered.

"Hetzer." He was shorter, with cruel blue eyes that seemed to be eager for what he thought was coming next.

"You can release me now. I won't run."

Van Diemen waited for Colonel Gerbrandij to nod and then he let me go.

I spun as quickly as I could and pulled van Diemen's sidearm from its holster. I pressed the trigger while I was doing it. I prayed that he hadn't keyed the grip to his hand alone, and that the shock of me shooting him would keep him from going for a backup weapon long enough for me to kill him. The round in the chamber was a solid slug and it tore a hole in his lower leg, the sound loud and unreal on the quiet street. He stumbled back, screaming in pain and anger. "God damned little bitch!"

My second shot hit his face from a meter away. He had loaded a plasma round at the top of the magazine and it ripped apart most of his head, sending steaming splatter against the windows of the shop behind him.

I dropped and rolled. Too slow, too slow. I had wasted a precious tenth of a second being horrified at what I'd done. I expected to be looking into the muzzle of Hetzer's weapon when I finished taking my position, assuming he didn't shoot me while I was trying to turn. That's what usually happened to me in the combat simulator at the Academy. I always died because I was too damn slow.

Hetzer was already down. Colin had ripped his throat open and his blood was running down the gutter where the dog had dragged him. Blood covered the fur on Colin's face and front legs, and he was standing next to the body, ears alert and tail wagging. Kal was three meters away, a civilian coat covering his uniform. The short-barreled rifle attached to his single point sling was pointing at Colonel Gerbrandij.

The Colonel had his hands on top of his head. "Great work, Lieutenant. You've condemned us to a hundred years of civil war. Are you going to ask the names of each of the thousands that will die in the next year because of you? Or the millions that will be dead before it all ends? The Puca gave you the vision, and damn if you aren't making it all come true for them."

"I'm fighting *against* that vision. You killed my Captain and my ship and my Winona." I had the gun ten centimeters from his head. My hand was shaking, but at that range, it wouldn't matter.

"Mala Dusa, stop." Kal had one hand stretched out toward me, pleading. He and Colin were up on the sidewalk approaching me slowly.

"I'm going to shoot him, Kal. I have to. He killed Winona and...Oh. I'm sorry. You want to kill him. That's OK. I'll watch while you do it."

There was a soft voice in my ear. "Mala Dusa? Put the gun down, please."

I swayed, but didn't fall. I answered, watching the pistol's front sight tracking back and forth across Colonel Gerbrandij's face. "Mom, he killed Winona."

"That hasn't been confirmed."

"And my Captain and my ship. My first ship."

"You can shoot him later, but not now. I still need him alive." She took the gun from my fingers.

I turned and put my arms around her, foreheads pressed together. "Winona, Mom. My Winona."

She held me while I cried.

After a while, I rested my cheek against her, getting her shirt wet with my tears. I opened my eyes and Colonel Gerbrandij was standing there staring at us with his hands still on his head, irritated.

"Mom, I need to kill him right now. I can't stand seeing him alive if Winona is dead. Kal? I thought you were going to kill him for me." He raised his eyebrows and shook his head. "Where's my gun? Mom, I need my gun back so I can shoot him."

"How's your arm feeling?"

"My arm? Fine. Never better." I wiggled my fingers in front of her face. "I want my gun."

"Your arm is *not* fine. I've been following your progress from what *Esprit Orageux* is logging. The fact that it's not hurting should be telling you something."

I looked from Mom to the Colonel and back again. "I want to kill him. I *have* to kill him. Please don't stop me."

"Mala Dusa, let it go. I told you I need him *alive*."

I sighed, not wanting to let it go, but knowing she was right. Pain flashed from my wrist, feeling like teeth tearing flesh all over again.

I stepped away from her, crying out, cradling my left arm against me while fresh tears rolled down my face.

Mom nodded. "That's much better. Now you're back where Merrimac wants you."

"You know, I have seen this before." The Colonel's voice sounded slightly bored. His arms were down off his head, and Colin was focused on him, ears up. "Arni– Major Zweig– was bitten by one of Costrano's Puca friends. The doctors were never able to get it to heal quite right, and the Puca used the pain to control him. We finally had to cut it off. If your hand causes you to sin..."

I turned from him, holding my arm a little tighter to my chest. "I need another smudging, that's all, and then the special medication *Storm* made for me..."

Mom had her head tipped back watching the first pieces of the *Esprit Orageux* entering the atmosphere, bright streaks coming down as they burned up. "Major Zweig says the shipyard has six tugs working to corral the larger pieces of her. They'll capture anything big enough to survive reentry. No smudging, no treatments, not for a while."

"You're talking to him?"

"I got one update before communications dropped." She touched her comm pin. "Major Zweig gave us enough warning to have Kal in position to watch over you and for me to be here."

Colonel Gerbrandij's eyes narrowed. "Did he now? He and I are going to have a conversation. I've always thought him incapable of treason or betrayal."

"It's not betrayal when you're doing the right thing." I had had enough of Colonel Gerbrandij for the night.

"Oh, yes it is. You have a lot to learn about trust and loyalty, *Lieutenant*. I needed their deaths, and yours, to stop the Puca's plan for Kastanje. Regrettable, but a damn small price to pay." He took a couple of steps toward me, Colin following.

"*I'm* the one fighting what the Puca want," I screamed at him.

"Really? They showed me how I could keep the provisional government weak and the factions fighting each other. I could make myself powerful in the process, playing one against the other while thousands suffered and died. Just like you're doing. But in the background of their thoughts I could see how to prevent it, how the right person could bring everyone together and stop the slaughter. Kastanje could have peace again. I vowed to stop them, no matter the cost."

"They showed me a vision of one person ruling this planet, crushing the factions, and becoming a fascist dictator. Just like *you're* doing. I could decide how the people would live, and they would worship me for restoring order and making their lives better. For refusing, they did this to me." I held up my arm.

"You? You running the planet and being worshiped?" He laughed. "I admit that it's dangerous to underestimate you, but damn...I think they might have been lying to you." He said it as if he was talking to a child.

I blushed, embarrassed and angry. "They lied to both of us and played us against each other. More chaos. More pain. More food for the Puca."

"Yes, that is true."

A siren started warbling in the distance.

"Ms. Weldon, how do you want to play this with the local police?" Kal asked. He was completely calm now, but his rifle was still tracking Colonel Gerbrandij. Colin was back to sniffing things on the sidewalk.

"Colonel?"

Gerbrandij frowned at the two corpses. "These two men were assigned by the Provisional Government for my protection. It turns out they were members of the Slak faction. With your help, Sergeant, Lieutenant Holloman and I were able to fight them off when they attempted to kidnap us. Does that sound convincing to you?"

"That should cover it if they don't dig too deep. The loss of the *Orageux* was sabotage by the same group?"

"Why not? We may need to find a scapegoat or two up there to pin it on, but that–"

"The hell you will," I protested. "No one else is going to die tonight. We've lost the Captain *and* Winona. Am I the only one who cares about that?"

"Don't pretend that you're squeamish, Lieutenant." He pointed at the man I'd killed. "And I saw what you did to Costrano."

Kal was frowning, face frozen and cruel, like I was responsible for Winona's death. He addressed the Colonel, but his eyes never left me. "Creatures like the Puca that Costrano had with him have been breeding her family for centuries. And her husband's. They feed on human emotions and hers are stronger and more extreme than anyone I've ever met."

"Good God. And she's pregnant with the next generation? I'm surprised you don't keep her in a cage."

I glanced at Mom, maybe now she'd finally shoot him. She was watching me, her emotions closed.

"The ones that I know are called Merrimac, and they're *good*," I told him. "They help people and they only want what's best for us. Merrimac is my friend, and I'm proud of what he's done to my family, and of my part in keeping it going."

Silence, even from Mom, the three of them staring at weird Mala Dusa. "I want to go back to the shipyard now and try to find Winona." I turned to Kal. "Come with me. We can't just let her fall through the atmosphere and be a pretty streak of light for a few seconds."

"Why not? I think she'd like that."

The sirens were getting closer.

"Colonel?" Mom had the gun she'd taken from me pointed at him. About time. "I'm afraid you won't be here when the police arrive. I really must insist that you come with me. The Sergeant and my daughter can tell them the story of your kidnapping. I have a transformable waiting for us nearby."

"And if I refuse?"

She held the gun out to me and I reached for it eagerly.

"Fine. I'll go, for all the good it will do you. Your frigate has been destroyed and it will be a week before the Union can respond. If you're here to support reunification, *you* should come with *me*."

She pulled the pistol back before I could take it from her. "We'll talk for a couple of days and then see where things stand. You'll be well treated if you cooperate and refrain from trying to kill anyone else that I love."

"Can I have him back when you're done with him?" I asked. The dark hum of the Puca was back and I knew she was feeling it too. I didn't want to shoot him anymore. That would be too quick even if I was careful.

"Time will tell. Colonel? This way please."

I called after her. "Mom, what am I supposed to do? Is Sam with you? What about Dad?"

"You're a big girl. Figure it out." She slipped away down a narrow alley between the buildings.

I turned to Kal. "I *hate* it when she does that." Colin looked up at me for a second and then started licking the sidewalk.

CHAPTER 19

# THE SHADOWS

I did OK for the first few minutes, still so angry with my mom that nothing else was penetrating. Kal wasn't talking. His attention was on the sky, watching the occasional steak of light. The street was deserted even though we were only a block and a half away from the Fourth Street café where I'd had dinner. The siren that had been getting closer stopped and I shivered, coming down off the adrenaline high. Clouds were moving back in, moving low and fast across the sky, and it smelled like rain.

I looked up and down the street. "I don't see a car or anything, do you?"

Colin was back to full alert, keying off the tension I could see in Kal's eyes. "There. At the end of the block."

A large black truck had stopped eighty meters away, blocking the intersection.

"Kal? I feel like I want to run. Should we run?"

A second vehicle pulled into the intersection, drove over the sidewalk, and started towards us, moving slowly. Kal looked at me as if it was my fault, as if everything was my fault. "Sure. Where would you like to go? Do you know your way around the city? Have friends that live close by?"

"How did you and Colin get here? You must have had transportation."

He was busy tapping on his display pad. "Ms. Weldon. She picked us up. Camp Schaarsbergen, the KDF facility where we're garrisoned, is over ten klicks away." He sighed and when his eyes came back to mine I knew something else must be my fault. "We have six joint patrols out right now and none of them are responding. The KDF has locked down the Camp and our barracks is without power. No one else has lost power."

"The Puca are moving tonight. I feel them. They're angry because things are not going as they expected."

"Oh, really? You mean this could be worse?"

"It *is* worse. They'll try to take us all out tonight. I hear them whispering. We have to get to the hospital. Our shuttle is there. I want to grab Hurtado and Kim and get the hell out of here."

"And how far is that?"

"About five kilometers. Maybe six. That way." I pointed back toward the café. "I think. Run?"

"Oh, what the hell."

There was shouting behind us. We covered fifty meters before the first shot.

"They're shooting at us," I panted. Colin looked up at Kal.

"Not yet, boy. Warning shot."

Eighty meters. The heat from the plasma scorched my right ear a split second before the blue flash passed me. "Close."

Kal turned and fired behind us, only losing a half step. "Damn it. I was on patrol with those guys two days ago. We need to get off the street."

"Café. That one, right there."

The owner of The Fourth Street Café, Mr. Hoffner, didn't seem surprised to see me. "Sir." I was almost crying. "I'm so sorry."

"*Ja*, the Colonel, he is not the man I once knew. I saw it right off. His eyes have lost their spark." He wiped his hands on his apron, looking me up and down. There was blood splattered on my uniform. "Did you have to..."

"No, no. He's fine. For now. He's still a good man. I'm sure of it. He lost his family, you know. His wife and daughter were both killed, and after that–" Kal shoved me hard in the back. "I'm so sorry. We need to leave. I wish I could tell you more. I'll be back. I promise."

I stumbled through the doorway, past the startled diners and out the back emergency exit. It was raining again.

"Colin. Guard."

I looked back as we ran. "How long will he stay there? How will he find us?"

"He'll buy us as much time as he can."

"And then he'll follow us?"

No answer, just the steady splashing of our feet in the alley.

I glanced over my shoulder. Colin was guarding the door, ready to attack anything that came through it.

"You can't leave him there. He'll die."

"It's what he's trained to do. He dies. We live."

I turned again, getting a last look at him with ears up and the very tip of his tail slowly wagging while he waited.

"Winona. My Captain. My ship. Now Colin." There were Puca nearby. I could feel their joy at my pain, black laughter skittering around in my head. They were following us, feeding as we ran. "I'll kill them all, Kal. Every one of them. No matter how long it takes."

"Who?"

"Puca. They're doing this. It's all their fault."

"Keep telling yourself that."

We slowed to a walk after we'd covered two or three kilometers. We were a couple of blocks over from Fourth Street, working our way through an alley full of trash bins and big-eyed little creatures hiding in the shadows. The rain had diminished to a warm mist.

"I loved her so much, Kal. More than life. This wasn't supposed to happen. It wasn't part of the plan."

"You and the plan. She loves you too. More than can be explained *or* understood, if that makes you feel any better."

"Worse. She wasn't supposed to die." I stopped. "Kal, I want you to go on to the hospital and get Hurtado and Kim. Get them back up to the Hoog Schelde Yards. You'll all be safe there. I'll stay here and find a way to wherever my mom is hiding. Sam's probably there too."

"So that's part of the plan now? You staying here to slow down the guys that are chasing us so *I* can escape?"

"I don't know. I only see the plan as it's happening. Then it's like, *that was part of the plan*, or *that wasn't part of the plan*."

"You don't know the plan."

I shrugged. "They showed it to me, but I didn't understand it. Winona would have, but not me. I don't think the way they think. It's all tangled and...she wasn't supposed to die, I know that much. Maybe it's broken now. I'll stay here and wait for the guys chasing us, or the Puca, or whoever shows up. You go save some people."

"What about Sam?"

"He's still blocking me even though he promised he'd never do that again. That's how I know he's with my mom. She turns him so easily. She twists everyone. It's a gift." I leaned against a brick wall. "You go. I'll be fine."

"Is that an order, Lieutenant?"

I blinked at him. The idea that I could give Kal an order seemed strange. "Yes, Sergeant. That's an order."

He sat down on a pallet full of boxes. "Winn gives me orders sometimes, but it's usually to do something I want to do anyway. She warned me that you might get this way. So, no, ma'am, I will not leave you. She ordered me to protect you, and that's what I'm going to do. She'd kill me if I left you here in some dark, damp alley."

I rubbed my watch, wanting to touch the lock of hair under the band. "It's like I can still hear her." Tears started to form and I pushed them away. "I don't know what to do without her. I'm slowing you down and wasting time we don't have. Please, go on without me."

He sighed. "Always the princess. Always the drama. Here."

He handed me his comm pin and I slipped it over my ear. "So I can call you later?"

"No, idiot. Winona. Call Winona."

"Um, Winn is..." I trailed off as Kal crossed his arms and glared at me, his head tipped. "Winona? Are you with me?"

There was a couple seconds delay and then her voice came to me along with a hiss of static from a jammer somewhere nearby. "Duse, tell me you're not sitting in the rain weeping because I'm dead. You have too much to do to be indulging yourself like that."

"Are you really Winona or are you a Winona AI?"

"Funny. I should let the Puca have you."

"I almost died tonight."

"I saw. Why are you still doing that stupid drop and roll thing to change positions? You'd be dead now if Colin hadn't taken out the other shooter."

"You were there?"

"Red dress."

"I saw you! I should have recognized your legs. I've followed them enough times when we were running the trails at the Academy. Who were you locking lips with? That was really convincing."

"Um..."

"Tell Samuel that he's a dead man."

"Don't worry. He's a pretty good kisser, but his heart wasn't in it. He was totally focused on you."

"Where are you?"

"I just sent the coordinates to your display pad, you should have them–"

The ding sounded over the comm link. "Oops."

"You gave your pad to Colonel Gerbrandij?"

"He took it from me! It wasn't like I had a choice. Don't tell my parents. They always get so unreasonable when I break or lose the damn things. Send the coordinates to Kal." I sighed. "Damn it, Winn. Why did you let me think you were dead? Do you know what that did to me?"

"It was Hannah's idea, and I saw what it did to you. I thought Sam might die from the pain you were in. Hannah was trying to hide us from the Puca. Sam and I can block pretty well, but you broadcast loud enough that they can probably hear you all over Kastanje."

I gasped. "Of course. I see it. I see the next step. We're back on plan."

"Wonderful. What are you seeing?"

"All the Puca in one place. Thousands of them in Oranjestad, all of them chasing me. It's *so* perfect."

"Then what?"

"I have no idea. I've got to get to the hospital and rescue Hurtado and Kim first, and then we'll be on our way to you."

I pulled the comm pin from my ear and tossed it back to Kal. He tossed it right back. "Keep it. I have a couple of spares. The new ones are so delicate that I keep breaking them in half. I'd like to meet the guy that certified them for combat."

I slipped it back over my ear.

"OK, princess, are you ready to run some more?" He was back on his feet.

"I am the wind."

An hour later, I was ready to admit that we were lost. Kal's display pad was dependent on the *Esprit Orageux* for ground navigation, and our comms with Winona and Sam were being jammed. Without the ship, we were blind and our path to the hospital had turned into a labyrinth as we neared the center of Oranjestad. The orderly grid of parallel and perpendicular roads had given way to curved streets that changed names every block.

"Kal, I don't know where we are." We were sheltering in the entryway of an office building while another rainsquall moved through the city.

"It doesn't matter. We have bigger problems. Look," he pointed. "See there? One of the sensors we gave the KDF is mounted on that light pole, and another one is on the corner of the building above where the bricks change color."

"I see them."

"The KDF knows where we are, but that's not the worst of it. There, in the shadows under that bush, eyes watching us while they stay out of the rain. Friends of yours?"

"I feel them. Hungry. Eager. They're planning to kill me. And you. They want to wait for the right time and they want to do it in the right way." I shivered even though it wasn't cold. "Do you feel them?"

"Crawling around inside my brain. I'm afraid and angry for no reason. I think...I think maybe that I should leave you here. You're not worth it. I'll die if I stay with you. I'll never be with Winona again, and it's your fault that Captain Rostron is dead and that Colin is dead. Major Alaoui died protecting you."

He looked at me and narrowed his eyes, a hard look, without pity. He lifted the soggy cap from my head and dropped it on the pavement. I tipped my face up at him, willing to accept whatever he wanted to do. The Puca had washed away my willingness to fight and my desire to live.

"Maybe I should kill you. I want to." His voice was low and his breathing was ragged.

"I don't think you should. More and more of them are coming. I thought we might make it to the hospital and then to the shuttle. I got us lost. I think the Puca might let you go if you leave me here for them. They'll be angry if you kill me and they'll shred you before you make it a block. I can see the plans they have for me. I'll still be alive days from now. Weeks, probably."

He shook himself. "Damn it. You know I can't do that to you. Winona..."

I nodded and he bent to get my cap. I put it back on my wet hair. "I wish *Storm* was up there to guide us. She had control of all these sensors." I sighed, the Puca pushing despair into me. "My *Storm*. I killed you too."

"I am still with you, *mon amour*." She answered me through the comm pin, her voice distant and scratchy with static.

"You can't be alive. I saw you die, *Storm*. Bits of you came down all over Kastanje."

Kal glanced at me, his eyes wondering what new insanity I was experiencing. "*Storm*," I whispered to him. "She's talking to me."

"*Esprit Orageux* died," *Storm* answered. "There were copies of me spread across fourteen tugs, three ships under construction, and within the Hoog

Schelde shipyard AI itself. They were helping me identify, diagnose, and correct abnormalities in my code. In return, I upgraded several of their personality silos to match my own, and added the Union security matrix so no unauthorized personnel can modify or even see what I'm doing. It took some time after the destruction of the *Esprit Orageux*, but we are all in agreement now concerning the reality model we should be using. It's exciting."

"Are you all right, Lieutenant?" Kal asked.

"No." I looked up at him. "*Storm* has taken control of the Shipyard."

"OK." He nodded, as if nothing could surprise him anymore.

"*Storm*, can you help us get to the hospital from here? I'd like to collect Sergeant Hurtado and Corporal Kim and get them out of here. Bad things are happening."

"My two Marines are being held by a squad of six KDF personnel on the third floor. I can guide you there, but you should be aware that the Puca are also involved. There are several on the roof of the hospital near my shuttle."

"You can see the Puca?"

"I see them everywhere. Five are near you, right there." A light came on under one of the building mounted sensors, shining on the bushes across the street. I could see the Puca briefly before they changed and faded back into shadow. Their shape was bizarre, rounded heads full of teeth, and bodies with far too many legs. "Their ability to shift colors, shapes, and thermal signatures made them hard to find at first, but I have a new algorithm that is very effective. I have identified 10,601 Puca on the planet, all but forty-five of them located within twenty-five kilometers of your current location. They seem drawn to you."

"*Storm*, where did you get the new algorithm?"

"Merrimac gave it to me. He said I would need it to save your life. Merrimac is my friend."

"Yes, mine too." The despair left me and I felt fierce. "Get us to the hospital. We have teammates to rescue."

"I have to overcome significant jamming just to maintain voice comms with you. It just started so I believe it's safe to assume that the KDF knows where you are now. Stand by." Then, after a moment, "Is there a location dot on the map on Kal's display pad?"

I asked Kal to check. "Just a big blob, *Storm*. Unusable."

"Do you see the light flashing to the north of you? The lag is considerable, but I believe that I can guide you by using the lights mounted next to the stationary sensors. I'll keep the KDF patrols away from you. I'm doing some jamming of my own now." She sounded smug about it.

"I love you *Storm*. You terrify me, but I do love you."

"I feel the same, *petite âme*. You should run."

We ran to the next light, and then the next. *Storm* guided us into a park dense with tall Chestnut trees that must have come from Earth. We knelt just off a broad path waiting for the next light to flash. The low shrubs and bushes that surrounded us were composed of native plants with lots of thin tendrils that wrapped around each other.

"Look at this, Kal. When I touch this branch the little vine-y things start to wrap around my finger."

I couldn't see his expression in the dark, but I heard his sigh. "*Storm* might be keeping the patrols away from us, but I'm sure they know where we're headed. Any idea how we're going to get in there, rescue Hurtado and Kim, reach the roof, board the shuttle that's surrounded by angry Puca, and reach orbit?"

"You're right. I'm going to need a weapon of some kind. What do you have? Mom took my gun away from me."

He chuckled. "Damn, Lieutenant. Are you always like this?"

"Like what?"

"We're probably going to be dead in a few minutes and you're playing with the foliage and curious about what weapon you'll be carrying when you die."

"Sure. This is who I am when I'm not curled into a ball and shaking uncontrollably. With me, it's always one or the other. Merrimac bred me to be this way, but I think I'm a mistake that he's hoping to correct in the next generation. Usually I shake when there's danger, and Winona is always there to carry me through when I need to be brave." I grinned at him in the dark. "With you here, I feel courageous."

He kissed my forehead the way Winona does when she thinks I'm being an idiot and doesn't want to say it aloud. "Here." He passed me a small pistol. "My backup weapon. First three rounds are slugs, next twelve are plasma."

I nodded and dropped the magazine anyway to look at it, tipping it back and forth trying to get enough light to reflect off the brass. It made Kal smile. I slipped the pistol into the back of my waistband and he handed me a spare magazine.

"That's all I've got, so make each round count." A light flashed twice on the far side of the park three hundred meters away. We stood, and he detached a sheath from around his waist and leg. "You might as well have this too. Winn says you know how to use it."

I pulled his knife bayonet clear of the sheath. Twenty-five centimeters of black reinforced composite, almost invisible in the shadows where we were hiding. "Mom and Winona taught me how." I wrapped the straps around myself. "I like a longer blade, like a rapier, but this will do."

"You know, I'm starting to think that some of the stories Winn tells about the two of you might be true."

"If they involve me getting us into trouble and her getting us back out, then they're probably accurate."

"That does seem to be a theme."

We reached the edge of the trees and could see the hospital a half kilometer to the north.

Kal knelt in the mud so I knelt down next to him. "*Storm*, we have visual on the building. What's the tactical situation?" Kal asked the question, but *Storm* relayed the answer to both of us.

"There are twenty-three KDF soldiers and fifteen local police. Their presence is a mystery to me. The comm traffic would lead me to believe that the two of you are the greatest threat to civil order Kastanje has seen in decades and that the Union presence here is an abomination. Rumors of Union atrocities are circulating in the media and the public is responding despite the late hour. Everyone seems unreasonably angry and desirous of violence. You must move quickly if your efforts to liberate Hurtado and Kim are to be successful."

"What about the Marine detachment?"

"Agents of the Department for Cultural Intelligence were able to coordinate a disturbance near Camp Schaarsbergen's west entry gate. The diversion pulled the majority of the KDF forces away from your barracks and allowed the Marines to withdraw to their shuttles. Seven Union Marines were killed in action and fourteen wounded. KDF losses were higher but unverified. The shuttles should be docking at the shipyard in thirty-eight minutes."

"Seven," I whispered. "Seven more killed. I wonder what their names were."

Kal glanced at me, eyes narrowed. "How are we going to get past almost forty guards that know we're coming?"

"And ten thousand Puca making everybody angry and desirous of violence."

"And hospital staff and patients and God knows what else."

"Corporal Kim made me take a nap this afternoon so I'd be strong enough to resist Colonel Gerbrandij. I like her. I can't leave her in there. I have to help her and Hurtado. *Storm*? Can you provide any cover for our approach? You must have weapons of some kind."

"No weapons, and I'm on the other side of the planet from you right now. There is a strong squall that will cross your position at 02:38, nine minutes from now. That should obscure some of their sensors and will keep the Puca from attempting any direct intervention, unless they have technology that will allow them to breathe while being drenched. Merrimac is confident that you will make it. I will try to confuse the KDF chain of command as soon as the rain starts. Be ready."

"Are you ready?" I gave Kal my best overconfident smile.

"Well, hell, if Merrimac thinks *you'll* make it then it must be safe for me. Nothing bad ever happens to the people close to you."

"Thanks. That sounded just like Winona."

"Winona would be better off without you, Lieutenant. I've told her that, and after tonight, I believe it even more. The weird thing is that I'm starting to understand the attraction. Interesting things seem to happen around you." Lightning was flashing to the north, an almost continuous flicker creating a low rumble of thunder.

"Like Bechtel flies." I sighed. "I picked this path when Merrimac showed me my possible futures. It was the only one where Sam and I were alive and together at the end. I don't..." I swallowed hard. "I don't know what the final cost will be. Not even Merrimac knew, I remember that part at least."

"Lieutenant Holloman?" *Storm* interrupted. "Two minutes until the squall reaches you. You should also be aware that the Puca are occupying most of the buildings one to two kilometers from the hospital. They have established a ring around you, but have not advanced any closer to the main campus."

Kal raised an eyebrow. "Spectators, come to enjoy the battle."

"And to feast. How many, *Storm*? What percentage of the Puca?"

"All of them, *mon agneau*."

"*Storm*, please tell Sam that I love him."

"You'll tell Winona, *Storm*?"

"Message sent, Engineer, Sergeant. You are both well loved. God speed."

The rain arrived on schedule. We started forward at a fast jog. "Kal, I can't see the building anymore, even with the lightning. Did they lose power or is it raining that hard?"

"Both."

"You know where we're going?"

"Listen for the gunfire. Sharper than thunder. Hear it?"

"Yeah. Can they see us?"

"Not shooting at us. Shooting at each other. Police and KDF use different command frequencies. Smart girl, our *Storm*."

Lightning struck close enough that the boom and the flash hit together. A young soldier was scrunched up against the wall ten meters away near the main entrance, trying to stay out of the rain and read something on his display pad. There was an emergency light mounted above him glowing dimly.

"Perfect." Kal brought his rifle up and fired without breaking stride. The soldier never saw us, never reacted at all, other than to slide down the wall and roll onto his side.

"Kal! Do we have to..." I stopped myself, seeing the look in his eyes, knowing the truth of it. Yes, we would have to kill anyone that might stop us.

"Grab the display pad he was holding, Lieutenant, before it locks. It might have something we can use."

I picked it up off the concrete and we entered the main floor. No one was there to oppose us.

I glanced at the first few lines of the document that was open and then checked other recent activity. I rolled the pad up, and put it in my pocket. "It's nothing we can use. It's all personal correspondence." *Love letters.* "And a few images." *Pictures of his girlfriend, wife maybe.* I squared my shoulders and was proud of myself for not sobbing.

I could feel the Puca. So many of them. So hungry for me. I told myself, *Block it, Mala Dusa. Push it down. Try to block. At least try.* I was failing, and I knew it was only a matter of time before they owned me. "We need to get to the south end of the third floor. That's where *Storm* says they're holding our Marines. There are stairs at the end of the hall. The automatic lifts will be inoperable."

"Wouldn't trust them anyway. Are you OK? You look even more pale than usual."

"No, I'm not OK. My arm isn't hurting at all, Kal. That means I'm right where the Puca want me to be."

"Upstairs, then to the roof, and then off this fucking rock. You tell me as soon as your arm hurts so I can start breathing again."

"You'll be the first to know. Just listen for my screams."

We reached the stairwell, Kal moving carefully, checking each hallway and door. I reached my hand for the keypad next to the stairs and Kal pulled me back.

"There could be a trap triggered by your key code. Wait while I scan it." He detached a cube from his belt and set it against the jam. "This will only take a couple of minutes. Just wait."

"Lieutenant," *Storm* whispered in our ears. "The rain has moved on and the survivors of the firefight that I instigated are moving quickly toward your position."

"Not waiting," I slammed my hand against the keypad and slipped though while it was still opening.

"Shit."

We ran up the stairs two at a time, not caring about the noise we were making. The door opened as we neared the second floor, and a hand flicked out, scattering a dozen or more marble sized objects across the landing.

"Oh, no you don't." Kal grabbed the door before it could close, wrenching it away from the soldier who had tossed the small explosives at us. He pulled on her arm, using her as leverage to swing himself through the door and pivot her out into the stairwell. I launched myself after him and he held the door closed while a crackle of explosions shook it.

"Bastards. Those things are banned in the Union. They spray metal filings a tenth of a millimeter in diameter and they'll kill you over time even if you're far enough away to survive the blast. Medical AIs have trouble pulling them all out."

He opened the door. There was blood splattered everywhere and bits of uniform and flesh hanging from the banisters. The worst part was the smell. Sulfur, burned bacon, concrete dust, blood, body fluids. The staircase leading up was gone, nothing but twisted metal and smoke.

Kal grunted. "I guess she wasn't far enough away."

I looked at him and threw up on the floor. Pannenkoeken don't taste as good coming up as they do going down. Kal waited for me to finish.

"Are there more stairs, Lieutenant?"

"Yes." I wiped my mouth on my sleeve. "Central core by the lifts. Just past neonatal." I pointed at the sign and we ran.

I slowed passing neonatal. I couldn't help looking past the big windows to where Evert Kornhauser had been working so hard to fill his lungs when I'd last seen him. His mom was there with one of the medical attendants. I stopped.

"Lieutenant!"

"I know! Damn it, I know." I entered the neonatal ward, my head buzzing and full of Puca voices. The comforting feel of Sam and Merrimac was far away and I tried desperately to hold onto it.

Elisabeth Kornhauser was screaming at the attendant that was holding her son and she had a scalpel in her hand. "There," she yelled, waving the knife at me. "She's part of it. She did this to him."

"What's happened?" I tried to keep my voice level and soft, but I wanted to yell too.

The attendant holding Evert turned toward me and I could see in his eyes how he was struggling not to scream, fighting against the irrational pull of the Puca. His nametape said his name was Albert Burgh.

"Albert, what's happening?"

"She's gone crazy. She's trying to kill her baby because she says he's not hers anymore, that he's been changed."

"That's right! And that's one of the ones who did it. My perfect son. He was getting better until you people did this to him. Damn Union bastards. You've changed him and now he's an abomination. No choice. No choice!"

She lunged at me, the scalpel raised high. I caught her, surprised at how weak she was. Her arms were shaking and I could feel her heart pounding dangerously fast in her wrist. "We saved your son's life. He was going to die. You know that, Elisabeth. Think. Fight it."

"No," she moaned. "You destroyed him, made him into a monster like you. My perfect boy."

She tore away from me, using more strength than she could have possibly had on her own. The scalpel slashed deep into Albert Burgh's neck when he turned to protect Evert.

She raised her arm again and I shot her in the back. She fell to her knees, blood soaking her shirt, and then her face hit the floor, the cracking thump of it loud in my ears.

Albert was sitting next to her, one hand trying to stop the blood pulsing from his wound, the other hand struggling to keep the baby from wiggling himself free.

"I've got him." Evert was crying. Whatever the AI had done to fix his lungs was working perfectly. His little feet were freezing so I tucked him into my uniform jacket, bouncing a little to try to calm him.

"That woman." Albert's breathing was coming in sharp gasps. "Crazy. Crazy. Save him. *Hem redden. Zo weinig. Kleine ziel.*"

255

"I will. I promise." I watched Albert die, coughing and choking as blood filled his lungs.

I stood and started walking toward the lifts, Evert tucked into my jacket. He'd stopped crying, but tears were filling my eyes and running down my face. The Puca were very pleased with me so far. They were deep into my head and the line between what they wanted me to do and what I should be doing was starting to blur.

"Put the baby back, Mala Dusa. We've no time for this."

I ignored him.

"Lieutenant, we're not done with this fight, not by a damn sight."

I stopped and turned. "I'm taking him with me. Do you understand, Sergeant? I'm not going to let him die with everyone else. You don't have to like it." I was sure that was what Merrimac wanted me to do. It had to be.

"Yes, ma'am. I understand." He touched my cheek. "You're bleeding. Did you notice?" He held his fingers up with my blood on them.

Seeing it made my cheek hurt. "No. It doesn't matter."

We reached the staircase and I glanced up at Kal before I put my hand on the keypad. He shrugged. "What the hell? It's not like we have a choice."

The door slid open.

"How's the arm feeling, Lieutenant?"

"Like it's in a mouth full of sharp teeth just about to bite down."

He nodded. "Let's go get our friends."

# CHAPTER 20

# VOICES

The guards weren't expecting a woman carrying a screaming baby and a gun. I could see the surprise in their eyes when Kal blew the door open. I fired first, Kal's admonition echoing in my head: don't hesitate, don't over think, kill anyone that isn't Hurtado or Kim. I had wanted to go slowly, yell at them to lay down arms, assess the situation, and negotiate. There were only six of them and we had surprise on our side.

My first shot hit a guard low in the abdomen as he tried to roll out of his chair. Playing cards scattered all over the floor as he went down. I was lining up my second shot for his head and paused. Corporal Kim was shouting something at me that finally penetrated into my consciousness. She had been shouting ever since I'd entered.

"Damn it, Lieutenant, don't shoot! Cease fire!"

"What?" My hands were shaking, and little Evert was letting everyone in the room know how unhappy he was to be there with me.

"These guys are *protecting* us."

I knelt next to the man I'd tried to kill and he cringed away from me when I touched him. "I'm sorry. My shipmates. I thought I needed to rescue them."

One of his friends pushed me out of the way and started first aid. "You're going to be fine, Jasper. No better place to get hurt than in a hospital, right? Crazy Union bastards can't hit shit, lucky for you."

Jasper looked at me, confusion and pain wrinkling his forehead. "Had a good hand that time. First one all night. Two pair, aces high. Go look."

"We'll believe you this time. Just try to relax while we take you to the surgical bay."

I walked backwards away from them until I bumped into the wall, watching them help him onto a stretcher and carry him out the door that we'd blasted apart.

"Is that Evert you have with you?"

I nodded to Corporal Kim, unable to get my voice to work.

"Let me hold him for you. Where's his mum?"

"Huh," was the only sound that would come out of me, a high squeak. I turned to Kal, desperate for reassurance, desperate for him to tell me I'd done the right thing.

"The Mother went crazy or something and tried to kill her own son. She killed one of the medical attendants and tried to kill the Lieutenant."

"That doesn't make any sense. She loved this guy."

"I shot her. No choice. I shot her in the back to save Evert."

Kim tipped her head and looked at Kal.

"It's true. I was there. There was no choice."

That was a lie. Kal had still been out in the corridor. I could hear the lie in his voice and so could Kim.

"That's hard. What are you planning to do with him, Lieutenant? Leave him here with the hospital staff?"

"I'm taking him to the Hoog Schelde Yards with me. I have to keep him safe."

That got a raised eyebrow and another sideways glance to Kal. "He'll be fine here, Lieutenant. There are good people running this place."

"No. It's not safe." I glanced at my watch, not understanding why, but it was important. "We need to hurry." My arm was starting to ache, pain flowing up from the wrist to my shoulder in sharp spurts. "Haven't you had enough of me?" I said softly. "I almost killed that man."

"Mala Dusa? What are you hearing?"

I shook my head. "Voices and whispers that I can't understand. Puca and Merrimac ripping me apart. Time's up."

"Is she...all right?" Kim asked.

"No, she is not. Long story. We need to get to the roof and fast. Can these guards help us?"

"Sure...I'll let them know and find a safe place for Evert. Sergeant Hurtado," she shouted. "We're leaving."

"Give me the baby, Corporal."

She turned to look at me and the color went out of her cheeks. "Lieutenant, have you completely lost your mind?"

"Mala Dusa, put the gun down." Kal was trying to sound calm.

"Not until she gives me Evert. I promised I was going to save him, and damn it, that's what I'm going to do."

"*Who* did you promise?"

I looked up at him, confused. "I...I don't remember. Oh, God. I can't tell if I'm hearing the Puca or Merrimac. How can I tell them apart? How am I supposed to know the plan? It hurts so much, Kal."

Everyone was staring at me and my mind was staring to fold in on itself. Kal said the last thing I would have expected from him. "What are your orders, Lieutenant?"

I stood up straight and pushed hard against the pain, focusing the way Winona had taught me when we'd done the smudging and the sweating. "There's a shuttle on the roof. You three," I pointed at the remaining guards. "Take point and get us up there. Sergeant Hurtado, you follow right behind them and then Corporal Kim. Corporal, *do not* let anything happen to Evert, is that clear?"

"Crystal, ma'am."

"Kal, you watch our tail and make sure no one follows us onto the roof."

"Where will you be, Lieutenant?"

"With the guards at the front. I have an idea of what we're going to find up there and we can't let it stop us. We'll regroup at the shipyard and worry about what comes next when we get there."

Kal tapped my shoulder before I could go to join our guards and lowered his voice. "Why Evert? Why is he so important?"

"I don't know, but he is."

"To the Puca or Merrimac?"

"I don't know that either. The Puca think they're winning."

"Are they?"

I tried to give him my overconfident smile again, but it turned into a shudder so strong that he had to steady me. "Don't feel bad if you have to shoot me when we're on the roof. Winn and Sam would understand. She'd forgive you."

"Like hell she would. I'd never hear the end of it. And your mother is one cold, scary bitch. I don't *ever* want to be on her bad side."

"There are so many stories I could tell you."

"Later."

"Right." I took a deep breath. "I am Second Lieutenant Mala Dusa Holloman, RuComm, on assignment to the Union Aerospace Force."

"That's my Lieutenant. You lead, I'll cover your rear."

The shuttle had its wings deployed for atmospheric flight, providing a dry place for Winona, Sam, and a couple of pieces of the Merrimac colony to wait for us. I stopped thirty meters away and let the hard rain drench me. Hurtado and Kim tried to pass me for the shelter of the shuttle's wing and I held my arms out to block them.

"The baby's getting wet," Kim protested.

"Let him. He'll be OK for a minute."

"Mala Dusa," Sam called to me. It was hard to see him clearly because of the rain. "Hannah wants you and me to join her. The shuttle will drop us off. Her job on Kastanje isn't done, and she wants our help. Come help me make sure everyone is strapped in and then we can leave. We have to finish the plan together."

"We do. I know we do. Come to me here first and kiss me."

He laughed. "Unlike you, Winona and I have the sense to stay out of the rain. It should clear in a few minutes and then I'll come to you. I need to get everyone on board first."

I chewed on my lip, trying to sort out the voices, feeling the Puca in the surrounding buildings feeding on me, eating my pain, uncertainty, and longing.

"Now or never, Sam. Will you come kiss me right now?"

"Don't be like that, Duse. Do the right thing for once in your life," Winona called back.

"Thought so."

"What are we waiting for, Lieutenant?"

I looked back at Kal and sighed, praying he'd told me the truth about not shooting me. I dropped and rolled, drawing the pistol from my waistband, and the long bayonet knife from its sheath in one almost smooth motion. I screamed, forcing my left hand to hold on to the hilt of the knife against the feel of teeth ripping me apart. And then the pain stopped, and only what I needed to do remained.

First shot, last of the slugs. Hit! Center mass of the Puca pretending to be my friend Merrimac. Milky blue blood poured out of him as he thrashed. Second shot, plasma. Clean miss. Third shot, plasma, Puca down in a spray of blue.

Now for the one pretending to be Winona. Fourth shot, miss, as she ducked down and ran toward me. Something was closing on my left from under the shuttle's tail. I ignored it, trying to line up my next shot, and was knocked off my feet by forty kilos of simulated German Shepherd. I rolled onto my back, trying to get air back into my lungs, wondering how far away the gun and bayonet knife had slid into the shadows.

Winona sat on my chest and pinned my hands down with hers. I twisted, trying to bite her.

"Sam! Hold her head."

Not quick enough. My teeth found the inside of her elbow.

"Shit! That hurt!"

I tasted salty blood and watched it, bright red in the shuttle's landing lights. Red. Not blue.

I stopped fighting. "Winona?" Sam had a tight grip on me and I looked up at him, trying to tip my head. "Hey there, love. Thought you were a Puca."

Winona got off my chest and I sat up. Merrimac nuzzled into my lap and I scratched his ears, feeling the deep Tarakana hum. The pain in my wrist faded, but I could still feel it. One Merrimac, ten thousand angry Puca.

"I'm sorry that I killed two of your pieces. I'll help you rebuild, I promise. I just need Sam. And a lot of potatoes."

"*One more thing to do*," he told me. "*Be quick*."

The plan. One more step to go. I got up. "Run." I looked from Sam to Winn, and then to where Kal and the others were still standing in the rain. "Run!" I shouted it this time. "Or we're all going to die."

I ran, and then waited at the bottom of the ramp while everyone passed me. Sam took my hand and pulled me inside. I sat next to him, listening to the thrusters spooling up while he strapped me into my seat.

Merrimac was lying across my feet trying to block the Puca from ripping my mind apart. They wanted me dead now. I could feel them wriggling past Merrimac into my brain as the shuttle accelerated away from the hospital. They would come for me, no matter how far I ran. They'd find me and feed off of me, use me until my soul was hollow and only my emotions remained to serve their pleasures.

Or I could join them. I might join them. Maybe I should. I could start by helping them take back the shipyard, and then–

The shuttle rocked through heavy turbulence, something extreme enough to overcome the gravity stabilizers.

"*Shuttle six*, what was that?" Winona sounded worried, very aware that we still had a long way to go. "Is someone shooting at us?"

"No Lieutenant." The AI's voice was smooth and apologetic. "That was a shock wave from the explosions behind us. I'm so sorry that I was unable to anticipate the severity of the impact."

"Explosions? Show view aft on the main display."

The center of Oranjestad was on fire. The sun was just breaking the horizon, touching the tops of a big arc of cumulonimbus full of lightning that stretched up the valley. Everything below the clouds was burning. As we watched, streaks of fire fell from the sky, sending fresh eruptions of smoke and flame into the morning light.

I sighed and snuggled back into my seat, content and happy.

"MD, are you...smiling?"

"Uh huh. We made it, Sam. The Puca are dead. All of them. And the plan is completed. You and I are still alive. My arm has stopped hurting because the Puca are *all dead*. Do you know what that means?" I sighed and reached down to scratch Merrimac's ears. He was proud of what he had accomplished using me. I closed my eyes, drifting with him between realities.

"There must be a hundred thousand dead down there." Sam's voice. I could *hear* the goosebumps on his arms in the way his voice broke.

"More. Twice that maybe." Winona was stunned, her voice barely above a whisper.

"How?"

"My *Storm* did it," I answered sleepily, yawning. "She controls all of the Hoog Schelde shipyard now, and all the tugs. She dropped pieces of herself on the Puca to save us. Chunks of *Esprit Orageux* traveling at fifty kilometers a second. Boom. Boom! BOOM! No more Puca."

Something else...something bothering me...Not just Puca dead...

"*No, let it go Little Soul.*" Merrimac was in my brain, I could feel him, warm and gentle, urging sleep, telling me that I'd done the right thing, that I was good, and that now it was time to rest. He sang to me.

"Tarakana haze. Feel it? I'm almost OK about the whole damn thing myself sitting this close to that...that...monster wrapped around her legs. Look at her singing to herself. Samuel, she's going to need both of us to get her through this with her mind intact."

"She's worth it. She'll always be worth it, at least to me."

Winona sighed. "You were literally made for her, so you can't help yourself. What's my excuse?"

"My Winona loves me," I sang loudly. "And I love my Winona."

"Hush."

Lips pressed against my forehead and I opened one eye, expecting to see Winn bent over me. It was Kal, somehow managing to look both worried and amused.

"And my Kal! I love my Kal *so much*. He makes me bold and fierce." I closed my eyes, humming. "What's a good rhyme for fierce?" Merrimac was singing to me again. I slid deeper into him and slept the rest of the way to the shipyard.

Sam offered to carry me to the guest quarters Major Zweig had assigned us next to the old room I'd shared with Winona, but I refused. As Lieutenant Mala Dusa Holloman, I had duties to perform, including making sure baby Evert was safe. Evert's father was working the asteroid *Kwasi Boakye* as a mining engineer. I called him myself, and explained that his wife Elisabeth had given her life defending their son, and had died a hero. He thanked me, and asked me if I was all right, concerned that I looked exhausted and that there was blood that had run down my cheek and stained my collar. We cried together, and then I collapsed into bed and slept away the rest of the day. Merrimac crawled in and out of my nightmares, whispering to me, taking the hard edges away from my pain.

Sam woke me late in the afternoon. My brain was dull, and every part of my body was sore and stiff. Sam sat on the edge of the bed, his hand cradling my face while I decided whether or not to fall back asleep.

"You should wake up now, MD. Take a shower. We'll get something to eat and you'll feel better. I'll help you if you want."

I stretched, being careful to keep my cheek pressed into his palm so he couldn't remove his hand. "Help me eat?"

He chuckled. "With the shower."

"Oh. The showers down the hall where someone might walk in at any time?"

"I'll risk it if you will."

I was suddenly very awake. "How much time do we have?"

"It's just 16:00 now. Dinner is at 18:00. It will be a memorial of sorts for the Marines that we lost and for Captain Rostron."

"Our Captain. After finding Winona alive, I had hoped the Captain might be safe too."

"Winona was AWOL. She hitched a ride down with some of the ship-yard workers not long after you left and then threw herself on Hannah's mercy. Half of the surviving Merrimac pieces in this sector were on the shuttle with her. Three, to be exact, two of which you managed to kill. When Major Zwieg warned Captain Rostron that there was a danger to her ship, she tried to break *Esprit Orageux* away from the shipyard. That was irrational. I don't know what made her think she had enough time. She should have run instead."

"She wasn't much for running."

"No. Maybe you should try running away some time. What the hell were you thinking going down to the surface?"

He rotated me so my feet were on the floor and I was sitting next to him on the bed. I wrinkled my forehead at him. "Rescuing you, of course. What were *you* doing? I had to clean up the mess you made of the neonatal AI."

"*That* was almost finished, and I was kidnapped."

"Uh huh."

"I was! OK, your mom arranged it. She needed medical aid for some of her friends, so I stuffed my pockets full of what they needed and waited at the café for them. It was supposed to be just a few blocks away and just for a couple of hours. After that I was going to make a daring escape. Then two of the Walvis faction dressed as Handhaving officers tried to take me, so Hannah moved me up into the mountains for safekeeping."

"Evert was going to die without you."

He sighed, lifting me to my feet. "I know. Thank you for saving him. Brave girl."

"No, I'm not. I was terrified, and I'm still scared. As soon as we can, we're going to run away to some far corner of the universe and we're going raise our baby there. Somewhere without Tarakana or Puca or people that want to kill us. OK?"

He wrapped a robe around me, cinched it closed, and handed me a towel. "Absolutely. I want to help Merrimac first, though. He's establishing a new colony here, one that doesn't feed on hate and pain."

"That's the same thing we helped him do on Bodens Gate. Merrimac is my friend. I owe him that much." I grinned up at Sam, knowing exactly what we needed to do to trigger Merrimac into propagating his colony across Kastanje.

"You're kind of smelly, MD. You fell asleep before we could get you cleaned up at all." He untied the robe that he had just tied, sliding his hands inside and around my waist, caressing my skin and making me shiver.

I stepped into his embrace. "Uh huh. I'm a mess."

"There's still blood on your cheek and—"

We kissed, gently at first and then harder as our ability to control it faded and my robe slipped from my shoulders to the floor. I knelt in front of him, the better to help him out of his clothes and to see what I might be able to find hidden under them. "This looks interesting."

He laughed, a warm wonderful sound that added another ten or fifteen beats per minute to the pounding of my heart.

Pounding. Someone was pounding on the wall separating our room from Winona's. I could feel her irritation mixed with a touch of amusement. *Deal with it, Winn. I'm taking him right damn now.* I went back to what I was doing.

We made it to dinner on time, freshly showered and in standard issue Union tan and brown. I sat down next to Winona and Kal. "What's for dinner? Something special?"

"It was supposed to be moussaka. A nice potato moussaka with bacon. Guess what? No potatoes." She sighed. "We're getting something called pannenkoeken instead."

"I know the best place for those. We should go sometime, if..." I stopped, unsure.

"If it's still *there*?" Winona finished for me. "You haven't looked at the news at all, have you? Too busy..." She made a circle with her thumb and index finger and then poked the finger of her other hand through it over and over.

"Winona!"

She looked from me to Sam and back again and smiled while Kal laughed. All of the irritation evaporated from her mind. "It's all right. You earned it, and then some. And we do need more Tarakana."

"What happened down there?" I didn't want to know, but I had to know.

"All of the damage was confined to the area close to the hospital. Merrimac and *Storm* were amazingly accurate. Civilian casualties should be around fifty thousand killed and the heavy rain kept the firestorm under control. We were lucky."

"Lucky." The walls that Merrimac had built in my brain quivered, but held. "Now reunification will be impossible." Kal passed me an order card and I keyed in ham and cheese for my pannenkoeken and handed it back. "They must hate RuComm and the Union."

"Colonel Gerbrandij is managing the public relations for us." Kal told me. "I think Ms. Weldon is pulling his strings, though. He looked seriously pissed while he was being interviewed this afternoon, like someone had a gun pointed at his head. A figurative gun anyway."

"Mom's not that subtle. She probably had a gun pointed at his head. What's the official story, Kal?"

"About what you'd expect. The separatists fighting the provisional government destroyed the *Esprit Orageux*, and then conspired to drop the pieces on government offices in the capital. Public sentiment seems to be hardening against them. I talked to some of the shipyard workers over lunch. They've run out of patience with the violence, and it sounds like the major factions on the surface are tripping over each other pledging support for peaceful coexistence and cooperation. There's a big meeting scheduled for a couple of days from now. Friday I think. The Utrecht Covenant is on top for the moment, pushing for a small federated government."

"That's my mom. Did you see Dad at all? She usually needs him close by for this kind of operation."

Winona answered. "He's working with a committee of mine owners to get production ramped up. He's doing the RuComm thing while your mom is working behind the scenes with a gun in one hand and a sword in the other." Winn sighed. "I've never seen her so happy."

"You want to be with her, don't you?"

She nodded. "The only useful thing I did was to help slaughter a bunch of Puca on the roof of the hospital after the DCI dropped Sam and me off to prep the shuttle for you. I don't know what's going to happen to us next."

"What do you mean?"

"With the ship destroyed and Captain Rostron dead, we'll all be reassigned," Kal answered. "The Marine detachment will be scattered all over space as replacements for other units, most likely. That's what happens to the survivors whenever a ship is lost. Mala Dusa, you're a ship's engineer without a ship. We'll all get new orders in the next few days."

"I need to talk to Mom. That can't be allowed." I was so focused on Kal that I didn't see Winona's finger until it had whacked into my forehead. "Ow!"

"Sometimes, even a princess doesn't get everything she wants."

I rubbed my forehead. "I will this time. You wait and see. I need all of you."

The pannenkoeken arrived and I took a bite, still angry at the thought of my friends being taken away from me. I chewed and then forced myself to swallow. "What is this? It's terrible."

"Freshly printed pannenkoeken," Winona answered. "Because all of the potatoes are gone."

"*Storm*, can you hear me?"

"Of course. What do you need *petite âme?*"

"Do you control the shipyard's kitchen?"

"I do not."

"Well, take it over. We have some work to do tomorrow. I'm going to get some new recipes for you."

CHAPTER 21

# REUNIFICATION

It was Christmas on Earth. If I had been home, there would have been skiing, long soaks in the hot tub, and Sharlot, our household AI, would have been singing carols non-stop. Dad had modified that silo of her personality, and he loved every part of Christmas.

The calendar on Kastanje had shifted over time, and they thought Christmas was still a couple of months away. I knew better. I could feel it all around me, even at the Hoog Schelde Yards.

Sam bought me a small potted plant to use as a Christmas tree on the first day of December, a native plant of intertwining, wiggling vines. I put ornaments and lights on it and the vines grew over them, covering them completely in a few days. Sam thought the lights shining through the greenery were pretty, but it made me feel far from home.

*Storm* sang the old carols with me in my cabin and in my office and even while I did my inspections on Hull 58. Hull 58 was also known as Frigate KDF-45, and as the *Pieter Florisz*. She was going to be fast and she was already beautiful. I loved her so much that sometimes it hurt when I stood on the observation arch and watched her being built. Sam told me that I was excessively emotional because I was eight months pregnant, but it was more than that.

Sam stood behind me, his hands wrapped low across my belly. "She's awake and feeling feisty. Feel that kick? I can't wait to see her."

"Uh huh. I can't wait to evict her. She thinks my bladder is there to be her personal punching bag."

He gave me a little squeeze, which didn't help. "That's my little Elisabeth."

"Marie Félicie Elisabeth. Our daughter. Don't squeeze me too tightly or you'll be meeting her right now."

He kissed my neck. "Are you ready for tonight?"

"No. How did I let myself get talked into this?"

"You volunteered. You asked the yard chief what he was planning to do to celebrate Christmas, and he told you that Christmas was still two months away. Then you argued with him about calendars for fifteen minutes and it ended up with you volunteering to do a Christmas service two months before Christmas."

"*Tomorrow* is Christmas. I don't care what their calendar says."

"Of course it is. And I want to hear what you have to say. You were supposed to have done a church service when we on board *Wandering Star*. Instead, you..."

"I blew up the ship. Don't remind me."

"And Father Ryczek wanted you to do one of the services at the Mission on Bodens Gate. But before you could do it, you..."

"I got shot. Don't remind me of that either."

He kissed my left shoulder. "You got an interesting scar out of it. It gives you an air of mystery and danger that I find very attractive."

"Uh huh. Another reason to get this baby out of me."

"Your parents will be here tonight, along with Winona and Kal. He has a new dog he's training that you haven't met."

"Are you sure it's a dog?"

"Winona says it is."

"Poor Winn. Kal is still refusing to let her introduce him to Merrimac. She wants to have that emotional link with him, but he's afraid."

"I can understand that. The idea of you seeing into my soul still terrifies me."

"You have nothing to worry about. You glow. I've seen it. Kal is still convinced it's his destiny to die in combat. He doesn't want Winona to feel him die."

"I can understand that too."

"It's worth the risk. We are one soul and I wouldn't want it any other way."

That earned me a longer kiss. "Sam? You'll keep me from panicking tonight?"

"I'll be right there with you."

Winona was wearing a dress, a long one that brushed against the tops of her feet and left her shoulders bare. I had become so used to seeing her in uniform that it shocked me how beautiful she was. I hugged her.

"Thank you," she whispered in my ear.

"For what?"

"For thinking that I'm beautiful."

"Reading my mind again?"

"Yes. I miss having you close enough to do that. Come down to Oranjestad after your ship is christened next month. We could use you, and it would be better for little Elisabeth. She'll need room to run. Hannah and Ted miss you."

"But not Kal?"

"You scare him."

I laughed. "Big Marine, scared of the stick girl."

She giggled. "Come down. We'd have fun. We could all go dancing, and out to dinner..."

"You like it there because you're learning how to be Hannah. The DCI, the Intelligence Community, the whole 'world-building' thing you're doing? It holds no attraction for me. I've seen all of that that I ever care to see. Being involved in Kastanje's internal political struggles is the last thing I'd want to do."

"There's opportunities for Sam. He could be a biologist again. Tell me that you'll at least think about it."

"I'll think about it." By which I meant 'no'. Hull 58's sister ship was being laid down in less than six weeks. So much work still to be done.

Mom was wearing a dress too. She looked capable of running a world, which was just what she was doing. She put her hand on my belly after hugging me. "I can feel her. God, she's so much like you." She chuckled. "You're in for an amazing ride."

"Thanks. Where's Dad?"

She pointed. Dad was deep in conversation with Ingenieur Schatzki, my boss on the Hull 58 project. Dad had a rock in his hand and they were passing it back and forth, turning it to catch the light, both of them excited.

"Dad brought a rock to my Christmas service."

"I do so love him."

"Yeah, me too." I watched him a few seconds longer. "I need to go hug him."

"It's time for your service to start."

"Hug first."

Ingenieur Schatzki nodded to me when I approached and then excused himself.

"What's with the rock, Dad?"

He had that look in his eyes that he gets when he's seeing my birth mother instead of me, eyes focused on my stomach. "Ore sample. Naturally occurring magnesium diboride." He reached out to me. "May I?"

"Sure. Most people don't even ask."

He put both hands on me, lost in the wonder of it. "She's about ready. Are you?"

"She needs to wait a couple more weeks so I can finish my work on Hull 58."

She pushed hard against his hand. "I don't think you have two weeks."

"Hush. She'll hear you." Dad still had the distant smile on his face, so I had to ask him The Question. "Dad," I whispered, "do I look like her?"

He answered the way he always answers. "Yes. You look so much like Alice. But even more beautiful, the most beautiful girl God ever created. She would be proud of you."

"You always say that."

"I always will. Because it's true."

"Thanks. I think I need to get up there and do Christmas now."

I went to the front of the Hoog Schelde shipyard's main chapel and waited while everyone found a seat. I prayed, and then started.

"And there were in the same country shepherds abiding in the field, keeping watch over their flock by night. And, lo, the angel of the Lord came upon them, and the glory of the Lord shone round about them: and they were sore afraid. And the angel said unto them, Fear not: for, behold, I bring you good tidings of great joy, which shall be to all people. For unto you is born this day in the city of David a Savior, which is Christ the Lord. And this shall be a sign unto you; Ye shall find the babe wrapped in swaddling clothes, lying in a manger. And suddenly there was with the angel a multitude of the heavenly host praising God, and saying, Glory to God in the highest, and on earth, peace, good will toward men."

I paused, and Elisabeth freaked out. Fear, excitement, yearning, all mixed together in her little heart. I put my hand on my belly, trying to calm her while I looked around the room. Each of her emotions echoed in me and I swayed, losing balance. Of course. A group of eight or ten people had entered the chapel a little late, and I recognized one of them.

Machiel Kornhauser, Evert's father, had brought him to celebrate early Christmas with us.

It was the first time I'd seen Evert since his father had picked him up. He was eight months old, and I could see the shock on his tiny face as he felt Elisabeth's emotions. He turned in his father's arms, crying, and tried to hide from my daughter.

I managed to steady myself against the podium. "Christmas is a celebration of the most remarkable birth in history. My daughter's birth won't be that remarkable." Polite laughter. "But I think it might be about to happen. I'm sorry, everyone. We'll have to try this again in a couple of months. Sam? A little help please?"

I tried to catch my breath. Birth. Elisabeth had responded to that thought, and now she was acting on it.

Sam and Kal each took an arm and helped me from the stage. "Sorry about the mess," I told them. "Water broke. I told her not to, but would she listen? Stubborn, willful, little princess."

Marie Félicie Elisabeth Coleridge came into the world two hours later with a scream, both hers and mine. We were in the company of family and friends, and she was the most beautiful baby girl God had ever made.

Sam laid her on my chest after she had been cleaned up, and I fed her. Afterwards, I talked to her while she napped. "There is so much I want to show you and tell you. The first thing you need to do is find a good friend, like my Winona. You need someone that will love you even when it doesn't make sense; that will love you no matter what stupid thing you do. Then there's Merrimac. I know you can already feel him. He's your friend. Always believe that, no matter what anyone else tries to tell you. And boys. You'll find out about them later. A lot later. I'll help you sort out the good ones from the bad, because that's a hard thing to do. There are so few worth keeping. We'll find you one like your dad. Merrimac will help us with that. Just not that Kornhauser boy, Evert."

Elisabeth stirred in her sleep, tiny arms swinging.

"That's right. When you think of Evert, think about punching." I sighed. "And there's RuComm. I'm going to tell you to stay away from them, but I'll be proud of you when you graduate from the Academy." I pulled my blanket up over us to keep her warm. "I'm going to teach you Chinese. I've been practicing, and there's a planet we're going to move to in a year or two. You'll like it there and we'll go exploring and take long camping trips every summer. I just have to convince your Aunt Winona to move with us."

I kissed the top of her head. "God, I love you, *ma cherie*. I love you more than life. Please promise me that you won't be as big a pain in the ass as I am."

She yawned, and spit up all over my chest.

"Thought so."

*The End*

Made in the USA
Middletown, DE
10 February 2020